SENTINEL RISING

Wayward Orphans Book 1

JEREMY FLAGG

Acknowledgments

No book is complete without a serious ass-kicking from Trish Heinrich and the authors of Superhero-Fiction. Reaching the finish line for Sentinel Rising is directly related to the support of Chris Cary and Paul Chapman keeping me caffeinated, fed, and asking if I got my words done for the day.

The Children of Nostradamus Patrons
Jason Janes
Larry Wilson

To that Starbucks employee who knows I mean "venti" when I say "large." You are the true hero.

Children of Nostradamus Universe

The Night Quartet

Nighthawks

Night Shadows

Night Legions

Night Covenants

Morning Sun (Prequel)

The Dawning of Superheroes

Awaken the Daughter

Anoint the Daughter

Ascend the Daughter

Wayward Orphans

Sentinel Rising

Join the Adventure

PATREON

For More Children of Nostradamus
"Follow" My Patreon For Free
https://www.patreon.com/writeremyflagg

Chapter One

2039

"Last stop. The Tower."

Patrick winced as the voice of the pilot echoed in the small cabin. Despite craning his neck, he couldn't see past her to the front window as she manipulated the HUD display. He wasn't certain, but the forward momentum had eased and if he had to guess, the craft had begun its descent. Holding tight to the arms of his chair, his fear of flying transitioned to fear of the unknown.

"It's the only stop," Patrick muttered.

She didn't resemble any of the commercial flights pilots he had flown in the past. The woman's military uniform should have been the first clue that this wasn't going to be like other trips. No attendant offered him an in-flight meal or beverage on the thirty-minute commute between Chicago and the Tower. It was hard to believe that in minutes, he would begin a new life, and he wasn't sure it was for the better.

"Icarus to the Tower, looking for permission to land."

Permission? A window opened in the holographic

display, and a man on the other end appeared preoccupied. Patrick eyed the screen, trying to decide if he was one of *them*. There was nothing out of the ordinary. For all he knew, he could be an average person. Did the Tower have regular people living there? He had assumed everybody would be like him.

"Designation?"

"Icarus, pilot Sinclair, Pietra." A light from the display passed up and down the woman's face. Patrick recognized the facial recognition technology. Despite flying into the Outlands, they still had stringent security. He had expected tents with bonfires to cook meals. That image was pushed from his mind when he realized they had security protocols.

"Accepted," said the Tower's representative.

"We're ready to land."

"Standby, Icarus."

Patrick's nails dug into the foam padding on the arms of the chair. The idea of floating in the air caused the muscles in his stomach to tighten. If they didn't make it to the ground soon, he'd be emptying deep-dish pizza onto the metal grates under his feet.

"Why aren't we landing?" Either the pilot didn't hear him, or she ignored his question.

Patrick replayed the days leading up to boarding the aircraft, anything to take his mind off the flying tinfoil ball of death. When the landlord arrived to pick up the keys, Patrick had already finished packing the single bag of clothes. As they said their farewells, Patrick contemplated pulling back his hand, asking to extend the lease and continue about his business.

It wasn't until he was walking toward the door with all of his belongings that he heard the man mutter. "Kindling." It wasn't the first time Patrick had been the subject of the slur. Tension between people like him and the mundanes had never been good, but now they were downright dangerous. For who, he still wasn't sure.

But some of the people's fear was founded. Days prior, his boss had used the same slur during a review meeting and without notice— Patrick tried to push what happened next out of his mind. He glanced down at his right fist, fearful he'd see blood speckling his knuckles. Before the incident landed him in prison, he had decided to vanish into the sunset. Troy—the Tower—offered anonymity.

The man appeared on the display again. Patrick's eyes went wide when he realized the man was having himself a mid-day beer while on the job. The tech stared at a display he and the pilot couldn't see. "We're having technical difficulties with security. Continue standing by."

Patrick imagined Utopia had no issues. The Free Republic of America was quick to forget the role the Children of Nostradamus played in liberating the country from a blood-thirsty tyrant. A small band of humans with extraordinary gifts put their lives on the line to stop a mechanical army from killing the residents of Chicago. The eastern seaboard had been decimated because of one murderous asshole, and those rogues had stopped him. They should be legends, but the memory of men is short.

Chicago remained the last bastion, promising a peaceful coexistence where humans and Children could mingle without harassment. The city owed them a debt it could never repay. For a while, Patrick had hope. But bigots infiltrated the city, holding rallies and threatening to purify those they deemed unclean. With nothing left to lose, Patrick turned to the one place that promised him safety from persecution.

"The window is opening. You're cleared for landing."

With a sigh of relief, Patrick counted the seconds before the giant metal box of death reached the ground. On the back of the pilot's seat, a black GD raised from the smooth surface. It took a moment, but the GD logo covered nearly every piece of equipment in the vehicle. It was impossible to trust the overly biased media these days, but it appeared they were correct in associating the mega-corporate Genesis Division with the Children of Nostradamus.

The fear returned as he pictured himself on a table being poked and prodded by scientists. He didn't want the attention. Hell, Patrick would have been fine without anybody ever knowing he was different. The idea of coming to the Tower had been to blend in and be left alone. He was running, and if he let himself think about what he ran into, he'd break into a sweat.

The craft shook for a moment, and he suppressed a yelp. A second later, everything stood perfectly still. When he opened his eyes, the ship hadn't burst into flames. The pilot turned around, an eyebrow raised.

"We've arrived."

The door on the side hissed as it slid to the side, giving him the first glance of the Tower. He waited, debating if he was ready to take a step out of the aircraft and enter this new world. Here, he lived in limbo, part of neither world. He didn't like flying, but he enjoyed not having to face a new reality.

"They're good people."

He focused his attention on the pilot. "Who?"

"You're not the first person who thought about going back. It happens almost every trip."

"Are you…"

"Human." Her lip turned up. "I fought in Chicago. I'm not saying all Children are saints, but one of them saved my life. He saved my entire platoon. They're trying to make a life for themselves. I support that."

Patrick reached for the buckle on the harness, securing him to the seat. With a click, the straps loosened, and he was one step closer to saying goodbye to the normalcy he had experienced for the first part of his life. He reached down, grabbing the straps of his duffle bag.

"If you hate it here. I'll gladly take you back."

"You can leave?"

Her face softened at the question. "It's not a prison. Give it a try, and if you don't like it, I can take you back to Chicago."

"Do many people leave?" The person at the transportation office had said the same thing, but Patrick hadn't been entirely convinced. It was good to hear another person supported the statement.

"A few."

Patrick lifted his bag and stood. "Thanks."

"Good luck."

With a quick nod of the head, he exited the craft. They had landed on a metal slab further from the Tower than he anticipated. It was unlike anything he could imagine. The media had shown drawings and even an elusive photograph or two, but nothing had done it justice.

Troy had once been a small suburban town in upstate

New York. Small houses on cul de sacs, where kids could play until the sun went down. But this, the immensity of the Tower left Patrick feeling insignificant. It easily spanned a hundred stories into the air, growing narrower until it reached a spire at the top. Had it been a perfect rectangle reaching to the heavens, it might have looked like the skyscrapers in Chicago. But it appeared as if it had been twisted, creating beautiful curves as it stretched skyward. There were several other buildings nearby, small cubes compared to the monolith.

The engine of the aircraft roared, and he dropped his head, running from the platform. He didn't know what to expect. He thought there should at least be somebody there to greet him. For all they knew, he could be a terrorist. It didn't bode well for a first impression.

"Patrick, what have you gotten yourself into?"

The Tower sat in the middle of a lush green landscape. From here, he could see the fountains and water features that littered the compound. Green reached into the air on the far side of the complex. They either forgot to mow the lawn or they grew their own crops. The blend of agriculture, greenery, and engineering shouldn't have blended together, but they had found a way. Troy had become a technological Mecha in a rural setting.

Turning about, he stared at a massive wall. The media had never mentioned a barrier surrounding the compound. Nearly a hundred feet tall, miles of metal circled the Tower, separating him from the rest of the world. Patrick spun about, counting the pylons looking like guard towers. From here, he couldn't tell how thick the wall might be, but it certainly held a prison feel. Patrick thought about looking for an exit and walking back to Chicago. The uneasy grumbling in his stomach continued. Anxiety might be part of life, but as of late, it went from unpleasant to crippling.

Right now, he wanted to run.

"Impressive isn't it?"

Patrick froze.

"One-hundred and ninety stories. More if you include the subfloors, but we don't want to brag."

There had been nobody behind him a moment ago. He dropped the bag, closing his fist as he spun about. Heat passed along his skin, pooling in his hand. Living in Chicago, even the most stringent pacifists learned to throw a punch.

"Patrick, right? Kilgannon? Scottish, right?" The man hardly gave Patrick a glance before he corrected himself. "Caledonian, I mean."

"Aye."

"Me too. Well, that's what the orphanage told me. I envy the accent. We'll have to visit someday."

The man walked beside Patrick, his eyes fixed on the Tower. He was husky, with short-cropped hair and a perfectly-manicured goatee. Patrick thought if he put on some weight, in a decade, he and this stranger could be cousins. Slowly, his fist eased open. If the man was a Scot, he couldn't be all bad.

"The place is usually a bit busier, but we've been having a town hall most of the day."

"A town hall?"

"We're not like the rest of the country. We've operated without much regulation. Everybody here plays a role in keeping the Tower running. It used to be pretty easy. But we're over a thousand people now and between finding jobs and keeping the peace, we've started forming our own legal system. You can imagine that when somebody like Dwayne can summon lightning or turn themselves into a fireball, we have some unique needs."

"A thousand Children?"

"Seven-hundred and six to be exact. Some people bring their spouses. We have parents who come here for their children. We don't want to separate families."

"But the Outlands?"

"The radiation? Yeah, at first, that was a major concern. The shields keep out the majority of the radiation. We had difficulty with crops at first. We have a resident with the ability to process sunlight through photosynthesis, and she's been helpful in understanding the needs of plants in this environment. She's got the crops going this year."

"It's a bit overwhelming," Patrick admitted.

"Wait until you get inside. We'll have you go through orientation and somebody from the welcome committee will help you get acclimated."

"Thanks." Patrick tried not to think about the orientation, or learning fresh faces, or even figuring out his place in the community. He found it difficult switching to a new cell phone. The idea of acclimating to an entirely new society—his brain could hardly process.

"I didn't read your entire file, but did I see you worked in a library?"

Work. Patrick could discuss work all day long. "I worked in the stacks at the Chicago Public Library. I've been there since I graduated college."

"Librarian..." The man rubbed his goatee, rolling the information around. "We definitely have a job for your skillset."

Patrick had resolved that he would never work in the stacks again. "Really?"

"A decade ago, Troy used to be a suburban town. It was far enough into the Outlands that we were left alone without being near the massacre of Manhattan." Patrick had watched the newsfeeds as the slaughter unfolded. Nearly every resident of New York City had turned savage trying to tear one another apart and ended with streets lit up with napalm. "It took a while, but the Tower is the next evolution of our small community. New arrivals hardly know what this place used to be. We could use somebody to help maintain records of who we were so we know how far we've come."

"A reference librarian?" The knot in his stomach relaxed and suddenly he had questions regarding acquisitions, budget, and scope of the research. The anxiety pushed away as the excitement of returning to his career set in.

"I'm getting ahead of myself. I get excited when I see a fresh face. Patrick Kilgannon, how about we go and see what it's all about?"

Patrick started toward the Tower.

"Whoa, do you think I got this gut walking?"

Patrick turned around to see a black circle hanging in the air as if it had always been there. Despite the sun shining, the disc seemed to pull in the light. Patrick eyed the thing and then the man. He hadn't recognized the stranger at first, but every person in Chicago knew the powers of the Nighthawks, especially the man who led the rally against the robot army.

"You're him." This was better than the time he sat down at a table next to Jennifer Lawrence. Except this time, it wasn't a drag queen having a bite to eat between sets. The man stepped into the disc, half of his body being swallowed by the portal.

"Conthan Cowan. Nice to meet you, Patrick." The Nighthawk waved for Patrick to follow. "Welcome to the Tower of Troy."

"I'm going to be a goddamned Sentinel." Eve gritted her teeth until they threatened to crack. "At any cost."

"If you're always this melodramatic, we're going to have a problem."

Eve wanted to reach out and slap her partner. It wouldn't be the first time she let her emotions get the best of her and she reacted without thinking. The last time she attended a training session, she had nearly broken the arm of a classmate. She didn't want to be here, but she understood why they chose this post for her.

"I'm fine," she lied. "I'm good."

"That's what I want to hear. If you're going to be working with me, I need to know you're not going to explode." Kevin hung on the word 'explode,' making it clear he knew about her abilities. She turned away, trying to hide the embarrassment creeping into her cheeks. It shouldn't surprise her that the rumors started seconds after her meltdown had occurred. Then she remembered there was no hiding from Kevin's gifts.

"No judgment," he said. "My abilities are simply there. I've never had to worry about them turning on or off. I consider my lazy ass lucky."

High up on the wall, they had been dispatched to look at the mechanism that controlled the shield. Nearly thirty feet thick, the wall appeared impenetrable, but it wasn't the fear of attack that worried the inhabitants, it was the bombardment of radiation. While she and Kevin were granted a natural immunity, the humans inside the Tower didn't have the same luxury. She didn't want to be assigned to grease monkey detail, but at least she could be useful to their community.

Earlier in the day, Eve had sat at the kitchen table with her father as he looked over the paperwork of the new arrivals. Each folder detailed their skill sets, education, job experience, but she had always been more fascinated by their powers. There was always a detailed analysis of what they could do, but there was a line on each of them elaborating their limitations. None of the Children in the Tower had gotten away unscathed. When the Nostradamus Effect swept across the globe, it had given them abilities at a price.

"What's it like?" she asked.

"You're going to need to elaborate."

Eve pointed to her eyes, like that somehow made her cryptic question more obvious. He never turned to look at her while they walked along the wall. "Your eyes," she said, "you're…"

"Blind?" he asked.

When put bluntly, it sounded ruder than it had in her head. "Yeah, I read that you can't see. Obviously, that's not the case."

"I can't," he said, "not like you. The human eye sees by the light waves reflected and absorbed by an object. I haven't seen that way since my abilities turned on."

"Oh."

"I just see differently. I can see the electromagnetic fields generated by objects. Back there, when the blood rushed to your cheeks, yeah, I could see that. Every time your foot strikes the metal up here, I can see the burst of energy it creates."

Eve closed her eyes as they walked and focused on her feet. Each time the toe of her boot scuffed the metal, she could sense the vibration of energy. If she concentrated, she'd be able to feel electromagnetic waves pulsing off Kevin as if he were generating copious amounts of body heat. Unlike Kevin, she couldn't see the lines, but they were there, infinite strings in the universe that, if she reached out, she could almost pluck.

"Is that why they assigned me to you?"

He gave a slight clap at the deduction. "First smart thing you've said since we got up here."

There was no point in hiding her annoyance. Her father oversaw the work details, and it wouldn't be a coincidence that she found herself with the one Child at the Tower that shared a gift similar to her own. For all the gifts she could have been given, it was bad enough it was considered passive. But to find somebody possessing something similar, it took the thunder out of having superpowers.

"Why are you so fixated on being a Sentinel? They act like they're superheroes. Right down to the uniforms. It seems a little cliched if you ask me."

"I didn't, but thanks for asking."

They continued walking along the wall in an awkward silence, the question hanging in the air between them. They were approaching one of the pylons, a plaque on the outside with a giant '53' engraved in the metal. It looked like every other tower circling the perimeter, but somewhere inside, it held the key to opening and closing the dome. As she tensed the muscles in her arm, the wall seemed to come alive, breathing in and out with the hum of electricity. Underneath her feet, a current ran through the metal in a web of wire and circuit boards. Try as she might, nothing about the tower felt any different from the rest of the wall.

"Feel anything off?"

"How did you know?" There were others with unique abilities related to their eyes, but this was the first time somebody had been able to see her reach into the electromagnetic field.

"Whatever you were doing, it moved the lines. It looked like you tugged at them with your hands. Pretty impressive."

It was the first time Kevin gave her any sort of compliment. She shook her head. "Nothing. It was easy to feel disturbances when I wasn't surrounded by technology. Now, it's like there is always something brushing against my skin."

They reached the door, and he went to reach for the handle. Leaning back, he pulled at the door, trying to pry it open. "I get that," he groaned, "sometimes it's hard for me to see small details in this place. If I concentrate I can push past them, but I haven't quite perfected it yet."

He gave up, throwing his hands in the air. He glanced back at Eve and then at the door. The curl of his lip gave away the bruised ego. Gesturing to the door, he stepped back. "Think you can give me a hand?"

Eve raised an eyebrow. "How much have they told you about me?"

"Enough," he said. "Hurry up before my ego calls the whole thing off."

She stopped herself from calling him a jerk. He managed to hover somewhere between dispassionately annoying and distantly supportive. Anybody else she'd have flipped off, but she didn't think it'd quite do the job.

With one hand on the door, she put a foot on the wall and pulled hard enough the muscles in her forearms bulged. A lock snapped, and the metal scraped its way open. Every Child had other perks; some were a little faster, some more durable, or healed faster. But Eve, she was easily one of the strongest people at the Tower. Even that advantage hadn't landed her a spot with the Sentinels.

Kevin walked inside the pylon, a room almost twenty feet in every direction. She followed, pressing the pad just inside the door, turning on the lights. He didn't speak as he followed the walls, pausing every few feet to look toward the roof. She had to commend the thought behind the job assignments. Unlike anybody else, the two of them could follow the flow of electricity and find any disruptions.

A crackle in her ear made her swat at a phantom. "Eve, Kevin, have you spotted the problem?" She rolled her eyes at the sound of Needles's voice. He was one of the few humans that worked full-time at the Tower. His abilities with computers teetered on being a superpower on its own. She liked him when he wasn't at work. But when he was on the job, he became a tedious taskmaster.

"Not yet. We're in the pylon. Give us five."

"Aircraft on standby. Tick tock," Needles said. If there were a camera in the pylon, she'd have flipped him off.

"All right, let's see what you can do." Kevin stepped back while gesturing to the entirety of the room.

Eve wanted to believe he was being kind out of the goodness in his heart, but she felt judged. A man with a similar gift was pushing her to put hers on display. It felt just like the teachers in the training sessions. She and the dozen other kids spent hours practicing, utilizing their gifts to ensure they wouldn't be a danger to the community. It was day after day of the beginner-level exercises. She mastered the basics. Basics wouldn't land her among the Sentinels.

"Fine." She flexed her shoulders, cracking her neck. "Let's do this."

Her abilities didn't come with an off-switch. After years of being bombarded by the sensations her body produced in reaction to electromagnetic fields, she'd learned to ignore it. But even then, it nipped at her, begging for attention.

She closed her eyes and focused on the tiniest of pinpricks along her skin.

"It's beautiful to watch," Kevin said. "I've never seen anything like this."

She ignored his comments, trying to push away any distractions. Her own body produced the lines flowing from her body. Her father had once referred to it as her aura and showed her a book of psychics who said they could see the colors radiating from a person's body. Purple. Her aura was purple in her head, and she imagined it licking the lines of every object in the room. Without knowing the specifics of each device, the room hummed with electricity. The sound grew until it sounded like a symphony with each musician playing a different composition.

"What are you sensing?"

"I..." She found it difficult to explain it to a person with no understanding of science. But for somebody who could see her abilities in action, she felt foolish. "The room, it's alive. I can feel the electricity moving through the walls. So much power. It's almost over-whelming." The tiny pinpricks were getting sharper as she reached further, trying to find something out of sorts.

"Keep scanning the walls. Can you feel a spot unlike the others? A place where the power is—"

"Disrupted." The moment she found the spot, her aura snapped back into place, inches from her skin. The hum ceased and the prickling sensation vanished. Soon as she dialed down her abilities, an overwhelming feeling of isolation came rushing in.

"Not too shabby," he said.

Extending her middle finger in his direction, she walked toward the wall, where she felt the power out of sorts. Filled with boxes holding circuit boards, conduits, and computer readouts, she couldn't make sense of what she detected.

"You already knew where it was," she accused.

"Yeah." He nodded. "But it's not about me. I saw you reaching out and touching the fields. You need more practice."

"You're as bad as the trainers."

"With that attitude, you'll never be a Sentinel." Eve bit her tongue when she realized the man was prepared to help her reach her goal. If he had more insight into her abilities than the trainers, then there was a chance that perhaps she could grow beyond the passive ability to sense electromagnetic fields.

He approached the wall, eyes darting up and down, looking at the same lines of energy she had touched. He paused and then leaned in close to one of the breaker boxes. "Are you seeing this?"

She found the panel on the wall, the door bent, barely able to close. "Somebody pried it open."

"Indeed." He pulled it the rest of the way open.

She tapped the communicator in her ear. "Needles, we found the problem."

"We'll have a temporary fix in place in a minute," Kevin added.

Once the box opened, she could see one of the circuit boards nearly snapped in half. Tiny sparks jumping from the wires. "Can you fix it?" she asked.

"Yeah." He flipped a lever inside and pulled the broken part free. With a couple clicks of the computer, he was moving at a speed she couldn't follow. "I'm just going to temporarily bypass this mess. It'll work in the short term, but they'll need the tech crew to come out and fix it. But that's not the real problem."

"What is?" She cocked her head to the side, unsure of what made him scrunch up his face.

"Somebody came in here and did this." Now the worry made sense. "We have a saboteur on our hands."

"Shit," she whispered.

He tapped his ear. "Needles, you should have access to the shield commands."

"What's the situation?" asked Needles.

"Contact the Council." Kevin's face looked worried. Eve couldn't grasp the severity of the situation, but the next words tightened something in her gut. Kevin's tone turned grave. "We have a traitor."

Chapter Two

2039

Patrick fell to his knees, shivering. He tried to shake the freezing cold clinging to his skin. It was as if he had run outside in a Chicago winter buck naked. Before he could see if the other man had a similar reaction, he stepped into another black void and vanished. Just as quickly as the disc appeared, it vanished, and he was left to catch his breath.

"Oh no, you go ahead," he huffed. "I'm just going to take a moment to hurl." He squatted low to the ground, staring at his shoes. He fought to keep the deep dish from resurfacing.

"You never get used to it," said a young woman. She kneeled in front of Patrick, giving him a curious glance.

Her lack of hair made her eyes appear unnaturally large and even more intense. He let a shiver ripple down his body. Past her, he could see that Conthan had dropped him in the rear of a massive room. There were hundreds of people not paying the freezing man any attention. His stomach settled, and he dared to stand upright. She followed suit.

"Welcome to our first town hall."

"You're a…" He wasn't sure if there was an etiquette to asking somebody if they were human or not. Never being around another Child of Nostradamus, he didn't know if the question was taboo.

"Human. I'm one of the priests of the Church stationed at the Tower."

"Oh." She raised an eyebrow, and he realized it sounded more condescending than he intended. "I didn't mean it like that. I mean, of course you're human." He tried to recover, but he could already taste the rubber of his shoe as he wedged his foot deeper in his mouth.

"I'm Patrick." He held out his hand. "But everybody calls me Patches."

The smile was slow to form, and he felt relief as it crooked to one side, turning into a grin. "I know, Patrick Kilgannon. I'm your welcome committee."

"Of course, he brought me here for a reason. Don't mind me. This is all—"

"Overwhelming? A bit much? Hard to swallow?" She gave a slight laugh. "Should I continue?" She moved past his hand and grabbed onto his wrist, waiting until he returned the gesture. "I see you, Patrick Kilgannon. I am Sister Adelaide, but you can call me Adelaide."

She held his gaze as she recited the introduction. With only a few words, she managed an intensity that a man twice her size would struggle to radiate. She squeezed his arm and let it go, turning toward the front of the room.

"Don't fret, being nervous. Many who arrive believe they are terrified of new beginnings. In truth, they're frightened to let go of their former lives. We each grieve this death differently."

She couldn't be any older than him, and yet she spoke as if she had soaked up all available wisdom. He spotted the small node behind her right ear. The people in Chicago openly wore their enhancements. They opted for ocular replacements that glinted in the light or tattooed themselves to highlight the circuits just beneath their skin. The box behind the ear meant an organic computer augmenting the brain's computing. Did she have the work done before arriving at the Tower or was this her attempt to keep up with the cadre of powers housed here?

"Sorry to keep you all waiting," Conthan said at the podium. "I had to greet a new arrival before coming here." He winked in Patrick's direction, causing more than a few heads to turn in their seats.

Patrick ignored the people, instead turning his attention to the room itself. It reminded him of his freshman seminar lecture hall. The stadium seating must have at least fifty rows, and down at the front there was a small stage where a few people stood next to Conthan. They resided somewhere in the Tower, and by the view out the window, they were somewhere near the top. He gasped as he realized he could see the wall in the distance, small, almost insignificant. Beyond that, he had a view of the rest of Troy, a suburban town with houses like any other.

"We're not going to make this a long talk. We all have work to be doing and as you know, if we don't do it, nobody will do it for us." Heads nodded as Conthan spoke. He had their respect. As one of the fighters in the Battle for Chicago, Patrick understood why. Without his band of Nighthawks, the landscape of America would be much different. Though Patrick believed if it hadn't been for the dozen members of the rogue group, America would have ceased to exist.

"We can finally say we're seeing a return on the crops. We can say a very special thanks to Fiona for the countless hours. But there are two things I know we need to discuss. First, the Council has decided that we are going to start opening our doors to the world." He paused, and quickly whispers filled the room. By the audience's reaction, Patrick could tell it was a hotly debated topic.

"We have been transforming the Tower into a Sanctuary for Children and their loved ones. There has been a lengthy discussion about whether we have the infrastructure to allow foreign Children into our home. With each passing day, we surpass our expectations and I can thankfully say we're ready. We..." he paused, grabbing the sides of the podium as a grin broke out on his face. "Goddammit, we've done it. We've made a home."

The rows of people stood, clapping, hollering and more than one burst of light filled the auditorium. There was a current in the crowd, a general feeling of togetherness Patrick hadn't expected to see. Somebody whistled, the sound cutting through the air like a siren.

"Barbara," Adelaide said, "she gets easily excited."

"They just..." Patrick dug his hands into his pockets. "Use their powers like that?"

"Why not? It's no different from breathing. It's who they are." She smiled, the grin returning to her face. "Some people are more reserved. Those with dangerous abilities might refrain, but even they have a time and place. The Children within the Tower celebrate their more unique traits."

He couldn't imagine using his abilities in public like that. He didn't want people identifying him by some random gift. No, he wanted to be known for the things he could control. Patrick let out a little laugh. "I feel like the only guy wearing clothes at the nudist colony."

"Oh, we have those too."

"Wait," he gulped, "what?"

"When your skin creates a corrosive chemical, clothes are problematic."

"You're joking, right?"

She pointed to the stage with her chin. One of the men standing next to Conthan was shirtless and as bald as Adelaide. Patrick leaned closer to the woman. "Corrosive skin?"

"Shoots lightning."

Patrick's eyes lit up. The lightning wielder was still discussed in Chicago. "He's one of the Nighthawks."

Conthan continued his speech. "I'm glad to see you're as excited as I am. But it's going to be a challenge. We're expecting the population to double and we're going to need everybody to pitch in. You all will become the ambassadors for what we're building at the Tower. This part is less than thrilling, but it brings me to the second matter." Conthan stepped from the podium as the bald man took his place.

"Things here have been relatively peaceful. The few minor disputes that have arisen have been dealt with by the Council. But with people coming from around the globe, we expect there to be different customs, rituals, and…" He didn't look nearly as comfortable in front of the crowd as Conthan had. Patrick felt a bit of kinship with the man. "Frankly, we need to iron out a working legal system. Most of us have broken more laws than we can count."

"That's an understatement, Dwayne," Adelaide laughed. "Man overthrows a government and refers to it as breaking a law."

Patrick laughed at her comment. He wasn't the only one who found the statement comical. A good number of Tower residents joined in, chuckling at Dwayne's expense. The tension eased in Patrick's body. Here he was, among people who could easily demolish what remained of the Free Republic and they were laughing at the irony of a legal system that attempted to define them.

"Seriously folks, the Council—" Dwayne threw his hands up in the air at the continued heckling from the audience. It was hard to tell if he was smiling or grimacing. Patrick had attended more than his share of city council meetings when the library needed money. Other than the presenter being half-naked, this wasn't much different.

Conthan rushed to the microphone. "The Council has asked for volunteers with legal backgrounds to help. Apparently, don't be an asshole isn't as legally binding as I hoped."

"They're regular people, just like you and me." Adelaide knew exactly what to say. Something about the woman captivated him. Amongst these Children, there was an army, and she spoke as if she didn't harbor an ounce of fear. Before he could respond, she reached down, picking up his duffle bag. "Follow me."

"But the meeting..."

"You're more than welcome to stay and listen to him

rattle on about the dissemination of new rules for the residents. Or, perhaps..." She walked toward a door in the rear of the auditorium. "We go on a tour of the Tower and I can introduce you to your new home."

"Home." The word sounded foreign, as if by applying it to this location somehow gave it a new meaning. Chicago had been home, the library had been home, but the Tower...

"Home," he repeated. Not yet, but maybe someday.

Reading status reports atop of the world wasn't as fulfilling as Alyssa had hoped.

"They never end," she sighed.

She blinked and when her eyes opened again, there were dozens of screens filling her vision. If she had known leading the Sentinels would require so much paperwork, virtual or otherwise, she'd have remained a grunt. If she wasn't sifting through injury reports, she was signing off on the mastery evaluations for their powers.

Alyssa flexed her hands, closing them into fists. It had been days since she'd thrown a punch. For years, she fought for her life, for her very right to live. When that got boring, she helped lead a revolution to over-throw a corrupt government. At any point, she could have been killed, and here she was, staring at paper-work, flexing her muscles, longing for a simpler time.

She reached out and with a quick two-finger gesture, the screens vanished. Leaning on the railing, she closed her eyes and let the last of the setting sun caress her skin. There would only be a few more moments before the rest of the Council arrived. She savored the warmth, breathing deeply, hoping to smell the roses in the garden.

Alyssa's fingers tightened on the railing as a soft melody started playing in her ear. She smiled as the sound grew louder. "You could say hello like a normal person."

The music stopped playing through her earpiece and piped in through the speakers on the rooftop terrace. She rolled her eyes, finding it difficult to wrangle the edges of her up-turned lip. Normally, the roof held dozens of residents as they enjoyed the pool or walked through the raised rose garden. Tonight, it was reserved for the Council to convene, but for a short period before their meeting, it was all hers.

"Are you responsible for this?"

She flattened out the front of her tunic, admiring the ornate cuffs. Their resident tailor had delivered the garment himself. He had been tight-lipped about the source of the gift, but Alyssa had her suspicions. The garment fit perfectly, snug enough to be flattering but loose enough that her arms had full range of motion. It took a special kind of man to understand that, for her, function superseded fashion.

"It is quite lovely, Ned."

The piano music ended abruptly, replaced by a beat and synthetic strings. It wasn't her taste in music, but she could endure based on the gesture alone. She wandered into the garden and inhaled deeply, savoring the sweet smell of the roses. Alyssa had no problem owning the title of *living weapon*, but every once in a while, she missed the days of being thought of as a girl.

Ned didn't have any abilities like the Children of

Nostradamus. But to those who worked with him, it was hard to tell the difference. From his perch in the hub, he could see every square inch of the Tower. He had over-seen nearly every circuit and wire installed in the mono-lith. She didn't need to ask. He was watching her, admiring her from a safe distance.

"Will you be joining us tonight?"

"Dwayne has my reports." The voice in her ear was shaky, lacking his usual bravado. She wanted to ask if the hub really needed him or if he was hiding.

"The elevator's facial recognition had issues. I had to use my access code."

"I'm trying to keep an entire city running," he shouted. The switch in topic brought back his bombastic self-inflated ego. "Do you know how many people could do this job? That's right. None. Who needs superpowers when you have me?"

"I'm glad I make you nervous," she said with a smile.

The music cut off and the scent of roses faded, only to be replaced by a crisp smell that reminded her of rain-storms. There was only one man whose presence could ionize the air like that.

"Dwayne," she said, giving a slight wave to the man behind her.

"Oh good, I was hoping I'd catch you before the others arrived."

"Commander Rahim," he said, with a slight bow.

"Why do you insist on such a foolish title, Coun-cilman Ayer?"

"Touché."

"I needed a moment of peace before another one of these meetings." She returned to the railing while her companion joined. Dwayne Ayer, one of the original Nighthawks and the man who saved her life more times than she could count, followed her as she returned to her perch at the railing. As she pressed her arms on the metal, peering over the ledge more than a thousand feet below, he hesitated before doing the same.

"If Needles hears the battery isn't working..." She pointed to the metal gauntlet around his wrist.

"It is." He fidgeted with the device. "It's been a long day. Do you mind?"

"Just like old times," she said, taking a step back. The man's body crackled and sparks jumped between his fingers and from his arms to his torso. She shielded her eyes as his hands grew brighter. The air burned as a thunderous crack filled the rooftop. A bolt of lightning poured from his hand, surging upward in the air.

She had seen the force he wielded used to shred metal and blow holes through walls. But as the bolt diminished, it struck the force field surrounding Troy. The shield rippled, waves of blue and purple rolling outward, dispersing the energy. When his internal battery demanded he offload the building energy, it could be disastrous.

But, it could also be beautiful.

Alyssa smiled at the light show, hoping the residents of Troy were close to windows so they could take in the spectacle. Like many of the Children housed in the apartments below them, there were two sides to every ability. For Dwayne, it was the constant threat of unleashing the power at an inappropriate time. He had set more than one mattress on fire while he slept, and every once in a while a spark jumped from his shoulder to a nearby light. But thanks to Genesis Division's gadget on his arm, he had found some control.

"I wonder how long before Needles yells in my ear for hitting the shield again."

She held her tongue at his comment, turning away to hide the grin. Ned had a reputation, and she couldn't deny the accuracy of the claims. He pretended he had a temper just as much as he pretended to have a real ego. They were an act, a persona he developed when he became a freedom fighter.

"I see." Dwayne's voice gave away his epiphany. "I should have known you didn't get dressed up for a Council meeting."

"What are you insinuating?"

"Nothing, I swear." He held his hands up, backing away slowly. "Okay, maybe a little something. Can I offer you a piece of big brother advice?"

Alyssa felt flattered that he referred to her as a little sister. "Skits will be jealous."

"I'm not sure Skits knows how to be jealous," he joked. "Will she threaten to stab me? That's a good possibility. Hell, that's always a possibility. Don't worry. I have room in my life for more family."

"Dwayne Ayer, a family man."

They both paused at the statement. When she first met the brute, they lived in an abandoned hotel in Boston. Together they protected the remaining Children. There was no time for relationships and even if there was, the fear of losing somebody always hung over their heads.

"It's still weird when I think about it. I have a husband. I have a job."

"You have a kid," she said.

"Eve, she'll be the death of me. She reminds me so much of Skits."

Alyssa nodded. It was the truth. Slightly reckless, fast to anger, Eve resembled Skits in many ways.

"What's your advice?"

"Don't wait to tell him."

He had a way of cutting through the grief and saying exactly what she needed to hear. She took in a deep breath as her fingers ran along the cuff of her tunic. There were a thousand reasons not to tell the man. They worked together, and she hardly had free time for herself. But something in Dwayne's simple suggestion tugged at her heart.

"Father would hate him," she smiled.

"If it helps," he laughed. "Depending on the day, *I* hate him."

Alyssa nearly spat as she laughed.

Behind him, a black void opened in the air. Conthan stepped out in his usual leather jacket and t-shirt. Dwayne reached out, and for a brief moment, he and Conthan held hands. The simple gesture wasn't lost on her. She had to wonder if Ned would ever be a man she'd casually hold hands with.

"The others should be here in a minute," Conthan started, "but we have another problem."

"Skits is missing," Alyssa said.

"You know?"

Alyssa stepped away from the railing, closing the distance between the other two. "I was her partner for four years. She hasn't checked in for days."

"Have you spoken to Gretchen or Lillian?" asked Conthan.

Alyssa hadn't spoken to either of them since vowing

to never work another assignment for Genesis Division. The two women had begged for her to stay as one of their operatives. It had been one thing to infiltrate foreign countries and help save or protect people. But Lilian had started caring more about the interests of her corporation than the well-being of humans. Skits did it for the rush and, despite Alyssa leaving the wet work missions, there was no convincing her friend to do the same.

"No." Both Conthan and Dwayne's eyes went wide at the animosity coating the single word.

"I'll follow up with Gretchen," Conthan offered. Alyssa didn't dislike his friend and Lilian's right-hand woman, but she didn't want to open a line of communication.

"Great, just what we need, another problem." Dwayne's head shook back and forth, a frequent habit when discussing his sister.

"What else?" asked Alyssa.

"Eve and Kevin were working maintenance on the wall—" he threw his hands up, "—and they found evidence that somebody tampered with the shield."

Alyssa predicted that it was only a matter of time before their background checks on the citizens of Troy would fall short. Paperwork and computer records could be forged and with the growing population, Needles couldn't verify every detail.

Conthan let out a long sigh. "Do we know who?"

Dwayne and Conthan started to rattle off a list of the newest arrivals to the Tower. Alyssa ignored them, caught up in a growing conspiracy. When the Nighthawks first met, it had been at the meddling of a dead psychic. She manipulated each of them, bringing their orbits closer and closer together until they over-lapped. It had been an effort to save the world, and thankfully, they succeeded. But the psychic instilled a lifelong lesson in her.

Alyssa held up a hand, silencing both of them. "There is no such thing as coincidence. We know that more than most."

"What are you getting at?" asked Conthan.

"We'll deal with the wall. But I can't help but wonder…" Had they grown too comfortable in their new home? When they hid amongst the ruins of Boston, hunted by the government, they treated every day like a fight for their survival. "What if Skits' disappearance is related?"

Chapter Three

2039

"You've got to be kidding me. These people are crazy."

The window ran from one end of the living room to the other. Without curtains, it would be problematic during the day, but right now, he wanted to see the boundaries of Troy. Squinting, he found it wasn't simply dark outside, but the glass itself was tinted. He rested his hand on the surface, leaning in to see if he could make out the wall.

"Initializing."

He lurched backward, tripping over his own feet. His backside hurt as he landed on the hardwood floor. Inspecting the room, he couldn't find the source of the voice. The furnishings were modest; a small couch and coffee table facing the island divided the space between the living room and kitchen.

"Hello?"

Adelaide had deposited him at a vacant apartment on the thirty-second floor. She explained it was a mostly empty floor, the future home of the international refugees. The woman had been nothing but cordial since they met, but she refused to step over the threshold to his new home. She suggested he turn in early to begin orientation in the morning, saying power assessment is always rough on the first day.

"How may I assist?"

Patches repeated himself. "Hello?"

"Hello!" The voice was almost human, but a slight tinge of artificial in its voice didn't quite pass the Turing test.

"Who are you?"

"I am the computer. You can summon me by saying, 'computer' along with a wide list of commands."

"Computer? Don't you have a name? I thought all artificial intelligence computers had names." He had a voice-operated computer at work named Harold. They were generally the same, a long list of commands to help make life simpler. He almost missed growling at the computer as it misread every command he attempted to feed it.

"I am not an intelligent computer."

Patches climbed back to his feet. He chuckled at the computer's ability to insult itself. The window morphed from black to a reflection of the living room. Instead of a reflection of himself, there was a featureless person.

"What can you do, computer?"

"Computer, what can you do?" It corrected his syntax.

"You're sassy for an unintelligent computer." Patches tossed himself onto the couch. The man in the window stepped forward, shimmering until it appeared as if he stood in the living room. He had seen a hologram before, but nothing as impressive as this. The computer was see-through but opaque enough to take up space. Patrick tried to hide how creeped out he was by a living machine emerging in his home.

"Computer, what time is it?"

"22:43."

"Computer, tell me an interesting fact."

"The children of identical twins are genetically siblings."

"Okay, so you're a bit of a freak." He kicked off his shoes and pulled his legs onto the couch. The apartment was nicer than anything he ever had in Chicago. A librarian's salary wouldn't be able to afford this without at least one or two roommates.

"Computer, dim the lights. I should probably crawl into bed soon." All but two lights turned off, and the remaining overhead light grew faint.

"Computer, overwrite name. We'll call you Harold."

The image of the man scrambled for a moment and then returned. "You can summon me by saying, 'Harold' along with a wide list of commands."

Patrick laid back on the couch, resting his head on the collection of pillows near the end. It hadn't been a day, but so far, the Tower had exceeded his expectations at every turn. The two residents he met today were nice enough. It seemed as if the people here were attempting to create a utopia. He could get behind that idea.

"Harold, tell me about the Tower."

"Please specify."

His love of history got the better of him. "It's origins."

"Citizens have stated that the Tower has a 'rather fascinating' origin story." Patches closed his eyes and tried to imagine Harold as a real person telling him a story.

"Troy originally consisted of a suburban town located one-hundred and fifty-seven miles north of New York City. Situated west of the Outlands, most of its inhabitants were relocated after the nuclear power plants in the Northeast were breached." Patrick noted that the computer avoided using the usual term terrorist or freedom fighter regarding the explosions.

"After the Battle for Chicago and the Manhattan Massacre, Troy was added to the Outland territories. Its first new residents were Dwayne Ayer and Conthan Cowen. It quickly became known as the Mecca for the Children of Nostradamus."

Patrick hadn't expected to meet one of the Nighthawks today. As a smile stretched across his face, he couldn't help but admit he was smitten, or perhaps even a little jealous. He spent his entire life scared of the power housed in his body. But these Children, they used their abilities to fight for justice. They were heroes—and he was a librarian.

"Harold, who are the Nighthawks?"

"Named after a painting by American painter Edward Hopper, the Nighthawks are a rogue group of Children of Nostradamus and one human. The psychic, Eleanor P. Valentine, to prevent the telepath, Ivan Volkov from creating a global catastrophe, selected these individuals."

Patrick recognized the woman's name. Many still believed she was a terrorist who attempted to kill a president. More than one modern history book labeled this Daughter of Nostradamus as a domestic terrorist or foreign assassin. He was glad to see that whoever programmed the computers had seen to prevent misinformation from being cataloged. He was more than excited to see the library tomorrow and discover how he could help preserve an accurate account of history.

"Harold, what is the origin of the Tower?"

"The Tower was created to house the Children of Nostradamus. Funded and developed by the acting CEO of the Genesis Division, Lillian Day. The Tower is considered a sovereign nation within the Free Republic of America."

Patrick closed his eyes. His mind wandered, fighting off sleep to come up with more requests for the computer. Rolling onto his side, he curled into a ball on the couch. There were so many questions bouncing around in his head, but he couldn't convince himself to ask.

"Good night, Patrick Kilgannon."

"Patches," he muttered as sleep carried him away.

"You've got to be kidding me." The words came in breathy bursts as she eyed the transparent figure standing at her side. Her hands rested on her knees as she attempted to control the flow of oxygen to her lungs. Drip by drip, the sweat rolled down her face, clinging to her nose before it sailed toward the floor.

"Computer, run the simulation again."

"Eve, I do not recommend—"

"Computer override. Run the simulation again."

The black bodysuit tightened. Each node weaved into the fabric responded with a slight vibration to the current running through the floor, walls, and ceiling of the room. When it finished, the suit grew heavier.

"Computer, increase resistance."

Muscles flexed as her suit grew heavier. Like most Children of Nostradamus, she was stronger than a human. But unlike the other Children, her ability to sense the electromagnetic field was secondary to the strength in her limbs. Eve knew that even among her people, she was strong. The suit compensated, slowing her and forcing her to work up a sweat.

"Begin."

The white room dimmed slightly as another figure materialized. Where the light from the floor and ceiling intersected, a hologram of a person stood. It had become her mission to defeat the featureless representation of the computer. On an easier setting, it wouldn't have been difficult, but she wasn't looking for an easy work-out. Eve wouldn't become a Sentinel by playing it safe.

With each simulated fight, the computer recorded data. The biometrics from the suit turned into bits and bytes, information teaching it to be a better opponent. For years, she trained with Alyssa, learning to be a competent fighter. Much like the computer, Alyssa learned from every encounter.

It stepped forward and threw the first punch. A left jab, a distraction, as it positioned its feet for a powerful right hook. Eve blocked the blow with her right forearm. The moment she struck the illuminated construct, the suit responded, the pressure feeling almost identical to an actual blow. Had it been a real person and she without the suit, its arm would have snapped in half. Instead, it followed with the right hook.

It bent its arm, feigning the punch and throwing its elbow. Eve leaned back, out of reach. She caught its knee, stopping it from striking her torso. Grabbing onto the construct, she lifted it up in the air and slammed it onto the floor. As she reached back to strike its face, it rolled out of the way.

The foot struck her arm and the suit almost tightened to the point of being painful. Its heel slammed into her chest, sending her into a backward somersault. Alyssa would scold her for relying on her endurance to absorb blow after blow. It wasn't enough to be the last person standing. You needed the strength to drag yourself from the match.

Eve changed tactics. She climbed to one knee as the construct charged. It raised a knee, attempting to strike her face. She grabbed it by the shin, guiding the limb too high to make contact. With a slam of her fist, she hit the inside of its other knee, snapping it in half. She maintained her grip as she stood, chucking the figure like a weightless pillow.

"Computer, I expected—"

The air behind her vibrated. She bent at the waist as a foot passed over her back. Fingers braced on the floor, she kicked back, striking something in the chest. Tucking into a forward roll, she spun about and saw the two-handed fist coming down toward her skull. She crossed her arms in an X, catching the force of the blow.

"That's more like it," she smiled. The only way she'd become a Sentinel would be if she could prove that she was more than capable without active powers.

Pushing its hands to the side, she jabbed twice at its kidney. She jumped to her feet, ready to go on the offense. She led with a punch, but the computer knocked it aside. Then with a knee, extending it at the last moment, her heel striking its stomach. It tried to gain the upper hand, but with the first block, she struck the inside of its elbow, snapping the arm in half. It spun, trying to strike her with a sidekick, but she ducked low.

Her knuckles hit the construct in the Adam's apple, forcing a retreat. But she snaked a hand behind its head, pulling it down as she brought up her knee. She wrapped her arm around its neck, grabbing her other arm for leverage. It struggled, but she refused to let go, tightening her grip until it went limp.

"Computer," she barked.

Even with the suit restricting her to the strength of a normal human, she found the fight to be easy. For a moment, she wondered if the computer had admitted defeat. The lights built into the walls of the room grew brighter until it was nearly impossible to see. Eve squinted against the light, her eyes almost burning.

"What are you—" She spat as something struck her torso, forcing her to keel over. Eve was about to try again when the suit registered another strike along her back.

The computer had robbed her of her sight and sent another construct to do what its brethren couldn't. She closed her eyes, bringing her arms up close to her face to protect herself. Swinging wide with her right arm, she hoped to catch it in the chest. She repeated the maneuver again, trying to make her arm as long as possible. The strike hit nothing but empty air.

Her knee bent as something kicked her from behind. She couldn't fight an opponent if she couldn't find it. The computer changed the rules of the game in order to provide her with the challenge she demanded.

With her eyes tightly closed, she tried to imagine where it would strike next. For a moment, she felt the construct standing behind her. She rolled to the side as it leaned in, ready to strike. There was no blow, a minor victory.

She couldn't see the hologram, but she sensed it. Eve summoned the part of her brain that accessed her gifts. There were so many electromagnetic fields in the room, it became almost as blinding as the light itself. The lines of energy moved swiftly, starting bold and thick and diminishing as the fields dissipated. Everything from the lights, the heat generated from her boots scraping on the floor to her breath generated an electromagnetic charge, and right now, they overwhelmed her senses.

The construct's foot moved through the air and at the last moment, she could sense the lines that made it visible.

"Oomph," she spat as the nodes in her stomach registered a firm strike.

"Elevated heart rate. Terminating—"

"Computer, override."

She closed her eyes and took a steadying breath. It was the first time she fought without her sight. She could dodge, deflect, and lash out against an opponent she could see, but this was an Alyssa-level fight. Her mentor would have sensed the movements almost supernaturally. How could she fight the construct if it didn't make any sound?

Something moved through the static noise. Tossing her arm up, she connected with the computer. The lines rippled, and she caught the construct's arm before it managed an uppercut. The hair on the back of her neck stood on end. She kicked backward, the heel of her foot hitting a new opponent.

"Tricky," she huffed.

Palm thrust forward. The force of the blow rippled

along her body. The energy radiating from the suit paled in comparison to the pulsing of her heart. Her blood pumped as the computer required effort from her to land each strike.

She sought the construct behind her. Pushing through the white noise, she could sense the human-sized figure. Eve pivoted on her heel and growled as she thrust both hands outward. The energy ruptured, the electromagnetic fields trembling throughout the room. The construct dissolved, the lines tearing apart.

Lights in the room dimmed, and she opened her eyes. One figure remained prone on the floor while the other had vanished. She eyed her hands, unsure of what had happened.

"Computer, what just happened?"

The voice didn't quite come through. It took a moment before the male voice returned to normal. "An electric disruption caused a failure in construct number two."

"Holy hell," she muttered. Holding up her hands, she smiled. It was the first time her passive abilities had manipulated the fields. "Computer, send work out data to my phone."

"Delivered."

The smirk spread across her face as she panted. "I'm going to be a Sentinel."

"Surely you jest," Alyssa said.

The woman sitting across the table shook her head. Removing her glasses, she folded them neatly and set them on the clipboard in front of her. She took a deep breath, collecting her thoughts. Along with Dwayne and Conthan, three other people sat on the Council, each overseeing a particular area of the Tower's operations.

"Maeve, are you asking what I think?"

She nodded, brushing her hair behind her right ear. "You know that the research teams have been studying your abilities. Some Children have abilities far too volatile to control. It has been one of our top priorities to find a way to safely and humanely suppress our gifts."

"Let the record show, I remain against power suppression," Alyssa quickly added.

Dwayne leaned forward, resting his elbows on the table. He tapped the band around his wrist. "If it wasn't for this, I would be a liability to the Tower. There are plenty of people who would like some sense of normalcy."

Errick nodded. "I agree with Dwayne. Juliet has to fear that everything she touches melts. Can you imagine how it would change her life?"

"It is part of who we are. It might not always be easy, but this is a solution too easily abused." They had discussed it at length when Maeve joined their community. A former Genesis Division employee, she served as the bridge between the Children and the scientists who worked in the labs deep beneath the Tower.

"How is it any different from treating cancer? Or a prosthetic for somebody who has lost a limb?" Errick asked. Alyssa admired the chief of their medical staff. He worked closely with Maeve, learning new ways to treat not only the Children in the Tower but develop new technologies to better mankind.

"Errick, please don't believe me naïve." Maeve was an ambitious woman looking to push the boundaries of science. Thankfully, Errick balanced her endeavors with his pragmatic nature. "This is not the same thing as a treatment for a medical condition. Our abilities are not ailments."

"Perhaps. But you're saying this as somebody whose gifts enhance their life. Shouldn't it be Juliet's decision?"

Alyssa shook her head. "I have no issue with augmentation or even developing methods to compensate for our abilities. But can you imagine if the Warden had access to technology that could suppress our abilities? He'd have stopped all of us. We'd have been defenseless. It's a dangerous road we walk."

Invoking the Warden's name quieted the table. It had become taboo to bring him up in casual conversations. Everybody on the Council had been the victim of his aspirations for world conquest. Alongside Dwayne and Conthan, she had fought to stop the man. Errick had spent countless hours in triage tents, using his abilities to mend deadly wounds. While not part of the war effort, Maeve found her colleagues slaughtered by the Warden. Each of them took a moment of silence to process the path that brought them to this table.

Maeve straightened her back, pushing the hair behind her ear again out of nervous habit. "We believe we are close to reaching a solution. It's tech-based and has to be calibrated to each Child. But it would suppress their abilities similar to the bracelet Dwayne wears."

"Reversible?" asked Alyssa.

"Temporary," Maeve said with a nod. "I know where you stand on this matter. We have intentionally avoided research that might lead to permanent removal of our gifts."

Alyssa didn't like it, not in the least. But at least the

woman still played by their rules. Part of the Tower's philosophy was community and transparency. The details of this meeting would be available for the residents to view by morning. Dangerous powers remained at the top of their priorities.

"My only other report involves Chimera." Both Dwayne and Conthan sat upright at the mention of the Warden's pet project. "Before you get your spandex in a bunch, it's not what you think. The research we recovered does have the potential for instilling powers into humans, but it is incomplete and it's at least twenty years away."

Alyssa remembered the human subjects housed in the basement of the Facility, a prison for people with powers. The Warden, a Child himself, conducted experiments with the former CEO of Genesis Division with the blessing of the President of the former United States of America. The trinity of evil.

"What good can come from his research?" Alyssa sat on the Council as the head of the Sentinels, the tower's self-appointed security force, but amongst the six of them, she remained the most reserved. It had been less dire before arriving at the Tower. They acted like the Home Owners's Association, helping introduce people to the community and settle the occasional dispute. Now, with near limitless resources and technologies at their disposal, she felt their hubris posed the greatest threat.

"He focused on adapting the abilities of Children and infusing them in humans. He had never been successful, and we have no intentions of continuing that train of thought." The air suddenly turned chilly as Maeve's abilities pulled the moisture from the air and lowered the temperature. The loss of control was a sure sign she was excited about the next words out of her mouth.

"We have found ways to duplicate some abilities with technology."

Conthan leaned forward, his eyebrow raised. "Really? Who's abilities?"

Reaching into her pocket, she pulled out a small box only slightly larger than a deck of cards. "That wasn't me chilling the air." She eyed Alyssa as if she had heard her thoughts. "It's limited in range, but I've effectively duplicated my abilities."

"To what end?" asked Alyssa, holding her hand out for the device. Maeve slid it across the table. It was compact and seemed innocent enough, but it had created a chill in the air around them.

"My abilities aren't much different from how a common refrigerator works. Matter of fact, most of our abilities are easily replicated. But there are a handful who could prove massive breakthroughs for mankind."

Alyssa followed the scientist's line of sight. Her gaze remained fixated on Conthan, and suddenly she understood the potential of this breakthrough. "You could create a transit system with Conthan's abilities."

"He wouldn't be our primary method of travel."

"I'm being replaced by a box?" Conthan laughed. "But it'd be nice not to be opening portals every day for the scientists to come and go. Or supplies. You know how boring it is to be the supply guy?"

"What about Errick's abilities?" Maeve asked. "The medical breakthroughs are numerous."

Dwayne nodded in agreement. "Errick and Maeve, meet with your teams, and let's make this the focus of our next meeting. What are the benefits and do they outweigh any pitfalls? Then we can vote if we want to move forward with this."

"End meeting," Alyssa said. The orb hovering over the table lowered slowly until it rested in the middle of their table. "Upload recording to Council channel."

"We're done?" Errick asked.

"No," Alyssa said, "but we have a matter to discuss off the record."

Maeve shook her head. "This isn't protocol."

Dwayne held up his hand. "Hear her out, and then we can decide as a group if we want it on the record."

Alyssa held her hand up, silencing the members of the Council. Just beyond the rose bushes, she watched a shadow stand upright. At most meetings, Ned locked the doors so they could meet without disturbance. Either their newest visitor had been here before they arrived, or they had sidestepped his security.

"Who is it?" Her voice didn't leave room for interpretation.

"Sorry, sorry," Eve said, and Alyssa's muscles relaxed as Conthan and Dwayne's daughter stepped out.

"Shouldn't you be at home?" asked Conthan.

"I thought..." Alyssa raised an eyebrow. Of all the Children in the Tower, Eve knew best their need for discretion during these meetings.

"I wanted to tell you about the wall," Eve said.

"We have your report," Alyssa said. "It should be sufficient."

"Oh," she replied. "Okay. I'll head out. I just wanted to make sure I didn't leave anything out."

"We'll be back shortly, Eve," Dwayne said. "I'm making steaks."

She nodded, giving a slight wave before she headed

out. Alyssa had read the report, and Eve had been far more thorough than any of the other maintenance crews. She'd need to talk to her and see how Eve was adjusting to her new role.

Alyssa eyed the sphere resting on the table. Even though it had stopped recording, she had no doubt that Needles, their sixth member of the Council, was listening intently. Unlike the five of them, he served as the only human, a reminder that not all of their population were blessed with powers. It also helped that he currently served as the head of technologies and infrastructure for the Tower. Nobody in attendance knew the Tower better than him.

"We have a traitor amongst us," Alyssa said calmly. "They disabled the control mechanism to the shield. Not only that, but when we went looking for the footage to discover their identity, they had disrupted the cameras. We have no idea who it might be."

Dwayne eyed her before looking at Errick and Maeve. "Do we discuss it on the record?"

Both shook their heads. "We're in agreement."

"If they were tampering with the shields, we have to assume it's because they either wanted out, or they wanted something to enter." Alyssa and Needles had already discussed the ramifications. He missed the meeting tonight to build a more robust method for finding the traitor. Unable to trust his staff, it all rested on his shoulders.

"What does it mean?" Errick asked.

"We don't know," she admitted, "but we've been training for this. Tomorrow I'm going to observe the other powers classes and see who we might recruit for security."

She omitted the information about Skits' disappearance. They were as open as they could be about the activities that occurred at the Tower, but the only people who knew about the Wet Works were the Nighthawks. Once the Tower was secure, she'd pay Gretchen and Lilian a visit and rescue Skits if she must.

"You're preparing for war," Maeve said in a whisper.

Alyssa nodded. "We've always been at war. But now the enemy has invaded our home."

"Not again," Errick muttered.

"This time we will be ready," she promised. "I'm activating the Sentinels."

Chapter Four

2039

"In the name o' the wee man."

Patches couldn't hide his excitement. With eyes wide, he tried to take in the massive room lined with shelves. When he thought he had taken it all in, he looked up to see a balcony running along the outside of the second and third stories. It wasn't as massive as the Chicago Public Library, but then he only worked in a small section of the massive building.

"This is all mine?"

"I've looked over your job placement," she held up her phone. The screen had the picture he had taken at the transportation office when he left Chicago. Next to it were the words, "Assignment: Head Librarian."

"I can't believe it." The shelves were bare, the middle of the room filled with palettes of unopened boxes. "Hopefully they gave you more information than that."

"Conthan wrote 'library stuff,' as your job description. So I'm pretty sure he's never set foot in one before."

The excitement of being in charge of his own library forced an audible giggle from his throat. This would have never been an opportunity in Chicago. Even if he received his doctorate and slaved away in the stacks, he'd only have been given the chance during his retirement years. To be twenty-four and in charge of his own library, it was…

"This is terrifying," he admitted. The excitement came laced with a sense of fear. He didn't know how the Tower worked. Did he have to get his acquisitions approved? Who would come in to check out the books? He hardly knew the demographic other than they had powers. He couldn't fill an entire library with research papers on the origins of the Nostradamus Effect.

"When I started here, it was much of the same." She walked to the closest box and peered inside. "You're the welcoming committee they said, make sure people adjust to the community. What does that even mean?"

He stopped marveling at the immensity of the space to study Adelaide. She couldn't be much older than him, but the way she spoke, it defied her age. She pulled back the top of a box and tore at the plastic. Holding up a single book, he leaned in to see the title. Basic Algebra.

"Okay, so it looks like I'm going to be in charge of the textbooks. I can handle that." It wasn't something he typically did, but he could manage. "I'll need to talk to whoever is in charge of education here."

"Professor Mary," she said. "You'll like her. The school isn't big, but she makes sure those kids are getting the best education."

Patrick opened the next box to find it filled with packing peanuts. He dug through to find a glass container inside. Brushing the tiny white flecks to the side, he found the case held a robotic hand. His eyebrow raised as he tipped the box, showing Adelaide.

"Jasmine Gentile," she said. "That must be her first prosthetic. Let me tell you, she was not pleased to receive that. You'd think the head of the Paladins would be grateful to receive a prosthetic from the Body Shop."

He picked up the case and inspected the metallic digits on the hand. It wasn't anything he'd expect to find in a library. "So, I'm holding somebody's hand?"

"Former hand. She's in charge of the Paladins, a military unit. If you've been to the commons in Chicago, you've seen her statue before."

He had, in fact, seen her statue many times. It was weird to be holding a piece of history in his hands. It wasn't a book, but he could catalog the artifacts and put them on display for posterity. He returned the prosthetic to the box.

"Okay, so school, history. This is going to be a bit of everything." His mind was swirling, trying to establish where he should start first. There were more than a hundred boxes stacked throughout the library. It looked more like a warehouse than any library he had worked in.

"Think | Look of | at it this way." Adelaide rested a hand on his shoulder. "You're | He's now the keeper of our | Children's past and that provides | gives us a roadmap | path to our future."

He took a step back from her. Her speech pattern turned almost robotic. He feared the woman might be in the throes of a stroke. It was the first time she spoke as if multiple people were having a conversation.

"What was that?"

"I | We are a collective." She pointed to the box behind her ear. "I | She am | is not a Child, but I | he is."

"But yesterday…"

"We | She is still a human | individual."

Adelaide's eyes glazed over as she stared into space. "Adelaide is a cherished priestess in the Church of Nostradamus. She has been with us since the beginning. Like many, she is part of a collective consciousness."

Patrick couldn't stare her in the eyes anymore. It was awkward to know he was talking to more than one person at times, people he couldn't see. He eyed a box, grabbing a book inside, focusing on the cover as he spoke. "So there are more of you in there?" Telepaths could rob a host of their free will and speak through them. People spoke about the Battle for Chicago, claiming a telepath caused it.

He glanced up from the history textbook to see she was smiling as she eyed him. "Like you, Azacca is a Child of Nostradamus. He broadcasts his thoughts on a specific frequency and the CPU behind my ear allows us to operate as a hive."

"So he can hear you right now? Don't you worry about privacy?"

She shook her head. "I am a humble servant dedicated to uplifting the titans sent to us by a higher power."

"You worship," he gulped, "Children?" He couldn't fathom why anybody would want to form a religion around people like him.

She laughed. "It's going to take time, but you're going to need to be open."

"To what?" He couldn't imagine having another person sharing his thoughts, or worse yet, hearing the thoughts of another person. He spent far too much of his life trying to maintain some semblance of privacy.

"You are not like other people." Her hand wrapped

around her neck and her finger tapped on the bump behind her ear. "I am not like other people. Be open to the possibilities. We are here because the outside world hasn't evolved with us."

He placed his arm on her shoulder as she had done to him earlier. "You know your pep talks are almost as terrifying as dealing with this." He gestured to the room with countless hours of work ahead of him. "A simple, 'you've got this,' would be fine."

"I don't know. Do you've got this?" Her eyebrow raised.

He set the textbook back into the box. "Yeah." He didn't have any clue how he'd manage, but he had to believe. "I've got this. Consider yourself my first volunteer and help me start opening boxes."

"I | We see you."

He bit his tongue. *That* was going to take some getting used to.

"Imagine sinking into the sand, relaxing your body one part at a time. Let the tension leave your toes and then your feet. As you work your way to your legs, imagine the sand supporting your knees. Keep breathing. Deep breaths in through the nose and out through the mouth."

Eve ignored the teacher's meditation. While he attempted a more holistic approach to accessing their abilities, she could only focus on the construct from the night before. She no longer belonged in a room full of passives. She had spent the night staring at her phone, looking at the biometrics of the suit the moment the construct disintegrated. None of the readings made sense.

She turned her head to stare in the mirror that covered one side of the studio. The multi-purpose room had been designed to accommodate everything from ballet to yoga. There were many like it throughout the Tower, offering everybody a chance to indulge in their hobbies. Right now, however, it housed half a dozen students attempting to find an inner calm so they could access their abilities.

Somewhere just beyond the wall, somebody walked down the hall with a purpose. Eve sat upright, imagining she could see through the stark white barrier to the person approaching. They moved quickly, passing through the fields generated by the electronics in the wall. The person slowed as they approached the door. Eve tightened her hand into a fist as her instructor sat up from his spot on the floor.

"Eve," he started, "is everything okay?"

"Somebody's coming," she said.

Alyssa pulled open the glass door to the studio, causing Eve to jump to her feet. It had been ages since she had the opportunity to train with her mentor. Once Alyssa created the Sentinels, she rarely had the time or energy to spar with Eve. She wouldn't confess it aloud, but it was one of the many reasons she wanted into the program. It would be like old times in their cul-de-sac, practicing in the front yard.

"Eli." Eve's heart sank as Alyssa spoke the instructor's name. Any hope that she interrupted their class to offer her a spot amongst the Sentinels vanished. "Do you think it would be possible to have a word?"

Alyssa stepped toward the door as Eli got up and

followed. Her face didn't give away any secrets. She finally turned her back so she could speak without any of them reading her lips. None of the other five students had the ability to hear beyond that of the average human, but Eve turned to them, shrugging her shoulders, hoping they had more of a clue. Their faces were even more puzzled than hers.

Eve cleared her throat, preparing to question Alyssa's presence, when the lights shut off. Had they been in one of the rooms along the exterior of the Tower, they'd make do with sunlight, but here in the middle of the structure, they all tensed in the absolute darkness.

"Margo," Eve said, "can you help us?"

A soft yellow light radiated off a girl barely in her teens. The classroom's mantra, '*All Powers Are Useful*' proved more insightful than usual. It wouldn't last for long. Eve had clocked the girl's abilities before, and within the first twelve minutes she lost ninety percent of her light.

"Don't be scared," Alyssa said, but Eve knew better. The perfectly even manner she spoke usually gave away her desire to keep secrets. When she eyed each of the students, she paused on Eve. "Eve, keep an eye on them." With a slight scuffle of feet, Alyssa and Eli vanished from the multi-purpose room into the hallway.

Eve spun around to face the five students. She wasn't the oldest, but she had her abilities longer than any of her classmates. She took inventory of their gifts, assessing any potential should this be more than a power outage.

"Eve, what's going on?" asked Paul, the eldest student. "Why did Alyssa ask you—"

"Shh," Eve pressed her palms onto the floor. "There's

no electricity getting in my way. I should be able to see what's going on."

The wooden slats under her hands were cool to the touch. The Tower had died. There were emergency lights on throughout the building, but the massive current that made it impossible for her to sense the world suddenly vanished. The fog cleared, and she could sense every square inch of the building and the surrounding grounds.

She pushed harder than she had tried before. There were people, tiny blips everywhere throughout the building. They moved quickly, running as if their lives depended on it. Dozens were moving toward the main entrance while plenty moved further into the Tower. Something out there caused a panic, alerting some while chasing clusters of Children away.

"Oh shit." Her eyes opened and she could no longer see the people, only feet in front of her. Instead, she felt the electrical pulses running toward the building. There were more than a hundred of them coming at the Tower in a well-organized manner. As they neared the main door of the Tower, they broke rank. A cluster moved toward the entrance while others ran toward the outer wall of the Tower.

"Synthetics." Eve fell backward, trying to shake the drunken sensation caused by her abilities. "There's a lot of them. They're attacking the Tower."

Margo started crying.

Nobody in this room was prepared for the horror approaching. Passives didn't have to train with their gifts in the same way the active powers did. There was no gym time, little to no creative use of their abilities. The former government had created these machines to keep the peace, and at every turn they had been used to hunt and kill the Children of Nostradamus. If a synthetic broke into this room, they would die.

"Are you sure?" asked Paul.

"I've sensed them before. But not like this." Dwayne had taken her along when a neighbor swore they heard noises at night coming from the woods behind her house. They had found a synthetic under a fallen tree. Eve had watched astonished as electricity poured out of her adoptive father's palms, frying the robot.

"I want everybody in the corner, away from the door," she said.

Paul picked Margo up and carried her to the corner while the others followed suit. She put her back to the wall, inching toward the door. If it opened, she'd worry about the consequences later. She spent years training with Alyssa, but never had she faced a real opponent. Her heart quickened, beating almost loud enough for her to feel the pulse in her fingertips.

Eve placed her palms against the wall, letting her abilities drift outward. She didn't need to feel the entire compound, just the area closest to them. The electromagnetic fields from the front of the building were being distorted. Dwayne—she recognized the bursts of lightning at his command. They were fighting. Almost forty Children pushed the synthetics back from the entrance.

"Oh no," she whispered. While they maintained the front of the Tower, the other packs had taken to climbing the walls. They were breaching the building in a dozen locations. The Children inside were scattered, running. Those that remained deep inside the Tower weren't fighters. They attempted to protect families and human loved ones.

Eve balled her fists. She didn't need to reach far to feel the synthetic stalking through the hallway. Only a few inches of wall separated her and a room of scared Children from a robotic killing machine. If she closed her eyes, she could sense the machine's movements, pausing every few steps to assess if there were any Children nearby.

It stopped. At this range, she could detect the synthetic staring at the wall. It only made sense that killing machines could detect faint sounds or even see through walls. Margo tried to stifle her tears, but the girl's sobs filled the room.

It was time to prove she could be a Sentinel.

Chapter Five

2039

Patrick stood in the dark, holding a mannequin clad in an old leather jacket. He had been trying to sort out its significance when the lights in the library shut off. After hearing the pilot speak with the Tower command yesterday, he wondered if the Tower had more growing pains than they let on in the brochure.

"I'm just going to hang out in the dark," he sang to himself. "Who needs eyes to see what they're doing."

Adelaide had left several minutes before the lights went off, claiming she needed to see to another recent arrival, but he suspected the dusty boxes causing her to sneeze had sent her running. "Not everybody appreciates the awesomeness of being a librarian," he said to himself. He waited for a moment, spinning around with arms stretched out. "What? Nobody? Sheesh, tough crowd."

The room turned red as emergency lights flared to life. He tried squinting at a book on the table in front of him but couldn't make out the text on the cover. "I suppose twenty-seven boxes are enough for the first day.

I wouldn't want to overwhelm myself with too much fun."

Something made a noise on the other side of the door, and he hoped it was Adelaide returning to offer extra muscle. At least with her there, he'd be able to ask more questions about his new home. Patrick walked toward the door when he heard a scream. Picking up the pace, he picked up steam, preparing to barge through the exit. There were more screams and then the air vibrated, causing the double doors of the library to shake.

He reached for the handle as the door flung open and a woman knocked into him hard enough to send him hurtling into a stack of boxes. His skin burned, starting with the spot that hit the boxes. The heat rippled along his skin, dispersing the heat until the sting was nothing more than an annoyance. There was no pain, just a warmth he couldn't control. He didn't have a chance to ask what was going on when the door tore off the hinges.

The red lights gleamed off the metallic surface of the robot. Patches' blood ran cold as his brain pieced together the reality looming before him. Every person in Chicago remembered the slaughter caused by the metal terrors.

"Run," he yelled.

"Shit." The woman ran, but tripped over one of the boxes littering the floor. She hit the ground, crawling her way past a stack of history textbooks. The synthetic followed, and with a single powerful stride, towered above her. She spun over and froze. In the red light, her face appeared straight from a horror movie, mouth gaping as if a scream would pour forth at any moment.

Patrick gasped as the synthetic grabbed her by the neck. Lifting her off her feet, she dangled like a broken doll, a helpless victim. He tried moving but found his feet wouldn't respond, as if they knew better than to confront the killing machine. "Let go of her," he yelled.

She held onto its forearm and braced her feet against its torso. Her body tensed and screeching metal filled the silence of the library. Then, kicking off, sparks lit up the room. She fell again, holding its severed forearm in her hand. The woman was strong, but sheer strength wouldn't stop a machine designed to kill their kind.

"Get out of here," she yelled. "I've got this."

He wasn't convinced. It wasn't the one-armed synthetic that worried him. Its sibling stepped into the broken doorway, looking to aid its brother. He didn't have time to regret coming to the Tower. Desperation lightened his feet, and he managed a step toward the hulking robot. He screamed as he lowered his shoulder and charged the synthetic closest to her.

It swatted at Patches, striking his back as he barreled into the robot. The warmth in his skin turned to a stinging burn. At any moment, it felt as if his body would burst into flames and he'd smell charred flesh. The synthetic came around for another blow and this time, when it struck him in the chest, he let loose a guttural scream. He forced the heat from his chest into his shoulders and arms.

As the killing machine snatched at his throat, Patches grabbed its wrist. The servo wheezed as it leaned forward, using its weight to overcome him. A whining filled the air as he pushed back, crushing the synthetic's arm. The searing pain throughout his body diminished enough to think clearly. He came around with the back of his other hand, striking its torso, sending it soaring into the air.

The second synthetic raised both arms, small guns springing from its forearms. Patrick froze, unsure if he should run or try to jump from the line of fire. His legs trembled and for a moment, he thought he'd piss himself before being shot through the forehead. Unlike the first, this machine had been painted, a blue stripe coating half its face.

The war paint only made it look more menacing.

"Blue," shouted the woman, "stop."

The synthetic paused, head cocking to the side. Patrick balled his fist, forcing his feet to obey. He hardly managed one step. He tried to decide if his body could absorb the impact of a bullet or if it'd tear through his skin and bury itself in his flesh.

The woman walked between him and the synthetic, her hands held up as if she attempted to broker a peace deal with the killer. "Blue, it's me, Eve. You wouldn't hurt me. Where is Skits? Is she with you?"

Patrick watched as its head tilted from one side to the other as if it understood her question. Despite the robot's perplexed expression, it never lowered its arms. Patrick didn't know who the woman was or why she thought she could reason with artificial intelligence.

"Blue, you know me." Her tone lowered, almost cooing.

The synthetic on the floor used its broken arm to push itself upright. Patrick prepared to throw her aside and die a hero when the blue synthetic lunged. He tensed, closing his eyes, but didn't hear gunfire, just the sound of metal scraping on metal.

"Thank god," she let out a long sigh.

Patrick opened one eye, scared he'd still be shot before the day was over. Blue had the other synthetic by the neck, pulling its skull apart. Even if the machine had saved her, the casual ferocity it demonstrated didn't make it any less frightening.

"What the—"

It chucked the corpse of its sibling before lowering its arms at its side. She ran up to the machine and hugged it like they were old friends. Patrick couldn't understand why anybody, especially a Child, would embrace one of the murderous machines.

"Blue, what's going on?"

"You know this thing?" None of this made sense to him.

She glanced back over her shoulder like she had forgotten he was in the room. "Long story. My aunt adopted him after the battle in Chicago. There was a platoon of them that helped the Nighthawks. Only Blue survived and he's been with her ever since."

"You don't say long story and then ex—wait, it's a pet? What about the others?"

"Never seen them before."

"What the hell is happening?"

She turned around, her face scrunched up, the anger seeping into her eyes. "We're being attacked. Can you fight?"

"No."

"A crushed synthetic says otherwise."

"I can't."

"What's your powers?"

"It's complicated."

"Dammit," she growled, "you're a liability."

"I'm—"

"Stay here and keep an eye on Blue."

"You're going to leave me alone with that thing? It'll try to kill me."

She placed her hands on the synthetic's head, standing on her tiptoes so they were almost face to face. "Blue, promise not to kill—" she looked over her shoulder again. "What's your name?"

"Patrick. But everybody calls me Patches."

"I'm Eve."

"You're not—"

"Promise not to hurt Patches?" The machine's head nodded up and down. "You do what he says. Treat him just like Skits or me. Do you understand?"

She patted it on the head before heading toward the door. "Patrick, keep an eye out. There's more of them. I'll be back to check on you soon."

Eve ran for the door and out into the hallway. She bolted left, leaving him staring at the synthetic. His skin continued burning as if ants marched along his arms and shoulders. It'd be hours before his skin returned to normal and he felt comfortable again. He had a silent battle in his head, trying to convince his feet to move. When they peeled off the floor and let him lean against a half-filled bookcase, he realized just how petrified he had been—and still was.

"I'm not a liability," he whispered aloud to convince himself.

Saying the words didn't change the reality, or made him feel better.

"Run," Alyssa screamed.

The lobby of the Tower had been full of residents. The synthetics broke through the doors and got into the open space. She regretted removing the ocular enhancement. Had she enough time, she'd break out her phone and go through the videos showing a dozen different fighting techniques. Perfectly curated after years of searching, she'd absorb every stance and maneuver, and without a single rehearsal, she'd be a master. There wasn't time to pause and let her abilities run wild. People were going to die.

"Computer, show me Rahim training selection."

The lobby was ten stories tall with floor-to-ceiling windows. The afternoon sun poured through the glass, illuminating the water feature in the middle of the room. Four bridges in the cardinal directions crossed over the water to a circle in the center, where a single great oak tree rose high into the air. On a typical day, it was a beautiful space to wander about with friends while discussing the latest gossip. But as one of the massive windows shattered, Alyssa realized their home had become a war zone.

The machine dropped from the balcony, the floor under its feet cracking. They were as terrifying as she remembered. The eyeless face stared at her while it raised its limb, the cannon on its arm emerging, ready to fire. The contact lens in her right eye showed a video of her training. Recorded months earlier, it sped along at high speed, almost too fast to comprehend.

As the gun fired, she jumped out of the way, sliding along the floor. She didn't have time to focus on the video. She rolled over, kicking her legs until she reached a crouching position. Her muscles responded as if she had performed the maneuver a thousand times before.

Perfect execution, just as she had seen in the video. Alyssa didn't need a tingling sensation to know her abilities were at work, she simply *knew*.

Two steps toward the machine, she sprung forward, rolling into a somersault, careful to watch for the cannons on its arm. The shots fired, and she hissed as the heat of the bullets passed dangerously close to her back. She sprung up, bending at the waist, one of her feet passed overhead, smacking into the skull of the machine. It grabbed her leg, just as she predicted. They were superior fighting machines, but whatever computers made up their adaptation algorithms still followed a routine. She strived on predictable opponents, ones she could learn from and adapt to.

Its other arm pointed downward, preparing to fire. Hanging on the arm, she twisted her body, grabbing its arm, forcing it to bend. Her body vibrated as two shots fired at its own face. She held still for a moment to see if the machine had any fight left or if she had penetrated its central computer.

"One," she kicked off, pulling her leg from its grip.

The video in her contact lens resumed playing. In a few seconds, she watched nearly ten hours of urban tactical strategies, along with mixed martial arts and weapons handling. She might not have the flashiest power in the Tower, but she counted herself as the most deadly.

Hiding in the center of the room, two people had pressed themselves against the oak tree, trying to stay out of sight of approaching synthetics. Neither had any active abilities to take on the robots. Leaning forward, she started in a mad dash to reach them before a trio of killer robots found their next prey.

She reached the bridge leading to the oak at the center of the lobby. The three machines were only feet from being able to turn and point their weapons at the couple. Pulling at a bracelet on her left arm, she separated it, letting the thin filament between the bands shine. If her body wasn't enough of a weapon, nearly every accessory on her served a dual purpose. Children who relied solely on abilities were never as prepared as her. If she was going to be the deadliest person in the room, she'd make every part of her become a weapon.

She reached the tree, startling the two Children clenching their eyes shut as if they could will away the danger. She put her back to the tree, waiting for the arm of the synthetic to appear.

"When I say run, go," she whispered.

The synthetic appeared to her side, and she created a loop with the filament, snaring its arm. With a sharp tug, the arm severed, falling to the ground. The machine spun about, lining up the weapon on its remaining limb. Alyssa ducked under and bobbed to the side, repeating the maneuver. The filament passed through the metal as if it were nothing more than clay.

"Run!" she screamed.

With a sweep of her leg, she toppled the synthetic, but not before one of its companions fired. She tried to roll out of the way, but the fallen robot blocked her escape. Her teeth clenched tight as she made herself small. The guns let loose a rapid succession of shots.

There was no sting, no bullets penetrating her sternum. She sprung to her feet, willing to take the bad aim as a sign to continue dismantling the machines. The bullets left its weapon and should have struck her, should have killed her. But they vanished. A small black void opened in the air next to the closest synthetic's head, the munitions emerging and striking it in the skull.

The cavalry had arrived.

She fell through a similar void before she had time to find its creator. Years ago, they had practiced the execution of these maneuvers until they had them perfect. She welcomed the unpleasant icy cold of Conthan's portals. Unlike other Children, his abilities defied science, or at least that's what the researcher said for the time being. Even as she entered the portal, somewhere, her body was already exiting in another.

She emerged behind the third synthetic near the tree. She dropped ten feet from the air, twisting her body to use the momentum to her advantage. Her fingers searched for a spot on the machine's back. The moment she found a grip, she leaned backward, forcing it to teeter and lose its footing.

She kicked off as it staggered, trying to catch its balance. She should have sailed headfirst onto the cement paver, but the cold enveloped her skin again. Conthan remembered. Knowing that the Nighthawks hadn't grown soft in the luxury of the Tower brought about a renewed sense of vigor.

His portal redirected her again, a sensation that always caused her stomach to churn. Instead of soaring toward the pavement, she was lunging toward the front of the synthetic. It could be prepared for a long list of logical reactions, but Conthan's abilities were sporadic and unpredictable, the perfect counter to machine thinking.

Alyssa clutched the synthetic's wrists, toppling it. There was no pressure point to push or windpipe to crush. Unlike the men in the videos, there seemed to be only one way to stop them. Knee on its chest, she let go of the arms and quickly pulled at its head. The metal whined, refusing to break as easy as the other.

Shots fired from the cannons and she ducked low to its body to avoid being struck. With another yank, something tore apart, leaving the head dangling like fruit on the branch. Its body stiffened, and she attempted another pull, this time yanking the skull free.

"Three," she whispered.

More synthetics flanked her. The machines had transformed into k9 looking creatures. She hated the dogs more than she hated the synthetics. Smaller and able to move more quickly, they were even more ferocious than when they transformed into featureless humanoids.

The black void opened over her head. Conthan would run out of juice in the next few portals. Like most Children, he had limitations on how far he could extend himself before his body rebelled. Each black disc he created connected to somewhere else in the world, and if it appeared over her head, he had a plan. She just hoped he could execute it before the mutts descended upon her.

The first dog lunged, leaping into the air, hoping to use its weight to pin her to the grass. She dipped low, dropping into a pushup as it sailed overhead. With one arm, she pushed off, spinning onto her back just as she saw a thin black bar exit the portal. Conthan had, in fact, been paying attention when she spoke to him during training sessions. Perhaps he wasn't a lost cause after all.

The attacking synthetic skid to a stop and was turning around, preparing for a second attempt. The videos had an assortment of weapons training, but there was none she favored more than the staff. It had been the first weapon she learned to use. At first, she believed it weak since it didn't have a sharp edge, but her opinion changed when her mentor demonstrated the ferocity contained in the long piece of wood.

Technology had improved on its design.

Alyssa reached up, grabbing the foot-long staff just as the synthetic tried for a second leap. As soon as her fingers clenched around the black metal, it extended to its full five feet. She braced the weapon, hooking the end into its chest. She sent it flying out of reach, but not before she tapped her finger twice on the weapon. The end flared to life, a bright flash of plasma burning through the metal plating.

"Four," she whispered.

Spinning her legs, Alyssa jumped into a crouch and prepared for the four oncoming synthetics. A jab to the neck, searing through the hydraulics, left one head hanging by its wires. Next, she brought the weapon down over its head, denting its skull.

"Five."

They were learning. Two became three, then four. There was no fear as they rushed toward her. The synthetics were mindless killing machines, and they'd sacrifice themselves if it meant getting to their prey.

Alyssa spun the staff, separating it into two pieces. She jumped over the first, landing in a somersault and springing to her feet. The glowing tip of the batons drove into the closest synthetic's metallic skull. She understood why Skits loved her abilities so much. Having a weapon that reached forty-five thousand degrees almost made it unfair.

"Six."

They transformed and swarmed her. She ruptured

the power unit in one before the other knocked away one of her batons. They were no longer attempting to take her out one at a time. They moved as a pack, realizing the only way to overpower the fighter was by sheer force.

Alyssa heard the shoulder cannon powering up behind her, an awful wheezing. The next thing she'd feel was the burn of a laser as it pierced her skin. She had been lucky to this point and only burned a few times. But as they tightened their ranks, there would be no place for her to jump, spin, or flip out of the way.

She turned in time to see the black portal open overhead. If Conthan thought another weapon would save her, he was mistaken. He could have opened the portal inside the synthetic, severing its body. If he had demolished the shoulder cannon, perhaps she could have fought off the machines. But, try as she might, kicking the closest synthetic only bought her a few seconds.

A figure fell from the portal, a woman. The shoulder cannon fired and a bright red light silently attempted to burn its way through the chest of the newcomer. The synthetic to her left raised its arm, attempting to eliminate the newest threat. She knocked the wrist to the side, spinning in close, using her body as leverage as she smashed the inside of its elbow. Metal bent, leaving it another useless limb.

Her savior punched the synthetic, her fist breaking through the metal chest. She tore at the casing, tearing out the power unit before turning to Alyssa.

Jasmine Gentile. The only woman who Alyssa had never bested in practice had fallen from the heavens to save her. Conthan had bent space and time to find the one fighter who could mobilize and unify the Children within the Tower to resist the synthetics. Gifted with the ability to change the density of her skin, the soldier came equipped with natural body armor. And based on the military tactical suit, she had been involved in her own operation before Conthan borrowed her.

"Alhamdulillah" Alyssa said.

"One," the woman said with a smirk.

"Don't stop," Eve said, urging two young residents to keep running from the main lobby. She had to take a breath to focus on her abilities, to ensure they weren't heading into danger. Thankfully, it appeared that most of the synthetics that infiltrated the wall were focused on the fray in the lobby.

The immediate area didn't have the rapid pulsating electromagnetic fields given off by the synthetics. She pointed down the hallway, letting her abilities reveal the lack of machines. "Go that way and don't stop. Find the adults." They didn't hesitate, wanting nothing more than to be away from the carnage on the ground floor.

On the fifth story, she was safe to look down into the wide-open space that served as the Tower's lobby. It was impressive, meant to be a beacon to all those who walked through the front doors. A massive oak tree stood in the middle, surrounded by gardens filled with exotic flowers. Four bridges in the cardinal directions stepped over water, leading to more greenery and seating for those taking lunch breaks. It was easy to forget while sitting next to one of the many sculptures that you were inside the world's most advanced structure.

From her vantage point, she could see the Children who attempted to turn back the tide of machines. A flash filled the space, a blinding light as if lightning had struck within the walls of the Tower. It was followed by the sound of screeching metal and then yelling. They were barking orders at one another, mounting a defense.

Eve wanted to join, to arrive in the nick of time to prove she was capable of saving lives and defending her home. The determination and anger left the door open for doubt and fear. She had led the synthetic away from the classroom, and it came with a sense of pride. But when push came to shove, she only survived because of Patches and Blue. If she couldn't stop one of the machines, what were the chances of helping stop an army?

In her head, she imagined she'd be the hero and that somehow, the world would be a better place with her protecting it. After a questionable save, doubt held her in place. What if she arrived and once again somebody had to save her? What if she wasn't the hero, she told herself day after day? What if…

She wanted to join, but she couldn't. Eve struggled to breathe, her lungs working against her until she thought she might hyperventilate. She clung to the banister over-looking the lobby below and found her legs unable to hold her weight. While she struggled to stay upright and not pass out, she watched the heroes, the *actual* heroes.

Alyssa moved like a dancer, each bend and twist more elegant than the last. She and the two synthetics on either side moved in concert. They'd try to grab, and she'd slide out of the way. She paced herself, looking for opportunities to strike. She kicked one while shoving an electrified baton into the hip of the other. Even when they tried to use their guns, she had moved out of their line of sight. It was shocking to see Alyssa's abilities outrace synthetics created to destroy her.

Eve let out a long breath, pausing before she inhaled. An hour earlier, she mocked her teacher for guiding them through a meditation. Now she tried to remember the sand supporting her body, taking away the stress in her joints. Her legs were growing stronger, but not enough to let her leap from the balcony and join the fray below.

"Jasmine?" The military's most well-known Paladin fell out of nowhere. Living with Conthan, she had grown used to him teleporting everything from himself to the left-over steaks in the fridge. But for him to call reinforcements gave away how bad the situation had gotten.

Unlike Alyssa, Jasmine lacked grace. A synthetic's shoulder cannon flashed as it tried to bore a hole through her with a laser. She hardly flinched as the beam of light struck her in the chest. With a growl, she back-handed the machine, sending it hurdling twenty feet to the side. A juggernaut, she pulled one of the synthetics away from Alyssa, tearing its arm and neck apart like they were paper dolls.

The legendary Nighthawks had reunited once again to make a stand against the robots. Eve's heart skipped a beat as an intense power source created a cascade of ripples in the electromagnetic field just beneath her. There was only one Child in the Tower that wielded that kind of power.

A synthetic flew from the balcony below, and a bolt of lightning hammered its chest with a deafening crackle. His fists were visible, stretching outward. There was no build-up as they flashed white. The bolt of lightning split into a chain, skipping along the ground until a pair of synthetics attracted the uncanny energy. They may have survived the first onslaught, but it grew brighter, enough she had to shield her eyes. Now, the synthetics were nothing more than damaged hard drives and melted circuits.

"See anymore?" His voice was loud enough that it filled the lobby almost as much as his lightning.

Jasmine finished tearing a synthetic in half with her bare fists before spinning about. "I don't see." She paused as Alyssa ran past, kneeling next to a person lying on one of the bridges next to the oak tree. "Dwayne, we have injured. You need to find Errick. Now."

"Can you find him? You're—" Dwayne's words were quiet, meant for somebody standing nearby.

"I can do it." She recognized Conthan's voice. For the past five years, those two men had helped make her the woman she was. But up to this point, she had only heard stories about their efforts. For a time, she believed them to be tales that grew with each retelling, but today they were proving their merit.

"Don't be a hero," Dwayne said. There was a tenderness in those words that cut through the tragedy and gave her a slight smile. If Conthan had been using his abilities to help bring reinforcements, he'd be nearly tapped out. Pushing himself further, he always ran the risk of his abilities taking control and leaving him a burned-out husk of a man.

"Never," Conthan said, "that's a job for the next generation."

She wanted them to be speaking about her. But as her

fingers dented the metal railing, there was little doubt they spoke about the Sentinels. Her heart wanted to plow down the stairs into the lobby and stand with the Nighthawks, but her body betrayed her.

Eve stumbled away from the banister, her legs folding at the second step. She collapsed, face nearly smacking against the tile. There was no way the next generation would be heroes, not if they were like her. Curling into a ball, the cold of the tile pressed against her face. The tears streamed down her eyes as she let out a sob.

Chapter Six

2018

"Are you crying, boy?"

The man's harsh voice rang in the boy's ear. The boy shook his head, but it was impossible to hide the tears running down his face. He stared at the young girl, unconscious in the middle of the room. Nearly two dozen pairs of eyes remained fixed on him, judging his actions. The other children in the room stood rigid, unwilling to speak, for fear of the man's rage turning in their direction.

"Boy, why are you crying?"

He stared at his hand, the sensation of her sternum breaking still reverberating through his fingers. The snap could be heard louder than her grunt. He had done that, broken the girl's bones. He had frozen until her chest resumed moving in a rhythmic manner. Tears rolled down his cheek, thankful he hadn't killed his friend.

"I-I thought I killed her."

"The clans kill all the good Children? Are you the best Scotland—"

"Alba," he spat out of reflex.

"The Queen should have eradicated the uprising."

Standing upright, the instructor paced around the fallen girl. The boy watched him while the instructor inspected the faces of the others watching their match. The room was massive, but the other kids stood on the edge of a giant circle to one side of the space. It had become their second home, a training facility where they were tested time and time again. He had seen the older kids use the space for matches, but today had been the first for his class. Luck abandoned him when Feral pointed in his direction.

The boy didn't want to fight his friend.

"Celebrate," Feral bellowed, "you're standing, and she's not. Given the chance, she'd have done the same."

The boy refused to believe she would have hurt him. The girl had been one of the few kids at the academy to treat him like a real person. He had never wanted to come to this cursed place, but the rules required him to serve. Despite the rigorous classroom work, studying abilities possessed by other Children of Nostradamus, he found a friend, somebody who hated the academy as much as him.

"Erica—" More than a few kids gasped. He shut his mouth quickly, hoping Feral hadn't heard his slip of the tongue.

The fast stomping feet caught him off guard as the man wrapped a hand about his throat. He pulled at the man's wrist as he was lifted from the mats. Feral lived up to his name, growling as the boy's legs dangled in the air. He had broken one of the fundamental rules of the academy. There was no stopping the man. He couldn't grab hold of Feral's fingers and pry himself free.

"Who are you?" Spit pelted his face as Feral shouted.

The edges of his vision blurred as his oxygen-deprived brain shut down. "N-n-nobody." He struck the floor, collapsing as he sucked in air, praying it wouldn't be his last.

"You are nobody," the man said. He returned to his walk around the circle, drawing the attention of the other students. "You do not have a name. You have no value."

Feral pointed to two of the recruits and then to the girl. There were no words exchanged as they scrambled to pick her up by the arms. Pulling her from the circle, a boy lifted her and headed toward the main doors, exiting the training room. He watched his friend being carted off, taken to the medical unit. He prayed they could save her.

"You," Feral pointed to another girl, one of the larger recruits, "take her place."

The boy hadn't crawled to his feet before she stepped into the circle. There were no formal beginning or end, no pleasantries as she approached him, slamming her foot into his stomach. The scream left his lips as he rolled away. He didn't want to fight, to hurt another person. But unlike before, he didn't know this girl.

"Defend yourself or undergo reprogramming."

The threat caused the others to gasp. There was no worse threat than undergoing the administrations of the Programmers. He didn't want to face them, to allow them access to his thoughts. It was win the fight or be tortured. It wasn't much of a choice, but as he jumped to his feet, he decided.

"Girl. Beat some sense into him."

Her fists answered. The first punch came wide, attempting to clock him on the side of the head. He ducked, but discovered her deception as she drove her knee into his chin. Teeth bit through his lip, and he tasted the blood filling his mouth. Next, she attempted to drive her elbow down on the back of his neck.

He pivoted, spinning out of the way and instead of putting distance between them, he stepped closer. Driving two knuckles into her kidney, she grunted. She managed a punch to the face, but unable to lean into it, it did little other than intensify the stinging in his lip.

They had taught them to be fast, to strike at every opportune moment, to never back down. He threw Feral's teachings out the window and swung an arm between her legs and under her armpit. The unorthodox maneuver made her freeze as he lifted her. By the time she caught on with what was happening, he reversed directions and slammed her onto the floor.

"Finish her," Feral growled.

The boy's breath came in ragged gasps. He stepped back from her, refusing to obey the man's sadistic prodding.

"Kill him." The command came as easily as pointing to the boys to remove his friend. The girl spun around on the floor, using the momentum of her legs to kick herself upright. Unlike the others, stubble already appeared along her scalp, another trait of individuality the adults attempted to remove. It framed her face as her brow furrowed and the sneer spread across her lips.

She favored her right side, awkwardly shifting her weight to the ball of her left foot each time she kicked. He blocked, as they had shown, absorbing the impact. On the second attempt, he dropped his guard and caught her by the ankle. With his other hand, he turned the toe of her foot until her knee cracked. She suppressed a scream while dragging her nails across his face.

He kicked, the snap of her other leg filling the room. Now she screamed as he shoved her backward. She collapsed, unable to support her weight. The other kids in the circle watched, the blood lust growing in their twisted smiles. Even Feral waited, desperate to see the boy's next move.

Kneeling over her, he wrapped his hands around her throat. She batted at his face, nails dragging across his cheeks, each cut stinging more than the last. His fingers tightened, pushing into the softness of her neck. Flailing, she stopped attacking and struggled to roll free.

The boy closed his eyes as her face darkened from red to purple. He tried to ignore the atrocity, instead focusing on his survival. If this was the only way to avoid the Programmers, he'd learn to cope with the guilt. Her body twitched one last time before going limp. He didn't let go, ensuring he had finished his opponent. Seconds passed before he heard Feral speak.

"Good boy." He snapped his fingers. "You might earn a name yet."

The boy didn't want a new name. He wanted the name given to him by his parents, the one his friends called him. There was no end in sight to this hell he had been forced into. If he could hold on a little longer, perhaps he'd be able to escape. He just had to survive.

"Take him to the Programmers."

Chapter Seven

2039

Needles didn't let being human stop him from having superpowers. He stood in front of a wall of computer screens, eyes darting from one to the next before the picture shifted to another security camera. In front of the projections, Alyssa could barely make out the scene before they shifted to the next set of cameras. She didn't feel she was quick enough to identify the label on the screen, let alone make out the people.

"Everything goes blank at the same moment," he said. As if on cue, all the screens cut out, leaving the wall empty. He folded his arms, tapping his foot as he attempted to make sense of the chaos. Alyssa knew it was his thinking face, a slight snarl caused by not being able to put all the pieces of the puzzle together. Anybody else might have seen it as his ego running rampant, which might often be the case. But this—he was worried.

"Hackers?"

"No," he said. "There was no transfer of data between the Tower and the outside world leading up to the attack. I checked if anybody uploaded a bogus code. Nothing."

"You think it was an inside job?"

He shook his head. "Have we met? I don't think. I know. There is no way that somebody could bring down the shield and open our front gate from the outside. That part had to be done inside. But they knew to cover their tracks by scrambling the security feeds. By the time the cameras turned on, the damage was done. They're good."

For him to compliment anybody was an event worthy of marking on a calendar. Needles didn't hand platitudes out freely. "But I'm better," he said.

The screens started coming back to life. One by one, the projections hovered in the air. Unlike before, only six came online, showing specific cameras throughout the Tower.

"What are you looking for?"

"To bring down the shield, they needed the power out. They're trying to cover their tracks. But they had to get to the sub-basement and I can track every camera before then."

There was no point in agreeing. He'd explain it to her when he found something of importance. For now, she was a passenger on this journey, so she gave him room to work. There were Children in the Tower capable of processing computer data like a casual thought, but even they struggled to keep up with his tenacity. Needles was an arrogant man. Ned, however was the opposite. She watched his lips move silently as he attempted to protect their way of life.

The screens began rotating through a series of corridors. Alyssa hadn't grown accustomed to Needles since he had worked with the neural link. The idea of having a tiny computer in his head didn't sit well with her, but the by-product meant a safer Tower. The computers responded to his commands without speaking, and in true form, she couldn't even attempt to keep up with how fast he moved from one to the next.

"There!" He pointed.

On the screen, a man walked with his head dropped, shielding it from the camera. "The back of his head isn't going to solve this case."

"Alyssa." Needles smirked as he turned to look at her. He paused as he made eye contact. The grin elongated until it blossomed into a smile. She held her poker face, refusing to give him any satisfaction. But she couldn't control the warmth in her cheeks as they flushed. In this game of chicken, Needles won. She took a step closer to the screen to hide her body's response.

"I would think by now you'd know I can work magic." If she didn't, he'd be sure to remind her. He had been the tech behind the resistance that liberated the Free Republic of America. The way he spoke, an unknowing listener might believe he single-handedly saved the planet.

Reaching out, he pulled the image of the man from the screen, so it stood independently in the space between them. With a twist of his fingers, the figure rotated. The computer filled in the gaps, the lines drawing in the missing parts of their mysterious culprit. With another twist, the features of the face emerged.

"How?" she asked.

"Everything about our bodies follows a mathematical formula. It won't be perfect, but it'll be damned near close. Then if the resident is on file, it'll identify them. I'll send all the information to your data pad."

"You won't need to," she said. "His name is Patrick. He's the newest arrival at the Tower."

A second screen displayed all the information they had on the man. "It can't be him unless there's an accomplice. Kevin and Eve found the problem in the shield control just as he was arriving."

"There's no such thing as coincidence," Alyssa mumbled.

Needles understood the words more than most. Much like her, a dead psychic had manipulated his future. Without Eleanor P. Valentine's involvement, he might have never become a freedom fighter. But had she never intervened, his childhood friend might also be alive. Dealing with the psychic's ramblings always left him furious.

"I swear, if we have to deal with mentalists again…" He threw his hands up. "I quit. Nope. Not doing this. I quit. Call the transport, I'm leaving."

Alyssa let him continue on his rant as she studied the three-dimensional projection of Patrick Kilgannon. Needles continued swearing, making sure everybody in the control center heard him profess quitting. When she turned around, she caught the eye of a tech who shrugged her shoulders and returned to staring at her computer screen.

"Is this the first time you threatened quitting today?"

He stopped. "No." The smirk returned. "And it won't be my last. Somebody get me a coffee. I have to make sure this damned building doesn't implode." He spun about, looking for somebody not engrossed in their work. "P-Dawg, get me some coffee. Extra espresso, black."

"They're your employees, not your servants."

P-Dawg rolled his eyes and set his data pad on the table. The slender man walked by, shaking his head. "It's easier to do it and not listen to him whine like a grown man-child for the rest of the day."

"P-Dawg, once you get my coffee, you're fired."

"It won't be the last time today," the man shouted back as he left the control center.

Alyssa returned to the screens. "I'm glad to see you're finding a home here, Ned."

The mention of his real name broke through the bravado he wore like a suit of armor. The man's larger-than-life personality suddenly seemed far more human. He stood at her side, watching the screen. He cleared his throat, almost sounding nervous as he spoke.

"I have plenty of reasons to make sure this works."

Alyssa felt the man's finger brush against her hand before linking with her pinky. Despite the contact, he kept his head forward, his eyes inspecting the monitors. She appreciated his nonchalant approach as she blushed. This time she didn't hide the effect he had and instead gave his finger a gentle squeeze.

"I'll send his information to your data pad," he said in a whisper.

"Please do," she returned. She let go of his hand and turned to walk away from him and into the control room. Lowering her head, she hid her face behind the fabric of her scarf, making sure nobody had any idea what had transpired between them.

Dwayne's words from the night before echoed in her head as she entered the corridor, taking her to the elevator. Something in her head told her engaging in Needles's advances was a bad idea. But in her chest, her heart raced as she thought about the mostly harmless man.

"Och, they did try to kill us."

Patches wiped the sleep from his eyes as he chugged coffee. The liquid burned his throat, but he refused to stop until he reached the bottom of the cup. The bitter flavor woke him as much as the caffeine. No amount of liquid energy would make up for the loss of sleep. He considered turning around and returning to his apartment. Unable to sit in his new apartment and dissect the many ways he could have died, he found himself in the library. At least here, he could be useful, but three hours was not enough sleep to greet the carnage left by the robots.

"Oi." The two synthetics hadn't been removed. The two torn apart robots, along with the ache in his body, served as a painful reminder that he could have died yesterday. He had been in the Tower for less than a day, and already something had tried to kill him. This had not been in the brochure.

Yesterday, the lights snapped on after leaving the Tower in the dark for sixty-three minutes. Conthan's voice over the intercoms had done little to settle his nerves. They counted nearly two hundred synthetics breaching the wall and making it inside the tower. There had been a long pause before he mustered the bravery to speak the next four words. "We have four dead." He didn't sound surprised or remorseful, just a statement.

Something about that bothered Patrick more than the dead itself. Would their families be informed? The authorities?

"You're in the library, remember this is your happy place. You can forget about killer robots attacking the most powerful people on the planet." He couldn't ignore the reality with two synthetics lying on the floor. Whoever sent them had made a huge mistake, but that wasn't his problem, at least not today.

He stepped around the machines, watching vigilantly for any signs of life. They had come chasing the girl, Eve. Was there a protocol for dealing with their depowered remains? Would somebody come along and pick up the bodies, or did it fall on his shoulders to clean up the mess? Where was Adelaide when he needed her?

"I can do this," he said to himself. He leaned his head back, hoping for a few more drops of the sacred offering to drip from the cup. When none came of their own accord, he started sucking through the small opening in the plastic lid.

Setting his coffee down on a nearby bookshelf, he took matters into his own hands. "I'm not scared of you heaps of metal."

He approached the one he had destroyed. With a light kick, the torso rattled, forcing him to retreat several feet. When it didn't kill him, he tried again, keeping enough distance between them if he'd need to run. The synthetic wouldn't terrify him, at least not more than usual.

His muscles still hurt despite the hour-long shower in scalding water. Patches couldn't remember the last time something had struck him with that much force. He wasn't as strong as other Children, but his abilities had protected him from having his ribs shattered.

"That's right, you bloody bastard." He grabbed its arm. "You see, I'm not some random bloke you can knock around. Hit me. I hit you. Harder."

He dragged the machine to its companion, leaving it in a pile. He had a thousand questions for Adelaide. If this was a common occurrence, he'd take his chances amongst the humans of Chicago. He didn't care if they offered him the position of a lifetime. It wasn't worth almost dying.

He sat down on a stack of boxes and eyed the machines, convinced they were pretending. At any moment, he'd hear the whining of gears coming to life. He wasn't helpless. He understood that he had powers. It'd take more than a synthetic to stop him, but he didn't like to dwell on the idea of what made him different from humans. Even as he thought about going toe-to-toe with the metal man, he lowered his head, unable to celebrate the minor victory.

"What am I doing here?" He flexed his right hand. There should have been bruising, or at least a soreness in his bones. "Great, Patches, you're a strong idjit." A minor pain rippled across his body as he struck the table. His body dispersed the force along his skin. If he did it hard or enough times, the warmth of his skin would grow hotter until he wanted to scream. He didn't understand most of it. The Nostradamus Effect was like a second puberty, and this one was even more disturbing than having a full beard at fifteen.

"Adelaide, where are you?" He whispered to himself. She had commented that he'd be required to do a power evaluation at some point in the next few days to see if he'd require any special accommodations. There were no ambitions of being a hero, the furthest thing from it. But he had to admit, the idea of learning to harness this ability for some sort of communal good spoke to him. He could be the librarian *and* help move heavy objects.

He walked the perimeter of the library, looking for Eve's rogue synthetic. With each dark corner of the library, he held his breath, hoping the machine had vanished. In the back of the room, he found it standing, its head drooping and shoulders slumped.

"Blue, are you in there?" He thought about poking the machine, but didn't dare do anything it might take as aggressive. Throwing his hands up in the air, he decided it wasn't worth the effort. He'd wait for Adelaide, or perhaps the girl who knew its name. Having it in the library raised his anxiety and even as he walked away, he continued checking over his shoulder, fearful it'd come chasing after him.

"Chicago is looking a whole helluva lot safer now."

He focused on something within his control, the library. There were so many boxes that needed unpacking. Textbooks had been the focus before the lights went out. At some point, he'd need to contact the person in charge of the school and ask how he could support the students.

Of all the things they had stored in the boxes, the mannequin had been the strangest. He eyed the leather jacket hanging on its shoulders. It could easily be a hundred years old, and with the softness of the leather, it had been well used. If it hadn't been a woman's cut, he'd have tried it on to see if it was as comfortable. But for the life of him, he couldn't fathom why the people here would want to keep such a random relic.

"They certainly have weird taste." He hopped off the boxes, got closer to the brown coat, and ran his hands over the sleeve. There were numerous cuts in the fabric, gashes that must go all the way through. For now, it could live in the library, but eventually, he'd have to talk to the Council and suggest they move their artifacts to a more storage-friendly place within the Tower.

"Patrick Kilgannon."

His hand slid down the body of the jacket, fixing the flaps on the pockets. He looked over his shoulder to see a woman standing patiently with her hands clasped together. The dark skin of her hands and face contrasted against a white shirt. Even her hijab was light gold, mimicking the stitching on the rest of her clothes.

"As-salamu alaykum," he said with a slight bow. He caught the surprise on her face as he stood upright.

"Wa alaikum as salaam," she said, returning the gesture. "How did you—"

"Your accent," he said quickly, "it reminds me of my granny."

Her demeanor remained rigid, almost formal, despite the elegant manner in which she dressed. Granny Kilgannon would have liked her.

"My parents are from Scotland, and my father's mother migrated from Saudi Arabia. Granny was determined to teach me Arabic."

"You do your grandmother proud," she said. She didn't move a muscle when she spoke, and he quickly got the impression that something was amiss.

"Something is wrong?" He pointed at the two robots on the ground. "Does it have something to do with them?" What if she knew there was a synthetic hiding in the back of the room? He didn't want to risk it. "There was a girl. She knew the name of a synthetic. It's in—"

"Mr. Kilgannon, my name is Alyssa Rahim. I am in charge of the Sentinels, the peacekeepers within the Tower. I need you to come with me."

"Is something wrong?"

She stepped to the side, arm gesturing for him to follow. He didn't recognize her from the photos in the newspaper, but every Child of Nostradamus knew the names of the Nighthawks. But unlike the others, they hadn't published her abilities and just labeled her as the "fighter" in the group. No dense skin, teleporting, or ability to wield lightning, but of the group, they chose her as the dangerous one.

He followed her from the library, trying to keep pace with her as she worked her way through the corridors. "We have some questions we need to ask you about the incursion."

"Does that happen often? Are we in danger?"

She didn't answer his question. She slowed as they approached a synthetic slumped on the floor. Two men were inspecting data pads while hovering over the machine.

"Do you require assistance?"

One man shook his head. "We're ensuring that their hive mind is shut down. We'll be pulling the data off their drives and giving it to Needles to scan."

"Good work," she said with a slight nod.

Patrick continued following her until they reached the elevator. She waved him in and followed. "Sublevel two," she said as she pressed her hand on the panel. A light scanned her face, slowing as it did two passes of her eyes.

"What's in the sublevels?" The lack of response had him worried. He tried to replay every moment since he arrived. He had spoken to almost nobody other than Adelaide and Eve. Were they mad that he used his abilities to save the girl? Were their rules in place that he wasn't aware of? No, that couldn't be it. Conthan had used his abilities multiple times that first day.

If Alyssa wanted to vanish him, nobody would be the wiser. He had told no acquittances in Chicago that he was coming to the Tower. Even his parents were in the dark. He vowed that the moment he returned to his apartment, he'd call them and explain the entire situation. He'd finally have the difficult conversation and come clean about being a Child of Nostradamus.

"We will try to make this brief, Mr. Kilgannon." The narrow corridor bordered on sterile. He tried to sort out where the woman was taking him. There were no decorations or signage to give hints about their destination. It could have been a long hallway in any building in the world.

"Patches," he corrected, "people call me Patches. Mr. Kilgannon is my father. I have a few more years before I'm old enough for that." Nerves were getting the best of him. He knew he was talking too much. No, not talking, spewing. He couldn't handle the silence any longer.

"Where are you taking me?"

"Here." She stood against a flat piece of wall. She pressed her hand against the white wall, causing the hydraulics to hiss. His eyes widened as a seam appeared, a door sliding to the side. The technology housed within the Tower continued to amaze him. But even his amazement couldn't override the sinking feeling in his stomach.

"Please have a seat, Mr. Kilgannon."

The moment he stood in the doorway, the uneasy feeling turned violent. He had watched more than his share of cop procedure movies to know that a single table in a room with chairs on either side was for interrogation. The moment he stepped inside, he'd come under fire. His fists tightened, and he thought about running, getting out of the basement and being free of the Tower.

"Please." The voice held genuine concern, the first bit of warmth to slip into her overly icy demeanor. His muscles tensed. He might have abilities like them, but he barely knew how to throw a punch. Alyssa put a hand on his shoulder, "Do not force my hand."

He shook his hand, relaxing the muscles in his arm. With a single step, he entered the room. "What is this about, Ms. Rahim?"

"We have questions about your involvement in the incursion."

"I have a feeling about him." Alyssa pressed her hands against the glass, stretching her muscles. For the last three hours, her prisoner had done nothing more than pace back and forth. His body language didn't give away any signs of being calm and collected. If Patrick Kilgannon had sabotaged the shields and let the synthetics raid their home, he wouldn't be tapping his fingers on the table to relieve nervous energy.

"If he did it..." Alyssa leaned close, studying his face. "He wouldn't look so guilty."

The woman to her left tapped the glass and spread her fingers apart, zooming in on his face. Jasmine had been torn from her platoon, summoned by Conthan with one of his portals. Unlike the Children in the Tower, she insisted that her place was out in the world, trying to make it better for humans as well as her kind.

"I'm not so sure. I've seen plenty of guilty men think they are too smart to be caught. Once you put the cuffs on them, they turn into blithering idiots."

Alyssa appreciated her friend's advice. "Jasmine, you know I could use a person with your skills to help train the Sentinels."

Jasmine shook her head. "There's no better fighter out there. I don't think you need my help training anybody. But I appreciate the offer."

"I can train them to fight," Alyssa admitted, "but I can't train them to be a team. Not like the Nighthawks."

The room grew quiet. Alyssa had been one of the first Nighthawks, and their friendship didn't start until after Jasmine attempted to kill her. What started out as a mutual hatred for a common enemy blossomed into a begrudging friendship. By the time they saved Chicago, Alyssa couldn't imagine stepping into a fray without the woman by her side. But despite that, it wasn't Alyssa who trained them to be a cohesive group.

"I miss her," Alyssa whispered.

"I remember the first time I laid eyes on the Angel of the Outlands." They both smiled at their former leader's mythical namesake. "I'm pretty sure God wasn't happy that I tried to beat up an angel."

"She wouldn't let you win without a fight," Alyssa added.

"God bless her soul." Jasmine made the sign of the cross on her chest before lifting her necklace, kissing the cross.

"Enna lillah wa enna elaihe Raijoun."

Jasmine took Alyssa's hand and gave it a light squeeze. Neither of them typically shared emotional moments, but Alyssa would always regard her as a sister-at-arms, a bond that would connect them until death. It was only fitting that Vanessa, the heart of the Nighthawks, reminded them to rely on one another.

"I'm going to talk to our friend. Please continue trying to reach Soo Jung. We could use somebody with the ability to detect if he's lying."

"Are there no telepaths?" Jasmine cringed the moment she said it. Ever since the Manhattan Massacre, telepaths knew to hide, especially from Children. The only telepath the Tower communicated with was the Prime Minister of Canada, a fragile relationship Alyssa didn't want to strain.

"None," Alyssa lied.

Seconds later, she entered the interrogation room where Patrick had laid his head on the table. Once the door shut, the room transformed into an infinite white space. No seams or exits made it look as if there were no walls. The table and two chairs served as the only furniture in the room, leaving it sterile and empty.

"Did you decide to stop staring through the glass and come talk to me?" Patrick didn't lift his head as he spoke. She had read through his files, and there was nothing to indicate he could see through the wall.

"This is not like television, Mr. Kilgannon."

"Patches," he corrected.

"Patches," she said. "The Tower is a sovereign nation, which means nobody will come to rescue you. I advise you to answer my questions honestly."

"Or your partner comes in here and roughs me up?"

He lifted his head, leaning back in his chair. Alyssa sat across the table, staring at him, searching for anything that would give away if he were lying. Soo Jung's abilities allowed her to see micro-expressions, and no matter how much the woman explained her abilities, Alyssa just couldn't see the subtle changes in a person's face.

"What do you know of the incursion?"

"I was in the library with Adelaide unpacking boxes. She left. Next thing I know, this girl with a shaved head comes speeding in. She's being chased by those things."

"Synthetics," she corrected.

"I'm from Chicago," he growled. "I know what a synthetic is."

"I noticed the damage in the library. The girl, Eve, did she fight back?"

"Fight back? I terrified the girl before I stepped in."

"How would you describe your abilities, Mr. Kil —Patches."

"My body absorbs kinetic energy. Hit me and it disperses throughout my body." He leaned forward on the table, folding his hands. "I get punched and I punch harder."

"Why did you come to the Tower?"

"I thought you wanted to know about the incursion."

Alyssa couldn't tell if the man was angry or if he attempted to bend the conversation to avoid the question. He wasn't a stupid man. "Humor me, please. Why did you decide to make the Tower your home?"

"You think I had something to do with the synthetics? You think I let them in?"

He stood up, the chair tipping over. Alyssa didn't flinch at the motion. He might have an impressive gift, he might be dangerous, but she could see with his erratic motions and pacing, he wasn't a trained soldier.

"I do not know what to think, not yet. Tell me about the morning leading up to the event."

"I told you, I was in the library. If you don't believe me, ask Adelaide. She was there with me most of the day. I was told to take care of the library and we unloaded boxes. What else do you want?"

"You still haven't answered my original question." He wasn't unique. Each of the residents had a history, some more colorful than the rest. Alyssa had as many secrets as the next person. The migration of Children to the Tower was built on collective trauma.

He continued pacing, hands rubbing together. The silence stretched long enough that it was clear she wouldn't move on until he answered the question. Knowing his reason for abandoning the life he knew wouldn't prove his innocence, but it'd serve as a stepping stone for connecting with him.

The feeling in her gut hadn't diminished. She had seen the footage showing this man heading to their generators. But a man capable of putting hundreds of lives in jeopardy didn't pace back and forth across from her. Even if he hadn't pulled the plug, she couldn't believe his arrival had been a coincidence, no matter what her instincts said.

"Patches."

He paused his pacing before slamming a hand down on the table. The metal strained, but he left a near-perfect indentation of his fist on the surface. He had a slight grimace before he let out a growl.

"Because I'm dangerous."

Chapter Eight

2039

"Clean up," she barked, "how many more steps down the ladder do I go before I'm mopping the hallways?"

Eve stared at the phone display while she shoved another spoonful of cereal in her mouth. Reassigned from working the wall to emptying synthetic corpses from the Tower, she fought the urge to throw the piece of glass. Yesterday she had hopes of joining the Sentinel program, and bit by bit her goal had been destroyed. She had a chance to show herself a capable fighter, and she froze. Worse than that, she nearly crippled herself with doubt.

She finished her orange juice and climbed off the barstool, and pushed it under the kitchen island. Eyeing the synthetics throughout the Tower, she tried to decide where she would start a day of mind-numbing work. Several of the locations had check marks, claimed by workers up before her. Eve was about to check the synthetic's closest to her home, but paused.

"Computer, show a three-dimensional map of synthetic cleanup."

The digital man stepped out of the far wall. With a wave of his hands, a map of the Tower filled her living room. Tiny red dots could be found just about everywhere on the lower levels. She stopped counting once she hit a hundred.

"How many synthetics attacked the Tower?"

"That information is unavailable."

She gave the man the finger. She hated when information was "unavailable," a polite way of saying Needles didn't want people to know. "How many synthetics remain for cleanup?"

"Two hundred and eighteen synthetics remain." Thankfully, he couldn't predict every inquiry the residents would ask. Sometimes it just meant searching for the right question.

"Computer, is there a pattern to where they entered the Tower?"

"That information is unavailable."

The computer was useful most of the time. Right now, she wanted a clear-cut answer and either it truly didn't know, or Needles hid something. The lack of information was telling on its own. "Needles," she tapped her chin, "what don't you want us to see?"

"Computer, put a pin in all cleanup sites." The red dots had thumbtacks in them. "Now calculate the distance from the pins to all locations in the map."

"Complete."

"Computer, what locations within the Tower share the most similar distances?"

"Eighty-two percent of the synthetic have an equal distance from one location."

Reaching into the hologram, she spread her hands

apart, zooming in. The computer transformed the location from blue to a vibrant red.

"The library," she whispered. She couldn't fathom why they would be interested in a room filled with books. "Is there something in one of the boxes? Patches?" She mumbled to herself, trying to sort out why it would interest the robots. If he didn't have the answer, then perhaps Blue would.

Something was amiss, and if Needles hadn't sorted it out yet, she could provide valuable intel to the Council. The uneasy feeling yesterday, as her body shook with nerves, seemed like a distant memory. Instead, her chest vibrated as she focused on her redemption. Suddenly, the hope of being a Sentinel returned.

"Computer, check off these synthetics. I'll remove them."

Two little check marks appeared. She grabbed her vest off the back of the chair and slipped it on, zipping up the snug garment. With the hood pulled over her head, she was out of the apartment and heading to the elevator. The hallways were empty, understandable after an attack.

With each strike of her foot on the carpet, tiny sparks made her skin tingle. She picked up the pace, almost running past the apartments to the seating area that held the elevators. Once she was inside, there was no resisting the smile spreading along her face. It was a tragedy that people had died. Late last night, she overhead Conthan and Dwayne in the living room, lamenting over their ineffective leadership. They cared about every person who lived in the Tower. If she could help solve a riddle about the synthetics, not only would she prove herself useful, but she'd be able to give the two men a direction to point their anguish.

When the elevator stopped, she squeezed her way through the door as it hissed open. There were people, plenty of them, roaming about the common areas. Spectators, people who left their homes to see what the fuss had been about. She noted everybody moved in packs, several people clustered together. They were scared and found comfort in numbers.

"Eve," came a voice from behind her. He shouldn't have been able to sneak up without being detected. The moment she turned her thoughts inward, she recognized the disturbance in the electromagnetic fields. She wanted to curse under her breath, but bit her tongue.

"Marcus, how are you?" One of Alyssa's star pupils, a rising star amongst the Sentinels. Eve didn't dislike him, she just didn't like not wearing an identical silver badge on her chest. Envy, the emotion had become a constant companion.

"Crazy what happened here." She waited for him to catch up before sneaking a glimpse of his face. Only a few years older, he had a chiseled jaw and muscles only obtained from daily trips to the gym. Despite having a mechanical left arm, the shape of the metal bicep almost mirrored his flesh and bone arm.

Eve looked to the floor, aware that she was staring at his physique. "Pretty stupid, if you ask me. Who would attack an entire community of Children?"

"Janet, Rico, and I took out a few of them. The bastard got my arm, though. Have an appointment with the Body Shop to get it checked out."

She had been too busy admiring his muscles to notice the arm hadn't moved. She found the hole and scorch marks near his shoulder. "Are you okay?" He was a nice guy. She almost felt guilty for having a secret grudge against him. "Everybody else?"

"We're good." He gave his upper body a quick shake, the metal arm lifelessly flapping. "I hate to admit it, but I was terrified. Seeing the real thing wasn't like the simulations."

The grudge slipped away as he confessed a secret almost identical to her own. "I agree. But we won," she said. "I've seen you train. I'm surprised you didn't lead the charge."

Eve regretted it the moment she said it. Her moral support came off far more flirtatious than she intended. He smiled. *Dammit,* she thought to herself.

"Marcus, can you give us a hand?"

Saved. He gave a slight wave with his functioning arm as he walked over to a group of women standing around one of the synthetics. It was hard to stay mad at the man as he walked away. He earned his spot on the Sentinels. His ability to vibrate his body on the surface might not seem impressive, but when he could shatter concrete with a touch, there was no denying the usefulness. It didn't hurt that his legs were as thick as his arms, leading to a well-sculpted back.

"Get a hold of yourself," she whispered. Dating wasn't on the menu while she trained. There would be no distractions until she wore a Sentinel badge.

Eve reached the library. The doors hadn't been repaired, one of them determined to stay upright with a single hinge holding it in place. They had moved the synthetics, piled to the side of the entry. She counted her breath, inhaling slowly through her nose and counting to seven as she breathed out through her mouth. She couldn't dwell on her shortcomings last night.

"Patches," she yelled. "Where are you?"

When nobody replied, she closed her eyes and let her abilities flood the library. Every outlet, light, and hidden wire vibrated. With the power surging through the building, she looked for spots where there might be human flesh absorbing the energy. Nothing. But she found a human-shaped object with a familiar vibration.

"Blue," she whispered. She checked over her shoulder to make sure nobody had come into the library. After the attack yesterday, having a synthetic in the Tower wouldn't be well received. Even when Skits had control over her pet, it was met with disgust as people recounted how the machines murdered their kind, leaving families broken.

Eve started toward the back of the library. It already smelled like a library. Dust met with a bit of mildew. Patches had barely unpacked any boxes, but the atmosphere was there. Shelves were scattered across the space, broken up by the palettes stacked waist-high. It reminded Eve of the library she had visited as a kid, except more sparse. Eventually, it'd be made just as grand, that is, if Patches ever showed up for his work detail.

Climbing over a toppled box, she worked her way toward the back of the library. Amongst the books piled on every available surface, one thing seemed out of sorts. Barring her from passing, a mannequin held a leather jacket. Eve had always wanted one, but couldn't convince Dwayne to have one delivered with the Tower's "essential" goods. Even the vest she wore had practical applications, woven with thin carbon fiber threads. It could easily withstand the impact of a bullet.

"This is a weird library," she mused. There was no point in trying to get Blue out of the space while everybody was out and about. If she was going to wait for the librarian, she might as well take a moment for herself.

The fabric was softer than she'd thought. As her fingers traced the arm, patches had been sewn on in almost a dozen places. One of them was ready to fall off, revealing a thin gash on the arm. With a quick glance, she could see the garment was covered in similar cuts along the forearms.

"Somebody took a lot of damage in this." In one of the cuts, she could see a sliver of metal. Holding her hand over the arm, she let her abilities wash over the cloth. Even at this proximity, the interference from the Tower couldn't hide the metal strips woven into the arms. "Smart girl," she complimented the owner. "You knew you'd be in a fight."

Eve opened the jacket, looking for any identifying markers. It was old, perhaps a century by the style. Whoever had worn it had been ready for the knife cuts. She wanted to meet the owner and find out if they had been successful. "What is it doing here?"

Deciding to indulge herself, she pulled the jacket from the mannequin, glancing over her shoulder to make sure Patches didn't suddenly walk in. It was as comfortable as she hoped, fitting her as if it had been made with her measurements. She buttoned the front and slid the belt into the buckle. "So this is what they did before bulletproof armor. I'm impressed."

Eve wished there were a mirror nearby so she could see if she looked as badass as she felt. Reaching into the pockets, she struck a casual pose. She debated setting up her phone to take a photo when her finger brushed something in the left pocket.

Slowly pulling out the paper, she found it was an envelope, folded in half, spreading it open, she saw it had been sealed shut. Turning it around, she gasped. In beautiful black ink, her name, written with sweeping gestures that left the word "Evelyn," looking like a piece of art.

Everybody in the Tower knew about the letters received by the Nighthawks. A woman able to predict the future had sent letters into the world to be read at pivotal moments in their lives. They acted as guides, redirecting them so that their paths crossed. Eleanor P. Valentine was the mastermind behind the team of heroes rallying against a man bent on destroying the world. Eve had read each of their letters a dozen times, obsessed with how a dead woman reached beyond the grave to change the fate of all Children.

The cuts on the arm of the jacket and the mysteriously placed letter connected. She was meant to pick up the jacket, to reach into its pocket and pull out this letter with her name on it. The owner of the garment had foretold every action. Eleanor P. Valentine continued to change the world, hopefully for the better.

"It can't be."

"You must be the bad cop?"

Patches had returned to his seat, arms folded across his chest, while Alyssa and Jasmine stood across from him. The taller woman did indeed look like the meaner of the two. The tactical vest and military fatigues made her look more intimidating. For him, it wasn't the fact she had threatened his life. No, it wasn't that at all. He had walked past her statue in Millennium Park hundreds of times. He sat in front of legends, and that made their questioning even more terrifying.

"Mr. Kilgannon, I'm going to ask you one more time." She didn't budge a muscle as she talked. Similar to Alyssa, the women wanted him to focus on their accusations. It kept them mysterious. He had seen more than enough television to know how this routine would go. "What were you doing in the generator room?"

He unfolded his arms and scooted his chair closer to the table. Jasmine Gentile, the military commander: malleable skin, able to mimic the density of any object she touched. He knew every fact available about the Nighthawks—every Child did. They were as close to a team of comic book superheroes as any of them would ever come. In the library in Chicago, they even had their graphic novel, a loose retelling of the Battle for Chicago.

He tapped his fingers on the table. Starting with his pinky and rolling through his fingers, then repeating the action. With each rotation, he struck the table harder, leaving his usual cool, calm, collected self.

"As I've told Ms. Rahim, I don't know." The words came out more of a growl than he meant. But after being kept in the room for the better part of six hours, his patience had grown thin. They didn't seem interested in him telling the truth unless it aligned with their accusations.

"If you think it's going to change, then you're both bad at your job." He shouldn't insult them, but it was clear they weren't willing to listen. Even as he spoke, their faces remained emotionless. "I've told you, ask Adelaide."

"We will," Alyssa said.

Jasmine sauntered around the table, standing next to him. She was tall enough that her height could intimidate most men. Patches had stopped being scared; the adrenaline drained from his body. He had reached a state of annoyance, and the longer they kept him, the snappier he'd get. He concentrated on the tapping, striking the table harder and harder each time, the skin along his hand tingling.

"Four are dead. Four. I want that to sink in. Four Children died, and we suspect it has something to do with you. You're not being honest with us."

They had his files. They could easily learn everything they wanted about him. They'd see a boring man who tried to do his part to make the world a better place. He was so boring it probably looked suspicious to them. *Good,* he thought. Around hour three, he decided the moment they let him go, he'd request to return to Chicago. The facade of a utopia filled with people like him faded away, and now all that remained was a taste of bitterness and resentment.

Jasmine grabbed him by the shirt, pulling hard enough that it jerked him from his chair. The fabric of his shirt stretched, threatening to tear along the seams. He grabbed her wrist, trying to keep the clothes on his body. His fingers pressed into her skin and he found it like rock, unmoving, cool, almost statuesque. Patches stared into the woman's brown eyes and realized she had come in willing to be more of a bad cop than he realized.

"I'm not asking again," she whispered. He looked down to see her other hand balling into a fist. The legend prepared to beat him, to force the answers she wanted from his mouth. He nearly spat as she jabbed him in the kidney. It should have hurt, should have felt like a fight-ending blow, but he hardly noticed the pain. The rapping of his fingers along the table had created enough stored energy to withstand the strike.

When he didn't speak, she repeated, this time drawing her fist back. Patches winced as the heat rippled along his skin. Somewhere inside, his body displaced the energy of the punch, absorbing it until he decided to redirect it elsewhere. It wasn't as much as the synthetic from the day before, but it was enough.

When she raised her fist, ready to strike him in the face, he had enough. The energy needed an outlet, a way to empty out before he turned into a literal ticking time bomb. The heat poured into his elbows, along his fore-arms and pooled in his palms. He let go of her arm and slammed both palms into her chest.

Jasmine buckled, launched backward, tearing the shirt off his body. The Paladin hit the wall with enough force it dented, ruining the optical illusion of an infinite white space. Alyssa spun about, narrowing her stance, arms raised, ready to jump in.

"Bad cop didn't read my file," he said. He backed up until he stood with his back against the wall. Patches didn't want to fight. He never wanted to fight. But he wouldn't let his jailers abuse him until he admitted something that wasn't true.

Jasmine shook her head, patting her chest to inspect the damage. She gestured for Alyssa to stand down. Patches balled his fists, ready for her to jump over the chair and hit him again. If she believed brute force would stop the fight, he was prepared to prove the tactic futile.

"I don't want to fight," he said. "Let me go." He knew the words sounded like pleading.

Jasmine pressed a hand on the wall, opening the exit. "We're going to find Adelaide. Until then, we're keeping you here under surveillance."

The Paladin had convinced herself that he was guilty. She didn't have an ounce of empathy in her eyes. She was more frightening than any account he had read. But Alyssa, as she left, she turned for a brief moment, eyes saddened. Jasmine might have written him off, but Alyssa believed, or at least that's what he told himself.

When the door closed, he was alone again. Patrick leaned against the wall, sliding down until he sat with his knees against his chest. The better life promised by the Tower was nothing more than a sham. He came here hoping to find his tribe, but so far, he'd been greeted by nothing more than anguish. The first day the robots came to kill him, and now the people were trying to do the same. The heat in his skin faded, and the only thing he could focus on was the growing pit of despair.

Patrick wanted to go home.

Chapter Nine

2039

February 13, 1992

Eve Cowan,

I never wished for this jacket to hang in a museum as a decoration. In my youth, barely older than you are now, a man refused money for it, saying it might hold one more adventure. For me, it had many. You know me as the aging psychic who gathered the Nighthawks, but I wasn't always Eleanor Valentine. I grew into my name, a mantle filled with wondrous people in locations around the globe. As I write this, I long for the days of my reckless youth.

Even after death, I still have a role to play in the future.

I could not see the outcome for the Nighthawks, only a likely future. But since you hold this letter, I know they emerged victorious. Just like with your fathers, I cannot reveal a roadmap to what will happen, and for that, I am truly sorry. Time is a fickle mistress, and I am but a vessel through which she speaks. Let my words incite action. What action, only you can decide. While I attempt to predict

Eve finished reading the letter for a third time. As she spoke it aloud, she paused at each word, digesting the psychic's claims. Conthan received his letter from a dying artist, and Vanessa had delivered Dwayne a letter. Each envelope found its way to the recipient in a way that demonstrated her mastery of reading the future. Eve couldn't believe that all this time, even before her birth, a letter had been written to her. Now she dissected its meaning, trying to understand what Eleanor P. Valentine asked of her.

"When fate calls," she mumbled, "answer."

Conthan's letter had been opened and closed so many times that it dissolved at the seams. He kept it in an airtight case in the study. Dwayne had to rewrite his own, having lost it over the years. They talked about how the woman changed their lives with a simple stroke of the pen.

Eve sat down on a stack of books. Eleanor knew the future, had seen the outcome of their lives, but she played a dangerous game. More than once, as Conthan found his way into the vodka, he debated if the letters changed fate or if they cemented what was already meant to happen. Fate, was it written in stone? Or did the psychic defy the natural flow of events?

"I see why he raves while drunk," she whispered. Eve thought she understood his ramblings. But the magnitude of his questions didn't compare to what she was feeling as she ran her thumb over the indentations of the stationery.

"Okay, so what does it mean?" She could solve this problem. If Eleanor called on her to make a difference, she was ready. Eleanor offered her a chance at redemption after freezing during the attack yesterday. Becoming a Sentinel remained a priority, and if she completed the task for the psychic, she'd be able to make an argument to Alyssa.

"When fate calls," she repeated. "What the hell does—"

Chiming filled the quiet library. She froze. A second later, the chime filled the air. Eve looked up from the letter, refusing to believe the message from Eleanor had been literal. "Really? A phone?"

She shimmied off the boxes and followed the sound of the ringing. Sitting on the edge of a table, she saw the clear piece of glass. Somebody had left their phone in the library, and now it vibrated as somebody attempted to call.

"Eleanor," Eve said, "really? A cryptic message to tell me to answer somebody's phone?"

Eve hovered over the piece of glass, looking at the word, "Incoming" blinking on the surface. Underneath the blinking word, "Unknown caller." Eve picked up, wondering if when she answered Eleanor herself would speak on the other end. With one glance at the letter, she flicked her thumb across the screen.

She held her breath, unsure if she should speak or wait for the person on the other end.

"Alyssa, we have a problem."

The voice was familiar, somebody Eve had met in the past. She couldn't put her finger on it, but it was somebody she had had conversations with since moving to Troy. Her voice caught in her throat as she bit back the need to respond.

"Did you hear me? Skits is missing."

"Shit," Eve spat.

"Who is this?" The front of the phone switched to an image of a woman with long purple hair. Gretchen. The woman who'd bought Eve her first bottle of hair dye. She had spent many nights dining with the Nighthawks, a reunion of sorts. It had grown less frequent since they had erected the Tower.

She debated hiding or putting her thumb over the camera. But it was too late. Gretchen's face didn't look amused. "Eve, what are you doing with Alyssa's phone?"

"She must have forgotten it. What happened to Skits? Where is she? Why didn't you call Conthan? He needs to know."

"Whoa." Gretchen pressed a button on the phone and a hologram of her hovered over the glass. Genesis Division created the holographic technology, and under Gretchen's guidance, it had progressed quickly. Most of the Tower's construction had her to thank. But as she took over more responsibility with the international tech giant, those dinner parties became less frequent.

"Slow down." She pressed her hand against her cheek as she paced back and forth in a room hundreds of miles away. "Conthan doesn't know."

"Shouldn't he—"

Gretchen shook her head. "No, no. No, he doesn't need to know about this. He is already pissed that Alyssa and Skits—"

"Wet Works," Eve finished. The walls were thin and when she stayed up late reading, she could hear Conthan and Dwayne discuss things they wanted to keep secret. Conthan bordered on enraged when he found out that Gretchen used Alyssa and Skits to run errands around the globe. It took her some time to realize that their disappearances lined up with devastating events in the news.

"You know?" Gretchen didn't sound happy. "But yes." Gretchen never lied to her. Eve thought of the woman as part of their non-traditional family, the more serious aunt. Eve hadn't thought about it until now, but she missed those dinner parties. Each of the Nighthawks had endured unspeakable horrors, but when they reunited, they dined and spoke about the future. They toasted to Eleanor—

"Gretchen, where is Skits?" The letter. If Eleanor wanted her to have this conversation, something here was important.

Gretchen continued shaking her head. Even in the hologram, her purple hair shined. She had done away with the mohawk and spikes and adopted something a bit more tame, but she refused to be somebody who blended in. "I don't want you getting involved. Tell Alyssa—"

"I got a letter." Eve didn't know how else to make Gretchen listen. Did she screw up Eleanor's vision by revealing its existence? She tried to avoid dwelling on the causality of a psychic's intentions.

"What?" Gretchen approached the camera, leaning in. The smaller hologram studied her face. "What do you mean, *a letter*?" Her tone shifted, knowing full well that this simple statement could change their lives.

"I found a letter addressed to me. It's from *her*."

"Dammit."

There was a long pause as Gretchen parsed the information. Eve imagined she was having the same internal debate. The madness of dealing with psychics now made sense. She waited for Gretchen to speak, nervous at what was going to come out of her mouth.

"She saw this phone call?"

Eve nodded. "I think so."

"Eve, do you know what it means? Did she give any details?" Eve repeated the last line of the letter. Gretchen paced back and forth, the tiny hologram appearing to walk in place as the woman had a quiet conversation with herself. Eve didn't know if she was supposed to share the letter's meaning. Minutes after Eleanor entrusted her with a mission, she already blabbed. She understood why Conthan still spent nights staring at the sheet of paper in the study. It was enough to drive anybody mad.

"I called to speak with Alyssa. Skits is missing. I assigned her a recon mission in Boston."

"Wet Works." The moment Eve said it, Gretchen stopped pacing. She picked up the phone, so the hologram transitioned to just showing her face. "I overheard Conthan and Dwayne talking about it. Alyssa used to work for you, right?"

Gretchen nodded. "Skits reached Boston and then went dark."

Eve walked to the back of the library. She found Skits' pet powered down between a row of bookcases.

"Did Blue go with her?" Eve asked.

"I'd assume she never goes—"

Eve held up the phone, showing the face of the machine. Unlike his brethren, he held a swatch of blue paint down the side of his face. They had used it to identify a group of synthetics reprogrammed by Needles to help fight in Chicago. Of the squadron, only this one remained. It wasn't a surprise Skits kept him like a robotic puppy.

"What's he doing at the Tower?"

Eve's eyebrow raised. It was unlike the Tower to keep secrets from Genesis Division. The Tower only existed because of their partnership.

"I don't know how to say this, but we were attacked. A few hundred synthetics came knocking at our doors. People are dead, Gretchen."

"There's no such thing as coincidence," she mumbled. Eve had spent the last five years hearing the Nighthawks repeat the phrase. Now with a letter folded in one hand, a mysterious lost puppy, a forgotten phone, and Gretchen's call, Eve understood. For a year, she spun her wheels, trying to earn a position amongst the Sentinels. But in a few brief minutes, she found her path changed, something greater.

"You were going to ask Alyssa to go to Boston."

"Yes," Gretchen nodded.

"I'm going to Boston, Gretchen." She wanted redemption for not fighting the day before. It was no longer a wild attempt to earn respect and become a Sentinel. After freezing on the balcony, she needed to prove to herself that she could conquer the fear.

Eve eyed the letter. Did Eleanor know? Had she put this opportunity in her lap just when she was ready to give up?

"I'm going to Boston."

Gretchen protested and then bit back her tongue. There was no point in arguing when a psychic had already predicted the outcome. Eve stared at the letter as the determination set in. She didn't know how she'd manage it, but somewhere in Boston, she'd find the answers she needed.

"Be safe," Gretchen said. "Remember that the future is not fixed. Even Eleanor understood we have free will."

"There are no coincidences," Eve smiled as the words left her mouth.

Eve had a mission.

Chapter Ten

2039

Eve stared at her bed, the clothes draped across the comforter. Once she started going through her trunks, she found it outlandish how much tactical gear she had accumulated. According to the internet, girls her age were concerned with makeup, dating, and experimenting with alcohol. For Eve, her hobbies focused on sharp things. She wondered if Dwayne or Conthan realized how many knives had found their way into her collection.

"This is so much better than makeup," she said.

In the middle of the knives rested her tactical gear. Within the Tower, only the Sentinels wore these outfits, but with Nighthawks for guardians, Gretchen had made her an outfit tailored for her abilities. Capable of stopping a bullet, it seemed like a logical item to take out on its maiden voyage.

While she searched for the shoulder bag under her bed, she found herself eye level with a photograph. Sitting atop the hood of an old car, she couldn't remember the last time she smiled like that. Dwayne had worked as a mechanic years ago and they had rebuilt the engine, converting it to an electric motor. Conthan held a hose off the side, spraying her and Dwayne. For a moment, she felt a bit of guilt. They had once been in her position, recipients of letters that changed their fate. With a simple statement, she could tell them, and with Conthan's abilities, she'd be in and out of Boston in no time.

It was nearly eight, and Conthan and Dwayne would begin their nightly ritual of curling up on the couch to watch another horrible rom-com. They were like an old married couple, except one could rip through spacetime and the other shot lightning from his hands. She grinned at the thought.

Cracking the door open, she could hear the two men whispering. For all the technology housed within the Tower, they had done far too little to soundproof the living quarters. Privacy didn't exist, which made for some extremely awkward breakfast conversations. She could have asked for her own unit, but she found it comforting to have her second family close by.

"They still haven't found her," Conthan said.

"Did Azacca have anything to say about it?"

Eve had met the priest many times. The man had been pleasant enough, a polite gentleman, but his abilities, they left her uncomfortable. She couldn't imagine her mind linked with another person, broadcasting and receiving thoughts as if they were a jumble of phone calls. His speaking took a while to get used to as he switched from individual thoughts to the hive mind. The idea alone gave her a shiver.

"Nothing," Conthan said, "but he assures me she is okay. Based on her thoughts, he believes she's sleeping."

"What about the new guy? I saw you port into the town hall with him."

There was a long pause. Eve debated going out to speak with them, to confess about the letter, but curiosity won. Before she laid the letter on the table, she wanted to hear what was happening to the man who saved her life.

"He seemed nice enough. He's timid. You could tell by the way he reacted to everything that it was overwhelming. I'm not sure he's ever been around other Children before he met me." For Eve, it made sense. He hadn't exactly been the most confident fighter.

Conthan let out a slight chuckle. "He's Scottish, with an accent."

Eve nearly laughed out loud. Leave it to them to go from discussing crimes against the Tower to boys they thought were cute. They were indeed an old couple, and she loved them all the more for it. It didn't hurt that Conthan was right. Patches did have a sexy accent.

"Do you miss it?" asked Dwayne.

"Scottish men with accents?"

"Mind out of the gutter. The adventure. Being out there doing what we did."

"Do I miss running from things trying to kill me? Or being covered in blood daily?" Eve reached into her pocket, reaching in deep enough to touch the letter. Did Eleanor promise her the same bloody escapades?

"I never thought I would say this," Dwayne said, "but I do miss it. I can't explain it, but I've never been that close to a group of people. Every day, we were thankful we had air to breathe and stale coffee to drink. Look at us now. We get irked when Eve leaves a dish in the sink."

She grimaced, hoping they wouldn't notice her half-filled bowl of cereal resting in the bottom of the sink.

"Don't get me wrong," Conthan said, "I wouldn't change the past. I wish I didn't almost die as often as I did. But there were good things that came from being a superhero."

Ew. Eve tried to block out the sound of them kissing. It was one thing to eavesdrop on their personal conversation, but the moment she heard shirts come off, she'd need to turn on some music.

"Dwayne, think of everything we lost."

"To Vanessa," Dwayne said.

"To Dav5d," Conthan added.

"To Sarah."

There was a clink of glasses. Eve had listened to the stories about how Vanessa sacrificed herself to stop the Warden. Conthan had paintings in the gallery near the lobby filled with depictions of their time as Nighthawks. Dav5d had been captured and while neither of them said it, there was a look of guilt on Dwayne's face that explained how it ended for their friend. But Sarah, that was a name she had never heard spoken before.

Eve pushed the letter deeper into her pocket. If she walked into the living room and confessed Eleanor selecting her, they'd be dragged into the hero life once again. The letters created a burden for each recipient, but in that moment, she decided it would be selfish to involve Conthan and Dwayne. They had earned their retirement.

"Do you think Patrick had anything to do with the incursion?" Dwayne asked.

"Kid is green. Either he's a talented actor or he's important and doesn't know it."

"I saw Needles's projections. They were interested in him."

"He'll stay in holding for the night. Tomorrow we find Adelaide, confirm his story, and then decide if he stays or gets banished."

Eve wanted to pat herself on the back, impressed that she had come to the same conclusion as Needles. He'd be furious to know she discovered the pattern before him. But it'd be worth crushing his ego for even a moment.

"Crap," she whispered. She hadn't thought about Needles in her plan to escape the Tower. If he was sitting in front of his screens, he'd be able to track her. Each door she opened would set off an alarm until she reached the gate, leaving the Tower. She'd need clearance far higher to get away.

Sliding her hand into her other pocket, she touched the glass of Alyssa's phone. It was a long shot, but the phone gave her a reason to visit Needles. Perhaps she'd be able to blackmail him into helping. A plan formed, but first, she needed to finish packing and wait for Conthan and Dwayne to retire for the night before slipping out.

Her plan hadn't started and already it had gotten complicated.

Patrick stared at the metal tray on the table. He imagined a dinner while locked up would be nothing more than lumps of mush, but the Tower maintained higher standards. Separated by raised dividers, the meal consisted of a steak and greens, but when he reached for the utensils there was no trust between him and his captors.

He held up the plastic knife. It was laughable. In fact, he couldn't help but roll his eyes and let out a sigh of disbelief. He turned to the dents in the wall where he had thrown Jasmine. With a few seconds of stomping his feet or punching the wall, he'd have enough potential energy stored in his muscles to knock the door from its frame. But despite the awesome strength hidden behind a mild-mannered man, they gave him a plastic knife.

When Alyssa deposited the tray, she admitted they were having difficulty finding Adelaide. At first, the statement hadn't raised any red flags, but now he worried something might have happened to the welcome committee. She was an odd duck, but he enjoyed the warmth of her smile.

"So, Patches," he poked at the steak with the knife, "you run away from Chicago to this wonderful utopia. You're here a day and find yourself in jail. Somewhere in this, there's an irony tragic enough that Shakespeare would laugh."

He stabbed the steak with the fork, leaving it sticking straight up. He thought about how nervous he was the first day, standing on the platform waiting for the transport to arrive. Stepping into the aircraft, he'd nearly hurled, and the trip had been little better. Once his boss fired him, he lived on frozen pizzas and barely changed out of his sweatpants each day. Life had spiraled quickly, and he hadn't known what to do. The world wanted to pretend that Children were equals, but he had seen the dark underbelly of mankind. They wanted to be righteous while they discriminated.

After six hours of binging television and devouring

every bit of junk food in his apartment, a knock came at the door. He brushed the crumbs from his shirt and answered, trying to remember how to interact with another human. The man wore the blue uniform of the post office. In his hand, he held a letter.

"Been sitting at the office for a while, young man. It must be important."

The letter. It was *her* fault he sat in a white prison cell.

Patches had showered and sat on his couch, reading it once, twice, and then a third time. She was the reason he came to the Tower. The woman who once attempted to kill the President of the United States had mailed him a letter laying out his future.

The words were no less clear now. He reached into his pocket, thumbing the paper. Sliding it out, he cursed himself as he opened it, starting from the first line once again.

February 13, 1992

Patrick Kilgannon,

History distorts the truth. I suppose had I lived, the world would be a very different place. In your library, there are a hundred books that have made my name synonymous with traitor, but it could not be further from how I lived my life.

Despite having died before your birth, I have delighted in watching you mature from a wayward teen into a scholarly young man. This statement will be confusing at first, but I have faith you will unravel its implications. You do, after all, remind me of a man I once loved. Beneath his pursuits of academics beat the heart of the reluctant hero. Like you, he too once hesitated.

The world you've created unraveled for reasons beyond your control. There is no amount of empathy that can take away the sting of a man who must abandon his life. Instead, I'll appeal to that wayward teen who found himself in trouble more often than not. There is a place for you in this world. But the woman who will show you the path is far from where you stand now.

Through my many lifetimes, I have learned free will is mightier than fate. So I present you with a choice. Will you turn on the news?

With Regards,
  Eleanor P. Valentine

Even reading it now, he feared he put his trust in the wrong person.

She never visited the command center. It was bad enough she had to work on the maintenance crew with Kevin and listen to Needles barking in her ear. But as the elevator opened, she found the brain of the Tower to be relatively empty. Through a small lobby where scanners read every biometric she had to offer, she entered the large open space Needles used as his office.

There were screens being projected all about the room. Some of them held charts and information about specific residents, but most cycled through the security cameras. Despite the bombarding visual stimuli, Ned remained standing at a single screen. She let out a long sigh as she prepared herself to go toe-to-toe with one of the most aggravating men in the Tower.

Walking up to Needles, she could see Marcus in the frame. The Sentinel used his artificial limb as a shield when another synthetic fired. He got close enough to grab its chest plate. His body blurred, and the synthetic thrashed about until the parts fell to the lobby floor. Eve grew jealous, not of his affiliation with the Sentinels, but that he jumped into danger without regard for his own safety.

"What are you doing here?"

"Oh," she said, "I wanted to speak with you."

His eyebrow raised for a moment before his face lit up. She realized he wasn't looking at her at all, but over her shoulder. With a quick spin, she saw Alyssa meander into the room. Eve held steady, trying to think on her feet. She couldn't bribe Ned with Alyssa's phone if she were in the room.

"Alyssa." She gave a slight wave. "I forgot to grab it. But when I was moving the synthetics from the library..." She eyed Ned, giving him a narrow-eyed gaze that should burn the flesh from his bones. "I think I saw your phone on the table. I forgot to grab it."

Alyssa shook her head. "You must be mistaken." From her trousers, she pulled out a sheet of glass. "It must belong to Mr. Kilgannon. I'll retrieve it shortly. It might have information about his partners in the incursion."

Eve fought to control her face. It had been an outright lie, but Eve couldn't confront her without raising further questions. She watched as the woman walked, studying every movement. Alyssa had the grace of a dancer, and even casual movements seemed well rehearsed. Eve couldn't put her finger on it, but the tightness in her stomach confirmed that something was amiss.

"Have you learned anything from Patrick?"

She shook her head. "He has no alibi to put him in

the library. Multiple residents stated they saw him working his way toward the generators before the power outage."

Lies. Eve had seen him with her own two eyes. The man defended her. Without his help, there was a good chance the synthetics would have shot her in the back of the head.

"He scrubbed the footage leading up to the incursion. We're missing something important, but I haven't quite put my finger on it."

Alyssa stood next to Needles, inspecting the screens. Eve didn't take her eyes off the woman, staring far longer than was socially acceptable. She had to remember to turn away, or she'd give away her suspicions. Eve gasped as Alyssa casually reached out and grabbed Ned's hand. The hacker seemed just as shocked by the gesture. After years of studying with the woman, Eve knew without a doubt that Alyssa would never show signs of affection in mixed company.

"Is something wrong?" Alyssa asked.

"I'm missing movie night. Dwayne and Conthan are going to kill me. It's the one time they let me choose. I'm determined to make them watch a horror movie." She couldn't stop blabbing. "Conthan will hide his face. Dwayne will laugh. It'll... Sorry I can't stay and help."

It was time to test her skills at subterfuge. She gave Alyssa a hug. "Promise we'll get back into the studio," she said pulling away, "I miss dance classes with you." Lies, even Needles would see through the facade. Nobody violated Alyssa's personal space unless she initiated it. It was common knowledge, just like Alyssa had trained her to fight, not dance.

"Once things calm down, I'd like that."

Eve threw an arm around Ned's neck, her mouth close to his ear. With a barely audible "Shh," she slid the phone from her pocket to his. She squeezed him tightly as she pulled his ID. If he was as smart as he claimed to be, he'd see that something was amiss and be able to track down the source. If this wasn't Alyssa, he might be the only person in the Tower with the smarts to unravel the mystery.

"Take care, you two love birds." The more nervous she became, the more she spoke. She might not be cut out for the spy stuff. But as she exited the control room, she eyed Ned's badge. With this, she had a clear exit from the Tower, but first, she had one more stop to make.

Chapter Eleven

2023

They strapped him to the chair on what would have been his twenty-third birthday. This had become a second home, the single chair with leather straps. The walls were covered in ceramic tiles, an off-white that left them feeling dingy. Eventually, they'd pull out the tray of tools and the process would begin just like it had before.

Instead of focusing on the horrors about to happen, he tried to recall his family. Somewhere, he hoped his parents were celebrating with a caterpillar cake. He imagined they lit candles, one for each year, and that they sang, "Happy Birthday." The thought of his father blowing out the candles made him smile. He hadn't seen them since the academy had stolen him from his home.

Even as he pictured the man standing over his birthday cake, he couldn't recall his father's face. Bit by bit, the Programmers had robbed him of his history, erasing the things that made him human. It had become a game, the frequent trips to be reprogrammed. While others at the academy fell in line, frightened by the bogeymen hidden in the basement, he welcomed the challenge.

Oliver arrived, one of the very human technicians assigned to make him a more compliant recruit. The humans in the academy served one purpose, to make the Children of Nostradamus a formidable guard for the Queen. The humans maintained their names, a reminder that they were beneath those with gifts.

"I wondered when I'd see you again."

Growing from a boy to a young man within the academy had been one continuous battle for survival. He excelled in his studies, at the top of his class in science, history, and politics. But most of all, they knew him to be the best fighter. He'd have been a favorite of the instructors, except he continued to defy orders at every opportunity.

He wasn't in the mood for banter, not with his captor. Oliver pulled a chart from a nearby table and flipped through the pages. It was an unnecessary act, performed out of habit. Everybody, from his instructor to his class-mates to the Programmers, knew about his resistance to the cause. If his abilities hadn't been one of the most powerful, they'd have killed him long ago.

"Your brain has a knack for repairing itself. It looks like we are going to need to be more aggressive in our treatments this time."

Treatments. The man laughed as he pulled against the straps, holding his arms in place. Straining his biceps, he tried to pull free, but his captors had learned their lesson. He glanced at his surroundings, but other than the chair and a tray of medical tools, nothing looked capable of helping him. He turned his head to the observation window and squinted, hoping to see through the one-way glass.

"You should know by now—" The technician stopped speaking. "Look, I don't want to hurt you. But until you learn to control your actions, you're a danger to yourself and all those around you."

"Since when is freewill dangerous?"

Oliver tossed the clipboard onto the table of medical instruments. His usual calm and dispassionate face transformed until it he looked possessed. With teeth clenched, he grabbed a syringe. Without warning, he jabbed it into the man's side, taking care to avoid touching him. With a push of the plunger, the next wave of drugs flooded his system.

"Your people's free will led to a massacre." The man always assumed Oliver was English, but as the anger escalated, his accent thickened. "My family lived in Dumfries when the clans returned."

The man stopped tugging at the restraints and leaned back in the chair. Everybody knew about the carnage that took place that day. He struggled to recall his parents again. Even as he conjured the image, they remained faceless. Had they belonged to one of the clans? Did he? The memories had fragmented, and he could only catch glimpses of his life before the academy.

"I'm sorry."

"My sister..." The man stopped speaking, avoiding the demise of his loved one. The man empathized with him, and didn't want horrible things to happen. When the clans returned, uniting under the name Caledonia, the British slaughtered any who opposed the absolute rule of the Queen.

"Those are not my people." But they were, maybe.

The world grew cloudy. He fought the effects of the drugs, as they made it difficult to focus. Pulling at his restraints, he could barely wiggle his arm. He summoned an image of the Flag, a rich blue bearing St. Andrew's white cross. Every trip to the Programmer resulted in him losing more of his identity, memories from the before-times. They'd rob him of his humanity eventually, but they'd have to work at it.

"May the Queen clean those heathens," Oliver spat in his direction.

The technician would gladly have killed him by plunging a knife into his neck. His neck had turned a dark shade of red, and it crept upward along his face. As his body went limp, Oliver eyed the instruments on the table, plotting the many ways he could walk away vindicated.

He stepped closer, pulling gloves from the table, first pulling them over his left hand, then his right. Grabbing small white squares from the tray, he placed them on the man's temples, pressing until they stuck on their own accord. Next, he lifted another syringe, jamming it into the man's neck harder than necessary. He twisted the needle, causing a sharp sting as he pushed the plunger.

"We're just about ready to begin." Oliver signaled to the glass, to the invisible operators of the small plastic diodes. They were cowards, hiding their identities, so he couldn't hunt them down one by one. Given the chance, he'd kill each one in the slowest possible manner. His jailers deserved nothing short of agony.

"Your gifts are to blame." It was a common tactic, pushing the blame onto the recruit as if they were responsible for every atrocity they endured. "Your brain's ability to regenerate continues to rebuild neural pathways. We believe we've found a way to help you."

Help, the man nearly scoffed. "We want to remove these self-imposed restraints. After today, you'll be able to properly serve your Queen."

The phantoms entered through the walls, summoned by the drugs and electrical impulses zipping through his skull. Many of them were faceless, the details of their clothes or mannerisms fading away until they were naked apparitions without definition. There were a few who maintained their features, memories of a life the academy wanted to obliterate.

"Let us help you."

His abilities attempted to regenerate the damage done to his brain. As quickly as he could see a nose or an eye, they vanished. Without his memories, his connection to the time before the academy, he'd be like Feral, a tool used by the crown. They wanted his identity wiped away, replaced by their prime directive: serve the Queen at all costs.

The ghosts entered the room and left of their own accord, memories being stimulated by the computer. But amongst all the unknown figures, one girl stood in the middle, bald and with the kindest eyes he had ever seen. Unlike the others, she maintained her form, her features holding firm despite the technicians' best efforts. She was the last new face he experienced before they attempted to turn him into an empty vessel. Serving as a gateway to his former life, he refused to let them destroy her memory.

"Erica," he whispered.

Chapter Twelve

2039

Patches sat down as the hydraulics in the door started hissing. He had played out the scenario, bursting through the door and trying to escape. Knocking Jasmine aside might be easy, but he had already played his hand. Escaping wouldn't be the problem. It'd be getting out of the Tower before somebody struck him down with lightning. His resolve to fight drained, and he prepared for another round of questioning.

The door slid open—and the girl from yesterday appeared.

"Come with me if you want to live."

It took him a moment to digest the situation. "Did you just quote—"

"Whatever," she barked. "I'm getting you out of here. You can stay, or you can come with me. But we need to go now."

"And be a criminal? Are you daft?"

He wanted out of the cell, but his innocence would eventually grant him freedom. If he stepped out with this girl he barely knew, he'd be a criminal. He'd never be welcomed at the Tower if he fled.

Patches looked down at the half-eaten steak as the thought sank in. Earlier, he had wanted to leave and return to Chicago. It was the first he thought about staying. It was difficult for him to admit, but part of him wanted to be amongst his own kind.

"Look, you wouldn't understand," Eve started, "but the synthetics were after you. They were closing in on the library. I don't know why you're in the middle of this, but you are."

"I'm nobody special." He couldn't fathom why killer robots would be after him. Everything about him was ordinary, other than being a Child of Nostradamus. "Why would they want me?"

"I don't have time to explain. This offer has an expiration. Do you want to be free or not?"

She leaned out of the doorway, inspecting the hallway. There was no hiding her impatience. Eve was in a hurry to be anywhere but here. The look on her face was sheer guilt. Even if they made it out of the basement, there was no way they'd get through the wall.

"I'm staying."

"Dammit," she threw up her arms in defeat. "This isn't how it's supposed to happen. She had a plan. Maybe you weren't part of it. Maybe I was supposed to go on my own. Goddammit."

Patches pushed his chair out, standing. Eve's breakdown should have been alarming, but he'd repeated those words before. *She had a plan*, he thought.

"She is far from where you stand," he whispered, reciting the line from the letter in his pocket.

"What? Never mind," she turned, prepared to leave him.

"Eleanor wrote you a letter," he said.

"Wait, what? How could you know that?"

He dug into his side pocket and pulled out a sheet of paper. It never left his side. He had studied it word for word, pining over each letter, hoping he could make sense of the psychic's intentions. He memorized every comma and descending brushstroke of a skilled author.

Eve's jaw went slack, words escaping her. Patches hadn't considered that she was a person and not a descriptor of a place. But with her wearing body armor, backpack slung over her shoulder and keycard in hand, he couldn't imagine a woman further from where he was. Had Eleanor seen this very moment?

"There are no coincidences," Eve whispered. "It's a saying the Nighthawks repeat. They were each given a letter. Eleanor made sure they met so they could fulfill their destinies."

Patches eyed the door. Anxiety pooled in his stomach and he struggled to keep the bile from climbing into his throat. If he thought about it, he'd have a nervous breakdown and he'd be no closer to solving the riddle that kept him awake for weeks. Instead, he barreled to the door, bumping her to the side as he staggered into the hallway. If he didn't think about it, the worry couldn't take hold.

"I didn't think you had it in you," she admitted.

"Go," he said, "before I regret this."

"Are you—"

"Go," he growled.

"We don't have time to get your things." She moved with purpose, stomping down the hallway. He watched her head swivel as she eyed the cameras in the corners of the corridor.

"Won't they see you helping me escape?" He was convinced there was no way they'd make it out of the Tower. The security was like a government building, with cameras and locked doors at every turn. The Tower might be transparent and open with its residents, but they attempted to take safety precautions. If only there had been enough in place to stop robots from killing them.

"Yes," she said. "Needles is watching every step we take."

"Won't he stop you… us?"

"I don't think so," she said. He caught her giving a slight nod to the camera. She flashed the ID card in front of the elevator handprint. "He's on the Council. His badge should unlock the doors."

"Don't think so? *Should?*"

"I'll explain it once we reach the gates. Just stay close. Once we're topside, you need to act casual. Curfew is in effect, but we might bump into the Sentinels."

"Are those more robots?"

"Security team. You've met Alyssa. If you see her, run."

"But—"

They stepped into the elevator. The door hissed shut and Patches realized they made an awkward pair. She looked as if she was ready to leap tall buildings, and he was late for a job interview. He rolled his sleeves up, untucking the rest of his shirt as he attempted to embrace the casual look. Of the two of them, she looked far more out of place, well, any place except maybe the Tower.

"Why are you doing this?" he asked.

"The synthetics were converging on the library. I went to speak with you and found the letter. It told me to answer when opportunity rang. Then a phone—"

"Bit on the nose," he said.

Eve didn't hide the eye roll. "It was Gretchen looking for my aunt. She's gone missing. Kidnapped. Everything is linked. There are no such things as coincidences. You, the synthetics, Skits, the letters. We need each other."

"I didn't need—"

"Me? You were doing so well on your own. Perhaps they would have let you out. But Alyssa isn't Alyssa. At least, I don't think so. Something is going on here. I haven't sorted it out yet. But you're not safe."

Patches leaned back, using the rear of the elevator for support. In an elevator ride, Eve had gone from rescuing him to spouting conspiracy theories. He should have laughed at the preposterousness, but the growing pain in his stomach was anything but humorous. With every breath, he feared he might buckle over and hurl.

"You don't look good," she said.

"Trying not to vomit."

"Don't get it on me."

"Your concern is touching," he said.

The elevator came to a stop, and the door opened. He started forward, and she held her arm out, blocking his path.

"What?" She might be dressed like a superhero, but he didn't appreciate her acting like his personal savior. He might not be the most capable person in the tight space, but he wasn't useless, not entirely.

"We have company," she said.

"We have company," Eve said.

She sniffed the air, a faint scent of burning invading her nostrils. There were a dozen Children in the building who combusted because of their abilities. But only one who made her skin tingle as he warped the electromagnetic fields about his body.

"Shit," she hissed.

"What? Tell me," he said. "The Sentinels? Is it them? Synthetics?"

Nowhere in the letter had it mentioned that saving the poor man would require listening to his anxiety-induced ramblings. She wanted to turn and slap him like in the movies. With a strike of her fist, he'd hopefully return to normal and stop being a blithering idiot.

"Stay close. Keep your head down. I think we can get away before he finds us."

"Who?" he asked. She ignored the question, not wanting to have him turn around and run.

With electricity flowing through the Tower, the white noise made it difficult to use her abilities. If she closed her eyes, she'd sense an infinite number of lines generated in every direction. Some were stronger than others, some moved faster, but through the white noise, she could still detect *him*—Dwayne. His body vibrated with power as he allowed the electricity to coat the surface of his skin. The man was on a mission, and she feared that he'd discovered her absence hours before she intended.

"Walk quickly."

Eve grabbed Patches' hand and pulled him along. There was no point in being subtle. If Dwayne was looking for her, it was to stop her from leaving the Tower and doing something reckless. Even if he wasn't her biological father, he took the role seriously. She was old enough to have moved out with a family of her own, but he somehow balanced her independence while keeping a vigilant eye.

More disturbances. They were a sprint away from the lobby, but in this hallway, massive rooms opened on either side. She eyed the open space to their left. Each room contained a bit of Children history, brought to the forefront by local artists.

She pushed Patches into the room that served as an art gallery filled with statues. Each was easily twice the size of the person they resembled. Pulling at Patches, she headed toward the statue resting in the middle of the massive room. The art gallery would normally have Children gathering, hiding away while surrounded by stunning works of art. It had become a popular place for the school to take field trips by day and lovers to meet in the evening.

She pulled her conspirator behind a gigantic statue of a woman with reptilian wings. The Angel of the Outlands served as the anchor piece in the collection. The woman frozen in bronze appeared to be launching herself upward from a pile of rubble and, at nearly twenty feet tall, it served as a suitable hiding space.

"What—"

"Shh."

Eve closed her eyes, pressing her palms to the floor. There was so much noise, a constant bombardment from her abilities. When she accessed that part of her brain that allowed her to see electromagnetic fields, she had to fight back or be overwhelmed. While her heart sped up, she found a moving object that almost created a void compared to the rest—a man, walking down the hall at a leisurely pace.

"Sentinel," she whispered.

She ducked low behind the statue, pulling Patches out of sight. She placed her hand over his mouth to make sure he wouldn't give away their location. With her eyes closed, she searched for Dwayne. It was bad enough that her father was on the warpath, but now, with Sentinels closing in, it would be impossible to escape.

Eve wanted to curse, angry she hadn't paid more attention to her teacher when he instructed them on how to ease into their abilities. Perhaps if she had been a better student instead of acting like a petulant child, she'd be able to pinpoint her father's location. Instead, it was like shouting in a massive room, echoes without a way to pinpoint the origin.

The void of lines vanished, turning down another hallway. She held her breath, unsure if they'd turn around and head toward the gallery. Her abilities could detect nearby disturbances, but the moment she searched for anything further away, the static from the building made it impossible.

"We need to go," she whispered.

She pulled at his arm, nearly dragging Patches along. If necessary, she could toss him on her shoulder and make a run for it, not that it would look suspicious or anything. If Eleanor thought he was important, she wouldn't have lied, but Eve had to admit, she'd hoped for a more willing partner. His nerves were less steel than hers, and that didn't bode well for whatever adventure awaited them beyond the wall.

The hallway emptied into the east side of the lobby. If

they ran around the edges of the courtyard, they'd be at the doors in just a couple of minutes. From there, they needed to run through the fields and reach the wall. Needles' badge might open every door inside the building, but she wasn't entirely sure it'd open the barrier put in place to protect them. But seeing as it hadn't been doing such a great job, she hoped they could climb and be free.

"Do you have a plan?" Patches asked.

"Running is a plan." He groaned in response, but he didn't object any further.

Her feet moved quickly. There was no going back. If Patches couldn't keep up, he'd be left behind. Leaning into the run, she found her rhythm, passing the garden and rounding the center of the lobby. Halfway to the exit, she had no doubt they could make it. Patches followed, only a few feet behind. If she got caught, it'd be a slap on the wrist. If *he* got caught, who knows what they might do. In the Tower, they hadn't created laws dealing with treason. It'd be a shame for Patches to be the first.

She barreled into one of the panels of steel used to cover the shattered glass from the attack. It hardly budged as she smacked against the metal. The glass along the lobby looked beautiful, but it was nearly a foot thick and able to withstand the blast from a grenade. However, lasers were not on their list of weapons to prevent. She imagined the architects reconsidered that dilemma. With a shove, she found that whoever put it in place had melted the edges, locking it in place.

She fumbled with the keycard, eyeing it as she approached the doors that'd allow them out of the tower. Even Patches caught on to the panic attempting to take hold.

"Will the key open the door?" She was prepared to press the badge against the lock when Patches absent-mindedly pushed the door open.

Eve didn't question her luck. Perhaps it was an oversight, or maybe another person received a letter suggesting they leave a door open. Or perhaps…

"Eve Ayer." She cringed at the stern tone.

Shit, she thought. Dwayne stood outside, waiting like an overprotective father. At any moment, he might ask to smell her breath, checking for booze or sniffing her shirt for the smell of smoke. Despite their many disagreements, he had never put his foot down, and now, as power cackled along his skin, he was making a stand.

It was only more dire as a synthetic with a blue face stood next to him. She didn't know how the man found out about Skits' pet, but it couldn't bode well for her now. Without Skits commanding the robot, Eve and Dwayne were the only others capable of feeding it commands. He might not know what was happening, but the scowl on his face meant he didn't like it.

"I found your letter."

It had been a brief note, just to make sure they didn't worry about her while she fulfilled her destiny. At the time, it seemed like the polite thing to do. She didn't think he would poke his head inside her room like she was an infant.

"Dwayne, we need to go." She rarely used his first name, but with the amount of power wrapping around his body, dad seemed too informal.

"Like hell you do. Not with him."

Eve reached out, pushing Patches behind her, preparing to use her body as a shield. Dwayne might wield lightning like a god, but even he couldn't control the primal force of nature. At this range, he'd strike her as quickly as he would Patches.

"What are you doing? You can't go breaking people out—"

"He had nothing to do with yesterday."

"You don't know what you're—"

"He saved my life. I led the synthetics away from the classroom. They were going to kill me." It stung to admit she couldn't handle herself against a couple of robots. "He saved me."

"But—"

"Something is going on here. Something bad." She froze. If something got to Alyssa, could they have gotten to Dwayne as well? She pushed her abilities outward, rolling them along the ground until they slammed into Dwayne. The lines flowing around his body were chaotic, intense, and ready to burst forth. Whatever was going on, she confirmed the man was himself.

"Tell him about the letter," Patches whispered.

"Explain yourself," Dwayne demanded. His fists remained balled. The bracelet on his wrist blinked a bright red, ensuring all knew it had reached its capacity.

"People aren't acting like themselves," she said. It could have just been Alyssa, and even now she second-guessed herself. Had it been that out of character for Alyssa to hold Needles's hand? Everybody knew it was inevitable, but Alyssa refused to partake in speculation. For a split second, Eve doubted her conviction.

"No," she said out loud. Patches had been seen going to the generators. Fact. It would be impossible to be in the generator room and the library at the same time. Fact. Eleanor's letter. Fact. As she cycled through her checklist, she stood taller, certain that she was doing the right thing.

"I can't explain it. But if you're Dwayne..." His eye rose. "Then, you can't trust your eyes."

"You're not making sense."

Eve let her abilities brush against the metal cuff on Dwayne's wrist. The amount of power contained in the piece of hardware paled in comparison to what rested at the center of his body. She could sense it just beneath the surface, seeking an escape. How he managed this much self-discipline, she'd never understand.

"There are no such things as coincidences."

Eve raised her hands, letting them caress the invisible lines of the universe as if she were feeling the current of a small stream. With a turn of her hand, the lines pushed around her. She imagined grabbing the lines, redirecting them. The stream diverted and slammed into Dwayne. She held steady and grabbed at the lines produced by his own body.

"I'm sorry," she whispered. Instead of redirecting the stream, she stomped in the waters, sending it splashing in all directions.

Dwayne convulsed as lightning poured out of his body. She ducked, dropping flat on the walkway. A bolt slammed into Patches, sending him crashing into the glass wall.

It ended as Dwayne slumped to the ground, steam rolling off his skin. Eve rushed to his side, prepared to check for his pulse. The man's chest rose and fell with a slight snort. It was only the second time her abilities had disrupted the fields she grew up sensing.

She spun on her knee, prepared to run to Patches to see if he was okay. Her eyes widened as he picked himself up from the cement, shaking his head. Yesterday he had taken a punch from the synthetic without so much as a grunt, and now he absorbed a bolt of lightning. The man might not be as useless as she first thought.

"Blue, you're coming with us."

The robot's head nodded in compliance. She waved Patches over and watched as he staggered. He gave himself a pat on the face and struggled to walk in a straight line.

"Are you okay?"

"I…" He touched the charred remnants of his shirt. "I think so."

"We need to run for the wall. There is a small building near the exit. We can find transportation."

He flexed his fingers, stretching his upper body as if he were preparing for a workout. As he got closer, Eve could see the glow of his eyes, an emerald green light with wisps of smoke shedding from his tear ducts.

"Keep up," he laughed.

He charged past her. It looked less like running and more like he was flying between steps. Each leap sent him five, six, twenty feet toward the gate.

She growled. "What the hell?"

Alyssa's guilt refused to be suppressed by chamomile tea. She set the cup down on her kitchen table and stared at the ornate teapot. It was hours past her bedtime, but her mind continued to race, a blur of events over the last twenty-four hours.

"I'm not seeing the obvious."

After an hour of turning back and forth in bed, she admitted defeat. Whatever demons rested on her shoulder, they wouldn't be easily silenced. With a final sip, she decided it would be best to meet them head-on at the source.

Minutes later, she had changed from her robe to a more casual outfit. She glanced at a mirror, satisfied that it blended effort with comfort. Most importantly, she raised a knee to her chest. It allowed for mobility should the need arise. It was an unfortunate reality, but she preferred to err on the side of caution.

The hallways were empty. Even if the synthetics hadn't attacked, the residents of the Tower were amicable and listened to the rules set by the Council. There might be a complaint here and there, but they had developed an understanding. Rules weren't enacted unless necessary, and they did their best to communicate the reasoning. Conthan felt it important that they begin the Town Halls on a regular basis to continue an open dialogue and continue a mostly transparent governing. So far, he had been right.

Nearly every floor had resident quarters. She walked softly, counting down the numbers as she went. This floor held a few families, but most were occupied by a single person. With the industrial carpeting, Alyssa didn't make a sound as she passed by the last door before reaching the elevator.

She pressed her hand against the panel next to the elevator. It blinked red before beeping. She tried it again and found it refused to respond. Eyeing the camera, she wondered if Ned was watching his computers? With a quick wave, she waited only to find the door didn't open.

"I suppose even the mighty Needles must sleep." She pulled out her ID card. Opening the hand scanner, she slid the card into the slot. The light turned green, and the door opened seconds later.

Alyssa stared at the camera inside the elevator. The man insisted that no part of the Tower remained hidden. He argued for them to be installed within the apartments, but Conthan and Dwayne refused to violate the citizens' privacy. The vote had been split, and she remained the deciding ballot, a common occurrence amongst the Council. They weren't perfect, but as a new nation, they weren't doing too bad, or at least that's what she told herself.

The elevator slowed, entering the sub-basement. A hiss sounded as the hydraulics pulled the doors open. Within the sub-basement, there were multiple levels reserved for research. Genesis Division had taken up shop, working in conjunction with Children to advance mankind. Alyssa didn't want them here, not after their involvement in the death of so many people she cared about. However, their presence allowed her to keep the enemy close.

This particular floor housed spaces used by the most dangerous residents. The rooms had been constructed around their abilities to resist acid, or lightning, or ear-piercing screams. Some residents required more attention than others to prevent their abilities from wreaking havoc.

The doors to her left housed those cruelly affected by the Nostradamus Effect. For these residents, when their abilities developed, it transformed into a curse. Amber slept here at night, fearful she'd start a fire in her sleep. Malek had been delivered by the Paladins, his lungs unable to breathe anything other than pure nitrogen. There were at least a dozen and the number of occupants below the surface grew, and that left Alyssa's heart heavy.

On the right, there were numerous labs where a dedicated group of scientists worked during the day, helping to minimize the effects of these Children's abilities. They might try to build a utopia, but it wasn't pretty for all residents.

The lights remained off, other than the strips glowing along the floor. She didn't understand most of the science being performed in these rooms. Even reading the reports, she relied heavily on Errick to translate. Not knowing what they were up to made her nervous.

She paused at the last door on the left. Pressing her hand against the panel, she waited for the familiar hiss as it slid open. When it blinked red, refusing to open, she decided Ned needed to stop putting the entire Tower on his shoulders. The door finally opened when she physically swiped her ID. Unlike the apartments, even those for the more secluded Children, the room contained a single tube. Wires from the ceiling fed into the top of the cylinder, causing a slight hum in an otherwise empty space.

"Ya Allah. May he grant you peace, Elliot." Suspended in a blueish liquid, he bobbed up and down as oxygen bubbled around his body. Wires were attached to his body, providing constant communication with the hub. Seeing him inside, nearly lifeless, she thanked Allah for bestowing a gift she could master. Many, like this young man, not all were so lucky.

She forced herself to stare, letting the uncomfortable reality wash over her like the faint blue light cast from the suspension chamber. The medically induced coma was the only thing keeping Elliot inside from dissolving into nothing. Even now, the fluid in the tube only slowed the skin from evaporating. The others forgot the young man came to them seeking help. Despite a dedicated team of researchers working to overcome his abilities, the Council had already hopeless reality sink in.

"I will visit soon. We have many more pages to go before they defeat the White Witch." Alyssa offered a slight bow before pressing the button to close the door. While she felt the weight on her shoulders lessen, it wasn't the real reason she came to this level.

She hurried down the hall, heading toward where they detained the librarian. There was no need to keep him here when they could just as easily secure him in his quarters. She wasn't done with him, or at least, she wasn't done sorting out his role in this matter. But her gut continued to press on. He was not the malevolent person they first believed.

Rounding the corner, she found Conthan standing in the hallway, in front of an open door leading to the librarian's cell.

"Conthan," she said, "what is going on?"

"He's not here," he said.

"Who?"

"The prisoner. He's escaped."

Alyssa stomped down the hallway until she stood at the open door. The only sign he had been there was the half-eaten steak with a fork sticking upright in the center. She pushed aside the gut feeling. Alyssa would deal with it when they found him.

She studied the door, looking for tampering. With how quickly he threw Jasmine across the room, she suspected he could have blown it clear off its hinges. She hoped to find a clue as to how he escaped, but it was as if he had vanished without a trace. The only person capable of that stood next to her.

"Did you teleport him?"

Conthan scrunched up his face at the question. She admired the man, but it wouldn't be the first time he went rogue. His emotions had a tendency to control his decisions, and if he had feelings about Mr. Kilgannon, they could have clouded his judgment.

He didn't protest. She asked again. "Did you?"

"No," he butted in. "I came down to talk to him. He could be dangerous. Anybody willing to let synthetics into the Tower shouldn't be given a second chance."

Again, he let his emotions dictate his thoughts. Alyssa loved him like a brother, but there were many times she struggled not to slap some sense into him. Only a couple of years older than her, he required more time to mature.

"I doubt he had anything to do with the synthetics."

"I saw the same footage as you. He clearly got caught heading to the generators. What more proof do you need?" He slammed his fist against the wall, far more infuriated than she expected. He hadn't appeared this distraught when they first found out, and now he acted as if the world rested sorely on his shoulders.

"Something is..." Alyssa stepped close enough to the man that her eyes aligned with his chin. He stood his ground as she studied his face. "You're not like yourself."

Conthan turned his head as he let out a long sigh. "Alyssa…" He stepped away, putting his back against the wall. "I'm going to be honest with you." He leaned over, bracing his hands on his thighs. "I'm tired. When will humans give us some peace?"

Alyssa nodded. "It sounds as if you could use a couple of days for yourself. After that, you can take a personal inventory."

He ran a hand over his stubble and along his scalp. "I suppose you're right."

"I usually am." No hubris, just a matter of fact.

"Well, I'm going to head upstairs."

As he walked away, Alyssa held still, studying his posture. For a larger man, he always walked with determination, a sign he had grown from a girthy boy.

"The elevators are barely reliable right now. You might want to teleport."

"I'll take my chances," he shouted without turning around. "I need a chance to clear my head."

He turned down the corridor, his steps growing distant. Alyssa gave her head a light shake, trying to digest the conversation. Others might accuse her of being shy with how little she spoke. Observation wasn't the same as silence. Holding her words, she could study people, their actions, their words, and how the two compared and contrasted. The same pressure in her gut that believed Patrick Kilgannon was innocent lurched, convinced again, an obvious piece of the puzzle eluded her.

Not so long ago, she and Conthan had been fugitives, hiding away from the world. Trapped in a small house, with barely enough space to house her team, they became intimately familiar with one another. While she tried to relearn her ballet positions, he treated her as a model, grinding charcoal as he captured her movements. They served in the trenches together. A union oftentimes more intimate than lovers.

"Allah protect us," she whispered, "the Shayatin whisper in our ears."

Alyssa touched her chest, feeling for the star and crescent necklace hiding beneath her tunic. She clutched it as her mind raced with a cacophony of worry. Cutting through the questions about Mr. Kilgannon's escape, one phrase repeated itself.

"Who are you, really?"

Chapter Thirteen

2039

Patches squeezed his arm around Eve's waist. There was no way to cling to the girl without feeling like he was copping a feel. The first time she weaved between abandoned cars on the road, he'd stopped caring. If touching her breasts meant not being thrown from the motorcycle, he'd justify himself later. She hardly noticed as she leaned forward, turning the throttle, causing the motorcycle to zip through a forgotten town.

His parents had traveled from Scotland to Canada and settled in Chicago. Despite their worldly travels, he had never set foot outside of Illinois, that is, until Troy. With no friends or family, he found himself grasping to the message left for him in a letter. While it had been signed by Eleanor P. Valentine, it could have been forged as a cruel joke. In less than a day, he'd nearly been killed and thrown in jail. Now he was a fugitive from the only people willing, or so he thought, to accept him.

"Fuck," he grumbled.

The bike slowed, the revving engine shifting to a

light purr. He pulled his cheek from her back, daring to peek through clenched eyelids. Eve's hair continued whipping about as she eased back on the throttle. The small town could have been anywhere in America, a quaint series of houses built by the same contractor, with only slight variations between them. One had a sprawling veranda and the next a small porch with a screened-in porch.

Patches ducked under a chunk of asphalt spat up by Blue as the robot sped past. Eve's pet synthetic managed to almost keep pace once they slowed. He should have been impressed by the robot's speed in canine form, but it made him realize there was no reason to run from the buggers. The robot had been one of the herd sent to kill them, and now she treated it like a puppy, with claws, guns, and other deadly devices.

The bike slowed to a roll. He sat upright, hands gripping her hips. They had reached a series of blockades. It might have been normal in this part of the Free Republic, but it wasn't an occasional overturned vehicle. Somebody had built a wall. Cars had been turned on their side, blocking the roads, a wall that stretched almost until the tree-line.

"What is this?"

"Welcome to Troy," she said. "There's a safe house on the other side of this blockade. We can get supplies there."

"A safe house?" He didn't understand why the Children of Nostradamus would need a safe house when they had an entire compound to keep them safe.

"You're kidding, right?"

As Eve climbed off the bike, and turning, she

stopped and stared. Her eyes were stunning, even if they were currently judging him. He found himself blushing, embarrassed by how little he knew about *his* people. It had gone on the list of things he wanted to explore as he set up the library, but it appeared that was a pipe dream.

"What are you scared of?"

"Not all of us are superheroes," he said.

"Not all of us are ashamed."

The words stung. For a while, he attended a support group in Chicago that catered to people with gifts. Nobody in that dingy basement wanted to be special—they wanted to be normal. They shared affirmations, reassuring one another they *were* human. When life got busy, he stopped going, but he still whispered the mantra from time to time. I am human.

But here was a woman who reveled in her gifts. With a single statement, she cut him deep. He wasn't ashamed, not that he was different. Even as the thought crossed his mind, he struggled to believe his weak lie. As he eyed his hands, he understood that he'd give up his powers in a heartbeat.

"Give me a hand," she waved him forward as she stood in front of the barricade. The cars had been stacked three high with sheets of metal filling in the gaps. He spotted the welding marks and wondered why a people just shy of gods needed a wall for protection.

"What were you trying to keep out?"

"Outlanders. Zombies. Humans. Synthetics. You know, the usual stuff. We never had problems, but you can't be too sure."

"Zombies? You've got to be kidding."

She slammed her hands against the back of a car,

shaking the wall. She leaned against the car, bracing her feet before grunting and giving it another try. They could easily climb over the cars if they were willing to ditch the bike. "Can't we climb?"

"There aren't many solar cars and the gas will have gone bad in the rest. I don't want to be stuck here without a vehicle."

She had thought out her plan, at least for the next hour. It was more headspace than he had given the problem. If it wasn't for her, he'd be locked in a cell. It hadn't crossed his mind what the next logical step would be. Thankfully, the one thing Eve didn't lack was a sense of conviction. She'd move forward with or without him.

"Would they have killed me?"

She stopped pushing. "Kill you? No. The worst punishment they've ever given was banishment, and that guy deserved a lot worse."

Her eyes dropped, and he got the feeling she was reconsidering her answer. For the first time, he had a chance to really take in the girl who had saved him. The bodysuit clung to her skin until it reached her chest. Even the belt with pouches and boots was jet black, almost to the point they absorbed light. The only part that added bulk was on her chests and wrists, extra chunky bits protecting her heart. Eve might balk every time he used the phrase superhero, but if she had a cape, the uniform would be perfect.

"They might have killed you. Not our people. But the imposter, who knows what they would have done."

"Imposter?"

She shrugged, not offering any more answers.

Patches let out a low growl. "Look. We aren't going

to be best friends here. But we have these stupid letters and you said there are no coincidences."

"I wonder if this is how they started?"

"They?"

"The Nighthawks," she said. "They received letters. Dwayne teases that Conthan was a mess when they first found him. Maybe you're my Conthan."

She knew how to deliver a backhanded compliment. Great, another superpower he'd have to deal with. He had a thousand questions about her, the Tower, and her connection to the team of Children who saved the world. They'd have to wait. For now, he started with the straightforward questions.

"Tell me about the imposter."

He stepped around her, giving one of the cars a push. He attempted it again, putting some muscle into the gesture.

"I'm stronger than most." She wasn't bragging; she spoke it as if it were a fact. Patrick understood enough about the Children to know not all were created equal. Nearly all had enhanced strength, but it varied from one person to the next. He always wished he'd been more durable, but it was the lack of getting sick he cherished the most. In Chicago, the flu could put the strongest man on his ass, or at least that's what he'd heard. A healthy immune system sat squarely in the benefits column.

"The imposter?" He didn't want her sidetracked.

"The synthetics were heading to the library. They wanted something there. But you weren't there."

"I was apparently sabotaging the generators."

"Correct." She touched her nose, while pointing at him with her other hand. "Unless you can make copies of yourself, something was wrong. So you couldn't have done it. It means somebody that looks like you is in the Tower. The day before, we found somebody had gummed up the shield system. Now we have a conspiracy."

Patches pounded his fist against the car. Where there should be pain in his palms, there was only a warmth. "Keep going," he said as he smashed his fist against the metal.

"I went to see Needles about it. He's the guy in charge of our security. He's the only person who could have gotten me to your cell and out the front door."

"How'd you know he wasn't the imposter? If I were going to topple the Tower, I'd start with him."

"I had to risk it. Thankfully, Needles has a very *distinct* personality."

On the fifth smash, Patches stepped away from the vehicles. His skin felt like fire, millions of tiny needles pricking at his arms. His hands should be sore, perhaps even raw, but they vibrated. He tried steadying his breath, but the kinetic energy stored in his body needed an outlet.

"Then Alyssa showed up. It wasn't her. I've known her for years, and whoever wore her face didn't do their homework. I don't know if it's one person causing mayhem, or if they're replacing key players."

"Adelaide," he growled. "She was acting weird. Couldn't remember our conversation from the day before. I didn't know if it had something to do with the voices in her head."

The hurt came from inside his body. He forced the burn into his limbs as he braced himself against the wall.

Patches didn't need to understand his abilities for them to work. Perhaps when they had time, she'd be able to give him insight. But what he lacked in knowledge, he made up for in showmanship.

He thrust his hands forward, fingers digging into the metal. The pavement under his feet cracked as he pushed the vehicle. Shrieks of metal filled the empty town as he toppled the stack of vehicles. As the burning faded, he tossed the car to the side a dozen feet.

"Seems I'm stronger." He winked at her between gasps of air.

"Should we knock?"

"You're insufferable," Eve said.

Patches shrugged. "Not the first I've heard that."

Eve's fingers touched the doorknob, searching for the small dent caused by a new couch. For years, she walked in and out of that door, thinking she had found a home that accepted her. Conthan and Dwayne had treated her like blood. When she broke the rules, they scolded her, but most of all, they celebrated her every victory. The first time she paralleled park, or when she learned a new song on the guitar, it seemed there was always a cake being made. Together, the three of them had made this house a home.

"Eve, you okay? We don't have to—"

She pushed hard enough the lock broke the door jamb. Even after years of being vacant, she imagined the smell of burned pot roast and ozone. Neither man could cook, and if it hadn't been for her introducing them to online cooking tutorials, they'd have starved. They weren't prepared to be parents, but they hit the ground running. But try as they might, saving the world hadn't prepared them for a teenage daughter.

Once inside, Patches leaned in close to a collage of photos hanging on the wall. He tapped the glass before looking over his shoulder. "Are they nice guys?"

She nodded. "They're family."

They had decided as a household to leave most of their belongings behind. She had taken the photos that warmed her heart, but much of the house was just as they had left it. Dozen had left a protective coat on her memories.

"What do you know about the church?" she asked.

"Nothing really. You'd hear rumors from people about how they worshipped Children, but from what I gathered, most avoided them."

"Their founder is a man named Raymond Valentine Davis."

"Valentine as in…"

Eve dragged her finger through the dust on the front of the television. "Yup. You can say she's like his grandmother." With a quick gesture, she wrote the name Eleanor into the dust. "A mentalist killed his family. Rage filled the void in his heart. When it came time for him to decide the man he wanted to be, he decided on good."

"I'm not sure what about this moment requires story time?" Unlike many people in the Tower, she had firsthand knowledge about Eleanor Valentine and her mysterious ways. Patches might think the letter served as a marker to change his fate, but the psychic had never been that short-sighted.

"We call him Preacher. He's the founder of the church along with Azacca and his priests." Eve still hated the modern aesthetic of the couch. They had moved it into every position in the living room, and it never quite fit. Conthan refused to listen to reason and Dwayne had shrugged his shoulders. It had served as neutral territory in the evenings as they watched black and white movies. "The Nighthawks weren't the only ones to fight against the Warden. The Church joined in the cause. Ultimately, it was Preacher who saved the day. When I got booted from my house, he found me."

Patches had grown quiet. She glanced over her shoulder to make sure he hadn't wandered off. The man with dark hair and a healthy beard on his face listened without commentary.

"His father delivered the letters for Eleanor before she died. She set him on a path. He'd become the first victim of the Warden. He had a child who saved the world. The same child brought me here, and then to the Tower where I found the letter."

"It's all connected," Patches whispered. His voice held a bit of disbelief as the epiphany set in. Eleanor had that effect on her victims. He understood.

The letter in his pocket, the thing that changed his life forever, wasn't done. There were a thousand more choices to be made, and each one would lead him closer to fulfilling his destiny. "Eleanor altered the world. She's working through us. Hell, she might have seen this very moment."

"If that's the case, then no matter what we do…" He pulled his hand from his left pocket. "Our future is scripted."

"This is why we don't talk about Eleanor. A woman I

never met knows the outcome of every decision I will make. Is she telling me what to do, or by telling me, did she change the outcome?"

"Jesus," he said, "my head already hurts."

"I need to know you're in this with me."

"I'm here."

She walked past Patches, watching him move from one set of photos to the next. Before her parents kicked her out, she had been naïve, but reality had robbed her of a childhood. Part of her admired his innocence, the other mourned how quickly it was about to be torn from him.

"That's not what I mean," she said.

"That's what I feared," he joked.

In the hallway, Eve opened a door with stairs leading into the basement. She gestured for him to follow. "If she gave us those letters, something big is coming. She must have screwed up in a past life for all the things she's trying to prevent." Eve flipped a switch on the wall, but no lights miraculously vibrated to life.

"You want to know if I'm going to bail when things get tough?"

He had saved her when she froze. He didn't hesitate springing into action to rescue her from certain death. In the heat of the moment, he acted. Eve pondered if the man had any interest in becoming a Sentinel.

"Do I have a choice?" He was learning.

"I don't think so," she admitted. Perhaps she could accomplish Eleanor's chore on her own, but if that were the case, the psychic wouldn't have included him in this task.

"I don't want to be a hero," he added.

The words were raw and honest. She had been

fixated on becoming a Sentinel for the last year. She couldn't fathom why a person wouldn't want to be a hero. They were the ones who charged in and saved the day. Surrounded by people reluctant to accept the role for most of her adult life, she couldn't imagine a different goal.

"I do." It had consumed her, a singular goal. At least it had until the synthetics had attacked.

Without the vibration of circuits and wires in the wall, she could sense the electromagnetic fields in the room. Imagining her body pulsating with lines of electricity, she could see the room as clear as if the lights had functioned. Her built-in sonar revealed that nobody had tampered with Dwayne's safe room.

Eve stepped around the workbench and the tray of tools on the floor. She wrestled with the unfairness bestowed upon them by Nostradamus. Her ability to sense electromagnetic fields didn't compare to whatever Patches could do, that gave him his uncanny strength. Yet, despite the imbalance, he wanted to be a librarian while she wanted to be a fighter. The world had a cruel and sick definition of humor.

"How is this a safe house?"

Light filled the space as Eve opened a large metal door built into the wall of the basement. It wasn't the prettiest setup, and Dwayne had never gotten around to installing the keypad to operate the door, but it served as the repository of all things Nighthawks.

"If we're going to Boston, we're going to need some supplies. And you're going to need a change of clothes."

"You brought me here for a t-shirt?"

Patches let out a gasp as Eve finished swinging the door open. Stepping to the side, she revealed two mannequins wearing leather bodysuits. It was one thing to see people in the Tower walking around in street clothes, but it was another to see a uniform. It was an early prototype of the one she wore now, but it should help Patches control his abilities.

"You've got to be kidding me."

Pointing to the one on the right, she gave him a smile. "Get changed. I'm going to look for some rations and then we head to Boston to save Skits."

Patches touched the chest of the mannequin. The minor bumps along the surface were a surprise on the glossy fabric. It was exactly as he remembered. In the comics, Dwayne's uniform suppressed his abilities, keeping the lightning from erupting at inopportune times. It was a shock to see that the costumes were real and not the creation of an artist. What else might have been factual in its pages?

He had never seen video footage of the Nighthawks in action. He imagined them to be awesome, wielding their abilities like powerhouses. So far, he had met four, and none of them lived up to the grandeur detailed in the comics. Much like him, they were ordinary people, who just happened to have supernatural abilities.

He stripped, debating on if superhero uniforms provided enough space for underwear. He erred on the side of caution, not wanting to soil another man's formal attire. Sliding down the zipper, he paused, questioning what he was about to do. Up to this point, he could pretend he was a passenger, an unwilling victim of circumstance. But the moment he put on the lightning wielder's clothes, he'd say goodbye to the sidelines.

Staring at the thick rubber soles of the boots, he assumed they had tailored it for Dwayne's lightning. If somebody had helped the man master his chaotic abilities, perhaps they could do the same for him. Every bump and bruise thrust him one step closer to becoming a time bomb. No, they designed this for somebody willing to throw themselves in the line of fire. This wasn't the uniform of a lowly librarian.

He choked down the bile in his throat, coughing. Eve was determined to play soldier and rush into danger. Going with her had been the exact opposite for him. Every decision so far had been to take him away from the bad things. He set the uniform on the ground and grabbed jeans and a t-shirt off the wall.

"Sorry," he whispered. "I'm not a hero."

The clothes almost fit, slightly loose in the chest and gut. He slipped on his sneakers before leaving the vault. Patches stopped, turned around, and eyed the uniform. Eve had brought them here for his benefit, swearing that the letters were the catalyst for something bigger. Patches didn't want bigger. He wanted a quiet night in his flat away from the curse of being a Child.

Reaching down, he pulled the letter from his discarded pants and slid it into his pocket. He wasn't quite ready to ignore the psychic's warning. Grabbing a backpack pushed against the wall, he shoved the uniform in the biggest pocket. At least now, he wouldn't have to disappoint a dead mentalist and the only person who seemed to trust him.

Slinging the pack over his shoulder, he shoved away the idea. Once Eve realized just how useless he'd be in a fight, she'd go searching for a new partner. Perhaps that was his role in this disaster. He was meant to motivate her into action.

"Not a hero," he whispered as he headed up from the basement.

Chapter Fourteen

2039

Patches tightened his grip, clenching his eyes as Eve leaned left, swerving around a parked dump truck. Just as quickly, she threw her weight to the right, causing the motorcycle to lean toward the ground, missing a burned-out minivan by inches. Eve had thrown caution to the wind and ignored his squeals each time his life flashed before his eyes. Looking over his shoulder, they had long since left Blue behind. Even in his canine form, he couldn't match her reckless velocity. She assured him that the synthetic would catch up. Patches preferred the robot remain behind, one less killing machine to deal with.

Well into the Outlands, he expected to see nothing but death and decay. The media had painted the area as a nuclear wasteland, filled with delinquents who refused to join society. The buildings were in disrepair, and plenty of vehicles littered the road, all pointing away from Boston. But nature had done its best to reclaim the land. Plants and grass inched across the road and hid the front of buildings. Humans destroyed the power plants, irradiating New England, but nature refused to surrender to their machinations.

"It's beautiful," he shouted.

They moved through a sprawling area somewhere between the border of Massachusetts and Boston. The buildings didn't quite resemble a city, but it appeared as if it had been densely populated before the power plants forced a mass exodus.

They continued on the wrong side of the road, and he realized the cars facing the other direction were fleeing. His chest tightened as they approached a yellow sedan with a "Baby on Board" sticker. Even as they whipped by, he spotted the bleached white occupants resting in their metal coffin. They were driving through a graveyard of those who couldn't escape. Had the radiation killed them quickly? Or did some continue on foot once the traffic turned dense? The more questions he asked, the more he didn't want answers.

The Outlands was too kind a name.

They continued onto the interstate, maintaining a speed that made him tighten his grip around Eve. It felt as if they had been traveling for hours, and he was certain his thighs would ache from straddling the motorcycle for dear life. He nearly cheered when Eve slowed. The hum of the engine had dwindled to a dull roar, and now the ride was almost pleasant. They slowed and Eve steered toward an off-ramp leading to a broken-down rest stop.

The engine died, and she put a foot out, propping them up. "It's going to need to recharge before we keep going." She gave him a second to slide off before she threw her leg over and started pushing. Had it only been a couple of hours? The ache running from his knees, along his thighs and to his tail bone swore it had been weeks.

Other than the Tower, he had yet to see any semblance of life since leaving Chicago. The Outlands had a bit of romantic isolation to it. The silence, other than the rustling of grass and trees, let him imagine he was in a fantastical world. It came crashing down as he eyed the parking lot, where skeletons rested. A natural disaster didn't lay this kind of waste to the world. Man had done this. Seeing the destruction wrought by a handful of freedom fighters reminded him of the darkness of humans. What horrors would he continue to see?

Patches had to shake the descent, to stop himself from questioning the list of poor decisions he could have made. He didn't want to imagine how it got worse. Instead, he wielded his coping mechanism like a weapon—awkward humor.

"Great, maybe we can grab a burger and fries." He pointed at an old fast-food joint. It appeared as if there were several stores, all housed under the same roof. The moment he cracked the joke, he regretted it. "Milkshake would be awesome right now."

"Do you hear yourself sometimes?" she groaned.

His knees threatened to buckle with the first few steps. Eve, on the other hand, pushed the bike like this was a typical weekend getaway for her. Everything about the woman said militant. She lacked any noticeable personality other than determined annoyance. He wanted to like the person who rescued him from a jail cell, but so far, there wasn't much of a person to connect with.

"Are you always such a hard ass?"

"Excuse me?" she asked, annoyed.

"You haven't spoken more than three words, and I'm pretty sure you were barking orders."

"Pardon me." She pushed the bike through the parking lot toward the building. "I'm a bit focused on saving my aunt," Eve growled through gritted teeth.

"What did you want to be when you grew up?"

Eve stopped pushing. It was a simple question, something any two people could talk about without getting deep. It was either because of nerves or his refusal to sit in silence with her, but he needed something, anything, that gave her another layer of depth.

"I'm going to be a Sentinel."

Patches frowned. Her ability to remain focused bordered on pathological. He'd play therapist and ferret out the woman's reasoning later. For now, he wanted a simple answer. "Are you daft?" His accent got thicker when insulting. "When you were a wee lass, what did you want to be then?"

Her eyes narrowed, and she attempted to suss out the meaning of his question. She let out a long sigh, relenting to his off-the-wall question. "Fireman. Policeman. Doctor. Unicorn wrangler."

Patches snorted. The woman had a track record of wanting to help people. Her determination to be one of the Sentinels made sense. But he couldn't let this go without commentary. "Do you bribe them with cotton candy? Or is there a special unicorn call?"

She rolled her eyes and continued pushing the bike. He was just about to ask about being a police officer when she turned around. "Everybody knows they eat marshmallows." He chuckled at her pronunciation. Mallows.

"Just so happens my people are from Scotland and our national animal is the unicorn."

"Your people should ease back on the Scotch."

"No arguing from me there," he laughed. "But everybody knows unicorns eat jelly beans."

"Your unicorns are drunk too." He couldn't be sure, but he suspected she grinned. It was the most personality he had seen from her. He could live with talking about magical creatures all day.

"What would you name your ranch?"

"Rainbow Road Ranch."

The speed with which she threw it out forced a smile on his face. "I'd visit that ranch."

"Your turn." She propped the bike on its kickstand and positioned the solar panel to catch the afternoon sun. Taking a seat on the steps leading into the rest stop, she squinted at him. "What did you want to be when you grew up?"

"Librarian."

"That seems..." She searched for a kind word. He'd grown used to people giving him grief over his occupation. The idea of being surrounded by books written by dead people didn't appeal to the masses. It was no unicorn wrangler. "Boring."

"I'm surrounded by thousands of worlds. Whenever, there is an adventure waiting for me. I can be on a boat hunting whales or helping overthrow an ice queen. There's nothing boring about it."

"Why read about it, though? You can go on real adventures."

"Like this one?"

"I mean..." Her brow furrowed as she thought about it. "Yeah, I guess."

"Funny you should say that." He plopped down on the stairs leading to the row of shattered glass doors into the rest stop. He tried to make himself comfortable by leaning against one of the cement columns. "I stepped outside my comfort zone to go on an adventure. I gave up my life with books and got on a plane and went to Troy. So far, synthetics have attacked me. I got thrown in jail." He held up two fingers, pointing to a third. "Oh yeah, and Jasmine Gentile assaulted me."

"See!" She smacked his knee. "You're on an adventure."

He dropped two fingers to give her the bird. "Give me a book any day."

There was a lull in conversation. Eve got to her feet and peered inside the smashed glass of the rest stop. She pulled the handle of the door, breaking it off without opening. She kicked, knocking it off the hinges. Patches admired her willingness to use her abilities as if they were no big deal.

A few minutes later, she came out. "Empty. It'll make a decent place to sleep tonight."

"We're sleeping here? What about Boston?"

"Bike needs to charge. That should take a couple of hours, and I don't want to drive into Boston as the sun sets. If something held Skits hostage..." She hadn't figured out what could hold Skits captive. But the pause, the worry on her face, that made him nervous. "Yeah, we want daylight."

"So what are we going to do in the meantime?" He cringed at the statement, realizing it came off far more lewd than he anticipated.

The smile spreading across her face should have been

alluring, but it read equal parts sinister and amusement. "I'm going to give you an adventure."

"You said you wanted an adventure?"

Eve pulled her arms from her suit, tying off the excess fabric behind her back. Patches didn't seem thrilled with her idea of fun. If they were at the Tower, they'd be wearing impact suits and fighting hologram robots. But out here, somewhere between Boston and New York, they didn't have the luxury.

"I was thinking more like foreign cuisine. Our definitions of adventure do not overlap."

She had met people like him before. Her partner on the wall, Kevin, had started as a reluctant Child. They didn't want the responsibility that came with their gifts, or worse, they were scared of their abilities. Kevin would never be a fighter, but he found a middle ground that allowed him to embrace his differences. If she were going into the heart of Boston on a rescue mission, she needed to assess her partner's willingness to fight.

"Explain your abilities?" Eve asked. It's how Alyssa started every assessment with the neophytes. Describing their own gifts revealed more than just their abilities. Alyssa would find it amusing that one of her most difficult students had become the teacher.

"I don't know how to describe it."

"I'm going to punch you in a moment," she stated, "so figure it out."

His back straightened. He had offensive abilities. She'd seen the dent in the cell and the way he pulled the wall apart. Now she had to convince him they were more than just a fluke and that they provided value.

"My skin burns and then…" He stared at his hands, "I get strong. Wow, that sounds stupid."

"I sense electromagnetic fields. Let's save the 'who got it worse' competition for later." She watched him give a slight nod. Good, it was already progressing. "How do you get strong?"

"It just happens."

"That's not how these things work. We're all strong by default, but even I'm not as strong as you." She had watched him at the barricade, punching the metal. He might not have words for it, but she had a suspicion.

"When I get hit, it hurts, but not like it should. Suddenly I'm strong."

"You have never researched your abilities?"

Patches shook his head. "What good is punching stuff for a librarian?"

Eve bit back her words. With the strength hidden underneath his shirt, he could change the world. Even a mundane job like working at a library would be made easier with strength without limits.

"When that synthetic threw you into the wall, that's how you did it? The impact made you strong?" It made sense now. He wasn't the only person with the ability to transfer different types of energy in their body.

"Yeah. It doesn't really hurt. I mean, not like I imagine it does for other people. It doesn't matter if it's stubbing my toe or walking into a wall."

"Patches," she said trying to keep the smirk off her face. "Do you walk into a lot of walls?" The man could be a ferocious fighter, but he acted as if his powers had only developed yesterday. If she had those gifts, she'd have been bench pressing cars.

"Not at all." He waved her off. "I don't want to give away my third-degree black belt."

"Your body is acting like a battery. You're storing kinetic energy. Eventually your body has to get rid of it."

"How the hell—"

"I live with a man who wields lightning. Same thing happens to him. Once his body can't hold it, he has to empty the battery. How much can you hold?"

"I've never tried—"

Eve's fist connected with his jaw. She opted to make it a light punch, but enough to down most humans. There was no point in breaking Patches, at least not yet. Taking a step back, she waited for him to speak.

His hand touched his cheek. His head lifted as he ran his fingers over his neck. There wasn't blood, no split lip, or even a red patch from her fist.

"Describe what you're feeling."

"Shock. I'm a little surprised that you punched me in the face."

"I don't care about your emotional well-being. Physically, describe it."

His eyes widened as his head shook back and forth. "Your knuckles, they hit, and I felt it in my whole body."

"I'm stronger than—"

"Than most, I know. That was a love tap." The shock turned to a shit-eating grin. "My upper body vibrated. It didn't hurt. But the heat rippled along my skin. I can absorb more than that."

"Force distribution, that's impressive."

"It is?"

"Your skin is distributing the force of the impact

along the rest of your body. It must take that kinetic energy and store it." There might be more nuance to what he could do, but it was enough to get the ball rolling. For somebody to not have a broken jaw, there must be some weight behind their abilities.

Patches eyed his fists. Eve didn't understand how somebody with that much potential refused to use their gifts. Being able to sense the fields given off by objects did nothing to help her in a fight; despite that, she persisted. If she dwelled on it for long, her envy would turn to anger. Instead, she dispensed a more aggressive version of Alyssa's mentoring.

This time, she leaned into the strike. Putting her weight behind the blow, she slammed her palm into Patches' chest. The force sent him soaring through the air, his arms pinwheeling as if it might somehow save him. Had he been human, she'd have crushed his sternum. Even as a Child, he might suffer from a few broken ribs. As he hit the grass and rolled onto the sidewalk, she worried she'd been too aggressive with him.

Patches came to a stop. At first, she thought he might sob the way his chest went up and down. He bolted upright. "Burning. My skin is burning. It's been worse, but it feels like needles pricking along my skin." He pointed at her, growling. "You punched me again!"

"Can you hold it?"

He patted his chest, inspecting the damage. "You're not that strong," he spat at her. He rolled over, crouching over the pavement. Eve's eyes went wide as he drew back his fist. As he slammed his knuckles into the concrete, the slab cracked. He repeated the gesture once, twice, three times. He'd made a crater, the cement pulverizing into powder.

"You're exerting your powers. Is it draining your internal battery?" As he stood, a grimace formed on his face and she knew the answer. It also offered another series of questions, but she'd have to deal with those after he tried to return her sucker blows.

"Describe it." She narrowed her stance and brought her hands up, ready to deflect his fist if he dared to attack. Eve's abilities rolled outward, enveloping the man. Closing her eyes, she could sense the rippling waves rapidly emitting from his hands. The man stood out like a sore thumb, a bright spot that rivaled the energy flowing through the walls of the Tower. Her abilities provided a unique insight into his gifts, but she'd have to study him when he wasn't bitter about her techniques.

"Closing your eyes? Are you a Jedi Master?"

"I am watching you with my abilities. Heat, electricity, everything gives off electromagnetic fields. The hotter or charged something is, the faster and more dense they are. Right now you're—"

He swung.

Good boy, she thought.

She leaned back, letting his fist drift inches away from her face. His approach gave away his lack of training. The man relied on his arms to provide the power and he didn't follow through with his second attempt. She pushed his arm across his body, sending the punch horribly wide. As her skin connected with his arm, the fields vanished. Poof. Gone.

"Impossible," she gasped.

She braced for the impact. With a strike aimed at her chest, she caught the man's fist. Her feet slid along the grass, sinking into the ground. Even with prep, she couldn't stop him. Staggering backward, she fell into a somersault and settled on her knees. The pressure of the punch should have erupted in a shower of waves, almost deafening. But again, they vanished, absorbed by Patches' gift.

"You can control if you absorb the impact," she said. His eyebrow raised, confused by the statement. "Sometimes when you connect, you absorb the kinetic energy. But with that punch, you didn't absorb anything. You expended it."

Patches stopped his pursuit. She understood why Alyssa required them to delve into their abilities. As a Child of Nostradamus, raw talent wasn't enough. He truly hadn't experimented with his abilities, not even enough to control them. It was rare that a Child didn't have a basic understanding of their gifts before coming to the Tower. Kevin might hate being special, but he could wield his abilities with accuracy.

"When you hit the pavement, you absorbed the impact. But when you knocked the car out of the barricade, you exerted energy. Patches, you can control this."

His eyes widened at the prospect. Eve wondered if this was the satisfaction Alyssa felt when she enlightened her students. Her mentor had files and assessments to pore over, but when seeing a Child in action, that was the only way to know the extent of their abilities. But as his jaw dropped, she realized it was different for him. Knowing nothing about his gifts, it was a massive step toward controlling his power. He wanted control, and she could at least start that journey.

"You're charged and ready to go," she stood, brushing the mud off her knees. "I promise I won't smack you again. But let's try something a bit different."

She held up her hand, offering a sign of peace as she stepped closer. His body didn't relax, anticipating another sucker punch. She adjusted his shoulders, narrowing his gate while turning his hips.

"You're incredibly strong, but that's useless if you can't land a hit. So let's go over the basics."

She stepped back, raising her hands, clenching them into fists. With a nod of her head, he followed suit. "You can't imagine hitting the target. You have to imagine striking past them. Lean into the blow. Your power, even *your* power, comes from your body, not your arms."

Patches threw a punch, turning his body into the move. His face had transformed from the aloof sarcastic twit from earlier into a determined man.

"We can teach you to control your abilities."

His eyes softened. Behind the snarky quips, she touched upon something that spoke to the core of his being. Patches didn't want to be a hero, but he did want to be normal. She'd peel away the layers of fear until he felt comfortable in his own skin. It's what Alyssa would do. She imagined that back at the Tower, her mentor was smiling at her efforts.

"Let's get started."

Alyssa maintained a neutral expression, as if it were painted on her skin. The sun had started to set, and her thoughts were as cloudy as the sky stretching across the fields. Something was amiss in her utopia, and she couldn't quite place her finger on it. In the complex's corner, they posted the first crosses over freshly disturbed earth. None of them expected needing a cemetery this early.

Patrick Kilgannon had fled the compound with Eve. The girl was one of the most focused members of their community, and she'd have never done anything to jeopardize her future. It pained Alyssa each time she denied the girl's application to the Sentinels. Eve could floor any of the recruits, but she had seen what the military had done to Jasmine, turning her into a warrior without an identity of her own. Alyssa didn't want that for her mentee. In one day, she had stolen Ned's keycard, freed Patrick, and attacked Dwayne.

"Eleanor," she whispered, "I've seen your meddling before. What are you up to?" They each recited the phrase as if it were a mantra. "No such thing as coincidence." They carelessly threw it around every time they found themselves dealing with an awkward situation. But now, Alyssa sensed the words were dangerously accurate. Had the psychic inserted herself into their lives again?

The last time Eleanor Valentine meddled with their lives, they nearly died saving the planet. Her actions weren't good or bad. They transcended such an easy classification. Eleanor's altering of fate could be described as complicated. Once they sorted out her intentions, the picture had become clear. Alyssa needed to stop reacting, being the victim of circumstance. It was time for her to turn proactive. If her suspicions were true, she needed to hunt for clues.

Tonight would provide her first round of playing detective.

"Alyssa, we weren't supposed to meet tonight." The man didn't make a sound approaching. With his size, they could hear his footfalls slapping down any hallway. *Good*, she thought, *he teleported*. She had thought of the advanced technology available to Genesis Division. Try as they might, they hadn't unlocked a method to transfer abilities to others. If he teleported, he was the real Conthan.

"We have a security matter. I need to find who I can trust."

"What do you…"

Alyssa held up an orb. "Computer, play footage." The scene of her and Conthan talking outside the cell played on mute.

Turning around, the shock written on his face reinforced her sentiment. "We have a shapeshifter here. That wasn't Patrick Kilgannon who sabotaged the generators."

Conthan leaned in, examining the exchange between Alyssa and *him*. Bit by bit, his eyebrows furrowed and eyes narrowed. It was bad enough when somebody caught themselves in an untrue rumor, but to unknowingly cause one, it violated personal space. Her friend grew angry.

"Are you sure?"

She eyed the projection. "Evidence suggests yes."

"Great, this night is just getting better. First Eve, now a shapeshifter. Do you think they're connected?"

Alyssa didn't speak. Those who fought the Warden carried battle scars, and with a silent moment, she spoke volumes.

"Oh. It's *that* kind of connected."

The slightest nod confirmed his assumption. Alyssa thought of the man like a brother, a confidant bonded by a traumatic experience. Now, he served as her first ally in uncovering a conspiracy. Whatever role Eve and Patrick played, they were carrying out their part of destiny. It was up to her to make sure they had a home to come back to.

"Are they a Child? Why would they open the barricade to synthetics? We're not seeing the complete picture."

Alyssa watched as Dwayne and Errick pushed open the glass doors leading onto the terrace. She'd test them one at a time until she established their identities. First, she'd make sure the members leading the Tower weren't attempting to topple their utopia. Then she'd move on to the Sentinels.

"It will be a long night," she said.

"We're testing them?" Conthan might not want to be a fighter. He didn't want to be a leader, but he accepted the responsibility. Despite his attempts to shrug off the role, he was dangerously smart and adapted quickly. If things turned sideways, she couldn't ask for a better partner.

Reaching into her boot, she pulled out a knife.

She ignored the pain as she dragged it across her forearm. A thin line of blood appeared, and Conthan hissed at her decision. She held up her arm, approaching the residential healer. The knife in her dominant hand remained pointed upward, prepared to lunge should he fail her test.

"Errick, I need your gifts."

"Dwayne, lightning, now," Conthan added.

Dwayne's lack of eyebrows made the eye raise almost comical. Alyssa held out her bloody arm, almost thrusting it at Errick's chest.

"What has gotten into you?"

"Do it." She held up the blade as an incentive.

The man's palms were already warm as he pressed them around her arm. He ignored the blood and a second later, the wound knitted itself together. One down, and one to go.

"Dwayne," Conthan said. "Do it. I'll explain after."

The lightning jumped between his body and his hands. Tiny sparks rolled along his arms, crackling as they snapped. To emphasize his abilities, he pushed his palms upward, a bolt firing into the sky. Alyssa's nose scrunched at the burning scent filling her nostrils. Unless the shapeshifter could mimic their abilities—they were the genuine deal.

"We had to be certain you're not shapeshifters."

"Wait, that's real?" asked Errick.

"Florence Grace." Alyssa made it her job to know the abilities of every person within the Tower, but anybody should recognize the actress's name. "The first."

"I remember," he said. "They teach that in school now."

"There's—" Alyssa rested a hand on Conthan's shoulder, giving him pause.

Once upon a time, Conthan or Dwayne might have called the shots. She had been content to let them take center stage, but things had changed. Each of them navigated a world in which they sought to thrive. It was time for her to earn her reputation as the security advisor and the mentor for the next generation.

With as few words as possible, she explained the situation. She'd be repeating it another dozen times before they had it sorted. As she finished, she stepped back, letting the three men digest the information.

"We can't test everybody by their abilities," Dwayne said.

Errick nodded. "Is that why you didn't invite Maeve and Needles?"

Alyssa nodded. "Maeve's abilities are internal, and even she mentioned there is tech being developed to replicate them. Needles, on the other hand, it'll require an interrogation to sort that out."

"It could be anybody," Conthan said.

"Or everybody," Errick added. "Doubting the people around us is just as dangerous as misinformation."

Alyssa appreciated the man's more holistic methods. While the Nighthawks had a tendency to charge in and leave a wake of chaos, Errick grounded them. She had to admit, his doubts weren't unfounded. "The moment we're out of sight of one another, we become suspects."

"Where do we begin?" Dwayne asked.

Alyssa turned to see the camera pointed in their direction. From his perch, Needles had his hand in nearly every aspect of the Tower. If she were going to topple a kingdom, she'd start with the king. They each mumbled as they followed her line of sight. While they might help, they understood she had a personal stake in this particular interview.

"Gather the Sentinels," she said. "They all have active abilities. You should be able to identify them. Once you do that, hold them. I fear we might need a military force before this is sorted."

"Ariel," said Conthan. She hadn't thought about the mentalist in years. "The code word when we see each other."

"Unless the imposter is watching now," Dwayne said, using his eyes to point toward the camera.

"I'll see to him now," Alyssa said. Her relationship with Ned had barely entered the courting phase. Now, before they had a chance to be a couple, they would return to being brothers-at-arms. Dwayne's words to her the other night remained at the forefront of her mind. She hadn't taken time to process her own feelings, and now she was considering laying them on the table in front of the most arrogant man she had ever met.

The black portal sliced through the air silently. Dwayne stepped through, followed by Errick, leaving her alone with one of her dearest friends. As Conthan held his arms open, waiting for her to accept the gesture, she understood some relationships do not require blood.

"If he breaks your heart, I'll kill him," he whispered.

"Your chauvinistic attempts aren't necessary."

He leaned back, fearful he had said something wrong. Leading the security team, she dealt with male egos every day. But only Conthan feared offending her on a personal level.

"I'll kill him myself," she smiled. He laughed, his whole body shaking as he stepped into the portal. Now to interrogate her suitor.

Chapter Fifteen

2039

The sun had set and he should be winding down. Instead, Patches' heart kept thumping in his chest and he couldn't help but be excited. Eve spent the better part of the evening showing him how to stand when fighting or how to mix up punches, but more than that, somebody had taken a moment to make him feel useful, normal even.

"Does it always feel like this?" She reclined in one of the booths in front of a fast-food counter. "I mean..." He'd been pacing for the last ten minutes, trying to burn through the energy. Despite adding more than a mile to his boots, he couldn't sit still.

"At first." At first, he thought the small lantern on the table had been for his benefit, but he discovered Eve used her abilities as little as him. She could have seen the entire room with her abilities, but she relied on mundane eyes. "When you learn to ride a bike, all you can think about is how awesome it is to master the balancing act. Eventually, it'll be second nature and you just do it."

"Aye." He walked over and closed the lantern,

casting them into darkness. "I don't get why you don't use your gifts. You act like your muscle is the only perk."

He waited for her response. The seconds dragged and before he knew it, the lantern pulled away from his hand. Her face lit up, the shadows along her pursed lips making her appear angry. "Not all of us have active abilities."

"Sounds like you're making excuses. I had this teacher a few hours ago, lovely lass. She insisted I should learn to integrate my abilities into my every day. I think she might be onto something."

"Are all Scots this sarcastic?"

"My granny would have read you up, down, and back again. That tongue lashing could have been a—"

The lantern fell from her grip. Her hands shot up, covering Patches' mouth. Everything was consumed by the moonless night. The glass on the lantern smashed, tiny fragments sliding along the dingy tile. She held her hand in place, body tense. It wasn't perfume, but each time he inhaled, he could smell the earth on her hands.

"Blue," she whispered, "is that you?"

The synthetic had been stationed on the steps leading up to the front door. Once she had given it the order, it transformed into a statue, vigilant and unmoving. The robot didn't offer him any semblance of security. From his point of view, it was a killing machine sent to annihilate the Children in the Tower, and it didn't matter who treated the thing as a pet.

"There's a disturbance. Electrical impulses are getting closer. They're like the synthetics at the Tower." He appreciated that she could sense the world around them, but he couldn't make out her eyes despite being inches away. She held him tightly, her hand on the small of his back, keeping him from moving.

"I think they're on the road, maybe thirty of them. There's something wrong with their power units. The lines are erratic. I think they're broken."

When she pulled him toward the bench, he followed. The glass of the lantern cracked under his foot, the tiny snaps echoing throughout the rest stop. She sat him down on the bench. He didn't resist. Reaching out, he grazed her jeans, resting his hand on her hip. He narrowed his eyes, trying to make out which direction she faced, but all he could see was black.

"Are they coming for us?" His voice was soft, barely a whisper, but it sounded as if he shouted in the room.

"They're moving west." The sound of metal hitting the concrete was distant, but not far enough away to provide any security. If those feral machines came running for him, they'd be screwed. A building full of Children had barely stopped the killers, and here in the open, they'd be easy targets. The earlier sensation of feeling powerful drained from his body, and now he fought to keep from hurling.

"They're almost gone," she whispered.

The skin-tight suit she wore didn't leave much to the imagination. Even with the panels of body armor protecting her most vulnerable areas, where his head rested formed to the curve of her hip. The material's weave gave it a slight texture, and he rubbed his hand along the suit until her hand caught his. He about pleaded that he had been more interested in the clothing than the person wearing it. It was mostly true.

"We have company," she said.

As she pulled away, Patches realized he was left

alone in the darkness. She might be able to sense the synthetics in the darkness, but he was helpless. No, not helpless, powerful. He tried to remember what Eve had taught him earlier. He might not have mastered his abilities, but they were there for him to use. His heart thumped against his chest again, partly from the earlier rush, but also from the fear he was about to be torn limb from limb.

"Eve," he whispered. She could be inches from him, or she could be running out the back door. He prayed that the would-be warrior hadn't deserted him. "Are you..."

A pair of red dots stepped into the dining area of the rest stop. A place that had once been capable of handling a few hundred patrons suddenly seemed small, almost intimate. He imagined the canines sniffing the air, seeking their prey. It was foolish to think they imitated the animalistic forms. Instead, they probably used infrared or some sort of high-tech scanning to identify their victims. These stragglers could probably hear the blood pounding in his ears.

Patches inched to the edge of the bench. His muscles tensed as he braced his feet against the metal legs, ready to spring into action and make a run for it. If he was lucky, their feet would slip on the tile and he'd be able to reach the rear exit before they caught him. He'd flee as fast as—no. He pushed the thought from his mind. The running for had gone on for months. He wasn't helpless. It was time to stop running from danger, from himself.

The bench creaked as he stood. If they attacked, he'd absorb the force of the blow. If they tackled him, he'd be okay. He tried not to think about the weapons mounted within their bodies. Before today he would have avoided conflict, and after a single session with Eve, he debated if he could withstand bullets. She might have saved him from the Tower, but her sparkling personality was going to get him in trouble.

"Come and get me, you wankers."

They were good last words.

Deep breaths. Eve inhaled through the nose. She counted to three before exhaling through the mouth. Repeat. Eve struggled to push away the growing panic attempting to set in. Her feet grew heavy, and each step backward felt as if she were dragging cement blocks. The breathing might help her stay grounded, but her pulse raced as if she were in the middle of a rigorous workout. It wasn't the first time a panic attack had tried to squeeze the air from her body. Eve fought to push away the images of the balcony, watching her friends fight the synthetics.

"Come and get me, you wankers." Her companion, a man who barely understood his gifts and wanted nothing more than a normal life, prepared to take on two of the killer machines. If it were Alyssa, she'd already be charging into battle, throwing herself into danger without a thought of the consequences. Her mentor would disapprove of the cowardice, of Eve's body betraying her.

Inhale. Exhale. Inhale again.

Eve couldn't see the synthetics with her eyes. It was almost a sensation that if she didn't focus, it could be written off as a sixth sense. But she knew they were standing several feet apart, and that their heads turned in Patches' direction. Her abilities weren't as impressive as turning her skin into metal or shooting electricity, but at this moment, they were more useful. Her body tensed, accessing that figurative muscle that harnessed her gifts. It rolled outward, and she had a clear sense of the tables, overturned chairs, and Patches stumbling into a trash bin.

The batteries charging the synthetics were like bright beacons, enough that she could almost see the interior workings of the machines. The hydraulics hissed as the synthetics transformed from four-legged creatures to their upright forms. Like her, they could see in the dark, giving them an advantage over her blind friend.

She growled. He had been right, and she hated him for it. Being able to bench press three times the weight of a human wasn't her only gift. She was a Child of Nostradamus, imbued with an ability that nobody else on the planet shared. It made her unique, and perhaps it was time she started using it as such. Eventually, she'd punch her way out of a problem, but perhaps not denying this part of herself. Maybe that was the missing component.

Patches had gotten their attention, and he was about to get pummeled. The arms of the synthetics vibrated with power, the energy weapons, housed underneath metal plating, charged. He might be able to withstand a punch, but she wasn't sure if he could disperse the impact of a bullet or, worse yet, a laser.

"Be careful," she barked, "you're not invincible." Alyssa would be disappointed if she got the man killed. This morning he wanted to be a librarian, hidden away amongst his books. It was on her that he believed himself capable of taking on a synthetic. She grit her teeth, hating that she needed assistance. "Blue, I need your help."

One of the synthetics faced her.

The power in its arm died down as it approached. The hands shot out, reaching for her neck. It didn't find her to be a threat, not enough to wield one of its arsenals. The metal touched her skin, the fields of its hand intersecting her own. Her boots remained heavy, and she struggled to push away the growing anxiety. The two red eyes were two feet away, judging her, finding her unworthy of anything other than a crushed throat.

Anger. Rage. It smothered the anxiety in a tidal wave. Her teeth ground together and her muscles seized as the heat rushed through her body. Eve watched as her abilities flared, creating a clear image in her head of the synthetic tightening its grip on her throat. As if they were moving through a dense liquid, she brought up her hands, grabbing the machine's fingers. Her muscles resisted, but they couldn't resist her stubbornness.

Today wasn't the day she died. "Not today," she whispered.

The metal bent until its thumb snapped. It thrust its hand forward, jabbing her in the throat. Before she coughed, Eve slammed her foot into the torso of the machine, knocking it backward. She buckled over, gasping for air. Every attempt to suck in oxygen seemed as if she stood in the vacuum of space. Massaging her neck, she feared she'd fall unconscious before she stopped the machine.

The lines of electromagnetic energy vanished, and the darkness rushed in. The machine could be standing over her and she'd never see the killing blow speeding toward her face.

Sparks lit up the rest stop as metal struck metal. Blue, Skits' salvaged synthetic, risked life and limb to keep members of the Ayer family safe. It had survived the onslaught in Chicago, and since then, followed her everywhere. Eve always joked that it needed a collar and leash, but right now, she was equal parts thankful and annoyed that it provided her a chance to gain her bearings.

She sucked in oxygen like it might be her last breath. Each punch from Blue's fist lit up the room and Eve could see the flash of waves. Getting to her feet, she couldn't let her aunt's pet be destroyed. Leaning forward, she charged, bringing her hands together in a single fist. Eve swung, pounding the synthetic in the chest, hurling it backward.

She didn't slow. Even as the forearm expanded, the red light inside indicated a charged laser. Eve let loose a battle cry. Furious, she jumped as the laser flashed. The suit might be made for ballistic rounds, but she didn't want to test if it could withstand an energy weapon. Rolling, she spun on the floor, kicking with the toe of her boot, sending the machine's weapon high into the air. The second shot scorched the ceiling while she climbed on top of the synthetic.

The stub of a hand crossed her face. Her mouth tasted of blood, and it would only get worse if she didn't put the synthetic out of commission. The lines of energy radiated up its spine, the power core giving the metal limbs life. Holding its arm, stopping another punch to the face, she reached into the open cavity of its neck. She braced her knee and pulled, tearing wires from the monster's body. The sparks were bright enough to be blinding, but it meant its battery disconnected from its brain.

One down, one more to stop until they could claim a pitiful victory.

Sparks flew as Blue pounded one of its brethren. It meant Patches only had to survive one remaining synthetic, or at least until its siblings arrived. He could do it. He was a Child of Nostradamus. One day he woke in his bed, different, basically a superhero. It had been years ago, but today, Eve gave him enough confidence to be dangerous. His brain clawed at the logic, but the thumping in his chest silenced its protests.

It made him confident and dumb.

The tiny red eyes sped closer, with a slight duck and weave, as if he might try to shoot the machine. The thin red eyes lifted into the air, defying the massive amount of weight housed within their chassis. It was going to pin him—crush him. Even if his powers did exactly what Eve promised, it wasn't going to be pleasant. At the last second, he threw his arms up, convinced this had been a horrific and stupid idea.

The metal connected with his arms, then down the length of his torso. He fell backward, landed on the tile, unable to stop his head from cracking the ceramic. It didn't hurt like he imagined. The limb pinning his hands should have crushed his bones. The bounce of his skull didn't disorient. Instead, his skin burned. The muscles throughout his body ached all at once. The synthetic hadn't broken him. Like she promised, his gifts had protected him.

The heat. He pushed up with his hands, lifting the machine off his body. Mechanical knuckles punched the side of his head, then gripped his face as if the synthetic might tear it off. Grabbing its arm, he twisted the appendage, bending the metal, causing a shower of sparks to lick his skin.

The heat turned into an inferno that hurt. But the increased pressure in his chest stopped pushing inward. His abilities were awakening, working to save him from death. The laser sprung from the synthetic's functioning arm. As he kicked, sending it into the air, a bolt of red seared along his bicep, confirming that he was far from invulnerable.

Patches howled.

The room went dark. The synthetic smashed into a bank of tables and chairs while Patches climbed back to his feet. Once the machine sprung upright, it would continue firing that damned weapon, and there was little he'd be able to do to stop it. His body struggled to cooperate, as he tried taking a step toward the synthetic. He'd had his share of drunken nights, and right now, he felt as if he'd had one pint too many.

He'd always relied on the fire pouring into his shoulders, arms, and hands. It allowed him to crush cement blocks, but it did nothing to make him quick. The fire in his arms dwindled, and he imagined the heat siphoning into his legs. It hurt, as if at any moment his thighs would cramp, and waiting for the ache to spread through his body, he wasn't sure improvisation was the right tactic.

With a yell, he jumped toward the red dots. In the dark, he couldn't tell how far into the air he managed, but the red dots passed harmlessly underneath. He slammed into something firm, one of the round columns situated around the dining area. He jabbed his fist into the concrete, breaking a hole, giving him something to hold on to before he toppled downward.

The synthetic refused to leave him be, and as the red lights turned in his direction, he knew he was a sitting duck. He let go, kicking off the column. He rushed downward, slamming into the machine. The bright red of the laser flashed. Even though it missed its mark, he hissed out in anticipation. Before it could fire again, he grabbed the laser and let the heat wash over his upper body. Wrapping his hand around the barrel, he tore it from the machine's arm. He repeated the maneuver, pulling its arm free as it attempted to wrestle with him.

"Just—" he buried his fingers into its chest and lifted the synthetic off its feet, "—die." His arms could carry the weight, but his legs buckled, and he dropped to one knee. Patches pulled at the fire in his body, pushing it into his bent leg, preparing for a shattered kneecap. With a downward thrust, he pinned the machine's spine over his leg. He let out a roar as the synthetic's body sheered, bending until the metal spine snapped.

The machine's chest tore open, and he swore he heard Eve screaming. Patrick Kilgannon, average librarian, had just defeated a machine built to end his people. The satisfaction was cut short as the room flashed white and an explosion wrapped around his body.

He had been victorious for a moment.

The shock wave of electromagnetic fields emanating from Patches made the hair on Eve's neck stand on end.

The explosion sent a blinding wave of light as it hurled him against the fast-food counter. His body slumped, unmoving. The room turned dark except for the bits of flame on the surrounding chairs and tables. As the black consumed her vision, her abilities worked in overdrive, and the only thing she could focus on was the surge coming from her battered partner.

"Blue, destroy any synthetics that enter this room."

Its hydraulics hissed as it scanned the room, looking for any stragglers. Its brethren didn't treat Skits' pet as hostile. Considering the arsenal wielded by the enemy, she'd take any advantage at this point. But right now, she needed to make sure Patches didn't die.

Eve hurried to his side, dropping to her knees. The power radiating from his body triggered her abilities, enough that it made it difficult to sense the features of his face. His body had absorbed the energy of the synthetic's ruptured power core. If he were awake, she'd coach him through releasing it. If he were like Dwayne, without an outlet, it'd slowly tear his body apart, destroying him one cell at a time.

"Patches." She gave him a firm slap across the face. "Holy shit." The impact of the blow, the heat created by the friction of her skin against his, should have sent fields flowing into the empty space around them. Instead, his body absorbed them, internalizing and storing the energy.

"Wake up." Even saying it felt foolish. She was lucky they didn't shred his body to pieces. She touched his body softly to prevent his abilities from activating. The burst of shrapnel had torn through his shirt and in more than one spot, her fingers grazed warm liquid pulsing from his gashes.

"If you die," she growled, "I'm going to be pissed."

The energy in his body gathered where her hand rested. Pulling her fingers away, she could feel the energy licking the tiny hairs on her arm. Eve cursed her abilities, wanting something more flashy or useful in a firefight. Twice in two days, she had taken this passive gift and wielded it like a weapon. With practice, perhaps she'd be as precise as a surgeon, but right now it was more like swinging a club.

"This might hurt." Eve pushed against his stomach, hands coated in blood. The energy pooled under her palm and she imagined the fields overlapping her own, intersecting and passing through one another. She couldn't see them with her eyes, but she imagined they were beautiful bursts of light exploding as they smashed into one another.

She grabbed at them with her fist, pulling them away from his body. The first attempt did nothing more than cause the energy to drift away from her hand. She tried again, focusing on the lines following her, pulling from beneath his skin. Despite the visualization, she could feel the energy sinking back into his chest.

The frustrated growl came out between clenched teeth. She preached Patches should learn how to use his gifts and here she was, like an infant. This was the reason Alyssa didn't want her on the Sentinels. Not that she wasn't a good enough fighter, it was that she ignored one of the most valuable parts of being a Child. Eve hated hypocrites, and here she was, the biggest one of all.

A flash of light sent her backward, landing on her butt. "Was that me? You? What the hell?" Every Child accessed their abilities through a manner unique to them. She took the aggravation, the anger at falling short, at disappointing her mentor, and pushed the rage into her palms.

The man's body glowed like a nightlight as she thrust her hand against his chest. She pulled at the lines, converting it to light and heat. The glow intensified, and she feared the heat would eventually scold her hands. With a grunt, his body convulsed and a flash of light flooded the rest stop. Even through clenched eyes, she could see sunspots, blue and green dots dancing in her vision.

For a moment, she couldn't see the fields. Packed tightly together, they lost any definition, and she was well and truly blind. Dwayne's random burst of lightning created the same effect, and it'd pass with time. For the moment, she couldn't tell if Patches' body remained a super-charged battery.

"Patches, you need to wake up," she pleaded. "I'm going to be pissed if you die on me." They had barely started their journey, and she feared it ended before it began. If this had been Eleanor's plan...

"Ach. Why does," he groaned, "everything hurt?"

Eve let out a laugh. If he hurt, it meant he was alive. "Next time, don't be a hero."

"You were wrong."

"About what?"

"I'm invincible." Humor. She could live with his bad jokes.

She put her back to the counter and slumped down next to him. They weren't going anywhere in the dark, and for a moment, they were safe. She'd need to grab her bag and bandage his cuts and make sure none of his bones were broken. But they were alive, and this very second, that was all she could ask for.

"Back in the day, did the Nighthawks get beaten this badly?"

From the stories around the dinner table, Eve knew this was only the beginning. To fulfill Eleanor's cryptic destiny, they'd need to survive more than a couple of wayward synthetics. But for now, she celebrated their first victory.

"We won," she mumbled.

"Aye," he added. "I still want that burger and fries."

She wanted to smack him, but now that he mentioned it, she did too.

Chapter Sixteen

2039

Needles had gone more than a minute without blinking. Others considered him insufferable, obnoxious, or even an egomaniac. They weren't wrong, and Alyssa wouldn't dare argue with them. Her first encounter with Ned had been in a sewer bunker where he helped lead a resistance against a corrupt government. He hadn't done it to serve himself, despite what he might say. The hacker persona shielded a gentleman, sometimes too well. As he insisted in a staring contest, she questioned her affections for the buffoon.

"Are you done with this juvenile test of wills?"

"I don't know." He touched a button on one of his monitors, turning all the screens in the command center blank. "Am I?"

"We both know I could strike a dozen pressure points and have you singing."

"Maybe you could."

It was unusually quiet in the command center. Ned complained he needed more hands, and when they assigned people to work with him, he claimed they were inept. The man was running on caffeine and stubbornness. He might not be a Child of Nostradamus, but she wouldn't dare call him an average human. But if he didn't allow his staff to support him, Alyssa feared he'd be shoveling dirt for his own grave.

"Where's the staff?"

His arms crossed his chest, and he leaned back, studying her. His suspicious nature came from years of living underground and rallying people to a cause that left a trail of bodies. But something had him on alert. Like the cat who ate the canary, he couldn't help himself. Ned knew.

"We are at an impasse," she said. The shapeshifter had done its job well. Trust had been shattered and paranoia already strained the closest of relationships.

"We are."

"Ned…" She rubbed the bridge of her nose, staving off a growing pain behind her eyes. "I have no way to test you like I can Conthan or Dwayne."

His eyebrow raised. Direct honesty was a trait he found difficult to digest. Normally, she'd enjoy watching him shift uncomfortably, but tonight she was on a mission.

"Nor can you test me. Without active abilities, we have to go about this the old-fashioned way."

"So what? Am I supposed to ask what your favorite color is and hope the imposter hasn't been inside your apartment?"

Alyssa took a step forward, maintaining a narrow distance between their bodies. She could feel his breath rush along the fabric covering her forehead. She made the man uncomfortable, a feeling she was sure he hadn't experienced in years. The tattoos crept up his neck, reaching underneath his jaw. Among the many pictures inked into his skin covering his chest was the name Dav5d.

To her, Dav5d had been a comrade, a companion in the fight to survive in the Outlands. His gifts made him socially awkward, his brain wired to see calculations but unable to process a simple smile. It was one thing she loved about her friend. She had been an *"other"* as a youth, and it was something they shared. Each of the Nighthawks had been a misfit and together they somehow merged as a family. If Alyssa thought about Dav5d for too long, her heart might sink or tears would threaten to stream down her face. His death had left a void in her heart. But that wasn't why Ned immortalized the name on his skin.

Years before Dav5d joined them in the Outlands, he had been a teenager, a hacker who thought he could make a difference. The world had ignored him, except for his best friend… Alyssa reached out slowly, her hand hovering just above Ned's chest. His body tensed as she rested it over his heart.

"You are the most arrogant, pompous, and self-aggrandizing man I have ever met."

"Well, you know what they say—"

"Shut up." The words were harsher than she expected. Somewhere in the Tower, she hoped Dwayne was smiling as she embraced his brotherly advice.

It was unlike her to be this forward. It was unbecoming of a woman to make the first move, but the thought of Ned mourning the loss of his best friend highlighted the man behind the persona. "Do you miss him?"

"Who?"

"Dav5d," she whispered his name, fearful that her voice would catch in her throat.

"Oh." His face lowered until he made eye contact. Alyssa, the fiercest fighter in the Tower, was scared that this man might step away, leaving her hand hovering and empty.

"Every day." His voice lacked any bravado. There wasn't another person in the Tower who could disarm Ned, but the hurt in his voice forced tears from her eyes. "I'm the man I am today because of him. Some people throw that out there, but he literally trained me. He wanted to join this hacker organization. I tried to talk him out of it." Ned let out a laugh. "Can you imagine if he listened? We'd all be dead."

She let the silence fill the space between them. He broke his gaze, looking toward the ceiling as he wiped his thumbs under his eyes. "Every damned day."

This was the man who won her attention. It wasn't about courtship or him attempting to woo her. She had genuine feelings for him. "He'd think you are doing an optimal job. You're performing beyond the expected parameters of a human."

Ned laughed, nodding his head. "Optimal. I'm jealous that you got to see the man he became. The smartest man alive and not an ounce of common sense about him."

"I envy you knowing him in a simpler time." Like many in the Tower, they carried their trauma, comforted knowing that every person had a similar story. Most chose not to dwell on the wounds, but for some, they had yet to heal. "He was loved, Ned. For so long he didn't grasp that word, *love*." She couldn't choke back the tears any longer. They streamed down her cheeks. "But he understood it before he died."

Ned rested his hands on her cheeks, his thumbs wiping away the tears. It was no longer a question of identity. They recorded none of their stories in a place for an imposter to study. Only a select handful knew about the sacrifice Dav5d had made to ensure the world had a brighter future.

Her hand covered his, and she savored the feeling of his palms. If her parents were alive, they'd have scoffed at her choice of suitor. They were from a different time, a part of a world slow to change their ways. They'd have tried to convince her otherwise, but just as they had accepted her determination to study ballet, they'd support her decision.

He leaned in close. Her heart raced, unsure. Part of her wanted to continue being touched by him, but much like her parents, she lived by a code of conduct others rarely understood. His lips touched her forehead. A chaste kiss. One hand remained on her cheek while the other touched the one resting over his heart.

Alyssa savored it a moment longer before modesty won. She retreated, taking a step away from him. One might think she refuted his advances, but the smile stretching across his face said otherwise. Not only did he pursue her, but he respected her boundaries, and for that, she could never express her gratitude in words.

"Alyssa Rahim." He gave a slight bow. "I shall speak with Conthan and Dwayne and ask that they accompany us for dinner."

She bit her lip, failing to hold back her smile. Not only did he subtly mention asking the closest thing she had to brothers for their approval, but he also offered to have them chaperone. He was so much more than the eyes of the Tower, and she hoped more people forgot Needles and met Ned.

"After we save the Tower."

"Of course," he said, waving his hands over the monitor, restoring the screens. "Duty first."

Chapter Seventeen

2024

"The Knights of Windsor do not rely on numbers." Feral spouted his gospel, the rules for what made the perfect soldier. Unlike the black bodysuits worn by the recruits, his lacked arms. Their instructor wanted them to see the muscles flex under the overhead lights.

"We are Knights. Our ferocity, our unwillingness to surrender defines us," they chanted.

The newest class of recruits had joined them for his postulations. Sitting on the side, along with the rest of the older men and women, the man studied his classmates. He rested on his knees, his butt sitting atop his heels as they did every time the teacher wanted to force his words upon them. But he hardly listened, staring at a young woman across the circle.

"Not all of you will survive. But those who do, you will serve as the Queen's finest."

At least five years younger, her dark eyebrows raised as she digested the man's words. She had yet to be indoctrinated. The longer she remained, that look of innocence would be replaced with indifference. Her mouth moved as she silently repeated his words. The gesture reminded him of somebody he once knew. He tried to place his finger on it, but the further he fell into his past, the more vague events became.

They had erased him. The act of having his memories wiped away was terrifying in its own right, but to be aware of their meddling, he understood why people feared the Programmers. No, something about the way her lips whispered their instructor's words. The memory was of somebody he knew more recently. There were so few people in his life, it had to be one of the instructors or…

She once sat on his bed. But like sand, he couldn't hold on to the memory. The quicksilver thought pointed to an erased memory. His past had become riddled with fragments he couldn't piece together. Closing his eyes, his attention turned inward, to the pulse of his heart. Unlike the others, he underwent regular sessions with the Programmers. They claimed his gifts set him apart from the rest, and they ran tests at every opportunity. Drawing blood and fastening him into the chair, they probed his body and mind.

"The Americans are mounting an army. But they lack your conviction, your dedication. They hide behind their technology and deny their abilities." Feral's speech varied little from day-to-day, but it always maintained a hostility toward Americans.

Accessing his abilities, he attempted to correct their experiment. The blood in his veins warmed until his entire face felt flushed. Even as his blood turned hot, his abilities searched for something, anything, to rectify. He had just about given up when he recalled the girl's face, eyes closed and lying on her back. She had—*he* had killed her.

"Here, in this space, I will remake you into warriors."

Even as he thought of the girl, his first fight at the academy, he couldn't picture her face. She had barely struck him, a weak blow of the knuckles. At the command of Feral, he thrust a palm against her sternum. She died before his classmates reached the medical unit. They had attempted to scrub a weak moment in his memory, to turn him into a soldier. The Programmers hadn't succeeded, not completely, but try as he might, he couldn't see the face of his friend. His abilities couldn't undo the damage, and right now, he wanted to see the face of his last genuine friend.

"I will—"

"Die." The man opened his eyes, standing upright while his classmates stared in disbelief. The room remained quiet, not a single person willing to whisper about the foolishness.

"You?" Feral laughed. Their last physical altercation has been years prior, when Feral threatened to kill him. He wasn't the same scared teenager who shied away from authority.

"Maybe it's the accent," the man said. "Should I repeat myself?"

Feral paused at the insult. It was obvious the man's size and aggressive attitude allowed him to avoid confrontations. He hid behind his name. But it wouldn't help him, as the blood in the man's body burned with rage. Even if he lost, even if he died, he wanted the satisfaction of hurting the source of his grief.

The man stepped into the circle, anger pushing one foot in front of the other. His eyes locked into Feral, and he refused to blink, even as the instructor's eyes turned an ominous yellow. Once they stood nearly chest-to-chest, he clarified that he no longer feared the man. If he didn't do it for himself, then he did it for…

"Erica," he whispered.

"Again?"

Feral's arm rushed for his neck. The man stepped to the side, hooking his foot behind the instructor's, and leaned forward. Feral stumbled backward, giving up his position as top dog. Retreating, for any reason, was seen as a sign of weakness. The Knights of Windsor would rather die than be seen as losing ground.

Feral's mouth let loose a growl, revealing the source of his name. The growl turned into a howl and the instructor swung as hard as possible. Despite the man throwing up his forearm to block the punch, it hit hard enough that it forced him to step back before he could absorb the impact. Despite what Feral taught, retreating wasn't a cardinal sin, not when it gave him the advantage.

Feral's arms were wide, and he'd attempt a bear hug, a signature move. If he succeeded, every bone in the man's upper body would be crushed, impaling his organs. Delivering an uppercut, he halted the advance, sending a spray of blood across his classmates. Only the youngest of them flinched. The others watched in anticipation, radiating blood lust.

"You killed her!" he screamed.

Feral wiped the blood from his lip, surprised the man stood his ground. The anger in his face faltered as a grin formed. "If memory serves me, it wasn't me who killed the girl."

Feral's skin darkened. What looked like a tan at first

was a dark coating of hair. Even his canines extended, matching his yellow eyes. The instructor's namesake fit appropriately, leaving him resembling a werewolf. His genes called upon the last animal he touched, transforming him into a hybrid and in doing so, pushed away his human reservations.

"It was you." The words were slurred from teeth not fitting his mouth.

Feral lunged.

The man couldn't escape. It wasn't meant to be a strike, at least not a blow he could deflect. He raised his arms in defense, and Feral's nails dragged across his forearms, cutting through the fabric of his uniform and digging deep enough to strike bone. Before the man could retreat, another set of claws dragged their way up his torso and across his face.

Feral backed away, letting the others see the damage he had inflicted in a single blow. The wounds hurt enough that the man had to focus on not grunting—he wouldn't give Feral the satisfaction. The gashes along his face knitted themselves back together. His cells worked to return to their natural state, sewing up wounds, replenishing the spilled blood. Feral thought he'd win with a simple strike, but the man refused to offer him even the smallest victory.

"Healing," Feral spat, "such a useless ability."

"Mut."

Feral couldn't resist the bait. He swung, leading with his claws. This time, he missed as the man dropped low, throwing a leg into the werewolf's gut. Nails caught his calf, shredding the muscle. The wound stitched itself before he brought his leg back. He spun out of the way, avoiding a kick to the face, and stole a jab to the instructor's kidney.

Had he a knife or gun, perhaps he could have evened the odds. But Feral had transformed into a weapon, and all he had were knuckles and the toe of his boot. As he strategized how to strike next, Feral grabbed him under the arm, pulling him close. The man attempted to slip out of his grip, but found the man closing an arm around his throat. As he struggled, reaching over his shoulder in an attempt to drive his thumb into Feral's eye, he found himself helpless.

"You're as weak as Erica." The words were a final bidding, panted into his ear as the forearm tightened. He couldn't breathe and knew what came next. He didn't have to worry about being suffocating as a snap echoed through his body. The world went dark.

Nothingness. Time no longer had meaning.

Moments later, the air rushed into his lungs as his eyes shot open. Feral held him by the back of the neck, raising him in the air as he displayed his trophy. Despite his gifts repairing a broken neck, the pain pulsing through his bones was almost enough to make him unconscious.

"... dare to challenge me?" Feral roared. "There's only room for one top dog."

He reached up, pressing his hand on the tip of Feral's fingers. The instructor's grip tightened at the sight of his prey surviving a broken neck. The man stared at the girl's face and, for a moment, he swore it was the face of his dead friend.

It hadn't been intentional and he could blame Feral for killing Erica, but that wasn't the truth. It had been his hand that struck her, that killed the last kind person in his life. If death accepted him, he'd have taken the coward's way out. But thanks to the Nostradamus Effect, he'd never know peace, never be able to see Erika again.

The pity turned bitter and transformed into rage. If he couldn't end his life, he'd become exactly what they wanted, a killer. His first target deserved nothing less. He pulled at one of Feral's fingers, screaming as his blood boiled. The instructor's might-makes-right attitude, his lack of regard for life, served as fuel.

"I am that one," the man screamed.

The same ability that returned his cells to their natural state spread a wave of chaos through Feral's body. The virus he spread transferred from one to the next until the instructor's hand turned black, withering away into ash. He hit the floor, toppling. He spun about to watch the first time he used his abilities on another person. Feral's color vanished, swallowed by black streaks spreading through his veins.

Feral died before his body collapsed. *Now* the room gasped.

There was a new top dog in the academy.

Chapter Eighteen

2039

Boston had seen better days. Patches got off the motorcycle, staring up at the surrounding buildings. Unlike Chicago, the buildings weren't as tall, at least not in this part of the city. Most buildings were made from brick rather than steel, and plenty of them had crumbled. The Battle for Chicago had left the Loop a ghost town, but even a metallic army didn't leave this much destruction in their wake.

Like the road here, nature had declared war and stood the victor. Hundreds of birds lined the metal balconies overlooking the grass-covered streets. Almost fifty years ago, a cloud of radiation had swept through New England, killing its occupants. As the age of man fell victim to their own hubris, the Earth sought to repair the damage. Patches couldn't help admire the beauty in the peace, but it was cut short as he came to terms with the graveyard the city had become.

"This is Boston?" he asked.

"What's left of it."

"It looks like a bomb went off. The Nighthawks lived here?" The weather mirrored the gloom of Boston. What might have once been a vibrant city had the splendor sucked away until it looked like something out of a horror movie. The gray clouds rushing by overhead blended into the landscape. At least if it rained, there'd be a chance it'd wash away the dust desaturating the buildings.

"Not a bomb." Eve pointed at an airship in the distance, partly embedded in a row of what had once been skyscrapers. There were military vehicles littering the streets, destroyed and hurled through the fronts of buildings. Whatever they thought they were fighting had bested them. It dawned on Patches who they had been after.

"They came for the Children?"

She nodded. "This is why the Tower is so important. They thought they could live here in the irradiated part of New England and not have to deal with this crap. But the military didn't like people with powers gathering."

"So they tried to capture them?"

"Not capture."

The flat tone brought home the severity of their people's origins. For all his days in the library, he had never thought to research the Children or their involvement beyond Millennial Park. Hunted. Killed. The Tower suddenly made far more sense than it had when he first arrived. They hadn't lived in Boston for the luxurious accommodations. It had been about surviving.

"Well, this is far more bleak than I imagined."

"People fear *different*. Maybe someday it'll change. But for now, the many fear the powerful." Eve had a tendency to drop snippets of wisdom, and he wondered how much of it was her own thinking or that of the legends surrounding her?

"Do we scream her name and hope she answers?"

She smacked him in the stomach. He buckled over, hissing at the pain. Eve might be many things, but a suitable medic wasn't one of them. The dozens of cuts lining his torso had been filled with a white foaming antiseptic, and she'd slapped bandages on him like she was applying stickers to a wall. He wouldn't bleed to death, but he'd feel it for the next week.

He glanced down to see through the cuts in his shirt to the patchwork of gauze. So far, they were holding, which is more than he could say for his clothes. He'd gone from conservative suburban dad attire to feeling like he was the headliner of a grunge band. He tried not to smirk as he thought of band names.

"I can find her."

"Does she have a tracker? Did they say where she was when you picked up the phone?"

"You need to stop thinking like a human."

"We are human." Her insistence to the contrary irked him. Fine, they were different, but creating an artificial divide between people led to the Children being hunted. He refused to buy into the ideology.

They stood at an intersection of two roads. This part of the city had more of a small-town feel to it. In the distance, the buildings grew taller, those that remained. He didn't ask why she decided this was a suitable spot to go on foot. Every time he asked a question, she provided him with a new level of horror. Right now, he needed to exist in his happy, ignorant space.

"There's so much carnage. Are those airships? I've seen one hovering over Chicago when the president makes public appearances. Tanks?" He pointed to the vehicle sticking out from a fallen building. "Over there—"

"I get it. The military really hates Children."

Not at all what he was getting at. "You're daft woman. The military left what must be billions of dollars of tech to rust."

"You sound surprised."

"Why didn't they leave the synthetics?" He waited for her quip. Despite obvious signs of battle, the remains of synthetics had been removed from the battlefield. Living people, he understood, but to leave some the expensive death machines and take the rest, that made little sense.

A nearby wall had the impression of a body traced in crushed red brick. There had been a scuffle and either a synthetic or a Child had been beaten against the wall. Burn marks littered the bricks. Patches kicked a bit of grass that had pushed up between the cracks in the street. Metal casings rolled out, munitions discarded by a gun. It wasn't a battle where both parties walked away in one piece.

"They did," she whispered. Eve's brow furrowed every time she connected dots. However, she wasn't great at informing him. Their partnership still tended to be one-sided. She had warmed up to him, but there was still a great divide in their relationship.

He groaned. "You know something. This is where you explain it."

"The synthetics at the Tower, the ones passing at the

rest stop… they're not new machines." She turned around, staring him in the eye. Whatever was about to come out of her mouth wasn't going to be good news. "Somebody has been repairing them."

"Who? Why? Why!" The synthetics in Chicago had replaced the human police force, at least for the more dangerous jobs. There had once been factories dedicated to mass producing the killing machines, but after the Warden turned them into his personal army, America got smart. Now somebody was turning machine cadavers into their personal army.

"A hate group, maybe? They're sending them from Boston to Troy."

Patches shook his head. It didn't make sense. "And they have a shape-shifting Child on the inside lowering the shield? Smells wrong."

She gave him a pat on the chest. "Despite your accent, sometimes you make sense."

"Ach." Teasing him seemed to be the newest ability she manifested.

"It doesn't add up." Eve held up a hand. Her eyes closed as a loud clacking came from down the street. "Blue has caught up." Moments later, her robotic pet dog appeared.

Patches dared to ask the obvious. "He showed up with the others. Do you think he knows? Could he tell us?"

The synthetic skulked closer, as if it were stalking prey. Patches clenched his fists, waiting for it to trans-form. With each step, its body unfolded until it walked like a stiff human. The blue coat of paint on its faceplate was the only thing that separated it from the others. If he had wanted to cause mayhem, he'd have painted all of their faces blue… if they knew.

"They didn't know Blue was different," he said.

Eve touched the side of the machine's head, giving him a rub like you might a puppy. He couldn't be sure, but the synthetic seemed to lean into her, craving the affection. The Ayer family had somehow taken a robotic killing machine and domesticated it. It was equally, if not *more* disturbing.

"That's a lot of coincidences," he said. She narrowed her eyes into a death glare. At any moment, lasers would puncture his chest.

He held up his hands to surrender. "Wow, you people really do take that coincidence thing seriously."

She continued stroking Blue's forehead. "We're missing an obvious piece of the puzzle. If a hate group sent synthetics to kill the Children, they wouldn't be working with one. There's something in that we're not seeing."

"And Blue?"

She patted the robot on the chest. "What do you have to do with this? Does it connect to Skits?" The machine's head cocked to one side, as if he didn't understand. But after barking orders at the machine, Patches was certain her pet grasped what she asked.

"How do we find her? The city is empty."

Eve shook her head. "Not empty, a ghost town."

"Same difference."

The moment the words left his mouth, he knew they danced with danger. Eve's body stiffened slightly, somehow aware of something he couldn't make out with his eyes. Whether or not she knew it, her abilities gave her an unfair advantage. He was glad to see she had taken his advice and started putting it to use.

"Not when the ghosts are watching you."

Patches regretted the earlier thought. He wished she wasn't putting it to use.

Chapter Nineteen

2039

Ned tapped a button only he could see and nodded in Alyssa's direction. They remained alone in the command center, the operational hub of the Tower. Now a single sphere hung in the air, recording her and broadcasting it to every screen within the building. She had made an executive decision, and she prayed she could call on the best of her people.

"Assalamu Alaikom. My brothers and sisters." Alyssa closed her eyes, drawing a deep breath. She was a soldier, not a politician, and now she understood why Conthan complained about his public appearances. "There is an imposter amongst us. We have identified a shapeshifter as the culprit behind the failure of the shield that allowed the synthetics to attack our home."

These were the facts, cold, hard bits of information that they needed to hear. But as fear worked its way into the residents, she offered them hope.

"Many of you know me as a Nighthawk. While it might have shaped me into who I am, that is not who I am now. Like you, each one of you, I came to the Tower looking for a home. Some of you, I call family. Others are my students. For those of you I have yet to meet, I cherish the day we break bread. The Tower started as a place of safety. I call it home now, but it means something greater. The Tower is a promise for a better tomorrow. I see hope in the faces of its residents."

Her eyes narrowed and brows dipped low. "Somebody is threatening our home. Because of this, we will go into lockdown until they are discovered. Stay with your loved ones. Cherish this time of reflection while we ensure your safety. For the imposter shapeshifter, you are on alert. We will find you."

Ned gave her another nod. The orb lowered until he snatched it out of the air. He let out a sigh as lights blinked on his screens.

"You realize you just sent seven hundred people into a panic. They're going to claim their wives and husbands are the shapeshifter."

Ned had a point, and by the number of blinking incoming calls, the residents wasted no time. Steadily, more calls lined up in the queue. He would have his hands busy, but he wouldn't have it any other way.

"They may panic, but when this is over, we will be judged by our actions. Trust. We will need it when we rebuild. My days of being a covert agent are over."

He held out his hand, palm up. Affection, romantic affection, was a foreign concept, and she navigated it blindly. She placed her hand in his and enjoyed the closeness. He lifted her hand, kissing her knuckles before letting go. "Go be a hero. I'll handle this."

She nodded. "Lockdown the command center. If somebody comes through those doors, shoot first and ask questions later."

"I see you're adopting my philosophy on life."

"Shut down all communication."

"Alyssa, you're going to be on your own. Should we get Adelaide and Azacca to act as walkie-talkies?" In Chicago, they had used the Child's abilities to serve as a form of communication when the satellites had shut down. For now, she didn't want to involve the Church. Relying on them would only serve to make the growing cults more devout.

Ned pulled a screen out of the air, his finger ready to press the button.

"Conthan," she tapped her ear. "Transportation." She gave him a slight grin. "We're never on our own." The black disc appeared in the air. Ned pushed the button on the screen and her earpiece clicked. They had entered into a communication blackout, and only Ned could turn it back on. He remained stiff, a bit of worry creeping into the edges of his eyes, but inside he was loving the fact he single-handedly ruled the Tower.

"I'll be back," she said.

"I'll be waiting."

She stepped into the portal. The cold washed over her skin, robbing her of body heat. With a slight shiver, she stood in one of the training rooms. Conthan, Dwayne, and Errick stood with half a dozen of her Sentinels. It wasn't as many troops as she hoped for, but it would allow them to sweep through the Tower, looking for the imposter.

Matts covered the floor, still left from their last training session. One side of the room held mirrors going from floor to ceiling, allowing her to watch the students as she demonstrated restraint techniques. Since taking on the Tower's security, she spent more time in this room than she did in her own apartment. It had been months in the making, but they finally prepared her students to be peacekeepers. She'd feel comfortable with any of them watching her back. They proved themselves as they protected the residents from the synthetics. Each one of them received notes of praise for their swift thinking.

"Have the three of you stayed within eyesight?" She hated not trusting the people in front of her. They had survived hell together, and now her fists tightened as she waited for a response. Conthan's nod allowed her to release the tension in her arm.

"Ariel," all three repeated the phrase.

"I can find more," Conthan said. "But I only have a few more jumps in me."

"No, we might need you. The Tower is locked down. If the imposter is inside, they won't be getting out. We need to sweep each floor, secure it, and move on to the next."

"Alyssa," Dwayne lowered his voice so her trainees couldn't hear, "to sweep the Tower could take us weeks."

They didn't have that much time. If the shifter was loose in the building and capable of hiding from Ned, they'd cause havoc. She couldn't think of a better solution. Holding up her hand, she quieted the chatter between the others in the room. She had read every dossier, knew every ability in the building. With all the powers, there must be one that could speed up the process.

"Curses." There was one person who could scan the empty floors to speed up their search. "If Eve were here, she could scan the floors for any electrical disturbances."

"Kevin," Dwayne said. "He doesn't have the same range as Eve, but he can help."

"He'll be in his apartment," Alyssa said. She appreciated the assist from her teammate. Being the sole person in charge of the abilities in the Tower was more difficult than she imagined. After this, she'd start selecting Sentinels to take on more of the administrative work.

"We'll need to power down the Tower if his abilities are going to work," Dwayne added.

"No shields," she grumbled. "I don't like this. I feel like we're being led into a trap."

The earpiece clicked. Her heart tightened as she feared something had happened with Ned. "Alyssa, we have a problem."

"I thought I said—"

"There are synthetics at the gate."

"A-ozu billahi mena shaitaan Arrajeem."

"Not Satan, synthetics." She did not appreciate his humor.

"I know that one," Conthan said. "Something bad is happening."

Nine sets of eyes focused on her, waiting for orders. Once upon a time, she did the same to their former leader. Vanessa had given her life to save those under her literal wing. Alyssa had never taken a moment to explore the burden thrust upon the woman before every firefight. Now, as a room full of Children waited for her commands, she transformed from a soldier into a leader.

"The synthetics are here." She waved the Sentinels forward. "The other day wasn't an isolated incident. We're at war."

Ten soldiers against a metal army. It wasn't the first time the odds were stacked against them. They continued reacting, dealing with one emergency after another. Whatever conspiracy unfolded around them, she worried the synthetics were the least of their concerns.

The airship was far more massive than he anticipated. From a mile away, it looked big, capable of casting a shadow far and wide across the city. But now that they were a block away, he couldn't fathom how large the interior must be. With all the problems facing the globe, the former America, land of the great, wasted its efforts on building machines of destruction. Patches silently cheered for its demise and the rise of the Free Republic.

Once a massive saucer in the sky, the sky ship had plummeted to the earth. The crash landing had destroyed buildings, created mounds of overturned asphalt and wedged itself deep enough it probably pierced the subway tunnels. Even depowered, it remained impressive. Had he been the owner, even now, he'd return to claim it, to turn it into scrap metal, or at least strip it for parts. He had to wonder why the government decided it wasn't worth retrieving.

Eve tapped him on the chest, motioning with her head toward nearby remains. The synthetics no longer hid from sight. Patches looked to the roofs, spotting two, with another just inside a hole blown in the wall of a building. Eve had grown quiet for the last several hundred feet, and nothing about her withholding snarky comments boded well.

"Why are we walking toward the synthetics? This is a bad idea. This feels like a very bad idea."

He pulled the straps of his backpack tight, expecting they'd chase after him. A bandage on his torso pulled at the skin, reminding him that his body wasn't in top working condition. Despite the pain, he tensed his chest and arms, searching for the thread connecting him to his abilities. The pain made the muscles in his body ache, but it provided clarity and the thin line turned into a steel cable. If they attacked, it might be him that did the chasing.

"Talk to me, oh stoic one."

"There's thirteen synthetics. All of them are refurbished. The power cores in these models are fluctuating more than the one that knocked you unconscious."

"It sounds a lot better when you say, 'The one I destroyed,' thank you kindly."

Eve stopped walking, holding her arm out to stop him. Blue continued, his feet clacking on the pavement. "Blue, stop." Something was setting off alarms for his companion and he didn't want to discover what made a superhero panic.

Blue continued, ignoring her command.

"Blue," she barked, "stop!"

Patches pushed her hand out of the way and grabbed onto the rear shoulder plate of the synthetic. It did nothing to stop him, but it continued walking, deeming him insignificant. He tugged, slowing its departure before letting go. He could have stopped it, knocked it to the ground, but he didn't dare kick Eve's puppy.

"The ship is powered. That's what I was trying to sort through." She fell in line behind the robot, following, waving Patches forward. "If I had time, I might be able to tell if Skits is inside. But it's dense. Whatever is powering the ship gives me the shivers."

"So, let me go over this again." He held up his pointer finger. "No plan." Middle finger. "Surrounded by synthetic bombs." Ring finger. "Puppy robot that isn't listening to you." Pinky. "No idea if it's a trap. Should I break out my other hand and continue?"

"I liked it better when you didn't talk."

The damage grew worse as they reached the nose of the fallen airship. It had crashed into the building and pulverized everything it touched on its descent. The street widened here and off in the distance he could make out the spire of a church. Earth coated the front of the ship and grass had sprung up, making this massive piece of technology look like a relic. Amongst the old stone buildings of Boston, it only seemed fitting that the city transformed the metal into another piece of history.

"Do we knock? Doorbell, perhaps?"

Out of the corner of his eye, the sun gleamed off a synthetic standing on rubble in an alley. The machine turned around, walking away from them. Patches spun about, looking for any of the ones that had been watching them earlier. It seemed they retreated in a painfully slow manner, even more disturbing than running killing machines. Blue froze close enough it could have put its foot on the craft.

"You saw them leave?" he asked.

"Uh-uh."

She held out her hands, palms down. A second later, she shook them and repeated the action. Growling, she stopped. "I can't sense anything this close to the ship."

What would the Nighthawks do? Would they chase down the synthetics and dispatch them one at a time? Perhaps Conthan would teleport inside the ship and provide recon. A team of superheroes would have their act together enough that something as simple as a military warship would fall in seconds. Patches didn't believe he and Eve would kick ass and take names any time soon.

"You ready to fight?" Eve whispered the question.

Patches curled his fingers. One synthetic nearly killed him, and she thought they'd survive a dozen of them attacking? He didn't voice his fear, but that didn't stop his stomach from growing uneasy. A single session with Eve had him wanting to prove he was more than a reluctant Child, but reality forced him to face the truth—he was just dangerous.

"I'm ready," he whispered. He spoke without throwing up. It was a step in the right direction.

A hiss erupted from the ship. Partway up, past the cockpit, a hatch opened. Had there been someone living inside the ship all this time? Eve narrowed her stance, as if she were going to throw punches.

"What do you think it is?"

It wasn't Eve who answered his question.

"This best be bloody good, mate."

"I said," Alyssa barked, "open the gates."

She slowed her run until she stood in front of the wall. The metal monstrosity stood out against the green fields in this portion of the compound. The cement road cut through the grass and expanded to allow shipping vehicles access to the Tower. Along with the forty-foot-tall wall came an invisible barrier, its hum barely audible. While the wall might appear impressive, it only existed to create the shield on the other side.

The ground shook as metal scraped on metal and the doors retracted. A section of the wall split, rolling back so she could see the other side. She expected to see thousands of synthetics, an army to put an end to their community. Alyssa let out a sigh of relief when she saw there were only a few dozen of the machines.

"Is the shield holding?"

"It can hold indefinitely against these rust buckets. I keep telling you, nothing is getting through without my say so." Ned's voice had returned to its typical smug tone. Alyssa believed what he said. They were safe for the time being.

"Computer, play Alyssa hand-to-hand."

Her right contact lens clouded and a series of videos played. Curated by her, one video bled into another, showing martial arts, grappling, weapons handling, and clips of previous fights. At almost one thousand percent speed, she focused, muscles twitching. It pushed her limits, absorbing this much information all at once. She'd be lucky if her body retained the memories for more than an hour. But if they were still fighting in an hour, they'd have lost.

Done.

"Open the shield."

"Whoa, what?" Conthan jumped in front of her. "Did you say open the shield?"

"If they're going to keep coming in waves. We're going to dispatch them as such." She turned around to see the six Sentinels in their black body armor. "Sentinels, are you ready?"

Heads nodded. Amber stepped forward, raising her fist in the air. "This is *our* home." Nodding heads turned into clapping and hollering.

"She's right. This *is* our home, Conthan. We will fight to protect it." She pointed at Dwayne as the lightning jumped from his palms to the ground. He was powering up, ready to launch the first volley. "Conthan, Dwayne, stand down. Provide support should we need it. This fight isn't for the old guard. It's time for the next generation to inherit our kingdom."

Conthan hesitated and made sure the frown on his face emphasized his displeasure with her decision. For a man who complained about not wanting responsibility, he was the first to take up arms to protect their people. He had come a long way from the sarcastic brat she'd first rescued in an art gallery.

"Go," she said. "Let us fight for our home."

The black disc appeared and Conthan stepped inside, emerging next to Dwayne, giving her and her troops space. She eyed the six soldiers. They had trained for this, and she had no doubt they'd succeed. But fighting in a classroom and fighting in the field brought with it a mental component she couldn't teach.

The Sentinels were barely kids. They should be considering colleges or what movie they'd see on Friday night. They had robbed the Children of Nostradamus of their innocence, and for these six, their youth. They joined willingly, but it didn't make Alyssa any happier knowing they signed on the dotted line. She had turned kids into weapons.

Alyssa prayed.

With Allah's blessing, she turned back to the killer robots ready to destroy her home.

"Ned, open the shield."

Chapter Twenty

2039

Eve balled her fists, bringing them up to protect her face. Turning, she glimpsed the voice. The British accent didn't prepare her for a man wearing a metal mask, covered in a frayed robe that almost hid his ratty clothes. Behind him, a dozen synthetics formed a semicircle. They found the man responsible for fixing the machines and sending them to the Tower to kill their friends.

The mask resembled the faceplates of the synthetics, expressionless and cold. By the grime coating his hands, she assumed he had been here for some time. It was the weathered knuckles that gave away his age. This old man had attempted to slaughter the people in the Tower. There were fresh graves because of his actions. Eleanor Valentine herself had interceded and sent Eve on a mission to rescue Skits. This man knew Skits' whereabouts. Her blood boiled, and she ignored the speed of her thumping heart.

"I'm not going—"

No witty banter. She cut him off, dropping low and

sweeping her foot behind his legs. He tumbled, and she stayed low to the ground, prepared to leap forward.

"I guess we're doing this." Patches slammed his foot against the ground. He repeated the motion a second time, then charged. Alyssa didn't have time to be shocked by his courage. The synthetics turned to face the overly confident Child.

The man on the ground raised his palm. Metal spread along his skin, covering his palm before glowing red and firing a laser. She rolled out of the way, surprised at the technology at his disposal. Even the Tower didn't rely on nanotechnology. A burst of heat near his feet sent him sliding backward and, with a quick change in direction, he shot upright, hovering several feet in the air.

Despite a community full of Children, none of them had the ability to fly. It was a myth perpetuated by comic book companies. He played his hand, demonstrating the tech at his disposal. Grasping at her abilities, she found his entire body vibrated, emitting more energy than a typical human filled with enhancements from the Body Shop.

"Blue, I need you." Despite the command, her own synthetic step forward to snatch the man out of the air. Whatever he had done to Blue, she'd make Ned fix it before Skits found out. For now, she and Patches were on their own.

She lunged, tucking her shoulder as she somersaulted, striking the pavement harder than she anticipated. With a quick push, she soared upward in a line that would allow her to wretch him from the sky. He prepared to punch, and with her momentum, she could only catch his hand. Her arm shook from the force, his blow almost as strong as Patches after absorbing her punch. Before she could fall to her feet, he grabbed her by the neck.

"I'm not going back," the man growled.

He spun, hurling her closer to the synthetics. She held the sides of her head, making sure she didn't receive a concussion that put her out of commission. A machine was on her, knee pressed into her chest, trying to pin her.

"Not today." She slammed her fist against its head, causing her knuckles to sting. Blood smeared across its faceplate. It fell back enough to give leverage, allowing her to wrap a leg around its neck and pull it off her torso. Sitting upright, she could sense the unstable power source. Like the others, these were refurbished and barely functioning.

"Careful," she yelled, "they're ticking time bombs."

Out of the corner of her eye, Patches ripped off one of the arms and hurled it at the mystery man. Patches lacked grace, but his ferocity was impressive. He picked up a synthetic and chucked it at the mastermind, who dodged out of the way of the projectile as if it were a mild inconvenience.

A silent boom knocked her onto the pavement, pressure rattling her skeleton. She tried to sit upright and found herself too dizzy to do anything other than hurl. The ground moved back and forth, making it impossible to gain her bearings. Emptying her stomach, she fought to get to her hands and knees.

Synthetics had anti-crowd, non-lethal weapons, almost as dangerous as the lasers on their forearms and shoulders. The man had his hands raised, and she could sense the growing charge in his limbs. Another boom caused her heart to skip a beat, and she feared the battle had been lost.

The fields radiating from his tech hit her hard enough she could almost feel their impact. He had stripped the synthetics, stealing their technology for himself. One of the power cores attached in the small of his back powered his devices. Eve couldn't let him win, not if it stopped them from saving her aunt.

She held up a hand, pushing through the nausea. Like she had with Patches, she tried pulling at the electromagnetic fields, summoning them like magic. From this distance, they hardly moved. The growl started in her churning belly, and her muscles tensed. The fields around his body wavered, snapping like a thread pulled too tight. He landed gracefully, but the moment he looked down to inspect his boots, she realized she had disrupted his technology.

"Patches," she coughed, "switch."

The shield shimmered a bright blue every time the machines jabbed at it. The light reminded Alyssa of Skits' ability to generate plasma, and to some degree, they were the same. It was one of the first inventions based on a Child's abilities, a feat proving that Children and humans could create greatness when they worked together.

"Amber, Janet, Rico, my left. Marcus, Damien, Trinity, my right."

Alyssa stood close enough to the transparent barrier that the hair on her arms stood on end. The synthetic on the other side was only a couple of feet away. Pulling the batons from the holsters on her legs, they vibrated as electricity flowed through the metal shaft. The shimmer vanished and the first synthetic swung, its fist passing through where the shield had been. They didn't talk, but the hive mind the robots shared acknowledged the ability to engage.

The baton smacked the first synthetic, connecting with the neck. The arc of electricity sounded like a little bomb. Before the robot could snatch away the weapon, she hammered its shoulder with the other. Moving faster than the machine, she dropped, hooking a baton behind its leg and heaving back, forcing it to stagger.

"Now!" she yelled.

Marcus lunged, just as she taught him. His prosthetic batted away an arm as the forearm laser sprung upward. The artificial limb might be strong, but it was the flesh and bone limb that made him impressive. Holding the synthetic's chest, his arm blurred, vibrating fast enough parts of the machine rattled free. The metal compartment tore open, exposing the blinking red lights of the power source.

Amber moved in a blur. The piece in its chest vanished, hurled into the air before exploding. Faster than any other Child, she was onto the next, arm extended. It attempted to brace for impact, but couldn't compete with her gifts. Clotheslined, it dropped to the ground.

The Sentinels *could* do this.

The popping of bullets forced her close to the synthetic she first attacked. Sparks flew as she treated it like a shield, standing too close for it to strike easily. With a kick of her foot, she sent it in the machine's direction wielding a traditional firearm, an unusual sight on the more advanced military units.

She charged, surprised by the synthetic transforming into its canine form. She drifted over, tucking and rolling until she was next to another machine with the gun. They were everywhere. With a tap, the baton struck the weapon, causing the gunpowder to combust, removing the synthetic's arm. The canine spun about, lunging to tackle. Kicking off, she dove for the grass, the dog sailing overhead.

Trinity was flushed paperwhite, her pigment absorbing energy from the sun. With an uppercut, she removed the skull of a synthetic, knocking it on its back. Her body flashed red as a laser struck her in the hip. Damien put his hand in the laser's path, deflecting it, positioning his hand until it hit one of the robot's brethren. Alyssa let out a sigh of relief. As long as his skin maintained its reflective properties, he'd be fine. More than that, it impressed her at how her soldiers stood ready to support one another.

Trinity screamed as she dropped to her knees, cradling her hip. Alyssa didn't know if she had absorbed the high-intensity light. This wasn't a scenario they had planned for.

"I've got her," Damien shouted.

Her first conquest dropped to the ground, limbs twitching before its chest tore open, the blast sending shrapnel in every direction. Alyssa dropped the batons as she forced her limbs to go limp. The heat clung to her skin as she rolled along the grass. Jumping to her feet, she skidded to a stop to see Marcus slumped against the wall, his prosthetic limb shredded and warped. Blood coated the side of his face, and she feared one of her charges had paid the price for her hubris.

"Their cores," Amber shouted, "they're rupturing." In seconds she cleared the distance, fingers on Marcus's throat. She waited for a moment, making eye contact with Alyssa before nodding. "Alive."

Alyssa reached into her boots and pulled out two long, slender blades. "Computer, knife training." The contact blurred, and she watched hours of videos in a couple of seconds. Leaning back, a red beam flashed past her face, striking another synthetic in the chest.

"Head in the game." Damien used her own saying to encourage her. He was right. She was better than this, more capable than any other Child in the Tower. It was time to prove why she oversaw the Sentinels. Alyssa prepared to dismantle every robot on the field.

"Patches," Alyssa coughed, "switch."

"You're not taking me alive." The man's voice might be muffled, but it didn't hide the accent. Patches' father had always complained about the English, and watching the man in his post-apocalyptic costume, he understood why.

The burn had gone from irritating to painful within the first few strikes. Absorbing the energy from a punch was more intense than tapping his fingers on a table. He didn't have any outlet other than forcing it through his arms. His fingers crushed the synthetic's arm. When his knuckles connected with its faceplate, the metal inverted. With another blow, its neck craned backward.

He held onto the arm, leaning back and swung, hurling it at the masked man.

"A mask, seriously? Like a real supervillain?"

The man had dropped to the ground, digging his toes in to brace himself for the oncoming synthetic. He hardly flinched as he batted away the hunk of malfunctioning machine. Patches had a moment to consider how easily he brushed aside the robot. "He's a Child," he barked at Eve.

Pushing the fire in his limbs into his legs hurt, almost the same as when he absorbed the energy from the exploding synthetic. He growled as he pushed off, jumping at the man like a missile. Their assailant glided out of the way, clear of Patches' outstretched arms. Bracing his arms, he slammed into a part of the aircraft, his body pulsing, determined to expend the built-up force. Fingers dug into the metal, pulling away a piece of its hull as if it were paper. He spun, hurling it at the man, catching him in the torso.

"Take that, you bastard." He'd have to work on his smack talk.

A synthetic sprung from its canine form, transforming midair. The momentum caught Patches off guard, hitting him in the jaw, rattling his teeth. His abilities tried to diffuse the impact, but the fire had already gotten hotter than he'd ever experienced. He grabbed the machine's skull, squeezing until his fingers sank into its skull as if it were soft clay. He squeezed, crushing the mechanics inside. The body continued hammering into his chest with its fists. Patches howled as the fire consumed his body from the inside.

He didn't need to push the heat into his hands. Every part of his body burned, clouding his thoughts. He grabbed the synthetic's shoulder, tearing away pieces like they were twigs. Even as he expended energy, his body replaced it, bringing another wave of pain clinging to his bones. When he slammed his head into the robot's mangled skull, it sounded like a bomb went off. The synthetic flew into the air, its face collapsed inward.

"Now," he grunted through the pain, "for you." The masked man tried to pull the chunk of metal off his body. Patches didn't want to fight, didn't want to hurt anybody, but the man trapped on the ground had started this. He had killed Children. Common sense drowned in his pain. "You're going to pay."

Patches hopped to his feet and ran, moving faster than he thought possible. The man sat upright, but Patches caught him around the shoulders, dragging him out from the metal. He didn't stop charging with the man until he pinned him against a crumbling wall. Even as he struggled, Patches refused to give the man access to his hands. "Stop fighting," he growled as he slammed him into the wall again.

A synthetic crashed into the wall, Eve mirroring his tactic. In the minute he had taken to dispatch the man, she had decimated ten synthetics. The machines limped along the ground, limbs torn apart and skulls ripped from their necks. He didn't want to admit it, but they impressed him. The only machine left standing had a swatch of blue across his face, watching them, but not acting.

Patches turned back to his captive. "Who's hiding in there?" He leaned into the man, using his elbow to put pressure on the man's sternum. Killing had never crossed his mind, but he'd gladly hurt the old man to make sure he and Eve didn't die.

"No." The man squirmed. "I won't go."

He pulled off the mask, tossing it to Eve. An old man with a white beard dropped his head, trying to hide his face. He coward, trying to shrink, not the act of a villainous mastermind.

"Do you know him?" Patches asked.

"Never seen him before in my life." She kicked the synthetic in the chest, shoving it through the wall. She walked up to the mystery man, grabbing his hands, squeezing until the metal in his palms cracked. "He's covered in tech."

"Body Shop?"

The man howled as he tried to push off the wall. Patches grabbed him by the chest and slammed him into the wall again. The bearded man continued looking down, his head dipping as he flailed about. He could resist all he wanted, but with the fire screaming in Patches' chest, there was no way he'd escape.

"Don't kill me."

"Who are you?" Eve leaned in close, studying the man's face. She rested a hand on his forehead, pushing upward until they locked eyes. He glanced up, searching the sky for something.

"You're not Knights," he said, confused.

"Knights? No," she said, "we're from the Tower. The Tower, your refurbed synthetics attacked. They killed our friends."

"You're not Knights." Whatever that meant, he sounded relieved. Even with her about to crush his windpipe, they were less scary than these Knights.

"Who are you?"

He stared up. Both Eve and Patches followed his eyes, fearful that something from above might come flying down. "They weren't meant to attack your people. They're trying to protect me, from *them*."

"From who?" Patches gave him a slight shake.

"The Knights of Windsor."

"That explains everything," Patches said.

"It should."

Eve held fast to his forehead, refusing to let him break eye contact. Patches swore his skin would combust as he pressed harder into the man. The wall cracked, bricks falling away as the man's sternum threatened to crack.

"Idgit. Why did your synthetics attack the Tower?"

Patches' thighs tensed, cramping, adding to the mounting agony. It became difficult to focus, let alone have a rational conversation. They had come to save Eve's aunt and follow the goddamned letters from a dead psychic. This asshat, playing with broken synthetics, had to be part of the bigger picture. Eve kept saying they were no coincidences… if only he could focus.

His face grew slack as the thought struck him. "The shapeshifter is a Knight."

"They're coming," the man hissed.

Alyssa held nothing but pride for her recruits. They had destroyed a dozen of the cursed machines, foiling any chance of them reaching the Tower. But more than that, as their ranks fell victim, they defended one another. Alyssa wouldn't remember a finishing blow, but she'd remember the moment Damien and Amber protected their own.

The synthetics reassessed the existing threats. While

they might appear to be mindless machines attacking anything in their path, they were smart, powered by mankind's attempt at creating artificial intelligence. Deciding Alyssa was the biggest threat showed their ability to think, but as they closed in, they hadn't fully realized the gifts she wielded.

Alyssa eased her muscles, moving into a fighting stance. Her fingers tightened around the hilts of her favorite knives. Fused until the edge was only an atom thick, in her hands these blades were far more dangerous than any robot.

The time came to show why the Sentinels referred to her as their commander. With the next step, the synthetics were within reach. The knife in her right hand sliced the synthetic's throat. The cut severed the machine's spine, turning it into dead weight. Despite a new home and new roles, she remained a fighter. No longer did she take to a fight with reckless abandon, like she had in her youth. Now, with more to lose, it wasn't about the thrill, it was about surviving.

Grappling hadn't awarded them an advantage. One synthetic turned to its forearm canons. She spun as a laser passed harmlessly to her left. Her ferocity with any weapon came from watching countless videos, allowing her muscles to memorize the motions. Her grace, on the other hand, had been developed from years of ballet training. Pivoting on one foot, she kicked, knocking an outstretched hand out of the way. Turning, she leaned into the swipe, pushing the blade through the skull of a synthetic. She ducked as lasers flashed. Shrinking toward the ground, they tried to follow.

Her right blade lobbed an arm off as she chucked her left knife. With a plunk, it slammed into the chest of another synthetic, causing the power core to rupture and explode. Shielding behind the closest synthetic, bits of metal debris hammered its hide. It grabbed her remaining knife, squeezing until she let go.

With lightning reflexes, she grabbed the falling blade with her other hand. Gripping the hilt, she cut off the machine's remaining arm. Changing direction, she slammed the tip into its head, repeating the gesture twice before it stopped reaching for her. Several of its brethren dragged themselves along the ground, while only two remained upright. She wouldn't discount the fallen machines, but her priorities focused on the remaining upright killers.

Hurling the knife, it sank into an extended arm's canon. It shook its arm, trying to dislodge the blockage. Its other arm lifted, the compartment popping up, preparing to fire. She dropped into a crouch, expecting the laser to soar overhead. Instead, the red light vanished into nothing. Alyssa growled as a small black disc appeared next to its head, teleporting the beam so that it shot itself in the temple.

"Conthan!" she barked. The man couldn't sit back and allow her the satisfaction of being the sole defender of the Tower. Another disc appeared next to the remaining machine, and this time lightning poured out. The two men stood back almost a hundred feet, trying to look innocent as Dwayne shook off the last of the electricity.

Focused on the machines, she hadn't seen the Sentinels vanish. Conthan must have been busy teleporting her recruits to the infirmary and Body Shop. She had the fighting under control, but she appreciated them saving her students. There would need to be a long debrief and re-watching of footage to see how they could improve their tactics. But for a first fight, they had her respect.

Pulling the knife free of one synthetic, she sank it into the skull of those dragging themselves along the ground. They tried to fire lasers or grab at her ankles, but the damaged machines had been reduced to a nuisance.

As Conthan approached, she could see his eyes had transformed from their usual green to black. His pupils were hidden somewhere behind the darkness, a by-product of his abilities. "You over extended yourself." She had seen him do it a dozen times to save lives, but it meant he wouldn't be teleporting anybody else until he slept.

"They're being taken care of," he said. "Errick will make sure they return to active duty in a few days."

Alyssa pulled the knife from the last synthetic, sliding it in to the hilt in her boot. She hunted for its twin, unsure if it survived the blast. "I'm not worried about another day. I'm fearful that another fight will find us today. What if there are more?"

"We're ready," Dwayne said, the lighting crackling between his fingertips. Despite the powerhouse ready to fight, something about this sat uneasy with her. This was the calm before the storm, and if killing machines wasn't the worst of it, she feared they might not be ready.

"Ned." She touched her earpiece. "Close the shields."

She waited for the hum of electricity to pulse through the wall. Brushing off her tunic, securing her hijab, she grew concerned. "Ned, do you read me?"

The lights in the pylon flashed as the air shimmered. She watched as the barrier severed a synthetic in half.

The earpiece clicked before she heard Ned coughing. "Done playing?"

"Are you okay?"

"Whisky went down the wrong pipe. Back to the imposter?"

Yes. They would begin searching the entire compound until they found the shapeshifter. She prepared for a sleepless night. "You two." She pointed to Dwayne and Conthan. "Get Kevin. We need to sweep the Tower."

Now came the worst part of being a leader. She didn't want to see the wounded, injured because her teaching had fallen short. Alyssa hoped it was nothing more than scrapes, bruises, and the replacement of bionic limbs. Gripping the crescent moon underneath her tunic, she prayed Allah spared her students.

Chapter Twenty-One

2039

"You've come to see your team?" The woman wore a white lab coat and held a data pad, a sure sign that she was the person in charge. They hadn't found the imposter, and Alyssa had a moment of concern that this woman could be a Child in disguise. A shapeshifter made everybody a target, and she feared the growing paranoia was part of their plan. Alyssa stole a glance at the woman's name badge.

"Yes, please, Dr. Winston." Despite reading the background files on every Child of Nostradamus in the Tower, she couldn't keep up with the influx of human researchers in the lower levels. After the Fall of Manhattan, Gretchen had left the Nighthawks, using her knack for business to oversee the world's largest corporation. Now acting as the CEO of Genesis Division, she handpicked their human residents. Alyssa didn't like many of the projects being explored, but they had made strides to benefit humanity. It was hard to forget the corporation had once been run by a telepath hell-bent on wiping out mankind. But if it meant saving wounded Children, she'd keep her protests to herself.

"Good news. In time, they will be fine."

Alyssa suppressed the urge to let out a sigh. Standing tall, she held her hands behind her back, face void of emotion. While the others scoured the upper floors for the imposter, Ned sent her elevator to the basement. As the screen flashed the names of the floor, she tensed, fearful of what she might find. The Sentinels knew the danger of their positions, but she couldn't help but feel as if she sent kids to fight a grownup's war. Next time, she wouldn't ask Conthan to watch from the sidelines. Alyssa had let her hubris override her common sense.

"Marcus?" The image of his prosthetic misshapen and shredded to pieces would haunt her tonight as she prayed. She had to believe his sacrifice was for something.

The doctor flipped through the screens on the transparent piece of glass. Her eyes sped through the documents until she paused. Alyssa's back stiffened, worried she was about to hear bad news.

"Come with me." The doctor turned and walked down the corridor. They passed by windows looking into empty rooms prepared to receive patients. As she pushed through a set of double doors, she found a dozen nurses and doctors moving with a sense of purpose. Above the table, a massive light shone onto the table, flooding the small space with a brilliant white light. Alyssa begged Allah to watch over the man lying on the table. When one doctor stepped back, his gown covered in streaks of red, her neutral face shifted toward horror.

"Doctor... "

Alyssa waited for the woman to turn and speak. While the people in the room moved quickly, they weren't screaming or discussing Marcus's failing condition. She needed to hear from the doctor's mouth.

"His prosthetic is scrap metal at this point. We had to remove it, but there was damage to the limb. Our Body Shop cannot build him a new arm, but the doctors are prepping him for a speedy recovery. They'll have him ready to receive a custom-built arm."

"Alhamdulillah." Alyssa grasped at the necklace under her tunic, touching her fingers to the crescent moon. It wasn't the best news, but he was alive. For now, that would have to suffice.

"The others?"

"Cuts and bruises. They're resting now," the doctor said.

They painted the walls a pristine white, causing the overhead lighting to be even more dramatic. The area hadn't seen this much action since it first opened. Alyssa appreciated that the humans here ran a tight ship, efficient and ready to deal with any problems that might arise with Children. It didn't remove the fact they treated those with abilities as scientific curiosities. Alyssa never felt more uncomfortable than she did as researchers assessed her abilities.

"Is Marcus awake?"

The doctor's eyes stared off into the distance, her eyes blinking in a specific pattern. It shouldn't be a shock that the doctor had enhancements, perhaps a full retina prosthetic? It might make her a better doctor, but something about a person dedicated to preserving life being augmented left her uneasy. They had offered Alyssa enhancements to bolster her gifts, but considering her abilities focused on her muscles, she didn't dare jeopardize altering her body. Not only that, Allah made her as she should be, and she didn't dare tamper with his creation.

"No, it appears the procedure will take another hour. Then they'll wait until he's conscious before sending him to the Body Shop proper." The mention of the facility a level below sent a shiver down Alyssa's spine. The sight of metallic limbs hanging on the wall was more disturbing than it was enticing. While the shop itself was equipped to outfit those in need of enhancements in case they needed help to regulate their abilities, even they served as a research center. Outside of Genesis Division, the Tower boasted the world's most advanced cybernetics lab, a point Alyssa didn't find worthy of bragging about.

"May I see him?"

The doctor clutched the data pad to her chest. Her face softened at the request, picking up on Alyssa's need to ensure her recruit was safe. She stepped up to the table surrounded by men and women in their pale blue scrubs.

"Can we have a moment with the patient?"

"We're just finishing up. Nurse…" One man pointed at a nurse. "Monitor the electrical impulses in his bicep. I'm hoping we won't need to remove more of his arm."

The surgery was unlike the shows she had watched on television. Most of them were holding data pads connected to robotic arms assisting during surgery. With the amount of tech being utilized, it appeared more like Ned's control room than a hospital. The smell of disinfectant made her think of the last time she'd seen her parents alive.

The car accident had robbed Alyssa of her parents, and between the light and the smell, she couldn't fight the memories. Only a teenager, when Allah called upon them, she had fled the hospital waiting room. Barreling through door after door, she found herself in a vacant operating room where she admitted they were gone. Alyssa ran her fingers along her throat, recalling how she had wailed until her throat burned.

Marcus lay on a metal table, shirtless and already cleaned after surgery. While his skin might not show signs of surgery, the bloody gauze sat on a nearby tray serving as a reminder. His chest rose and fell, and she found her body mimicking the motion. It wasn't the prettiest of sights, but he was alive. Knowing Marcus, once his ego shrugged off a crushing loss, he'd be thrilled to have a more advanced piece of equipment attached to his body.

"Ms. Rahim, he will be okay. This is the demands of the job."

The doctor's words were meant to be comforting, to ease the guilt resting on her shoulders. The weight she carried continued to grow. "They're peacekeepers, not soldiers. No person should have to fight for the privilege of living." Despite their proximity, Alyssa watched the divide widen, a wedge created by their experiences. Even though the doctor worked alongside Children, she was not one of them.

"Thank you, doctor," she offered, "Please keep them safe." In her head she added, *because I didn't.*

Chapter Twenty-Two

2039

The cement crumbled between Patches' hands, rock turned to powder, sending a cloud toward his face. The pressure in his hands pushed, no burned, and expelling it did nothing to mitigate the fire in his blood. Before, when he absorbed energy, he could flip a switch to stop, even if it required concentration. Eventually, the concentration didn't do the trick. His powers were in control and they raked him over the coals. This was why he needed the Tower.

The ache had reached a sharp pain, razors cutting through his body.

"I can't empty out. It's hurting again. A lot." Admitting that made it worse. What started as tingling in his muscles went from achy to consuming. He stumbled, his brain refusing to focus on anything other than the agony. It was as if he held his hand over an open flame for too long. He was aware of every inch of skin, and right now, it felt as if the flesh was being peeled from his body.

Eve ran toward him, releasing her grip on the old man's arm. "I can help. I can try. I—" Her voice cracked.

Despite speaking the words, she didn't have confidence in her abilities. It didn't bode well with Patches as he buckled over, slamming to his knees. Even then, his body protected him from the impact while it cooked him from the inside.

She rested her hands on his shoulders. Her fingertips were like hot irons digging into his back. He howled, hoping to distract himself from the pain. On television, he had seen people go unconscious from pain. He hoped for it, prayed for it. He wanted to believe when he woke up, the pain would be a distant memory.

Pain. No. Pain *and* fear.

He'd been scared to use his abilities, scared for other people when his strength turned unwieldy. He never thought about what his gifts could do to him. From nowhere, he thought of being strapped into the aircraft as he approached the Tower. His body had been crippled with anxiety, shaking from the fear of abandoning a comfortable life. Conthan's warm greeting and offer of taking over their library had temporarily quieted his nerves. Little did he know it was only a pit-stop. Comfortable was a thing of the past.

Now there was only pain.

He wrapped his arms around his chest, hugging himself, trying to offset the pressure pushing outward. Even the light touch of his hands rippled through his body, giving way to more burning. He tried to imagine the library, but even the mental version of himself had buckled over in agony. He wanted to die. If death meant relief…

"I don't know what to do," Eve whispered. Her panic didn't alleviate the pain, if anything it added to the fear.

"We must hide." The man reached down, grabbing

his mask by a leather strap. He fitted it over his face while looking at the sky. Something had caught his attention, but Patches couldn't focus enough to search for it.

"They've seen my face."

"Nobody cares about you, old man."

"I made the system. I know. They know I'm here. They're coming."

"Shut up, can't you see he's in pain," Eve shouted. "Can't you—"

"Interesting." The mystery man had moved closer, his shadow stretching over him and Eve. The man thought of him as a science experiment. Patches wanted to clobber him, to turn the fire in his body into a rage. Right now, striking him would tear the old man's head clear off his shoulders.

Relief. For a split second, the fire vanished, replaced by the echoes of pain. Eve's hands broke through the heat—frigid, cold. His body remembered the agony, but he sucked in air, thankful for whatever she had done. Before he could exhale, the pain washed over his body, slamming into him like a sledgehammer.

Eve cursed before thrusting her hands onto his back. He hissed at the contact, trying to pull away from her manhandling. She refused to break contact. "I," *cold,* "can," *freezing,* "do," *relief,* "this."

He collapsed, fell forward, catching himself. The impact vibrated along his skin, proving it wasn't over. On all fours, he managed another deep inhale. Whatever she attempted to do, it worked, at least for a moment. Patches couldn't discern the actual pain from his body's memory. Did it still hurt? Or did his skin forget the definition of normal?

"Better," he coughed. "I can't turn it off." The words were weak, and he hated himself for it. His own body failed him. Yesterday Eve opened the door, giving him hope that he'd find his place amongst the Children and be able to wield his abilities for good. He scoffed when she offered him Dwayne's suit. But as he stuffed it into the backpack, a tiny part of him wanted to be the hero. Now, it was a foolish dream.

"I don't know what to do," Eve admitted. "Maybe we can reach Conthan? Errick can heal you." Her voice cracked, and he feared she would cry. "I'm sorry."

"The boy doesn't need healing," the masked man said.

"What do you know?" Eve's anger attempted to mask the tears.

"We're not enemies. They are the enemy." With the pain gone, Patches could concentrate on the man, on his insistence that he was the victim. Minutes ago, he attempted to kill them, and now he acted as if they were going to be lifelong friends. Patches found his intentions hard to swallow.

He squatted next to Patches, head tilted. Even with the faceless mask, Patches felt as if he were under a microscope. "I apologize for your pain. Fear has a way of making one crazy. You understand. I feared *they* had found me."

Eve bent down, wrapping her hand around his neck. Patches watched as the man's feet nearly lifted off the ground. "The synthetics at the Tower? They were yours." The metal boots hovered above the pavement. "You killed our friends."

Patches didn't move. He wanted to hit the man again, to unleash the rage bubbling beneath the surface.

Anger masked the pain, and even if the attack had been a misunderstanding, Patches hurt because this man was a coward. Powers be damned. He wanted the satisfaction of feeling the man's jaw crush under his knuckles.

"Fear," he repeated, as if that would satisfy the dead's loved ones. Eve let go of the man's neck, and he toppled to the pavement. Rubbing his throat, he coughed behind the mask. "They attacked because you stood between them and their goal. They fled Boston on a mission. I didn't have any way to stop them."

"Your excuses put people in the ground." Eve drew back her fist, ready to punch the man. Patches hoped she knocked the stupid mask off his face.

"Girl." The man was growing annoyed. "Do you want me to help your friend?"

"Eve," Patches forced the words past clenched teeth. "It's starting to hurt again."

She stopped arguing.

She put a finger against the metal mask, stepping in close. "Can I trust you?" The heat was already building. Eve could continue drenching him with her icy touch, but it still didn't solve the problem. He was out of control.

Eve's fear of engaging the enemy melted away. Since fleeing the Tower, it was the first time Patches saw past the determined soldier to the panicked girl. It didn't bode well for their mission, but he appreciated seeing her humanity.

"You can," he said with the slightest nod. "You are not my enemy."

Eve removed her finger, frowning at the man. Despite his assurances, she wasn't convinced.

"If you try anything, I *will* kill you." The soldier had returned.

Chapter Twenty-Three

2024

"You killed Feral."

While he sat on the bench in his ten-by-ten cell, his jailor stood just beyond the door, far enough away should he want to lunge. The jailor's companion, however, standing in his perfectly pressed suit, didn't have the same reservation. He stood inside the cell, well within reach. He didn't fear the man, but he should. If he wanted to escape, he'd be able to grapple with the suited man and be out the door before security arrived.

"Tsk. Tsk." The one inside his cell wagged his finger, warding away any thought of escape. With a slight spin of his wrist, the man rose to his feet, supported by invisible hands. His bare feet hung in the air, removing the ability to lunge or stand. He allowed his body to go limp and let the Child's abilities hold him in place.

"Nexus," the jailor said, "this isn't a contest. We are on the same side."

Nexus, the man recognized the name, another one of the Knights. The man had never met either of them before. The jailor wore a finely tailored suit, looking a far cry from any of the instructors he had encountered in the academy. Nexus, however, wore the signature suit with the silver crest on his left breast. There were many of them coming and going at the academy, but never had he seen the crown atop the crest. The subtle modification marked him as one of the Queen's private guard.

Focusing on their choice of clothing allowed him to ignore being stripped and thrown into solitary confinement. It had become his unofficial home, the only place he spent more time than in the training room. He'd grown accustomed to lying in the dark, refused water or food until the only thing keeping him alive was his body's ability to heal. After the degrading levels of humiliation, standing before the men naked seemed nothing more than an inconvenience.

Once Nexus displayed his ability to control the room, the jailor stepped inside. "I am not here to punish you. I am here to offer you an exit from the academy."

He didn't believe for a moment they were offering him freedom. The only way a Child of Nostradamus left the academy required a body bag. He wanted to hear the stipulations, the punishment he'd have to endure, to have any semblance of autonomy.

He recalled the look on Feral's face as his body betrayed him, dying before his very eyes. The instructor believed himself untouchable, and in truth, it only required a slight touch to best him. These two men in the cell feared him and his abilities, and they should. He was as dangerous as the man manipulating gravity.

"Why did you kill him?"

Nexus tried to maintain a neutral face, but the tightened jaw and clenched fist gave away his anger. He wasn't thrilled with the death of Feral. Perhaps they were friends or comrades at arms? The man found it difficult to believe, but maybe they had known one another when they went through the academy housed floors above them.

"He deserved it."

The jailor laughed. "I'm not arguing with you. I knew him well. He was reckless, arrogant, and greatly overestimated his abilities. If it wasn't you, another student would have challenged him and succeeded."

"He made me a killer."

"Boy, he didn't make you do anything. He offered you a choice, live or die. You chose to live, and rightly so. *You* decided to be a killer."

The words stung. It was easier to believe Feral had forced the hand that killed his friend. He spent so long being furious at the instructor, he hadn't stopped to think that there had been another answer. As he debated if he would die for his friend, he found himself an answer he didn't like. They had been friends because of circumstance, but he didn't want to die, not then. Should he have to do it all over again, he realized he wouldn't change a thing. More than the bruises and broken bones, his words hurt. Something inside snapped.

"I'm a killer," he muttered.

"Now that we have established the obvious, let's discuss your future. My superiors have taken an interest in you."

He hardly listened as he sank into the darkness of his own mind. The days turned to years as he thought about revenge. Watching Feral die had been the closest thing to satisfaction since arriving at this school for the damned. But he had killed the wrong man. Had he been brave enough, he'd have let Feral gut him until his abilities couldn't keep up. He should have sacrificed himself to atone for his sins.

But his powers hadn't let him die.

Nexus's hold over him relaxed, and his feet touched the cold stone of the room. Despite standing of his own volition, he was aware of the subtle pressure pushing his arms at his side. Nexus didn't trust him, and rightfully so. They were no different from Feral, robbing kids from their homes and turning them into a super-powered army. They were monsters, and there was only one way to fight monsters.

"Scotland has become troublesome and the Knights require a champion to calm the uprising. Will you be the one?"

"The one?"

"That's what you said before you turned Feral into charcoal. That you *are* the one?" The man turned around, stepping out of the doorway. "Consider this your graduation from the academy. You are no longer nameless."

"I didn't say yes."

His jailor let out a slight laugh. As he vacated the cell, he paused, turning back to the man. "Use your head, boy. You agreed the moment you stopped trying to die. You sealed your fate the moment you fought back. Come, Nexus."

Nexus laughed at a joke only he heard. He stepped aside, gesturing for the man to leave his prison. "Ceann, come. We have much to discuss."

A name.

Ceann, the king of monsters.

Chapter Twenty-Four

2039

"Registry."

They had climbed the side of the fallen airship until the old man pointed to a hatch. With a handprint against the metal, it hissed, powered by whatever he had scavenged in the Outlands. Without another option, she followed the man into his secret lair. As she descended into the belly of the military's former flying tank, she made a note to have Conthan speak with the President of the Free Republic about cleaning up their weapons of destruction should they fall into the wrong hands.

He had converted one of the synthetic bays into his personal workshop. Pulling at grates, girders, and wires, he had built a level platform for his workshop. Tables were scattered about, covered in technology she couldn't identify. The next platform up held a single bed, the mystery man's home. She was about to ask how long when he cleared his throat.

"My name is Registry," he repeated.

Eve laughed. It was the furthest thing from humorous. She desperately wanted to believe the man could help Patches, but he wasn't giving her much faith. He sounded more like an illustrated comic book character than a Child of Nostradamus. "No, really, what's your name?"

"Lass, what do you know about Children in the United Kingdom?" He pulled the metal mask from his face. Now that she wasn't determined to knock the spit from his mouth, she had a moment to study his face. Easily in his fifties, he reminded Eve of the bums on the beach in San Luis Obispo. But most of all, the man looked tired, eyes heavy with more stories than she had experienced throughout her life.

Eve paused her mocking. For all the talk Dwayne and Conthan did about the Children in North America, they never spoke about foreign affairs. She thought coming to Boston might expand her worldview, but with a single question, he called out her narrow point of view. She bit back the scathing words forming in the back of her head.

"That's what I thought." Instead of letting him catch her cheeks turning red, she turned to inspect his makeshift workshop. Pieces of the ship's interior were scattered across a workbench mixed in with remnants of synthetic technology. She spent her teen years working on cars, but she had never gotten into the world of computers. He, however, reminded her of the researchers beneath the Tower.

"At the Tower, we intentionally push Children away from adopting monikers. Apparently, some people prefer to live in a comic book."

"We're identified at birth. They take us from our families and strip us of our identities. We receive names once they have placed us in the academy. Those of us that survive to graduation serve the Queen." He slammed his hand down on the table, shaking the loose screws and bolts. "Does that sound like your comics?"

"Sorry." Her face burned, and she forced her eyes to the floor. She skipped guilt and went straight to shame.

"Still burning," Patches groaned through clenched teeth. "It's never been this bad. Every time," he hissed, "every touch..."

Laid out on a cot, Registry hovered over Patches. Pulling at the light dangling from the ceiling, Registry inspected her friend's wounds. When he couldn't find an obvious cause for the symptoms, he reached for a data pad.

"He absorbs kinetic energy and stores it as potential energy." Registry paused, resting the data pad in his lap while he stared at a writhing Patches. "His skin diffuses the impact across the surface of his body."

"If his cells can... then he must... but would that..." His half-finished thoughts trailed off, as if his brain were moving too quickly for his mouth to keep up. "Do you have any details about his cellular makeup?"

She shook her head, appreciative that he had already moved on from her earlier blunder. He rummaged around the table before holding up a knife. She jumped to her feet when he held up a hand, stopping her. "I need to look at his blood. I think I can fix him."

She jumped up onto the platform with them. With a quick swipe, she grabbed the knife from his hand. "How much blood?"

"A few drops."

Meeting Patches eyes, she gave him a slight nod, one hand hovering above his chest. She didn't dare touch him and make it any worse. With a quick flick of the wrist, she nicked his forearm, drawing blood.

"He's not broken," she growled.

Registry tilted his head, not amused by her retort. Registry held out his hand, waiting for the blade. He held it close underneath his data pad. Seconds later, graphics and data were pouring from the image. Behind the mask, she couldn't tell if it was bad news or if he was simply studying the information.

"Sorry," she whispered. If this continued, she might as well record herself apologizing and play it on repeat. "In America, there is a bit of a divide about Children. We're either gods or damaged humans."

"I know. They outlawed your church in England. It's discussed often." There was an audible "Ahh." She wanted to look at his tech and see what the man was capable of achieving. Was he like Needles, or did it somehow relate to his gifts?

"Interesting." He didn't bother with further explanation. "I can fix him. It won't be pretty, not with the spare parts from this obsolete bucket, but it'll get him right as rain for now."

"How?"

He let out a slight chuckle, similar to her earlier condescending laugh. "Do you have a degree in physics, anatomy, and electrical engineering? Oh, let's not forget geology."

"Geology?"

"Let me explain in laymen terms." She didn't take the bait and stood calmly, waiting for him to explain. Geniuses always explained as they pat themselves on the back. "His cells are not like ours. They're crystalline in nature and capable of conducting, storing, and expelling energy at extreme rates. Your friend here hasn't learned how to expel the energy efficiently."

"I'm in pain," Patches groaned, "not dead. Remember? I'm still here."

Registry removed the leather straps, setting the mask on the table. Moving to his workbench, he started pulling pieces of junk from the shadows. He continued to fidget with another pair of gloves, tearing at the spot where his first pair housed the lasers. Before she knew it, he'd created a heap of junk. How he believed the answer lay in broken circuit boards and crushed weapons was far outside her wheelhouse.

She shrugged as Patches looked at her. He rolled his head back, clenching his eyes shut. Eve moved next to the tinkerer, trying to make sense of his work. "Tell me about Skits."

He jumped to his feet and climbed several platforms. Crawling around on his hands and knees, he tossed her the arm of a synthetic while he held a robotic skull. He shimmied down, returning to his workbench. As the floor creaked, she had to wonder how long he had been hiding? Welding this secret lair couldn't have been a quick task, and rebuilding hundreds of synthetics must have taken him time.

"How long have you been here?"

"Three months." He shoved the mask against his face, fitting the straps around his head. Eve reached out, letting her abilities brush against the metal. For such a small piece of technology, it vibrated with power. "Electromagnetic fields? Interesting. Stop so I can work."

He not only detected her abilities but understood their function. Despite him working on saving Patches, she asked more questions about her own gifts. Within a few seconds Registry had analyzed her powers. What could he do with a day? She calmed herself, pushing the selfishness out of her mind. "Skits?"

"Assassin, sent by your government."

Her aunt was a walking storm of chaos and obscenities, but a killer? Eve found it hard to believe. For her to be sent by the government, she would have needed approval from… "Shit." Gretchen worked alongside the upper echelons of the Free Republic. She and Skits both knew the president personally, so it wouldn't be surprising if the Chief-and-Commander had delivered the order.

"She failed," he added.

"What happened? Is she okay?"

His shoulders slumped, and he turned his head in her direction. Even without seeing his face, his bowed spine coupled with a long sigh gave away his guilt. "I don't know. She saved me from *them*. If it wasn't for her, they'd have killed me. My death sentence is extended, you could say."

"She's in England?"

"Perhaps." He rolled his shoulders and pushed himself upright. Leaning over the table, he pulled at the synthetic's hand until it detached from the arm. "Leave me be so I can work. He's safe with me." He lifted his mask and met Eve's unconvinced gaze, "I owe her."

Eve didn't want to leave Patches with this stranger. Instead, she focused on the possibility that she had discovered Skits' location. With Conthan's help, she could teleport in, grab her aunt, and be back before the coffee finished brewing. Had this been Eleanor's goal all along? Was meeting Registry part of the mad woman's scheme?

Patches and Eve had come together because the synthetics attacked the Tower. Registry had sent them. They came to Boston in search of Skits thanks to a phone call. Now, the three of them were sitting in the aircraft. This was meant to happen. Eve didn't need to ask if they had reached the end of their adventure. The more her mind ran in circles, the tighter her chest grew. She tightened her hands into fists, trying to stop the rapid beat of her pulse.

"Get some air," he said.

"I'll be..." Patches could barely finish his lie, "fine."

The panic attack threatened to take hold if she didn't calm the torrid flood of conspiracies. She stepped off the platform jutting out from the floor. Standing on the floor of the actual ship, it sloped downward enough she worried about slipping. With a couple of steps, she reached the ladder and put her first foot on the rung. For the second time this week, she felt entirely useless. There was no saving her aunt thousands of miles away *and* she couldn't comfort Patches.

Halfway up the ladder, she stopped. "Why did they do it? The names, I mean. Why take away your names?"

Registry had already begun soldering. The tiny sparks spitting up along his skin didn't stop him from working. He didn't acknowledge her question, instead leaned into the work in front of him. She swung around, holding the rubber-coated ladder, taking another step toward the hatch.

"They assign our designations. First, they strip away our identities. Once they've put us through hell, they give us the pleasure of serving a benevolent dictator. Good or bad, our names define us. For the Children of Nostradamus in England, The Knights of Windsor define who we are. The worst part..." He stopped soldering to look in her direction. "We thank them for the honor."

The racing pulse paled compared to the pain in her chest. Registry's words echoed in her head as she climbed out of the aircraft. The sun continued beating down, leaving the air moist and thick. She looked up, trying to see what Registry had been staring at. Were there really satellites watching her every movement? Did they point at the Tower? Was there a watchful eye relaying their progress to a foreign power? Eve hadn't expected a trip to Boston to turn into an international affair.

"Eleanor," she cursed, "what have you gotten me into?"

The craft had broken through the wall of an office building, leaving the floor exposed to the elements. Blue stood unmoving, patient as always, a gargoyle standing watch over the city. She walked toward the opening on the third story and stepped onto the broken concrete. It was probably dangerous and, with her luck, the building would collapse. Nothing would surprised her at this point.

Blue didn't budge as she approached. Normally his blank face would watch her as she approached, almost eager as she ran her hands along its head. Once Registry finished helping Patches, she'd insist that he undo what-ever tinkering he had done to the synthetic.

Wrapping her arm around the robot, she leaned her head against the cold metal of its shoulder. Boston stood as a quiet reminder of what man could accomplish. It was only fitting that it fell apart. Eve didn't have much faith in anybody outside of the Tower. At this point, the only people she trusted were hidden behind its walls, and now, lying on a cot in an airship.

Holding Blue made her think of Skits, of the times she would barge into their house, a fury of energy and swears. Dwayne would roll his eyes, but Conthan delighted in how she tormented her brother. She'd come with gifts, stories, and Eve listened intently to every word. After a few days, she'd leave off on another mission.

"Skits, did you come home with blood on your hands?"

She didn't want to imagine her aunt as an assassin. Skits was intense and a force to be reckoned with, but not a cold-blooded killer. Conthan preached transparency, but was that a foolish sentiment? Did he mean transparent to a point? Eve had questions about the people she called family and how it tied together with a note from a dead psychic.

She tightened her grip around an unmoving Blue. Emotions running wild, she fought to keep them from surfacing. She refused to cry as she stared into a city filled with the dead. "Don't be scared. We're going to save her."

Eve wondered if the robot doubted her claims as much as she did?

Chapter Twenty-Five

2039

"It's gone." Patches flexed his hands, the metal wrapped around his fingers, barely able to bend. The gloves Registry made were bulky and weighed more than they should, but whatever sorcery they contained, the burning had subsided. "I feel fine." It was a bit of a lie, but after the ache turned into agony earlier, he felt terrific. Registry had followed through with this promise and turned off his abilities. Patches had a thousand questions for him. "How did you turn off my powers?"

Registry pushed a lock of gray hair behind his ear. Without the mask, he was nothing more than an old man with crow's feet etched about his eyes. He had muttered to himself nonstop while he worked. Patches quickly got the impression that he was a man who preferred computers over people.

"I didn't. I created a system to bleed you dry." Patches didn't like the word "bleed," associated with him after this ordeal. "You're a complex battery. The gloves draw on the energy in your body."

"So they're like a backup battery?"

"Similar to a parasitic battery drain."

Science had never been Patches' subject of choice. The tips of his fingers extended past the ends of the gloves. As he flexed his fingers one at a time, the metal groaned, resistant to the motion. Turning them over to look at his palms, he realized he was wearing the pieces of a synthetic. "Doesn't that energy have to go somewhere?"

"Some models of synthetics have laser systems built into—"

"Did you give me lasers? Do I have lasers now?" Patches' eyes went wide. The kid in the back of his head couldn't believe that somebody had built him laser gloves. While they might stop him from wanting to die, there was a cool factor he couldn't ignore.

"With time, I could build a more efficient system. But for now, kid, you get punched and you can shoot lasers."

He refrained from asking the man to clock him in the face. The toys attached to his hands were going to give him a freedom he hadn't experienced since his abilities manifested. Much like the training session with Eve, he took a step in a direction he hadn't allowed himself to dream about. A single training session had led him to the pain. What would the next bring? He sat back on the bed, aware that his attempts at being a hero had been met with nothing but agony.

"Do I have to keep them on?"

Registry shook his head. "This isn't a Body Shop. Your hands belong to you. I've never been a fan of the Knights chopping off their bits to augment abilities."

The idea of having his hands sawed off and replaced with synthetic-like fingers made his stomach uneasy.

Registry took Patches' hands, admiring the handiwork, flexing the fingers one at a time.

Patches watched the man's face. The fear from earlier had vanished the moment he started working. Patches dared asking another question. "I don't know if it's rude…"

"Class D. Technopath."

"Path? Like a telepath?" Patches pulled back from the man. A telepath had threatened the Nighthawks and the world. His ability to read minds had made him damn near unstoppable. It was his pursuit of power that left the Free Republic in shambles.

"No." Registry stepped back until he leaned against his workbench. "They slaughtered mentalists in England. I'm a Child just like you." He picked up the mask, spinning it around to see the inside. "When the Nostradamus Effect happened, it hit me almost immediately. I don't see the world like you. My brain interprets the mechanics of systems. Given enough time, I could build an aircraft like this." He patted the wall. "Or something like your gloves. Once I dissect the components, I can build it."

"Sounds confusing."

"It isn't flashy, but it's kept me alive so far."

"Why the synthetics?"

"I'm understanding why your education system is lagging." He tossed the mask on the table. "The Knights of Windsor will not ignore me, abandoning my post. They're going to come for me."

"Come to the Tower with us."

"You Americans and that damned Tower. It was one thing when you were scattered across the country. It would have been international warfare to hunt down every Child. But you gathered in one spot and painted a target on yourselves. It's not a matter of if, but when the Queen will use all her resources to destroy the Tower and everyone inside."

At first, Patches imagined a bomb going off, wiping out the Tower. He didn't know if the shields would hold, not against something like a nuke. After nearly destroying the country, he assumed they built it with a nuclear option in mind. Unless…

"The imposter? Somebody looking like me turned off the shields when the synthetics attacked. That's partly why Eve dragged me into the Outlands."

"An imposter?" Registry laughed. "Sounds like the Queen has already infiltrated your home. Mimic, her bones are more like ligaments and can mirror any organism she's touched. She's one of the Knights' more ruthless assassins."

"But why did your synthetics come after me?" He had been alone, left to put away books. Unless they had a library card, they had come for the library's solitary occupant. Patches gasped. "The synthetics converged on the library. But they weren't after me. They were after Adelaide, who—"

"Mimic," Registry said. "Those bloody robots didn't abandon me. They went hunting. I suppose I should have been more specific in their programming."

"What are they going to do? The Knights, I mean?"

"Do? This isn't like asking them to swear their allegiance to the Queen. It's genocide, kid. I've done everything I can for you. Time to be on your way." Registry pointed toward the hatch where Eve had vanished earlier.

The man had gone from storyteller to disinterested.

Now that the problem of Patches' powers had been solved, he didn't care about continuing the conversation. "You said they're going to find you. Why not come with us?"

"If treason against the crown isn't enough, what happens if I go to the one place they're watching like a hawk? Kid, you've gone mad."

For a moment, Patches considered slamming his foot over and over until he could shoot the man with his own gadget. Registry hid away from the world, and for what? More time? The man could use his gifts to help the Tower, to help *all* Children of Nostradamus.

"You're a coward," Patches said. "The Knights shouldn't be bothered with you."

Registry picked up the chest of a synthetic and dropped it on another workbench. His hand rested on the metal cadaver as he stared at an empty wall. "I have seen atrocities, watched living creatures eradicated because of scientific curiosity, or worse, fear. I'm not hiding here because I'm a coward. I'm hiding here because I'm smart."

Patches slid to the edge of the cot and stood, testing his legs. With one hand on the wall, he studied Registry and the way his fingers traced a wire protruding from the synthetic's neck. He didn't take a moment to look down, instead, letting his hands map out the machine. Each gentle caress appeared like a gentle maneuver one might try with a lover. There was something about the act that struck Patches as soothing, almost beautiful. He imagined his hands doing the same, standing in the same spot as Registry.

"Och."

Standing outside the transportation office less than a

week ago, he had a decision to make. Burying his identity as a Child of Nostradamus had become natural. Instead, he focused on his studies or getting lost in work. Every time he pulled the knob off his bedroom door, he found himself confronted by a stark reality, he was not like other people. For years, he lied to himself. If he could be an outstanding employee or a good friend, he'd be able to ignore an enormous part of who he was. But, thanks to Eleanor, he stepped inside the transportation office.

Registry served as a reminder, a version of Patches who continued the lie. The man lived in fear, closing himself off from the outside world. The many doubts and the endless list of scenarios of what might have been vanished. He thought Eleanor Valentine had robbed him of his life, but sitting here, watching Registry removing a synthetic breastplate, the lady of fate offered him a gift.

"You want a system to understand?" Patches dug his fingers into the pockets on the right side of his pants. Even with the gloves, he trapped the paper between two fingers. He stepped down onto the next platform and placed Eleanor's letter on the workbench.

"Eleanor Valentine sent me. You've already been recruited."

The moon hung in the sky despite the sun barely dipping along the horizon. The air in Boston had shifted from a cool breeze to being frigid. Eve hadn't moved from the office chair in hours. Much like Blue, she had transformed into a statue, both of their gazes fixated on a crumbling Boston. While her eyes focused on a shattered window in an office building two streets over, she had been busy.

There might not be machines outside of the aircraft creating electromagnetic fields. Nature had seen fit to produce her own. At the edge of her perception, energy ruptured from clouds as lightning hammered against the ocean below. In between strikes, something flowed through her body. She imagined a space in her chest flaring to life with her abilities. Patches had been right. She hid from her gifts, and as she inhaled through her nose, straightening her spine, she couldn't imagine why.

Eve reached out with her mind… and there was a sense of infinity. The walls of the building or the aircraft twenty feet away didn't barricade or limit her perception. Eve let the shiver flow from her shoulders to the base of her spine.

Alyssa had taught her to meditate, but her mentor never hinted at the beauty of Eve's gift. It might not win at arm wrestling, but for now, for this very moment, none of it mattered. As the energy of the Earth flowed through her, she smiled. Peace swept her away as her muscles relaxed and she slumped in the chair. It might not seem like much, nor would it make sense if she explained it to another human, but she felt at peace. If she could let go, detach from the body perched in a leather chair, she could join in the graceful movements that fields the world produced.

A loud bang startled her enough that she jumped to her feet. Reality came crashing in and she found herself surrounded by the mistakes of mankind. The hatch on the ship squealed as it opened, and another bang sounded as it smacked against the aircraft. Eve shook her hands, flexing her limbs, stretching away the hours of sitting still.

Abilities were frequently discussed over dinner. But it wasn't until Conthan sat down at the table with his eyes turned an obsidian black that they discussed the pitfalls of their abilities. When Conthan abused the portals, some part of the darkness within crept into his eyes. That day he had been helping the researchers transport equipment further than he had ever attempted. He described it as feeling omnipotent, but eventually it'd tire his body and he'd go unconscious.

Where Conthan overextended his abilities, she was more like Dwayne. Her gifts constantly bombarded her and if she didn't close off that part of herself, she'd go insane from the overstimulation. Dwayne described it as pure bliss, an adrenaline rush that he never wanted to end. Eve had written it off as him lamenting about his abilities, but now, she could see the appeal. How hard was it for him to withdraw, to pull away from the bliss, to deal with reality?

"Is this what you meant by losing yourself?"

Patches stood on the aircraft, waving like an idiot in her direction. Whatever Registry had done, it let her friend stand without howling in agony. He started in her direction and she didn't know what to say, let alone do. They had come here looking for Skits, fulfilling Eleanor's predictions, but they weren't any closer to saving her.

She didn't want to call it quits and admit she was a rebel without the skill to back up her ideas of grandeur. If she returned to the Tower, she could clear Patches' name and maybe stop the imposter. Perhaps that'd be enough. Then she could sit down and have a heart-to-heart with Alyssa. Maybe becoming a Sentinel wasn't her destiny? Maybe it was enough to feel in control of her abilities and benefit the community?

Eve stretched her legs, sorting through the difficult conversation she needed to have with Patches. The poor guy wanted nothing more than to fit in and be part of the community. She had demanded he flee, to go on an adventure and achieve a destiny set out by a dead psychic. Eve didn't like being a failure, but she might as well start with him. She'd be repeating this conversation once they returned home.

"We're going to the Tower," he shouted.

"Blue, follow," she said, jumping from the building onto the craft. She made a note of the new gloves dwarfing Patches' hands. She'd ask questions later. For now, she was thankful her companion wasn't a writhing mess on the floor.

"I know. It's time to call it quits."

"What? No." He pointed back to the hatch. "Registry is why we came here. He was the missing piece of the puzzle."

"Did he give you brain damage? Our only clue is that the Knights might have Skits. We're in over our heads."

Patches face went still for a moment before he buckled over, laughing. If he hadn't almost died twice in the last twenty-four hours, she'd kick him upside the head. She wasn't in a mood to deal with his antics.

He wiped a fake tear from his face and rested one of the gloved hands on her shoulder. "We didn't come here to save Skits," he said. "That wasn't Eleanor's plan. We came here to save the Tower." Eve didn't follow his logic. Coming here couldn't have been a tedious errand just to send them back where they started.

"Why? Why did she do that? She could have told us who the imposter is. Eleanor must have known. So why the Outlands? What about Skits?"

He shrugged. "I don't know about Skits. We can get to her. But are you telling me something isn't different?"

"Different?"

He pointed at the hatch. "That man in there, he's hiding. He fears his own shadow, and he'd rather cut himself off from the world than deal with his responsibilities." Even as he explained, Eve struggled to follow the enthusiastic man's words.

"You numpty, he's me. If I hadn't gotten on that plane to the Tower, in thirty years, I'd be him."

Eve raised an eyebrow. Had Eleanor sent them here to become better people? Was Eve's path less about the destination and more about the journey? It sounded like something a psychic would say. She inspected the sleeves of the jacket and the many patched cuts. The psychic hadn't been scared to learn the hard way, and perhaps that is how she preferred to teach.

"You must feel it too." He tried to pull it from her.

The energy radiating off the man was intoxicating. Reaching out with her mind, she could sense the fields generated by his abilities. Unlike before, there was a sense of order as they flowed into the gloves. Registry had given him a focus, much like the bracelet Dwayne wore. Days ago, she cursed her abilities, loathing that they weren't flashy and unable to grant her access to the Sentinels. Now, she understood her gifts had nothing to do with Alyssa's decisions.

"I feel it," she whispered. Patches' smile broke through the stubble and he didn't try to hide the excitement.

"I bet Blue feels it too." He patted the robot's chest.

"The imposter is a Knight and if they've already infiltrated the Tower, it means something bad is coming. We're the only ones who know the entire picture."

Eve placed her hand over his, gripping the glove sitting on her shoulder. They hardly knew one another, but it might be time to start treating him as her partner. Patches had pieced together a part of the puzzle. Eleanor hadn't sent them on a fool's errand.

"Shit," she said. This wasn't the Patches she dragged from a prison cell. Had Registry said something that lit a fire under his ass or did death do that to a person? "Let's get back to the bike. It's going to be nightfall soon. We can be there by morning."

"Bloody hell." Registry's voice echoed from inside the ship. Seconds later, he pulled himself out of the hatch. The man had secured the mask over his face, hiding his expression. Eve squinted, trying to see what he waved about in his hand. Eve recognized the folded sheet of paper that Patches carried with him.

"Kid is going to get me killed," Registry rumbled.

"You're coming with us?" Eve wasn't sure she wanted the man returning to the Tower. A few hours ago, he had been willing to take the coward's way out and die in isolation. What good would he be to them? Even if she had extra space on the bike, she'd have easily let him stay behind.

"No," he said. A rumbling started across the street. She had spent hours staring at the buildings of Boston, but she had noticed nothing that could make that much noise. When the debris shook clear, she could make out the shape of an aircraft similar to the one used to transport Children to and from the Tower.

"You're coming with me." And with that, he walked down the aircraft, heading toward the smaller ship.

"What the hell did the two of you talk about while I was out here?"

Patches shrugged as he followed the man. "You know, guy stuff."

Blue followed Patches without her asking. She cursed under her breath. It appeared she missed all the life-altering conversations today. She only hoped they could make it to the Tower before the imposter caused any more trouble.

"Dammit, Eleanor, what next?"

"Ned, why did you ask to meet?"

She crossed the garden on the terrace overlooking the fields between the Tower and the wall. The sun's lingering light vanished and the soft lamps scattered about turned on. The smell of lavender and roses made it one of the more peaceful locations within the Tower. However, the sight of Ned leaning on the railing gave her an uneasy feeling.

His hair had grown out, far longer than when she first met him, and standing on the terrace, the wind whipped it about. He wore his signature t-shirt with a punk band logo along with jeans far too tight to be comfortable. Just days ago, she wished to be standing here with him, admiring the view. Now that fantasy had become reality, she struggled to think of anything other than where she had put the Tylenol?

"More of me requires ice than not. I am certain tomorrow I'll be covered in bruises." He turned around and held a finger to his lips. By instinct, Alyssa turned around, looking for anything out of the ordinary. The man was punching buttons on a data pad. He tapped his ear and pointed to one of the cameras stationed on the ledge on a floor above them. Like everywhere else in the Tower, the terrace was monitored by his watchful eye.

He let out a sigh as he finished punching buttons. He tilted his head as if he couldn't tell if the cameras were functioning or not. "The imposter is in the command center. I can't lock them out for long. Whoever they are, they're smart."

"How? I thought we sealed you inside."

"Vent? Cable conduit? I thought it was Adelaide at first." He hung his head. "I ran."

"Living to fight another day is a noble cause. Can we gain entry?"

He shook his head. "Not without seeing plans for the Tower. I'm such an idiot. I let everybody down." Alyssa studied the man's worry, his teeth grinding as he bit back curses. It was a rare event for him to set his ego aside and demonstrate humility.

"If they're in the command center, it's not safe here," she said. "I can manually open the gates, but can you lower the shield?" She tried to sort out the best way to warn the residents. Ned was the only person able to send building-wide communications. Her mind ran a mile a minute as she constructed a plan that would protect as many residents as possible.

He didn't shrug, but the bravado that was Needles had vanished. "I think so."

"It will take us some time to inform everybody. Vacating the research levels could take hours." He checked his data pad before taking a step closer, closing the gap between them. With only a few inches, the scent of his cologne competed with the flowers.

"Alyssa." He whispered her name, barely audible over the breeze. He bit his lower lip, holding back the next words out of his mouth. Would he dare to kiss her? Ned took her right hand in his, giving it a squeeze. "We need to leave now."

He stepped around her, cutting their exchange short, heading toward the elevator. The likeness was uncanny. A spitting image of the man fought for her heart. For an acquaintance, they might have gotten away with mirroring his face and mannerisms, but she had seen the man's soul.

When she didn't follow, he slowed to a stop. His back straightened as he let out a long sigh. Ned turned around, massaging the bridge of his nose. "When did you figure it out?"

"Ned would have never admitted he lost a fight."

"I didn't imagine a human's ego could be that self-aggrandizing."

Ned would have found it hilarious to know the trait she hated the most had given away the imposter. She thought of the man standing in front of his monitors and had to push her feelings for him aside. She didn't want to imagine what happened to Ned for the imposter to be standing here. Their mantra remained—Duty first.

"If you hurt him—"

"You'll kill me? I don't think so." Ned's body transformed, changing shape as if he were made out of clay. They shrunk until Alyssa stared at a replica of herself, the clothes along her doppelgänger's body resizing to fit the smaller frame. If not for the punk t-shirt and jeans, it would have been believable. Alyssa wondered how far their abilities stretched. Did the imposter have the ability to duplicate fingerprints, eye scans, or worse yet, abilities?

Alyssa blinked rapidly, pulling up the videos in her right lens. When they didn't start playing, she tried again.

Her doppelgänger held up the data pad. "The great Alyssa Rahim, reduced to an average human, simply by taking away her internet." The imposter dropped the data pad, driving her heel into the glass. "So sorry."

The woman continued to make strategic errors. Believing that Alyssa was only the sum of her abilities was a mistake, a grave one. After years of training recruits and fighting off synthetics, her gifts weren't her only asset.

Alyssa narrowed her stance, putting weight on the balls of her feet. Raising her hands, she made a show of curling her fingers. The imposter's body molded again, growing a half foot, limbs expanding. It wasn't until eyebrows reformed that she stared at Errick, the Tower's resident healer. The irony of a killer taking his form wasn't lost on Alyssa.

"I was hoping this—"

"Shut up," Alyssa said. "No villain speeches."

"Villain? Coming from the woman amassing a super-powered army. That's brill. The same woman who acted as a puppet assassin."

Alyssa tucked away the woman's words to digest later. Right now, she had to focus on keeping her guard up. Unlike the synthetics that moved in predictable manners, a person, a seasoned veteran on infiltration tactics—

Errick's right hand shot forward, aiming for the gap

in her guard. With a quick smack of her forearm, she sent the blow wide. But it was a smokescreen for the left arm gunning for her kidney. Catching her arm, she slowed the man, but not enough to stop the jab from connecting with her gut. Before she could respond, he bowed backward. Flipping with enough gusto, he caught her under the chin with the toe of his boot.

Alyssa staggered backward, running her tongue along her gums, checking for broken teeth. He landed in a crouch, a smile stretched across his face. He was taking pleasure in his mission. Alyssa had encountered his kind before, the type who enjoyed the fight more than the goal they needed to achieve. They'd drag it out as long as possible, proving they were superior. It was a subtle difference between a soldier and a psychopath, but an important one she had never crossed.

He sprung forward in a somersault, right fist clenched. Alyssa had pulled the move a hundred times before and stepped away, leaning as far back as her balance allowed. He jumped upward, his right hand stretched, expecting to connect with her jaw, launching her into the air. Before he finished, Alyssa drove the heel of her foot into his chest. She might not be a graceful master fighter, but she still had the strength of a Child.

"Oomph."

Alyssa saw her disadvantage pivot. This man expected a showdown, a choreographed fight that wouldn't happen without the videos. She growled. There was more to her than her abilities. Alyssa had been graceful long before the Nostradamus Effect. The countless hours in the studio staring into the mirror, perfecting her pliers and glissers positions. Loosening her shoulders, she put the weight on the tips of her toes.

Alyssa slammed her forehead into the man's nose. Before she could retreat, his hands pulled her neck down, drilling it against his raised knee. The world turned black for a moment and she stumbled as she slid away. The man's confidence grew as he pulled his fist back, lowering his guard. It wasn't a beautiful execution, but she spun, ducking low with her leg out. Errick jumped back, avoiding the sweeping motion.

He wiped the blood pouring from his nose and gave a slight nod. "Creative. I like it."

Alyssa flexed her muscles, searching for any memory of the videos she consumed at the wall. The sensory overload had burned through her gift, cutting their duration shorter than normal. This imposter knew it would happen, but they obviously didn't understand the more subtle nuances.

With a smile, Alyssa jumped forward, somersaulting along the ground almost identically to the imposter. She prepared to launch an uppercut, tightening her right fist. Coming out of the roll, she switched tactics, staying low. While the imposter leaned back to protect their face, Alyssa's knuckles connected with Errick's groin. She landed a punch, hoping they felt pain like any other male. She couldn't roll out of the way fast enough, giving him time to drive his heel down on the side of her knee. Alyssa screamed.

"I'm going to bleed you dry," he growled.

She clutched her knee, praying it didn't break. He was on her, using his weight to pin her to the ground. Alyssa didn't resist, his knee threatening to snap her sternum. There was no point in struggling against his weight. Unlike the other Children, strength had never been part of her gifts.

"Scream, Child." All his weight pushed on her chest, making it impossible to inhale.

"No," she choked.

So focused on torture, the imposter had made the gravest mistake—Study your opponent. Know their strengths, their weaknesses, but most importantly, the arsenal at their disposal.

Alyssa reached into her boot, pulling a blade free before she jammed it into Errick's thigh, turning as she jerked it free. She tried for another strike, but he caught her wrist. Driving it onto the ground repeatedly, he forced her hand open, sending the blade out of reach. He ignored the wound, crossing over her to grab the weapon. As he shifted his weight, Alyssa bucked her hips, forcing him off her.

She scrambled to get to her feet, but as she put weight on her knee, she stumbled and fell. There was no way she'd be able to outrun the imposter on her leg. What little agility she had on her side had vanished. She could only hope the damage to his thigh leveled the playing field.

"First you, then your friends," he said.

Alyssa refused to go down without a fight. The Tower counted on her. The people inside were *her* responsibility. If she lost, it was only a matter of time before this imposter killed them all. Alyssa closed her eyes and asked for Allah's blessing.

"Today is not the day I die."

"Today is the day you all die."

Chapter Twenty-Six

2039

Patches stared at the backpack as if he might be able to burn a hole in the fabric with his gaze. While he sat strapped into a seat opposite Blue, Eve had taken up position behind the pilot's seat. Her trust had limitations, and she observed every button Registry pushed and switch he flipped. She agreed to get into the craft, but the way she grilled his every decision, proved it wasn't only Patches she was slow to warm up to.

The synthetic remained an unmoving hunk of metal, ignoring the safety protocols, going without straps. Eve found comfort in the machine, and he found himself trying to understand her affection for the thing. While its head remained fixated in a single spot, it was the robot's hands that provided a clue. For all the positions it could sit, both hands rested on its thighs. Patches looked down at the identical manner in which he sat.

"Smartass," he whispered.

His three travel companions fell into place like they had rehearsed this scenario, except for him. His hands clutched at the fabric of his jeans, trying to ignore the fact they were hundreds of feet above the city below. At first, he tried to focus on his abilities, turning the switch on and off. It came easy for the moment, his body having forgotten the pain from a couple of hours ago. His muscles might not remember, but he did.

"Stealth mode? You've got to be kidding me. Does it go invisible too?"

Registry glared over his shoulder. Even with the mask, Patches could sense the annoyance. The older man reached for a switch overhead. With a slow, deliberate motion, the aircraft seemed to stop midair. If the transport that brought him to the Tower in this, he might have felt sick the entire ride.

"Show off," Eve said.

No, he couldn't be productive, preparing to save the day. He studied the three pouches on the backpack. One of the zippers had been torn clean off and the pocket gaped. He wondered if at some point it had served as something other than a bag for supplies should the world come to an end?

He tried to avoid thinking about the contents, but once he memorized every bump in the fabric, he thought of the bunched-up suit inside. Eve had suggested it, hoping it'd serve as body armor like hers. It had belonged to her father during his glory days, back when he was a hero saving innocents. Patches had refused to put it on, not wanting to travel down a foolish road that would put him in an early grave. But as he wiggled his fingers, he realized his fight against fate was already lost.

"What do I do?" The psychic hadn't given him explicit instructions. He convinced Registry to return with them to the Tower. He had solved the puzzle she laid out in front of him. The identity of the imposter, every bit of it, he'd connected the dots. He had asked Eve if she felt different, and even she admitted something about their perspective had shifted. Eleanor had worked her magic.

He turned his head, staring at the woman's backside. She held onto Registry's chair, keeping a watchful eye on the man. Eve looked the part of a hero. Tight black suit able to withstand who knows what. She had stolen Eleanor's jacket and while it didn't look like part of her high-tech suit, it remained far more badass. How similar was she to the woman who once wore that jacket?

"Fuck it," he said.

He released the buckle at his chest and slid the gloves off his hands. Blue's head turned slightly, tilting as if the robot were perplexed. "Now you decide to get involved?"

"Ten minutes until contact," Eve shouted without breaking her vigilant watch.

Eyes fixed on the bag, he lifted the tattered shirt over his head, tossing it in Blue's lap. The ship held steady as he stepped up to the bag, looking down at a destiny he never wanted. If he reached inside, if he pulled the suit out, he'd be choosing heroics. Inside the bag sat the end of his mundane life as a librarian.

He pulled at the zipper.

The suit remained untouched, crumpled in the pack since he hid it away. Before reaching inside, he reached down to the fly on his jeans, unbuttoning and wiggling his hips to slide them down. He kicked off his boots, trying to focus on the material and not the symbolism of what this meant. He wasn't a hero, but he needed to be prepared for whatever they found at the Tower. There was no desire to fight, but a dead psychic had robbed him of that choice.

His jeans fell to the floor, and he kicked them off, the denim sprawled across Blue's lap. It was now or never. He looked over his shoulder to see the back of Eve's head. She was pointing at something on the display, mumbling in Registry's ear.

Pulling the suit out of the bag, he held it up, noting the lines of silver running about the chest. Picking at one with his nail, he discovered they were metal, some enhancement for Dwayne's lightning. With a swipe, he dropped his briefs. It was be caught putting on a show for Blue or the suit.

No matter how much he stretched the fabric around the neck, it returned to its original shape. Without a better idea, he stepped into the neck, bunching the material until his feet poked through the bottom. The interior was colder than it should have been and almost slick. He feared it'd pull at the abundance of hair on his legs, but it slid along his body without fanfare. Once his arms were in place, he found the limbs were snug, but the mid-section hung off his body.

Blue's head remained tilted to the side, his faceplate staring in Patches' direction. Shoving his feet back into his boots, he completed the look. With a simple change of clothes, he went from timid librarian to caped crusader. Nothing about this appealed to him. Next thing would be saving kittens from trees.

"Oh, bollocks." The suit wasn't complete. He picked up the gloves, holding them against his chest as he worked a hand into each. Like him, it wasn't perfect, not by a long shot. But it was a start, the beginning of a new chapter in his life. Whether or not he wanted the responsibility, it was going to happen.

"What do you think? Sexy?"

The robot's head looked up and down and then froze in place. Patches hoped for a thumbs up, but the lack of response would have to suffice. As he shifted back and forth, trying to find a comfortable placement for his junk, he realized superhero costumes required underwear.

Reflected on the machine's face, he saw potential. Registry and Eve had taken part in transforming him into a hero. Not only did he look the part, but part of him admitted doing good, wielding his abilities for the betterment of mankind … might not be the worst idea. He hadn't finished cursing the psychic on this journey, but for now, Eleanor had gotten her wish.

"It suits you," Eve said over her shoulder.

Yes, yes it did, he thought.

The imposter slashed at her face, the blade's tip drawing a line of red across her cheek. The lack of pain worried Alyssa, but she'd deal with the gash once she pummeled her double. With a kick of her good leg, she hit the woman's wrist, forcing the knife from her hand.

"Alyssa, they're coming. You've already lost."

Alyssa pulled herself along the pavement, making her way to the railing that circled the balcony. She recalled the last person who tried to kill her also liked to torture his victims with monologues. The doppelgänger was nothing more than a nuisance compared to the Warden. Alyssa could hear Conthan's voice in her head, mocking the imposter's need to explain their evil actions. Egomaniacs loved the sound of their own voices.

Her fingers wrapped around a metal cable strung between the metal bars of the railing. She stood, putting her weight on her usable leg. The wind picked up, running up hundreds of feet alongside the Tower, feeling like it might lift her from her feet. She hissed as her toes flexed, causing the damaged muscle in her calf to strain. The gash was bad enough that she'd need a doctor if she hoped to walk normally.

Her counterpart wasn't in much better condition. The imposter's abilities were only dangerous if she could plant a seed of mistrust. Standing here, she was average at best. Right now, Alyssa could manage average, at least she hoped she could.

"Your people won't threaten the Queen any longer." The imposter picked up the knife, blood dripping to the tip. The woman's hair caught the wind, fluttering about her face. Alyssa hadn't seen herself outside without her modesty clothing in years. Despite the patches of red on her clothes and blood smeared across her face, she was indeed beautiful.

"We have no interest—"

"Bullshit!" the imposter yelled. "You sent an assassin to kill the Queen."

Alyssa didn't respond. She knew exactly who the imposter meant. She should have suspected Skits' disappearance was linked. Once this was over, she'd address Gretchen and Lillian. They might operate the largest corporation in the world, but Alyssa would not leave until they dissolved their wet works operation. She'd speak with the president herself if she must and put an end to these political killings.

"The Knights won't allow you to destroy our way of life."

Was this all a misunderstanding? Why had Skits' been sent? When they worked as a pair, they only accepted missions that benefited mankind. They'd never have gone on an errand for political gain. But it had been years since she worked as Skits partner. Maybe the darkness had returned, except this time, it compromised Skits' soul.

Her form shifted, and once again Ned stood in front of her. This person knew there was some sort of budding relationship between them, but she had made errors every step of the way. She had observed and learned, but she lacked the respect that served as the foundation of their courtship.

He tightened his grip on the knife. She leaned forward, putting weight on the tips of her toes. Ned's double would charge, or at least hobble, thinking the knife gave them the upper hand. Alyssa's body wasn't going to endure another round of slashing and snapped kneecaps. There was no way to win with brute force or fighting prowess. If she died, she'd make sure she sacrificed her life, ensuring the community survived.

Ned's face scrunched as he let out a roar. He tried to run, closing the dozen feet between them, but it was more of a sideways hobble.

Demi-pointe.

Grunt. Pointe.

Pirouette.

Alyssa spun on the tips of her toes, the knife dragging along her ribcage, deep enough to strike bone. With the force of the turn, she raised her elbow, striking the imposter square between the shoulders. She and the imposter screamed, filling the empty night with guttural cries. Fighting her instinct to clutch the wound, she dipped low, wrapping an arm between the imposter's legs and thrust up.

Alyssa watched as Ned grabbed at anything that'd stop his descent. His fingers wrapped around the lowest cable while he dangled hundreds of feet above the court-yard in front of the lobby doors. He grabbed the wire with his other hand, the blood making it impossible for him to secure his grip.

"You can't do this," he pleaded.

Alyssa dropped to her knees, her left hand clutching the gash, soaking her tunic. She stared at Ned's likeness, the first man to climb the walls around her heart. She had friends, recruits, mentees, but he was the first one to send butterflies through her stomach.

"Alyssa, you can't do this."

She reached for the knife, convinced the majority of the red covering the handle had come from her body. The hilt had already gone tacky as the blood congealed. His whimpers grew pathetic, and Alyssa forced herself to stare into his eyes. Visually, they were identical to the original, but they lacked any semblance of a soul. Try as they might, Alyssa felt no stir of emotions for the person. In the pit of her stomach, she could only think of the bodies she buried in the field.

A surge of light poured from the shield, sending waves of blue and purple light across the sky. The night couldn't get any worse, at least not until something powerful struck their first line of defense.

"They're here," they laughed. "You're all going to die."

"Astaghfiru lillah. Forgive me."

Alyssa drove the knife into the imposter's hand between the first and second metacarpals. With a twist, the wire hummed as they let go. She watched as the hand vanished over the ledge. She waited for the sudden wet slap at the pavement below, but heard nothing.

Alyssa slid the knife into her boot and tried crawling but found her body refused to cooperate. Collapsing on the cement tiles, she rolled onto her back, holding the wound as tightly as possible. The tips of her fingers had grown cold, and she prepared for the onset of shock.

Whatever had struck the shield did it again, harder. The ripples of light cascaded across the night's sky, creating a wonderful spectacle. The splash of blues and purples would have been a lovely sight under different circumstances. Alyssa closed her eyes, not wanting to see what awaited her people.

"Allah, protect them…"

Chapter Twenty-Seven

2039

Blue shot upright, shoving Eve out of the way as the robot made for the door. They hadn't landed when the machine pulled at the handle. There was no hesitation as it glanced down. A second later, it stepped from the aircraft, jumping the forty feet below.

"What the hell?" Eve stuck her head out the door before leaning back in. "Something is wrong. Even if Needles wouldn't lower the shields, he should have responded to our hails."

"They're here," Registry said.

"How can you be sure?" Eve asked.

"I programmed your pet robot. He's hunting the Knights."

"Does that mean we're too late?" Patches asked. The ship touched down with a loud thud, knocking him into the seat. She grabbed a bar overhead to steady herself. The only sound was outside as the earth groaned at the several tons of metal coming to a rest.

Eve stared out the door, looking at the bright lights of

the Tower. From here, everything looked normal. With the sun gone, it truly served as a beacon in the middle of the dark. She had to believe they had arrived in time. Once she reached Alyssa, they'd mount a defense and then the Knights wouldn't stand a chance.

"Go," Registry said. "Alert your friends."

"You're not coming?"

"Did you think I came to fight?"

"You said—"

"I'm here for protection. Protect me. I'm an old man and somebody broke my toys." He gave a slight nod, a vote of confidence that they still had a chance.

"Let's go." Grabbing Patches' hand, she pushed him out the door.

"We're going to run?"

Eve drove her knuckles into Patches' chest, spinning him about. She prepared to throw another as he held up his hands to stop her. The middle of his palms glowed bright red. The gloves worked, siphoning the energy flowing off his body. Registry deserved accolades for his gadgets.

Patches growled. "We're going to talk about you and your sucker punches."

"Run." Even at her fastest, it would still take several minutes before they reached the wall, and then a few more until they reached the Tower. Patches slammed the heel of his foot on the ground. The impact sent a wave of warmth through his body. Without another word, she jumped from the aircraft, bolting toward the Tower.

Even with a head start, Patches passed her as if she were standing still. His steps were so wide it almost appeared as if he were leaping with every stride. She leaned forward, digging her toes into the dirt, picking up speed. Once they reached the shield, she'd need to punch a hole through it again before they could warn the others. If she were lucky, Needles would have detected the aircraft, and the Sentinels would be waiting near the gate.

But luck seemed to be a luxury she couldn't afford. Something struck the shield, sending waves of purple light spreading across the dome that protected the Tower. The electromagnetic fields wavered, as if somebody were generating as much energy as the shields. Of all the Children in the Tower, only Dwayne could affect her senses like that. Closing her eyes, she let her abilities rush out, searching for abnormalities. She couldn't sort out their abilities, but it didn't take long to find the man striking the shield.

Without warning, there was an uncanny void. The fields generated by the shield shut off. Eve hadn't realized how powerful they had been as the pressure pushing against her chest vanished. "Oh no." Patches wouldn't see it. Something was going horribly wrong. She feared they were too late.

"Holy shit."

From somewhere behind the wall, lightning erupted, soaring skyward until it dwindled to faint sparks. The second and third bolts did the same. Patches understood Dwayne had to periodically empty his battery, but it couldn't be a coincidence that it happened just as they arrived to warn the Tower about the Knights.

Picking up speed, he stepped on a rock, launching

himself into the air, passing over Blue, leaving the robot in his dust. They might be too late to prepare for the assault, but it didn't mean he couldn't help. Eleanor had set him on this path, and Registry gave him the tools to succeed. Eve knew the suit would be the tipping point. The moment he slid it on, Patches refused to hide. He might not have been trained like Eve, but he couldn't remain a bystander.

Tonight, he'd own the title: Child of Nostradamus.

He landed, feet sinking into the soil before he pushed forward. One pylon, scattered along the length of the wall, sheared off as if by magic. The tons of metal flew somewhere inside of the wall, causing the ground to shake. Beyond the wall, shouting turned to screaming. Patches couldn't figure out what could destroy the wall, but whoever did it, they were attacking. He prayed they mounted a defense.

"I'm coming," he grunted. Behind him, Eve fought to catch up. Her sense of civic duty had become infectious. He needed to harness his inner Eve, the reckless determination she had loaded into the chamber. The shy librarian had been swallowed, consumed by a need to find his people.

He reached the wall, surprised that forty feet appeared taller than he expected. Looking over his shoulder, he found Eve in the distance, closing the gap between them. Patches slammed his fists against the door, causing the metal to vibrate in a low hum. The force covered his body, a warmth settling into his muscles. The second and third strikes ignited the fire, causing his skin to tingle. Driving it into his legs, he imagined the energy pooling in his calves and thighs.

He jumped, sailing through the air as if he could fly.

As he peaked, he drove his fingertips into the metal of the wall, denting it enough for a grip. One hand after another, he drove his fingers into the metal, pulling himself upward. Hiding from his abilities for years, he'd never imagined the ways he could use them. Hanging thirty feet above the ground and hardly exerting himself, he had never fathomed the rush they'd provide.

Patches pulled himself over the ledge atop the wall. Reality set in. Fires burned where the fields had once been. The lantern illuminating the further reaches of the compound had gone dark. In the distance, the Tower's lights broke through the darkness. Another flash of lightning erupted from the courtyard. Patches had another long jog ahead of him before he reached the resistance, fighting an invisible assailant. He scanned the sky in the chain's direction of electricity, looking for whatever the man targeted, but nothing stood out. Were there more than just Dwayne? Had Conthan joined in? And what about Alyssa?

The lights in the gloves pulsed red as they absorbed fire in his muscles. It wasn't as impressive as shooting lightning from his chest, but it'd have to do. He hoped the Tower made a stand, and if gods willed it, he'd help bolster their ranks.

Ready to jump from the wall, he prepared for another sprint.

"You're held together by duct tape," Errick barked.

Alyssa hurt. The world teetered and wobbled under her feet, shifting as she made her way to the elevator. She grunted, hugging herself as a wave of nausea nearly emptied the contents of her stomach. Errick put a warm hand on her forehead, forcing his abilities to quiet her stomach.

"We're under attack." She soldiered on. "They need me."

"I've stitched up your cuts, but I can't replace blood. You're going to collapse. What use are you then?" He wasn't being reasonable. She didn't know who found her and dragged her to the medical bay, but she needed to help mount an effort against the imposter's allies. "Alyssa, you need to stop." Nonsense. She wouldn't stop until everybody in the Tower was safe and accounted for.

"You know how this ends." Even she had to admit, the words lacked the force she wanted. His job was to repair her body so she could continue doing her job. "Errick, do what you must." She grimaced as she stared him in the eye. "I'm getting in that elevator."

"I know." Not even Errick's threats of her body breaking could deter her. He pressed both hands to her cheeks and closed his eyes. The palms of his hands grew warm and for a moment, the pain receded and she thought clearly. But as soon as he pulled his hands from her face, the floor resumed its rocking.

"Come back in one piece," he said.

Alyssa nodded and made it to the elevator. She smacked her hand against the panel to the side. When it blinked green, the door opened. Stepping in, she braced her back against the wall and smashed the button for the lobby. It was impossible to ignore Errick's shaking head as he vanished behind closed doors. His lecturing would have to wait until they won.

She patted down her side, looking for additional

wounds. The blood had turned tacky, leaving her tunic stiff to the touch. The gash on her pants remained wet, clinging to her legs. The imposter had done a number on her, but thankfully, Errick closed the majority of her wounds. If he thought she would lie in a hospital bed while the Tower fought for their survival, then he underestimated her stubbornness.

As the elevator ascended, something caused it to rumble. She rested the back of her head against the wall, trying to ignore her body's warnings. Alyssa had never shrugged off her responsibilities, and when they needed her most, she'd be there to hold the line. The second shake gave her pause. Whatever was happening above her could not be good. Had the imposter's friends already breached the wall and entered the Tower?

Her worries were confirmed as the doors opened, revealing the lobby of their home. She expected there to be dozens of Children rallying, fighting back against whoever dared to attack them. Silence. There should have been Sentinels executing well-rehearsed protocols, but their protectors were nowhere to be found.

A flash of light gave away Dwayne's location in the courtyard. Bolt after bolt, lightning flew skyward. At the rate he unloaded, he'd be reaching the bottom of the well within seconds, and then he'd surrender to his abilities. It'd buy him another shot or two, and in the process, it'd kill him.

Alyssa put a hand against the wall, pushing off, letting the momentum carry her body to the rock wall surrounding a flower bed. It took a second to wrestle the dizzying sensation until it passed. At this rate, she'd only be capable of serving as a human shield, and that was if she could reach the fight in time.

The fight came to her as the windows lining the front of the building shattered. Capable of withstanding a tank, it should be impossible. The metal frames holding them in place warped, bending as if the building would collapse in on itself. Dwayne came flying into the courtyard, his body limp. He landed with a thud, rolling along the ground. She held her breath, praying he sat upright. He stopped on his side, unmoving, and no signs of life. One of their heaviest hitters had fallen. If she could find Conthan, he could…

"He'd already be here," she whispered. Conthan would have stood next to Dwayne if he could. His absence meant he was unable to teleport, or he was using what energy he had to save families in the Tower.

Hovering twenty feet in the air, Alyssa caught the first glimpse of the invader. Despite the long list of abilities housed within the Tower, she had only ever seen one person truly fly. If Ariel had survived, she'd have torn this man apart one limb at a time without breaking a sweat. Alyssa feared they might not be dealing with Children at all. "Mentalists," she cursed. To her knowledge, they were the only people with the ability to fly.

The light in the room flickered. The world grew darker, and she clung to the wall with both hands. Alyssa feared she was about to go unconscious from the blood loss. Shadows closed in. Sound continued to permeate the room, but even with a shake of her head, she couldn't see.

"She wore your face. *You* killed her."

Alyssa knew the woman's voice referenced her doppelgänger. Had they seen the body in the courtyard as they invaded her home? The man could fly, defeating Dwayne. Possible mentalists with telekinetic abilities.

What about this newest adversary? Having worked with telepaths before, Alyssa knew the difference between a mysterious voice and somebody speaking in her head. No, whoever this was, they were a Child. They had somehow made the world grow dark. Was it a sphere of influence or did she inflict blindness?

"She'd have done the same." Make her talk. Learn. Alyssa listened to the shattering glass and twisting metal. There were too many sounds to hear the footsteps of one person. She focused. If she watched the hands of a pianist, she could play. If she squared off against a boxer, she could box. Everybody believed her abilities only flowed through her muscles. A misconception she never corrected.

"Your reign ends tonight."

In the distance, crickets chirped. Three sets of feet were thumping against the pavement approaching the Tower. Dwayne groaned quietly, cursing to himself. Alyssa closed her eyes and let her body adapt, overcoming its newest challenge. The world grew louder until she heard the faint rhythmic thumping of a person's heart.

"You wage a war you can't win." Alyssa slid her hands around the rocks until she found one loosely fitted into the wall.

"First, I'll kill you for Mimic, then we destroy the Tower for the Queen."

Alyssa turned, hurling the rock in the speaker's direction. With a meaty smack, it struck. The darkness retreated, and she tried to shield her eyes. This time, the darkness creeping into her vision had nothing to do with a Child. Her body betrayed her as she collapsed.

Looking up, she saw a void of space. In the shape of a woman, there was an absolute void.

"How's it feel to know you're going to die?"

"Today is not my day."

Three sets of feet had reached the Tower.

Chapter Twenty-Eight

2039

With every step, Patches intentionally slammed a foot onto the path leading to the Tower. The shock reverberated through his body, and the tingling in his limbs transformed into fire. The gloves shone brightly, but not even they could keep up with the energy building in his muscles. Without thinking, he took one last step and shoved the fire into his legs.

The lightning had stopped, but hovering in the air, he found what it had targeted. A single man had laid waste to the Tower, bending the building's frame, and shattering the windows. Most of all, he noted the fallen Sentinels scattered about the courtyard. Patches' calves burned, and he thought he'd start screaming. He launched himself into the air.

The flying man didn't have time to turn. Patches stretched his arms out, prepared to grab onto the man's arms or legs, anything that would bring him crashing to the ground. His fingers latched onto the man's collar and both of them tumbled through the air, head over heels.

He pressed the palm of his other hand against the man's back and the glove fired a steady stream of blinding red light.

Now the man growled.

Out of nowhere, the force of a two-handed blow struck him in the back. Despite his abilities, his teeth clenched shut from the pain. When the invisible force struck him again, the burning intensified as bad as earlier that day. His grip slipped as they slammed against the balcony surrounding the lobby. Patches' fingers wrapped about the man's boot as he fell. The shoe resembled the gloves he wore. Tech, it covered the man in more equipment than Registry.

He let the glove siphon the fire from his body. Registry's gloves fired. He replaced one burning for another as the laser bore a hole through the man's suit. With a swift backward kick, the man's foot struck Patches in the nose, breaking the bone. The boot broke apart and Patches shouted as he toppled toward the lobby floor.

"Petulant Child," the man shouted. "You dare touch me?" Damned Brits, always thinking themselves superior to the rest of the civilized world.

Patches held out a hand as the pavement sped toward his face. His body trembled at the impact, his abilities blazing through his veins. Rolling onto his back, he held up both hands. The left glove was in tatters, bent in different directions, as were two of his fingers. His right glove, however, fired another shot. It should have struck the man's chest, but the beam of light changed suddenly, veering to the side.

With each subsequent shot, the agony in his body

dimmed. He didn't care if he hit the man. Right now, he needed to empty the battery. The man let go of the balcony ledge and dropped several feet away. Patches was surprised to see, even with one boot missing, his feet never touched the ground.

"You should consider yourself privileged to be struck down by a Knight of Windsor." Patches fired another laser, but the man held out his hand and the light seemed to hover in the air, frozen in space. It vanished as if it never existed. Somewhere on the man, he must have technology capable of generating a shield like the Tower. If he survived, he'd start asking more questions about how things worked.

"Bolt ya daft."

The man must be twenty years his senior, but the insult gave him a pause. If a few words were more effective than punches and lasers, Patches would quickly cut the man. If there was one thing his people were known for, it was their razor-sharp tongues.

"A Scot? I should have guessed your people would have aligned themselves with these infidels." He took a step closer, holding his hands in front of him at waist level. Patches wasn't impressed with the man's size. People with chests that far across were compensating for one of two things.

"Yer' dad sells Avon."

The man's hands balled into fists and a crushing pressure pinned Patches to the floor. With a flick of the wrist, his remaining glove contorted, pulled apart by invisible fingers. Without a way to direct the fire, he'd have to rely on his own abilities. With a low growl from the Brit, the pressure increased as if he had dropped a car on him.

"Feel your bones pushing into your organs? The gravity will grow stronger, and next the membrane of your eye will rupture." The man let out a slight chuckle. He found far more satisfaction in trying to kill Patches than he should.

"Feel honored to be killed by the legendary Nexus."

Great, not only was he a Brit with an ego, but he also referred to himself in the third person. Patches opened his mouth to mock the man, but the pressure grew intense enough to crack the pavement under his back. It should hurt, and perhaps it would if the man focused on a single square inch of skin, but his determination to pulverize his entire body fueled Patches' abilities.

"Damned bawbag, is that the best you've got?"

Without warning, the pressure vanished, giving him a chance to breathe. He was about to hurl a string of vile insults about the man's mother. Nexus threw his hands in the air and brought them down swiftly. All at once, his body grew heavy, driving into the cement like he was being struck by a speeding train.

"Jest all you please." The man stood over Patches, pressing his booted foot on his chest. "But it doesn't change the fact you're about to die."

Eve shielded her eyes as a flash of light flooded the side of the lobby. She had seen the dark figure, a living shadow. Nobody in the Tower had a gift that allowed them to bend light away from their bodies. But the bright burst of white light could only come from one person.

"Run," Eve shouted. Bastion's body gave off a soft

glow, expending the light absorbed from the sunlamps installed in his apartment. A cloud of darkness started at his feet, crawling its way up his legs. Whatever the void was doing, it couldn't be good.

With one final burst of light, Bastion evaporated the darkness. Free of the woman's influence, he turned and ran. There should be dozens of Children in the lobby fighting. Only a handful of Sentinels had guarded the entry to the building, and they had been impaled. Each of them, bodies crushed by some extreme force. This void and her Superman wannabe companion had decimated their ranks. Dead. Her friends were dead, massacred for wanting a safe place to call home.

Eve screamed, the sound tearing through her throat, primal, raw, enraging. It got the attention of the empty space. There were no features, no definition to her being, just a spot where light feared to tread. While Patches traded punches with the brute, she was going to beat this invader until they pissed blood. Her throat burned, and she pushed that anger into her hands, flexing her fingers until they made a tight fist.

Eve charged, prepared to barrel into the *thing* attacking her home. The scream returned as she caught a glimpse of Alyssa's hijab. Slumped over, they had bested her mentor in battle. If she had fallen, her attacker must be skilled, able to fight, and somehow she controlled light. Alyssa would berate her for not doing a tactical assessment before running into battle. Eve welcomed the scolding, because if Alyssa could give that silent shake of disapproval, it meant they survived.

"Foolish." The world turned black, not dark like the night, but an infinite black. The sounds of Patches and the brute trading punches penetrated the emptiness, but her eyes turned useless as she swung where she thought the woman had been standing. There was a scuffle of feet and she spun about in time to receive a chop to the throat.

Eve tried to suck in air, but found herself unable to breathe. She held her throat, trying to rub away the pain.

"Pathetic. We expected resistance, but your only talents are dying."

Eve managed a cough. With the tiniest breath, a fist struck her kidney, causing her to buckle over in pain. The woman had the ability to see, or at least know, how to work within her gifts. It made sense that the Knights of Windsor would be skilled if someone trained them from the time their powers developed. For anybody else, it might be a problem, but she was Eve Ayer and her abilities were just as impressive.

She stepped back as the woman's hand attempted to connect with her jaw. She brought up her fists and narrowed her stance, just as Alyssa had taught her. Listening to the battle in the lobby, she hoped Patches was doing better with the big guy.

"We thought you'd be formidable."

"Great, another talker," Eve croaked.

Eve failed to block the knuckles as they connected with her jaw. She let her neck spin, bringing up her hands to try and protect herself. They had trained the woman to use brute force, less effective than Alyssa's surgical tactics. Shielding her face didn't stop the thrust of a palm to her sternum. She staggered backward, completely unaware of where she stood in the lobby. At any moment, she could bump into a wall or step into the water features surrounding the massive tree.

Screw that, and screw her. Alyssa imagined the ball

of power hiding in her chest, the source of her abilities. Thrusting it outward, Alyssa sensed the hum in the walls, the near-deafening song of power radiating from the big guy and Patches. But within the darkness, her abilities hardly detected the electromagnetic fields. Whatever the woman could do, she created a world where energy refused to penetrate.

Except for the woman herself.

The lines radiating from her body were faint, vanishing into the nothingness, but even she couldn't mask a fundamental force of the universe. Eve closed her eyes, relying on Nostradamus' gifts. In any other situation, they might not be quite so impressive, but right now, it might be the only thing leveling the playing field.

"You're beneath—"

The toe of Eve's foot caught the woman in the stomach, interrupting her superiority-induced monologue. As she pivoted, she threw out her hand, expecting to follow the kick with knuckles to the woman's face. She ducked under the blow, going low to sweep her foot before she recovered.

Using her momentum, she skipped onto her other foot, hopping over the woman's outstretched leg. The second kick caught the woman's head, sending her rolling backward. She swore, believing that her abilities made her invulnerable. Eve found it ironic that the Knight relied on her gifts while she had just embraced her own. Between the extremes, that was where Alyssa had tried to push her. For once, Eve let her stubborn nature fall away.

"Perhaps I was wrong," the woman said.

"Very wrong," Eve spat back.

The ball of energy erupted and, through closed eyes, Eve could almost make out the form of the woman. Fields rolled off her skin, concentrated around her heart and the hot zones of her body. The room remained dark, but her abilities filled the space, giving her a glimpse of the world. It was beautiful. Kevin had never expressed the wonder of being able to see the world like this. It was a conversation she'd have if she survived.

The Knight came in a flurry. She jabbed, forcing Eve to lean to the side, lining her up for a punch from her dominant hand. Misdirection had been a favorite tool in Alyssa's arsenal when they sparred. Eve ducked under the fist, and then pushed the woman's arm so it crossed her body. Grabbing her shoulder, she thrust a knee, but had it stopped short.

Eve leaned back as the woman attempted to bash her nose with her forehead. They were evenly matched, and every punch and kick was blocked or barely hit with enough force to tip the scale. Eve thrust her hand forward, not to strike the woman, but to dip her hand into the fields being generated by her body. Like with Patches, she pulled, attempting to wrestle them from their natural state.

"You'd never have survived the academy."

Nothing the woman could say would berate her more than she had done to herself. She shoved aside the feelings of inadequacy that haunted her for the past few years. Eve tore at the invisible energy, destroying the fields. With a final swipe of her hand, something in her screamed, begging her to stop.

"Bloody hell."

A naked woman held out her hands, turning them back and forth as if she were seeing them for the first

time. Bald and bare-foot, Eve hadn't expected her abilities to pull the Knight out of her self-inflicted prison. The
newfound ability to manipulate the magnetic fields had
turned out to be more unpredictable than she imagined,
but now she could see what she fought.

"Fuck your academy."

Chapter Twenty-Nine

2039

"How did you—"

Eve didn't give her time to finish. She kicked, aiming for the naked woman's torso. The Knight caught Eve's foot, twisting, attempting to pull it out of its socket. Eve spun in the direction of the turn, the toe of her other foot crushing the woman's jaw. She hit the ground, rolling away as the woman tried a cheap kick to the guts.

Kicking her legs up, she flipped onto her feet, keeping low to avoid a wayward thrust from the woman. Eve could see she wasn't really a skilled fighter, and relied entirely on her gifts. A Child so dependent on her gifts, she crippled herself the moment they failed. Thankfully, Eve had never made that mistake.

The woman's eyes faded into the darkness as her skin reverted. It looked like a black liquid spread along her body, dragging her into the shadows. Despite the woman's insistence on killing her friends, Eve pitied the Knight's existence in the shadows. Had she been amongst her own people willing to foster her as a person, not just a Child, perhaps she wouldn't be a sociopath.

Eve led with an uppercut, intentionally drawing it short. Spinning, she drove her elbow into the Knight's abdomen. She threw her head back, skull connecting to the woman's forehead. A punch to Eve's back forced a hiss from between clenched teeth. Hooking her leg behind the woman's knee, she tried to knock the Knight over. But she managed to wrap her arm around Eve's neck, squeezing, trying to choke her out.

The world turned dark, as if a cloud were rolling outward, siphoning the light from the lobby. Eve couldn't focus on the electromagnetic fields, not enough to manipulate them as she had earlier. No, if she was going to win this fight, she'd have to rely on more conventional methods.

Grabbing the woman's arm from under her neck, she lifted it just enough to dig her teeth into flesh. The Knight let out a scream in Eve's ear, a high-pitched bellow. Eve's teeth touched, and she jerked her head, tearing the flesh free from her arm.

She spat the chunk of meat as she bent over, using the woman's arm as leverage. She could have hurled her, putting some distance between them, but it was time to stop the fighting. Alyssa needed help, and Patches, dear Lord, she had no idea if the man was still alive. This ended now.

Holding the Knight's arm around her neck, she kicked off the ground, leaning backward causing them to topple. The Knight's back slammed onto the pavement. Eve spun about, never letting go of her wrist. The Knight's body had nearly transformed back into a living shadow. Eve twisted the arm, causing a loud pop. Before she could retaliate or let out another blood-curdling scream, Eve drove the heel of her fist onto the woman's neck. Pulling at the arm for leverage, she rested her boot on the woman's neck, cutting off her windpipe. Now she waited.

The woman clawed at her leg, trying to find a break in her suit. Her legs flailed, trying to turn over and get away from the force of Eve's boot. But try as she might, Eve refused to relent, staring in the black where her eyes should be. The bodies in the courtyard, her friends, this woman had been part of that, a bringer of death. She wanted to make sure the last thing she saw was Eve's bloodied face.

The woman's body went limp, unconscious from the lack of oxygen. Eve didn't let go, instead she pulled the arm harder, driving her foot further. It wasn't enough to win, to be the bigger person. They wouldn't stop, not with the vitriol they spewed about the Children in the Tower. No, bullies like this only responded to one thing, a bigger bully.

Snap.

The darkness vanished. Eve didn't have time to consider what she had just done, not the blood smeared across her face, nor the grinding of her heel on a dead woman's neck. It wasn't the noble victory, and there were no feelings of triumph. The Tower was safer, one less mass murderer gone, but as the fury subsided, it filled with guilt. It would be a conversation to have with Alyssa later, when they were safe and sharing drinks.

Alyssa might need her help, but she fought the urge to check on her mentor. She needed to help Patches stop the remaining Knight. Before she could spot the man, she saw a massive shadow speeding toward the Tower lobby. The entire structure trembled as it pushed its way through the steel beams.

The ship. Registry. That fool, he had jeopardized every Child hidden in the Tower. It tore at the girders, the nose slamming into the pavement, a suicide run to kill the attackers. Patches and the second Knight were thrust upward as concrete flew into the air.

"Patches, I'm coming."

Patches hadn't thought the pain could be worse than Boston. The agony pulsing through every muscle felt like being consumed by liquid fire. Burning alive from the inside hardly seemed like a peaceful way to die. He could lie on his back wallowing in self-pity and let this arrogant bugger win, or he could be a hero.

What should have been a growl turned into a scream. Whatever force the man wielded, the heaviness pinning him to the ground fueled his abilities. He pushed up, taking hold of the man's ankle. He tried to pull away, but Patches held firm. There was no longer a need to direct the fire, to coax it into his limbs. His fingers punctured the man's suit, his nails slicing through the skin until he could feel the bone.

The man's ankle crumbled in his hand, pulverized until even the fragments turned to a messy paste. There were no satisfying screams. The pressure pinning him to the ground redirected like a kick to the gut, sending him flying toward the broken entryway. Patches tried to turn off his abilities to stop absorbing the force. But as he struck a metal beam, his body shook and replaced what little energy he expended.

Even with a crippled leg, the man soared through the air, fist drawn, ready to strike. If Patches didn't expel the energy fast, he wasn't sure what would happen to his innards. Rational thought burned away, replaced by rage. Jumping to his feet, he clenched his fists, ready to brawl with the Knight. If he was going to die, he wanted to go out like a Child of Nostradamus—a hero.

He caught the man's forearm, pushing the punch out wide, but couldn't grab onto the limb. An uppercut struck Patches under the jaw, but hardly moved his head. Patches tried to drag his knuckles across the man's face, but his arm slowed as if moving through water. Before he could retreat, the man slammed both fists down on his shoulder, dropping him to one knee that cracked the cement slab.

"You're strong," the man admitted. The pressure returned, trying to drive him onto his stomach. "But strength without temperament is useless."

Patches forced his way to his feet, trying to muster a condescending laugh. The awkward grunting would have to do as he pushed through the wall of resistance, trying to grab the man's neck.

"External force gives you power," the man said, delighted at his own discovery. "What if we remove it?"

The force driving him into the ground vanished. He prepared to lunge, to sink his fingertips into the man's neck. He'd deal with the consequences later. Patches' legs kicked into the emptiness. Looking down, he found himself hovering a foot off the ground. By sheer will, he tried to propel himself forward but couldn't gain leverage.

Being weightless, free of external forces, he had a moment to breathe. His powers strained to find any energy to absorb. With each swipe, he found his muscles expending the fire, using up the power stored in his limbs. His attacker thought himself victorious, but he provided the momentary respite Patches needed to regain his composure.

"It's no use." The man's smug expression only made Patches angrier. Gravity. He must somehow be able to manipulate gravity. Did Registry create the tech that kept him afloat or was that his gifts? He held up the remaining glove to see it had been crushed, wrapped around his mangled hand. Soon as he saw the damage, he could feel the metal cutting into his skin.

Blue soared through the air, its K9 limbs stretched. Midway through the leap, its body twisted and transformed until it was human-like. Patches never thought he'd be excited to see a synthetic. But just like he and Eve, Blue had something to prove. He was surprised it didn't run for Eve, but he was thankful as the pain crept up his arm.

Blue managed to strike the Knight. At the speed it traveled, it should have spun the man about, but he hardly shrugged at the impact. The robot landed with enough force the concrete cracked. Blue wasted no time, reaching for the man, ready to drive its metallic digits into his flesh. But the robot's arms never managed to connect.

"Blue," he whispered. He wanted to cheer for the reclaimed piece of killing tech. When it couldn't snatch the Knight, the forearm canons shot up. The laser at this range should have vaporized flesh. But the beams of red light bounced off, shooting at the ceiling. Before Patches could lend his support, the robot dropped to one knee, then the other. Its body folded, metal bending until it appeared to shrink. Blue had tried to save the day, but the poor robot hadn't stood a chance.

"You were far worthier than any Scot I've encountered."

Patches could see the crushed synthetic, barely a nuisance to this Child. The crushed skeleton left it unable to walk or even claw its way along the floor. Its right hand continued reaching, trying for the invader. Eve was going to be pissed that her pet robot had been destroyed.

"Your name," Patches asked, "what is it?"

The Knight laughed. Did all bad guys have this level of arrogance at birth, or was it a class taught in primary school? Behind the man, Patches could see through the shattered windows of the Tower to the courtyard. Alyssa lay dead, her body crumpled in what could only be described as a splat. Despite the carnage, the Tower had a beautiful view. He only wished he'd lived there long enough to appreciate it.

"Nexus, Knight of Windsor."

Patches slammed his gloved hand against his palm. His body remembered the pain. With another hit, the man raised his eyebrow at the action. Patches repeated it, stoking the flames in his muscles, reunited with the burning.

It was Patches' turn to laugh. His body hurt as it shook, suspended in the air. It was borderline comical. Dressed in his body armor, the only thing he was missing was a cape. Even if what Registry said was true, their insistence on pretending they were superheroes struck him as juvenile. "That's a pretty stupid name."

Patches grunted, the fire flowing through his veins.

"It's time to give up, Child. You can't strike me."

"I wasn't planning on it."

Patches tucked himself into a ball as the screeching metal filled the lobby. The ship's stealth mode had rendered it a silent projectile. It no longer mattered as the transport ship tore through the beams. Nexus turned, holding out his hand to protect himself. No matter how much power he summoned, it didn't slow the battering ram. Falling short, the ship drove into the lobby floor, launching concrete into the air.

The weightlessness vanished and Patches found himself caught by debris.

Housed in the cockpit, Registry clung to the straps. His eyes were clenched shut as he prepared to be thrown against the window. The terrified Child had finally stood up to his bullies.

They were heroes.

The ship came to an abrupt stop, the wings snagging on the beams of the tower. He hit the ground and covered his head, trying to prevent a concussion. A cloud of pulverized concrete blacked out the room, and he could no longer tell if he was moving through space. A scream tore through his throat. But he couldn't hear it as the world turned black.

Patches closed his eyes. A hero.

Focus. The word screamed through her skull. There were injured, structural damage, and who knows what else going wrong, but she had to ignore it. There were no Sentinels coming to save her, no Nighthawks. The only people stopping a massacre from continuing were her and Patches. And Registry.

Registry had thought it a good idea to fly an aircraft into the lobby of the Tower. The idiot had decided that a wrecking ball was the only way to take out the big bad guy. There wasn't time to search for Patches to see if he was still breathing. Nobody moved as the dust filled the lobby with white.

If the Knight was unconscious, she wanted him to stay that way until she could snap yet another neck. Seconds earlier, she had killed her first person and already she plotted the death of the second. It shouldn't be such a simple decision, but if they forced her to play by their rules, she'd make sure she won by any means necessary.

The ship groaned loudly, settling halfway in the lobby. The window to the front had been smashed in, but she couldn't detect any movement on the other side. Registry was on his own until she found the Knight's body.

"A girl?"

"A Child," she spat back.

The man hobbled from the dust, a faint shadow unable to stand upright. When they arrived, he had been flying, but Patches grounded the titan. For somebody who left a trail of bodies in the courtyard, he didn't seem dangerous. He favored his left leg, dragging his right behind him as he moved. It didn't seem like a fair fight. He could barely hold himself upright. With a punch to the throat, he'd be incapacitated, begging for mercy. After the carnage he caused, she wanted him to plead for his life.

"A Child." He laughed. The arrogance made her blood boil. It wasn't enough for him to slaughter innocent Children, but he had to revel in it. If this was what the Knights of Windsor created, she'd personally see the entire institution burned to the ground. International invasion be damned. She'd go after each one of them if it meant keeping her people safe.

"That's what you wanted," she whispered.

"Let's be done with this," he said. The man could barely walk as he took a step toward her. Try as she might, her focus had been shattered. Now she had an arrogant prick in front of her and a dead psychic living rent-free in her head.

"This isn't the end." She wasn't foolish. Moving to the balls of her feet, she lifted her arms in case he somehow closed the twenty-foot gap between them.

"It certainly is."

"I'm not talking to you, asshole. You're not worth the attention."

The strike to his ego was as gratifying as a punch to the face. Unfortunately, he hardly flinched. "The Knights of Windsor will—"

"Die?" Conthan would be proud of the mouth she developed. "Cause the last person who said that to me is dead."

A falling piece of ceiling tile caused Eve to jump, holding her arms up just in case more followed. The debris sent another wave of white into the air, obscuring the man she was about to beat into a pulp. She didn't need to see the goon to sense him. The hair on her arms stood on end, and somewhere in the cloud, the electromagnetic fields distorted so far out of their natural rhythm, it sounded like two instruments slightly out of tune.

"Come," he said.

She lurched forward, dragged across the lobby on the

tips of her toes. She tried slamming her foot onto the pavement to stop herself from sliding. When that didn't work, she attempted to swat at the supernatural force pulling at her. The powder came alive, pelting her in the face until she couldn't open her eyes. He had effectively blinded her, stealing her most valuable asset, or so he thought.

The fingers closed around her neck, one at a time, as if he were in no rush. Another sociopath. He wanted to savor his victory. She fought against him, tried to shake herself free, but the same invisible force moved her arms to her sides, squeezing them against her torso. Her body went rigid. She held her eyes shut, letting her abilities drift outward. The power poured out of the man, racing down his arm and bombarding her with energy.

"A single girl," he yelled, "this is who challenges me?"

"Want me," she whispered, "to kill you, too?"

He pulled her closer, until only inches separated them. She turned her head, his breath wet against her cheek. He dragged out the moment, breathing loud enough it almost came out as a roar. Eve flexed her muscles, trying to break free of his hold. She was nothing more than a doll, a puppet, and he her master. If it came down to physical strength between them, she'd win every fight in both skill and strength, but the Knights relied on their powers.

"You couldn't if you tried," he whispered in her ear. She tried smashing her head against his, but his grip refused to give.

He lifted her high into the air as if she weighed nothing. The fields, whatever his abilities, were the reason a man unable to stand on his own feet was treating her like a cardboard cutout.

"You're all weak," he yelled. "Complacent. Pretending as if you are," he spat, "human. We are like gods. You hide from your gifts."

Eve relaxed her body, ceasing the useless writhing. The Knight had a point. Patches had said the same thing, calling her out for demanding he use his gifts when she refused. For years, she lived under the assumption that her abilities were worthless, unable to be used in a manner that benefited society. When she set her eyes on becoming a Sentinel, she blamed her passive powers when Alyssa rejected her. No matter how much she argued, the answer remained the same.

Eve stopped blaming her powers.

"With only two of us..." They both spun around as he made some sort of grand gesture. "We destroyed your home. The others will be jealous of the blood I spilled this night."

Tracing the fields generated by his abilities, she discovered the source. Just left of his heart, the lines were the densest, coming out in almost one continuous blur. She imagined herself reaching into the source, grabbing at the energy. Pulling it was like trying to scoop up water with parted fingers. They rippled from her influence, but she couldn't pull them, not like she had with Patches.

"Perhaps I'll return with captors, toys for my mates."

The growl came out louder than she expected. The power hit an invisible barrier, put in place by her sheer determination. She couldn't stop him from suspending her in the air, but she could gather the power, letting it build. His fingers squeezed, trying to silence her, but nothing would prevent her from calling out. If she couldn't pull at his energy, she'd redirect it.

The lines wrapping around her body wavered.

"What do you think of that?"

He wasn't just an arrogant asshole; he was a masochist. Pushing at the lines, she could feel his hand tightening, supporting more of her weight. She had always wanted an active ability, something she could wield in a fight. Now Eve wished she spent less time pining for a new power and more mastering her own.

"At least the Scot put up a fight."

Patches, the reluctant hero. She squinted, only able to make out the blurry outline of the Knight. There was no point in looking for him, at least not with her eyes. The jerk taunting her wasn't the only disturbance in the electromagnetic fields. There was another. The power didn't pour out of Patches like it did the Knight. His powers were going berserk again, and without Registry to help, it was up to her. Everything rested on her shoulders.

"So did the girl," she hissed.

Eve thrust the lines backward, pushing them through the noise until they struck the Knight. He staggered a single step. Her weight returned and he couldn't hold her without his abilities. The tips of her toes touched the floor. Her limbs pushed through the invisible force, muscles straining as she wrapped both hands around his forearm. She wished she could make out his face, the look of horror as he realized he had been bested by a girl.

"No," he slammed her in the stomach with his free fist. It struck her entire body, an invisible wall throwing her back. She rolled, taking him along with her. Bracing a foot against his stomach, she kicked, hurling him into the air. Being able to bat away his abilities didn't make him any less dangerous. Alyssa would refer to him as a caged animal, and now would be the time he'd be most lethal.

She continued the roll into a backward somersault and landed on her feet. She stayed low, listening for the impact, but there was no thud or oomph knocked from his lungs. Unlike the shadow woman, Eve's influence over his abilities hadn't done more than level the playing field. Rubbing her eyes, she pulled at the dust, but even with it clear, she couldn't see further than a few feet. The Knight had vanished.

Lights sparked above, and one of the aircraft engines smoked, sputtering enough to mask footsteps. He could stand behind her and she wouldn't know it. While manipulating the fields opened doors for her, she barely understood. It was the passive aspect of her ability, the one she hated, that served her the most in this fight.

"Come out, come out, wherever you are," she called.

The only source of power she could sense came from Patches. The man was lying on his side, curled in a ball. It was difficult to sense, but she knew in the middle of the tangled lines was a man in pain, and a man hiding. The Knight knelt over Patches' body, his arm raised, as if he was about to pile-drive her friend.

She screamed. The lines radiating from Patches' body stopped their chaotic pouring into the universe and redirected toward the Knight. As he brought down his fist, it was cut short, unable to close to distance to her friend's face. It didn't matter how it happened, just that she stubbornly held her ground.

"How are—"

Eve inhaled before letting out a blood-curdling

scream. Her throat turned raw, and she raised her hands, as if she were physically pushing against the Knight. His arms flew out wide, pulled in different directions. She turned her hands over, imagining her fingers holding his wrists. Eve pulled until each arm popped, pulled from their joints. She turned his manipulations against him, and for a moment, she understood his arrogant superiority.

With each step toward Patches, she wanted to pull the Knight's arms from his body, to tear him into pieces for the destruction he caused. When his screams echoed hers, she achieved a level of satisfaction. The energy pouring off Patches responded, flowing to where she imagined her hands held the man. With a turn of her wrists, the Knight's forearms broke, bone tearing through his skin.

The researchers frequently commented about one Child piggybacking another's abilities, but she hadn't imagined it possible, not with her measly gifts. But as the energy transferred from Patches to the Knight, she forced it toward his heart. He struggled, trying to use his gifts to wrestle control of his body, but the more he fought, the more she had to influence.

"Murderer," she yelled. "You killed them. No more."

He mumbled, barely audible over the blood pumping in her ears. Patches' body had nearly returned to its normal state as she borrowed the power created by his abilities. The Knight pushed, but he couldn't penetrate her rage. If the Knights wanted a fight, she was ready to give them one.

"I'm coming for you," she growled. "Each and every one."

The lines had grown so close together they appeared

as a spike that she drove into the man's heart. His screams demanded mercy, but she had no compassion for the psycho. She could make out his unmoving form as she stepped closer. It wasn't enough to kill him to save the Tower. Eve wanted her face to be the last thing he saw.

"In Hell, remember the name Evelyn Ayer."

She closed her fists and tore her hands down to her side. His chest tore open, blood splattering across Patches and the lobby floor. Unlike the shadow woman, there was no kidding herself. He wasn't unconscious. There was nothing left but a gaping hole in his chest, a tear reaching up to his shoulder where the collar bone had fractured and torn apart.

Her muscles twitched, sending tremors through her body. As she fell to her knees, the Knight followed suit, collapsing in a limp pile of flesh. The Tower was in shambles, and there was no way of knowing how many people they had killed. There was no telling if Dwayne and Alyssa were still breathing. There was so much to do, but all she could focus on were the blotches of red coating Patches. Where the dust had settled, it made his skin appear like alabaster with red speckling on top.

"P-Patches." With her throat on fire, she could barely manage a whisper.

Crawling over the rubble, she slid to her stomach, her head half on Patches' chest. She patted his face. When he didn't respond, she dragged her fingers through the blood to his neck. She almost laughed as the artery thumped. Her eyes hurt, filled with dust. She closed them, putting her arm over Patches, hugging the one good thing to come out of this disaster.

"Did we win?"

Eve let her walls crumble and the emotions struck her like a tidal wave. Fear, guilt, anger. A growing sense of relief shoved them aside. They'd worry about the ramifications of what happened later. For right now, his dumb question was all she wanted to focus on.

"We did, buddy. We won."

Chapter Thirty

2039

It was the first time they had used the dinner table in two weeks. Dwayne and Conthan had spent every waking hour since the attack rebuilding their home. Both men pushed themselves to the limit, and more often than not, she ate dinner talking to the computer. When the Nighthawks had first gathered, there were silent moments where the conversation tapered off, each of them staring at their plates. The quick glances from one to the next always made her feel as if they were keeping secrets.

Tonight, she understood the silence. Little bits of horror refused to be washed away with a scalding shower. Some atrocities remained etched beneath the skin. As they talked about installing tempered glass that Nexus had shattered, she could only see the hole she tore through his chest. Patches wacking up covered in gore. And as their eyes met across the table, they grew silent, sharing a memory both wished they could forget.

"Are you okay?" Conthan asked so often that he

could save time by recording a video. "I recognize that vacant stare."

She dropped a stack of dishes on the kitchen counter. Not that she didn't want to talk about it, there was no secret about what happened. She was thankful that Mimic had knocked out Ned and disabled the cameras. They might know what she did, but she didn't want her fathers to watch her cold ferocity. Despite them showering her with praise for her heroics, nothing about it felt right.

"Nightmares?" Conthan stopped clearing the table and sat down on their couch. He didn't ask for her to join. If she refused, he'd give her that look that made her wonder if he didn't have biological kids.

"Yeah." She moved to the couch, crossing her legs and getting comfortable. The bags under his eyes seemed to have darkened over the last few days. He only came back to the apartment to sleep. Once he got the bare minimum necessary for his powers to recharge, he'd be out opening portals to who knows where, getting and sending personnel and supplies.

"I still hear his voice."

Eve raised an eyebrow. Amongst all the Nighthawks, there was the dreaded "him." They didn't speak his name if they could help it, and even if they did, it got confusing, as the man in question had occupied more bodies than she could count.

"Ivan?"

He nodded. "At first..." He took a deep breath. Eve understood. It wasn't just baggage, it was an entire set of luggage. "At first, I thought it was because he was a telepath. Maybe he shoved this image in my head." He stared at his right hand, turning it over slowly. "If I think about it long enough, I can still feel his heart in my hand."

"Do you still have nightmares?"

"About that? No. The Warden didn't give me an option. That day, I freed Mark Davis from his own personal hell."

Eve didn't hide the confusion on her face. Whenever they spoke of telepaths, their vocabulary never seemed to explain the events properly. She didn't expect him to feel proud about killing a man. Even if the lingering gore haunted him, it wasn't at all like what she was feeling.

"The nightmares happened after."

Each time Eve heard the story, this is where it ended.

"I took his gun. I teleported to the aircraft that was flying away with the prisoners we freed. Jasmine held an old decrepit man, the husk of Ivan Volkov's first body. He had murdered Sarah. I pulled the trigger. It wasn't survival. It was revenge." Eve's mouth hung open, surprised that this man, her surrogate father, had killed in cold blood.

He scooted closer to the couch, resting a hand on her knee. He did it as much for him and as for her. Confessing, he opened Pandora's box, and the demons came flooding out.

"I still see his eyes."

"Me too," she said, "They're angry. But in the dreams, sometimes they're my eyes. I can't explain it."

"Would you do it again?"

That had become the million-dollar question. Not in the heat of the moment, with time to think it through rationally. Would she murder him again? Sorting through the possibilities, she stared at the ceiling, trying to keep the tears from flowing down her cheeks. She knew the answer, and she didn't like it.

"Yes." The dam broke before she could wipe them away. "Nothing would change. I'd kill him to protect everybody in the Tower."

"A word of warning for you." He reached out, palms up, waiting for her to fit her hands into his beefy paws. He closed his fingers, nearly hiding her tiny hands. "Dwayne once said this to me, and it has been my compass in dark times. When the killing gets easy..." His grip tightened. "I'll kill you myself."

His eyes were an intense shade of green, and they bore a hole through her. He wasn't repeating a memory. It served as a promise. Eve understood the sentiment. If she ever reached a point where killing became natural, and she didn't carry some semblance of regret, she'd want to be killed. She thought of Skits running missions for the government. Did she have this remorse? Eve imagined her aunt was beyond questions of morality. When they found her, it'd be the first question she asked. But now, morality sat at the core of her being.

She nodded. "Do other families threaten to kill each other?"

Conthan patted her on the leg. "The ones who love each other do." He gave a slight laugh. Yes, they might look and act like humans, but they weren't. Their abilities made them dangerous, and she was understanding why they created a community isolated from the rest of the world.

"Thanks."

He leaned back on the couch, studying her face. Conthan could pivot from one topic to the next, no matter the logical leaps. The slight smirk tugging at his lip served as his tell. Nothing good was about to come out of his mouth.

"Dwayne and I have talked, and we're going to speak with Alyssa. After the way you handled yourself, you've earned your spot with the Sentinels."

Eve had waited for years to hear those words. She should have jumped at the opportunity to be one of the elite. But there was nothing. No sense of urgency or validation filled her chest. It started as a gentle shake of the head. For two weeks, she contemplated the direction of her life, reevaluating her goals.

It took time, but she found a new ambition.

"I thought you wanted to be a Sentinel?" It wasn't a judgmental question, just confusion.

"I did, I mean I do, but sometimes we don't get to choose our path in life."

Conthan's face relaxed, and he crossed his arms, less than thrilled with the statement. His chest rose as he took a deep breath in through the nose and let it out with a grumpy exhale.

"Eleanor?"

The first night after the attack, Dwayne revealed to the Nighthawks about the letters received by her and Patches. Everybody tossed out speculation, asking what it meant. They even consulted Azacca and his priests, but ultimately, nobody could decide what Eleanor wanted to happen next. She knew. Patches knew too.

"I didn't know how to tell you," she started.

"When are you leaving?"

She lowered her eyes, concentrating on a coffee stain on the couch cushion. If she squinted enough, it resembled a dog. It shouldn't be that interesting, but she couldn't meet Conthan's eyes.

"I see." He stood up, and she feared he was about to storm off and the last sound she'd hear from him was the slamming of a door. "Let me get your bags."

"Really?"

"Evelyn Ayer." The full name always meant a serious statement was about to follow. "Years ago, I opened a letter from Eleanor. I can't explain the horrible things I've seen. The horrible things I've done. That woman nearly cost me my life half a dozen times."

"I see your pep talks haven't improved."

He held out a hand. "There are a thousand things I would have done differently, outcomes I wished never came to pass. But they brought me here, to Dwayne, to you. This isn't the life I expected, but it's one I'm proud to call my own."

The jerk made her cry. Crying once in the evening might be normal in the Ayer household, but twice was too much drama for her. She smacked his hand away as she stood and threw her arms around her adoptive father.

"Does this mean I'm a Nighthawk?"

"Copyrighted, missy. Come up with your own super-hero names."

She laughed. "Jerk."

Patches slung his duffle bag on the table just inside the library. With a deep breath, the scent of new books filled his lungs. No candle or air freshener could quite do it justice. The only thing better than the smell of fresh books, were old ones. Over the last two weeks, he had worked with the newly appointed head of education to get the library in working order for the school.

He had been terrified about first arriving at the Tower. He feared letting go of the life he had built in Chicago. But it hadn't been much of a life. Drifting through his days, he hid from his truth, and while his reception at the Tower started shaky, this place felt more like home than his tiny apartment ever had.

On the table, there were dozens of folded sheets of colorful paper. He pushed his duffle bag to the side. "What do we have here?"

He opened a bright green sheet of construction paper. He choked back tears as he read the scribblings. The youngest children had been practicing their letters, and when he grew tired of pushing boxes around the library, he'd sit down with them and check their work.

"Thank you for protecting my mommy." Patches wiped away the tears, his damp fingers leaving wet spots on the paper. Each of them carried a similar message, thanking him for his bravery. The last sheet, bright neon pink, had an addendum scribbled under her name. "I want to be a library when I grow up." He laughed between the heaves of his heart.

He found home.

"A weeping Scot," came the gruff voice, "why am I not surprised?"

"Reggie, nobody asked your opinion." At the mention of his new nickname, the man scoffed, annoyed. After days of being held in a cell, pumped for information about the Knights of Windsor, Alyssa and Jasmine granted the man his freedom. He had offered to overhaul the Tower's security systems, but so far, Needles kept him at bay. Instead, he spent time in the catacombs, helping researchers with their technology.

"I thought this was home?"

Registry pointed at the duffle bag. Patches nodded, grabbing the handles. "It is. It will be. But..." He didn't know how to explain it. Eve cursed the psychic's name, but Eleanor had shown him a world of possibility. She might hate the woman's meddling, but he was thankful the infamous Eleanor P. Valentine stepped in and gave him a direction.

"I have to see this through."

"Better you than me." He had asked Registry to come with him, to be their ace in the hole. Patches had never heard a man laugh so hard. Behind the joking and snide comments, Patches recognized the man's fear. It continued to serve as a reminder of who he might become if he didn't rally against the dread.

"Did you come here just to mock my life choices?"

"I wouldn't know where to begin, Scot." Patches owed the man a debt of gratitude, but it didn't extend far enough to consider them friends. Nestled under his arm, Registry held a metal case. His finger loudly tapped against the bottom, drawing Patches' attention. The unspoken stubbornness drew out an awkward silence until he finally caved.

"I've been wondering something since that night." Others referred to the fight as a massacre, and it was. Patches could still recall the sensation of congealing blood along his face. Before he realized what had happened, he could taste the copper. He needed the distance. "Why did you do it? You could have flown away."

"Survival. I hedged my bets. If you lost, they'd return to looking for me."

Patches wanted to believe somewhere in his living reflection there was an ounce of altruism, a personal battle to do the right thing. Even as he searched, he fell short. There was no point in projecting his own transformation on the guy.

"Regardless of your motives. Thank you. Next time I'd appreciate a warning."

"No promises." The man had a pleasant smile, not quite relaxed, but it was the first time Patches had seen it. Did it mean he was settling in at the Tower? Had he lowered his guard enough to become a functioning member of society, or would he be a recluse? Patches stopped trying to analyze the former Knight.

"The Body Shop in the basement, they're not nearly as brutal as the one used by the Knights."

"I thought you hated tech enhancements."

Registry leaned against a nearby table. The man had shaved, leaving a perfectly-manicured beard with more salt than pepper. He had even buzzed his head. The man might be handsome if it weren't for the personality that accompanied the package.

"I do. They're butchers. But they let me play with their toys. They don't question me while I'm working." Patches was surprised the Council let him roam freely. He caused a series of whispers whenever he entered a room. One heroic act wouldn't erase his bonds with the Knights of Windsor. "Most importantly, the technician is far too stupid to know when I've been up to no good."

Patches wondered if the man intentionally spoke like a villain in a comic or if it was an act to keep people at arm's length. If he was one of the good ones, he really didn't want to encounter a true bad guy. Unlike the awkward silences he experienced with Eve, Registry had no problem filling dead air with the sound of his voice.

"This is for you."

Registry turned around, dropped the case on a table and stepped back. When Patches hesitated, the man started his tirade. "Ungrateful wretch, are you going to open it?"

Patches let go of the straps and walked up to the case. The silver metal was thick enough to withstand a bomb. Patches glanced to the sides as his thumbs found the scanners. The locks popped, and the case released a slight hiss. The interior contained a thick padding of foam, but nothing else.

"Bollocks." Registry pulled away the top layer of foam and underneath rested a set of gloves. Both pairs were missing the pointer and middle finger past the joint. Patches didn't care about the material or the science behind how they worked. They offered him a measure of safety from himself. Between the cards from the children and now a gift from a crotchety old man, he found himself at a loss for words.

"I might have borrowed some of the Body Shop's tech. It's amazing what you can do with the right parts. The adaptive carbon steel-based nanotechnology should be more than capable of withstanding any blow you can muster. I've talked to the little buggers, and they're more than happy to regulate your internal battery."

Registry touched the wrist of one glove and it appeared to dissolve, leaving nothing but a slender metal bracelet. Patches let out a gasp, surprised by the size of the device. The old man rarely had anything positive to say, and more often than not, was taking digs at the others in the community. Patches wondered if it was all a defensive mechanism.

"Put it on, kid, before you insult me."

Patches picked up the bracelet, sliding it over his hand. It adjusted as it reached his wrist, hugging tightly, but not enough to hurt. "I don't know what to say."

"I'd prefer if you said nothing." It was an extremely effective defense mechanism.

"Superior craftsmanship."

As he adorned the second bracelet, Registry picked up Patches' bag, handing it to him. It was as close to a tearful goodbye as they'd have. With a simple gesture, Registry reinforced his earlier thought: this was home. The Tower had a spellbinding property that allowed them to become the best versions of themselves, and Patches was excited to meet his future self.

Taking his bag, he headed toward the library's double doors. He slowed his pace as he reached the exit. The butterflies were ferocious as they swarmed his belly. Unlike the ride to the Tower, they weren't conjured by the fear of the unknown. Eleanor had set him on an unimaginable journey, and for the first time since waking with abilities, he wasn't hiding. Somewhere beyond those doors, he'd find the Patrick Kilgannon he'd always wanted to be.

"Give them hell, kid."

Patches stepped through the door.

"I will, old man."

"Do you think this is a smart idea?"

Ned stood at the doorway of her home. The duffle

bag on her shoulder said everything she needed to. He knew there was no point in attempting to dissuade her. But it didn't stop him from pointing out the flaws in her plan.

"What about the Sentinels? They're a fine peace-keeping group, but they're not ready if something like this happens again. They'll need more training."

He tried to hide his insecurities and failed.

Alyssa understood the man's inability to speak his emotions and the coy manner in which he used her sense of duty to slow her exit. Unlike the missions with Skits, this wasn't going to be an in-and-out operation. None of them had any clue when they'd return, or worse *if* they'd return. His inability to speak his mind and be honest frustrated her.

"My story doesn't end here, Ned."

"When given the option of changing the world, know it cannot be done without you."

"Your debt to that damned psychic has been paid. This isn't your battle, Alyssa. Patches and Eve, it's their turn to shoulder this burden."

She set down the duffle bag, aware that Ned didn't back away from the doorway. He wasn't a large man, but with his shoulders lifted, he attempted to look formidable. The computer hacker, a keyboard warrior, was no match for Alyssa, and even he knew it. She couldn't tolerate his inability to speak his truth.

Her eyes locked with his. The moment she let silence fill the space between them, he grew restless. Fidgeting, he lasted seventeen seconds before he let out a sigh.

"Fine," he grumbled without her speaking. "Alyssa, I don't want you to go."

As he spoke those endearing words, his shoulders

slumped, and the bravado slid from his muscles. As much as she believed she needed to keep watch over the fledgling adventurers, she knew it wasn't the conclusion to her story. The psychic might have made use of her skills, but in the end, Alyssa knew her heart had a destination.

"Ned." She reached up, her fingers close enough to his cheek she could feel the stubble. Her voice trembled as she spoke his name. She wanted nothing more than to feel the warmth of his body in her hand. While she composed herself as a modest woman, not all of her thoughts were as chaste.

Telling the others about the imposter's mistakes, they quickly discovered the budding relationship. Nobody passed judgment. Their first official date, chaperoned by Conthan and Dwayne, had started rocky as Ned found it difficult to lower his guard and set aside his ego. She found him biting back his sarcasm and, more than once, stealing glances in her direction. But an off-hand comment about Conthan's foster home experience entered the conversation, and she discovered Ned shared a similar origin story. The conversation flowed, and she found the man had reasons to be guarded. For her, he put his best foot forward, and she believed even Conthan saw a man attempting to win her affection.

Her hand touched his cheek. Ned had become her sanctuary. "You are what I'm fighting for."

Ned rested a hand on hers, leaning his cheek into the touch. Their first touch came at a bittersweet moment. He closed his eyes, savoring the touch. Alyssa dropped the bag and put her other hand around his neck, pulling him close.

He resisted long enough to ask, "Are you sure?"

She pressed her lips against his. Instincts took over, and he put a hand around her waist, pulling her closer. His other hand rested firmly between her shoulder blades as he returned the kiss with enthusiasm. It surprised her to find he tasted like he smelled, a mix of masculine musk mingled with aftershave. Most of all, he tasted right, and she discovered she had been starved for too long.

Alyssa pulled him into the apartment, out of view of anybody who might be wandering the hallways. She paused, letting out a slight gasp. Her teeth gently bit his bottom lip, her body wanting more of the man. For all the control she showed on the battlefield, it deserted her as he gave her one final peck on the lips.

Standing on the tips of her toes, she pulled back, staring into his eyes. He rested his forehead against hers, chewing on his bottom lip. Alyssa had pictured this moment and found the reality exceeded her expectations.

"Your home needs you," he whispered.

Years ago, in a sewer, as she listened to the arrogant hacker talk about changing the world, she never imagined she'd willingly press her body against his. Ned's hands slid from her back, holding her cheeks. He planted another kiss on her forehead before pulling her closer, hugging her as if it might be their last.

"*I* need you, Alyssa Rahim."

Alyssa buried her face against his chest, refusing to let the man see the tears pooling in the corner of her eyes. He had done a good job as she contemplated abandoning her mission. As the man's walls crumbled, she found an even more beautiful man in his place, one she didn't want to abandon. *'I'll stay.'* The words fought their way from her lungs, determined to be whispered.

"Save the world, Alyssa. I'll be here when you return."

"I—"

He gave a slight chuckle. "Go. I'm your destination, not your journey."

Reaching down, he picked up the bag. Just like that, Ned said exactly what she needed to hear. It might not have been the easiest decision, but he understood her in ways nobody else could. She loved him, and without saying it, she knew he returned her feelings.

Stepping into the hall, he tossed her bag over his shoulder. And just like that, they returned to the roles fate thrust upon them. But unlike before, Alyssa wasn't just fighting for the Children of Nostradamus. An awkward man striving to reach his potential gave her new determination.

She closed the door and followed her future down the hall, starting the countdown until she returned.

Epilogue

2039

Patches awkwardly saluted the pilot standing outside the aircraft. Three weeks ago, the woman had flown him to the Tower. Her military uniform maintained perfect creases along the pants, far more formal than the suit she wore at their first meeting. The pilot winked, holding her position with arms crossed behind her back.

"I promised I'd return if you needed to leave."

"Not what I expected at the time."

"It rarely is, sir. Please make sure you don't hurl. I just finished detailing our ride." The pilot's face remained neutral.

Patches couldn't tell if she was joking or not. Stepping into the cabin, it surprised him to find a synthetic occupying a seat. When its head turned, he relaxed at the sight of a blue swatch of paint on its face. The last he had seen of Eve's pet, it had been transformed into a crumpled ball of spare parts.

A small yellow paper had been stuck to its forehead. He dumped his bag on a seat and pulled the note from

Blue's head. In three short words, Registry proved he was more complicated than the coward he portrayed.

"For the girl," Patches muttered, ending with a laugh. "You ready for this, Blue?"

The robot's head tilted slightly. He did not know if the machine understood it had been crushed and rebuilt. Where its body had been worn, long past its prime, Registry had made the new chassis sparkle. Blue raised his fist, slowly rotating it. The synthetic's thumb extended, giving him a good ol' fashioned thumbs up.

"He's always ready," Eve said from the doorway. "Question is, are you?"

Despite switching from the body armor to a pair of jeans and a shredded t-shirt, she still wore the leather jacket. They had spoken at length of this moment, the next leg of their adventure, and he couldn't deny the sense of relief at seeing her.

"Only one way to find out. How did your dads take it?"

She planted herself in a seat next to Blue, running her hand over his skull as if she were ruffling its hair. "I expected them to force their way in here with us, but..." She gave a shrug. "They kept saying their adventuring days were over. Then they tried to give me advice."

"Anything good?"

"Something, something, political disaster. Something, something, allies. Basically, don't do anything stupid. You know, typical Dad stuff." She threw up her arms, gesturing to the aircraft. The Eve he had first met, the woman who barreled into the library fleeing synthetics, was barely recognizable. It was hard to remember how much he'd disliked her when they first fled the Tower. He couldn't put his finger on what had changed.

Perhaps her inhibitions, her reservations, or the fact she now lived for herself. He liked this Eve.

"Ready to be stupid and save the world?"

She nodded. "Let's do stupid stuff."

"Far be it from me to argue." They both turned to see Alyssa standing at the entrance to the plane. Patches eyed Eve, his eyes widening as he nodded his head in Alyssa's direction. When she dropped her bag and took a seat next to Patches, there was a long, drawn-out, awkward silence.

"Please," she started, "I've been doing stupid stuff before either of you had powers."

"Do the others know?" Eve asked.

"They will."

Patches didn't know if Eve's mentor came as a chaperone or as a partner. Is this how it had started for the Nighthawks? Did a series of poor decisions bring them together until they saved the world? Life continued to surprise him.

"Never thought I'd be a Nighthawk."

"You're not," Alyssa started. "The Nighthawks are no more."

"Funny, Conthan said the same thing." Eve narrowed her gaze as she stared at Alyssa. Patches suspected them being allowed to go might have been influenced by the veteran of the group. Either way, he was glad to have some experience by his side. Now, when he screwed up, he'd have an audience.

"What's it going to be, Eve?"

"Seriously? Don't we make fun of Registry for his name? Nobody here is wearing spandex."

"Speak for yourself." Patches smiled as her glare of doom turned to him.

"I don't know."

Patches ran through the list of comics he read in his youth, searching for one that might lend itself to this trio of Children and their pet robot. Now that he had met the real Nighthawks, the magazines were over-the-top dramatizations.

"For years, you've tried to become a version of yourself based on the expectations of others. I rejected your application time after time because I needed you to become the woman *you* need to be. It took you long enough."

Patches snorted at how gracefully Alyssa had taken her jab. Shots were fired, and Eve opened her mouth to return the sentiment. She caught herself leaning back in her seat. He wanted to high-five Alyssa's ability to silence Eve. That alone made her the most powerful person in the aircraft.

The pilot climbed in, smashing the button that closed the door. Air hissed as the cabin pressurized. Seconds later, the engines powered up. Patches tried to focus on his hands, ignoring the growing unease in his gut. He could absorb the impact of a car crash, but the idea of free-falling from a mile above the ground still didn't sit well with him.

"Sentinels. I said I was going to be one. Here it is. It's decided."

"What?" He was confused.

"We don't conform to our roles, they conform to us." Alyssa leaned back in her seat, fastening her harness.

"Do I get a vote? I think we can do better."

"It's decided," Alyssa said.

"No really, can we put it to a vote?"

Eve gave him the finger. But even with the scalding

expression on her face, he couldn't help but smile. She struggled to keep the smirk from lifting the edge of her lip. Their first conversation had been about her wanting to join the Tower's peacekeepers. It wasn't according to the plan she had laid out, but she had achieved her dream.

"Sentinels it is."

And as they lifted into the air, they bid farewell to their home.

Continue the Adventure

For More Children of Nostradamus
"Follow" My Patreon For Free
https://www.patreon.com/writeremyflagg